THE

WIFE'S DREAM:

OR,

A PROFLIGATE'S LESSON.

BY THE POPULAR AUTHOR OF

"GALLANT TOM," "ELA THE OUTCAST," &c., &c.

~~~~~~~~

LONDON:

PRINTED BY E. LLOYD, SALISBURY-SQUARE, FLEET-STREET, AND SOLD BY
ALL BOOKSELLERS.

PREFACE.

THE author feels it his bounden duty to acknowledge his feelings of gratitude for the unlimited support and patronage bestowed on his labours from time to time, but more especially in the present instance, when their approbation has exceeded that lavished on any of his previous productions. The idea of the present tale was borrowed from the justly popular song of the same name ; but throughout the matter the author has endeavoured to engraft a moral on the minds of his readers, and he flatters himself that to a great extent his object has been accomplished, from the enormous circulation, both in the " Penny Sunday Times," and in its present form, the work has had. He once more returns his grateful acknowledgments and begs leave to remain

THE PUBLIC'S MOST HUMBLE

AND OBEDIENT SERVANT.

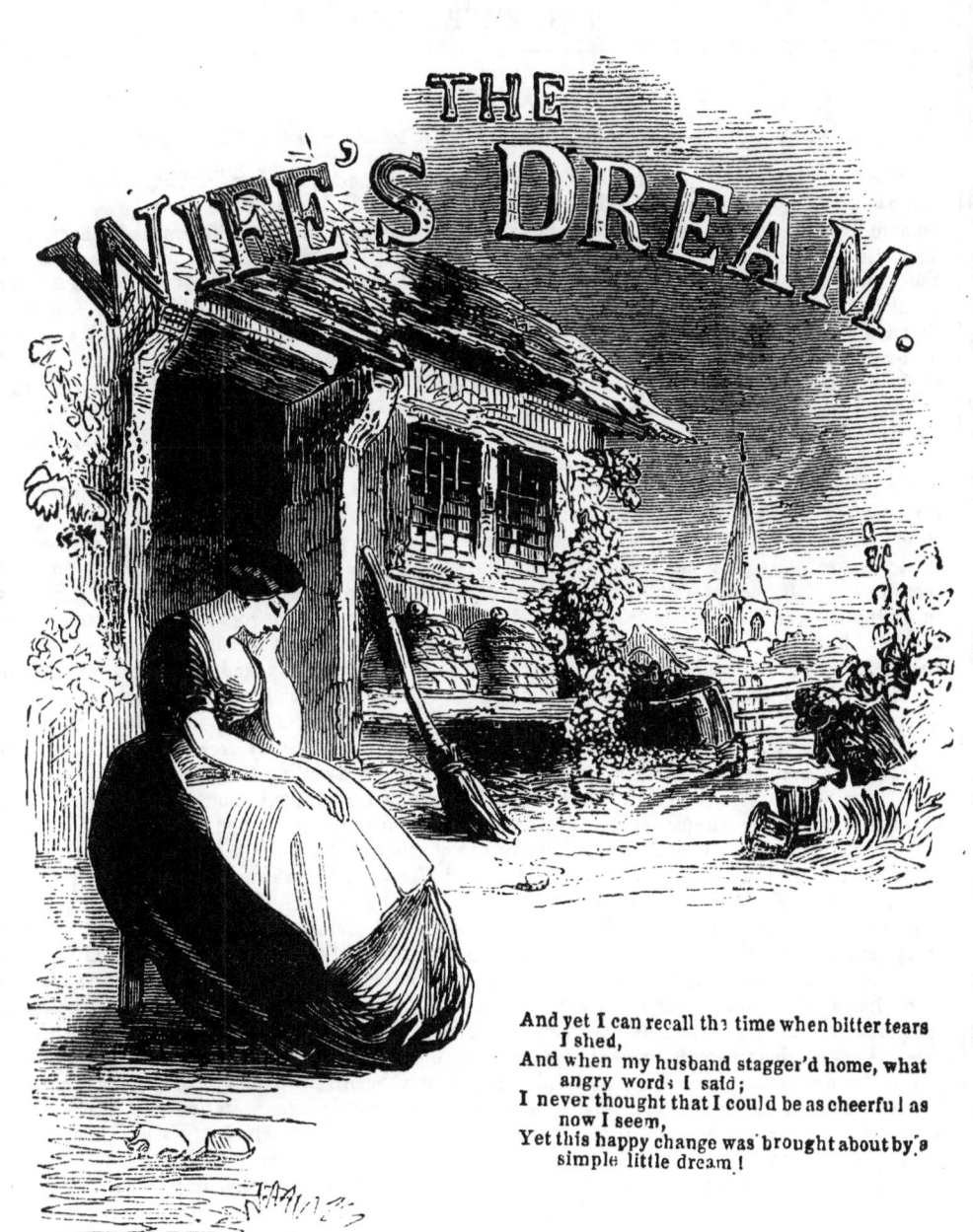

THE WIFE'S DREAM.

And yet I can recall the time when bitter tears
    I shed,
And when my husband stagger'd home, what
    angry words I said;
I never thought that I could be as cheerful as
    now I seem,
Yet this happy change was brought about by a
    simple little dream !

THE WIFE'S DREAM.

"Now tell me, Mary, how is it that you can look so gay,
When evening after evening your husband is away?
I never see you sulk or pout, or say an angry word,
And yet you've plenty cause for tears, if all be true I've heard?"

" It is because, my sister dear, a husband you ne'er wed,
Nor saw your children gathering round, and asking you for bread ;
You ne'er can know how it becomes a woman's lot through life,
To be, e'en to a drunkards fault's, a patient loving wife.

And yet I can recall the time when bitter tears I shed,
And when my husband stagger'd home, what angry words I said ;
I never thought that I could be as cheerful as now I seem,
Yet this happy change was brought about by a simple little dream !"

***—The author of the present Romance, for reasons which will appear in the course of the
work, has chosen to remove the characters, plot, and incidents from Ireland to England.

No. 1.

CHAPTER 1.

SATURDAY NIGHT.—THE CONFERENCE.—THE DREAM.—A WIFE'S SUFFERINGS.

It is Saturday evening—the labourer's weekly toil is ended; his few brief hours of relaxation approach, and some with cheerful hearts, though with tired limbs, wend their way to their humble dwellings, to find their only comfort in the bosoms of their families, whilst others, less domesticated and more improvident, though probably equally laborious, seek a false enjoyment in the society of some of their dissipated and reckless shopmates in the various tap-rooms of the great metropolis; and, under the maddening influence of the intoxicating beverage, squander that trifling pittance they have laboured so hard to realize, leaving their wives and children destitute of a meal on the only day of rest allotted to those who earn their living by the sweat of their brow. It is Saturday evening; the spade and the axe, the hammer and the anvil, the loom and the shuttle;—the plane and the saw, the fire and the furnace, everything which taxes the sinews of honest industry, for a brief period, per chance, is abandoned, and "home, home, sweet home," is the great and happy desideratum of all the prudent and well disposed "producers of a nation's wealth." The various shops abound with tempting eatables for the morrow's consumption; the various caterers for the public palate are on the *qui vive*; London is one great illumination, one blaze of gas light; pedestrians jostle each other in good humoured confusion; rival purveyors of animal and vegetable consumption bawl each other hoarse. The very donkeys seem to know, to their sorrow, that it is Saturday; the errand boy, to *his delight*, having Sunday in perspective, and numerous rambles of pleasure in anticipation, *does* know it; and all is bustle and activity. How the gin palaces are looking up; what innumerable members are *called to the bar*, many of them, alas! doomed to be summoned to and arraigned at a bar probably, at no distant period, of a very different description, and much against their will. There is a moral lesson in every shop upon which the eye rests; sound wisdom to be gathered from the countenance of every individual you encounter. It is Saturday evening, and the careful housewife is anxiously awaiting in her clean though humble dwelling the return of her " gudeman" from his weekly toil. A smile is on her healthy and intelligent countenance to give him a hearty welcome: the red fire crackles in the grate, before which is arranged to air on the clotheshorse, the clean linen intended for the Sunday use of themselves and their children. Already she has made all the most economical arrangements for their "marketing;" and perhaps, even the luxury of a trip to Gravesend, and all the delights of Windmill Hill, are in contemplation. Such a day of pleasure and recreation, and relaxation, will Sunday be to be sure; such a day of enjoyment of the blessings which an All Bountiful Almighty has provided for all His creatures, away from smoky atmospheres and densely populated neighbourhoods; far, far away in the green fields, beneath a bright sunny sky, and inhaling the pure air of Heaven! The children are permitted on this auspicious occasion to remain up an hour or so later, for it is the invariable custom of their parents to treat them to a nice hot supper no a Saturday night, that is, if they have returned themselves, and this has probably been the subject of their dreams every previous night in the week; and what a state of excitement and expectation are these little people in, to be sure; especially at the thoughts of the choice trifles which " Father" may bring them home in his pocket. Such is the scene which usually presents itself in the comfortable home of the honest, prudent, and industrious mechanic, on a Saturday evening; should he not unfortunately have been deprived of his independence, namely, the means of obtaining a commensurate living for himself and family by his own skill and labour. But it is sad to reverse the scene, and view the wretched habitations of squalid poverty, brought about either by misfortune or by suffering the reckless and destructive demon of extravagance to run riot, and to fatten on the very vitals of themselves and those who should be dear to them as their own existence. But we will draw a veil over this gloomy part of the picture, and come at once to our narrative. Follow us, reader, to the eastern part of the metropolis, to one of its most pestilential and crowded alleys, filled with crumbling lodging-houses, principally occupied by the lower orders of Irish, and the very refuse of the idle portion of the community. It is a small back-room we would introduce you to; age and neglect have blackened its walls; a keen current of air steals in at every broken pane of glass; there are but a few rotten ruins of furniture in the wretched room; a very small fire moulders in the crazy grate, before which two children, a boy and girl, are playing in unconscious innocence, while an infant is reposing in a cradle by the side. A small candle lends its feeble aid to illumine the cheerless place. The broken remnants of furniture are, however, arranged in the most precise order, and the floor is perfectly clean, showing that industrious hands have been employed upon it. This room was the habitation of Edward Langstone, and Mary his wife, with their three children. Edward Langstone was a skilful mechanic, who had constant employment when he thought proper to attend to it, and the wages he could earn were sufficient to keep his family in comfort and respectability; but a love of society, and the evil causes of bad associates, first lured him from the paths of rectitude, and losing all self-respect, he became a villain to himself and the affectionate and devoted partner of his life. It is Saturday evening, and Mary Langstone is seated at a table occupied at shirt-making, and anxiously listening to catch every sound that arose in the house, expecting the return of her husband, who had been at his employment all the week, and having in a fit of compunction carefully avoided his abandoned companions, solemnly promised that he would return home as soon as he had left the shop, and for the first time for many months bring her the whole of his wages, so that they and their children might for once in the way enjoy themselves.

Mary Langstone was a handsome woman of about thirty years of age. The traces of care and suffering were visible on her features, but still a smile of calm and patient resignation, and of hope beamed in her countenance, as she industriously plied her needle, rocking the cradle which contained her sleeping infant with one foot, and humming to herself in tones of plantive sweetness a simple ballad of the day. Her heart throbbed with expectation, and visions of renewed happpiness flitted across her imagination; but suddenly she left off singing, and putting down her work, she said :—

"How my eyes ache, for it is many hours that I have been thus occupied, and my weary task does not appear to progress at all; and when it is completed, how miserable is the pittance I shall receive for my labour. Edward tarries; he must have left the shop more than an hour ago, and should he have again been tempted by any of his abandoned associates, what will become of all the solemn promises he made me, and which have elated my bosom with hope and joy all the week? My heart misgives me. I wish he would come. Oh, Edward, dear Edward, could you but form a resolution to abandon the profligate career you have so long been pursuing, how happy we might be. But no, let me not despair;—you will not deceive me on this occasion;—for your own sake, for the sake of our beloved children, you will not. Let me not forget the warning of my dream; that awful—that awful though simple dream, which neither time nor circumstances can efface from my memory—I will no more upbraid you, dear Edward; all your neglect and ill-treatment I will endeavour to endure without a murmur; and may the all merciful God give me strength and patience to do so."

She paused; for at that moment the sound of footsteps ascending the stairs smote her ears.

"It is he," she ejaculated, hastily arising from her seat and opening the room door. She started back with a feeling of the most painful disappointment, when, instead of him she looked for with such eager anxiety, she beheld her sister. Laura Maysdale was several years her sister's junior; she was a most lovely, intelligent, and affectionate girl, who deeply sympathised with her sister in her unmerited misfortunes, and rendered her all the assistance in her power, though the means were very limited, as she was only a poor servant girl, and the principal portion of her trifling wages she received were expended in the support of their only surviving parent, an aged mother, who was stone blind, and was the inmate of one of the alms-houses a few miles from town. But many were the meals that the kind-hearted Laura procured for her sister, when she and her poor children must otherwise have perished with hunger. Mary quickly conquered her feelings, and greeted her sister with her accustomed smiles, and an assumption of cheerfulness she was very far from experiencing in reality.

"Dear Mary," observed Laura, embracing her affectionately; "this is Saturday night, and I am sorry that I could not find an opportunity of slipping out to visit you before, for I had so much reason to fear that you and your children would not be very well provided for. I have ordered a few coals and other little necessaries, which will be here presently—I have brought you a nice bit of supper from the cook-shop, a breast of mutton and vegetables, which will make you a comfortable dinner to-morrow; and see! here are two such beautiful slices of plum pudding for Bob and Nelly?"

The children, completely fascinated by the intimation, chuckled round their aunt, their "good aunt Laury," as they called her, and eagerly received the tempting fare, which they did ample justice to, in a remarkably brief space of time.

"My dear sister," said Mary, "how can I ever sufficiently thank you for your affectionate consideration? But indeed it pains me thus constantly to be encroaching on your benevolence, when you can so ill afford it."

"Now, now, Mary, let me hear nothing of that sort, I beg; what do I want? Am I not well provided for? I have a good kind master and mistress, though their limited income will not permit them to give me such liberal wages as they would wish; but they treat me the same as if I were one of their own family. I live well, have no more to do than is conducive to health, and I am content. But, bless me, how I am talking, and you are not eating. Now do make a hearty meal, dear Mary, while it is warm and nice, and I will see to making up your fire, which is at present in such a weakly condition that it is enough to freeze one to look at it."

Mary, to satisfy her sister, did partake slightly of the food, dividing a portion of it between the two children, while the affectionate Laura, (the coals having arrived) bustled about to replenish the fire, and to make everything as comfortable as possible.

"There," she said, with a look of satisfaction, "that is better. Edward has not come home, then ? Misguided man, I fear that nothing will ever bring him to a due sense of the madness and proflagacy of his career, and the heavy and cruel wrongs, he has and still is inflicting upon you and your poor children. He too, who is so excellent a mechanic, has always constant work at his command, and has the means of keeping you all in such respectability and comfort."

"Nay, my dear Laura," replied Mary, "believe me, in this instance you do Edward wrong he will be here anon, and I trust that to-night, at any rate, there will not be a repetition of those scenes I have too frequently expereinced."

Laura shook her head, doubtfully.

"He has been perfectly steady all the week," she continued. "Oh, what a week of heaven it has been to me. He has not lost an hour ; on the contrary, has made a good deal of overtime, so that the wages he will bring me home to-night will enable us to take a few necessary articles of wearing apparel from the pawnbrokers, and if he only keeps his promise, we shall soon be comfortable again, and enabled to leave this wretched abode."

"What delight would it afford me, Mary, should your hopes be realized ;" returned her sister ; "but alas ! Edward has promised you so often to reform, and so invariably broken his word, that I can place but very little or no confidence in him. It was an unfortunate day for you when you became his wife."

"Oh, he was once good and amiable, it was not until we had been some time in London that he was lured into his present evil courses. I still love him with all the fervour of the most devoted wife, and God knows how constantly I offer up my supplications to Heaven to enlighten his benighted mind and to restore us both to that happiness from which we have been so long estranged. But what a dismal theme is this ; let us abandon it, and talk upon one which is more calculated to inspire cheerful and hopeful feelings."

"My dearest Mary," said Laura, after a pause, "Heaven surely will reward you as you deserve for your constancy and self-devotion to the man to whom you have committed your fate, and from whose cruelty you have experienced so many trials. It has often astonished me how it was that your countenance could wear the smiles of gaiety and happiness when sorrows sufficient to break down the strongest fortitude were corroding your heart. The wild and guilty career your husband has so long pursued was enough to sink you to the lowest depths of despair and misery, yet have I never seen you sulk or pout, or say an angry word—tell me, how is this ?"

"Ah, Laura," replied Mary, "had you experienced what I have, which God forbid that you ever may, you would know how to appreciate my feelings more properly."

"I cannot comprehend your meaning, Mary."

"You are unmarried yet, Laura, and never saw your little helpless children gathering round you and asking you for that bread which you had not to give them. It is their dear sake which has sustained me throughout all my heavy trials. Ah ! my sister, it becomes a woman's lot through life to be, even to a drunkard's faults, a faithful, loving, patient partner."

"But oh, how few women are there, Mary," replied Laura, "who could continue to act with such exemplary fortitude and forbearance."

"The time was," sighed Mary, "and with sorrow and regret do I recall it to my memory, when my feelings were very different. Many were the weary hours I passed in weeping and bewailing my hard fate ; and when my husband would stagger home from his dissolute companions, how bitterly used I to reproach him—what angry words I would say to him, only aggravating the accursed demon that held possession of his reason. Never did I imagine that I could be as cheerful as I now appear."

"And how was this happy change brought about, Mary ?"

"By a simple dream, Laura."

"A dream !" repeated Laura, with the most unfeigned astonishment.

"Yes, my dear sister, it was a dream that wrought it all, but one that I can never forget."

"Is it possible ?"

"It is true," replied Mary.

"And you have never yet explained this to me," said Laura.

"I hesitated to do so, Laura, because I did not think I could trust my feelings with the recital. But listen."

Laura drew her chair closer to that of her sister, and listened with the most mute astonishment and profound attention while Mary thus proceeded—

"One cold winter's evening, I sat shivering in our fireless room, listening with anxious heart and aching head, as I had often before done to catch my husband's footsteps on the stairs. Awful were the thoughts that rushed upon my burning brain; black despair had set its hand upon me, and the raging of the tempest without, added to my misery. At one moment I was half resolved to plunge a knife into my bosom, and terminate my wretched existence; but the thought of my innocent children arrested my fatal purpose. 'But why should I thus torture myself?' I suddenly excaimed, 'for one who loves me not? Would to Heaven that he were dead. I never, never wish to see him more.'"

"Oh, awful!" ejaculated Laura.

"It was," coincided her sister. "I cannot even now think of it without a shudder of horror, but hear me out, sister. They say the wretched can find no sleep, Laura, but in that they are wrong. Soon, amid all my tears and anguish, in the midst of all my misery, sleep descended upon my eyelids; and busy imagination pictured to me in a dream the awful realization of my hasty wish. I saw my husband stretched dead at my feet, whilst my little ones were playing around him, unconscious of their sad bereavement. Frantically I threw myself upon his lifeless form, and covered his cold lips with my kisses, and madly endeavoured to recall him to life. 'Edward! dear, dear Edward!' I cried, 'oh, speak to me! My brain was wandering when I gave utterance to the dreadful words. I meant not what I said, indeed I did not. With all your faults, you are still, and ever must be the idol of my soul! Speak to me, Edward, or my heart will break!' 'Mercy!' exclaimed a well-known voice in my ear; with a scream I awoke, and found my husband standing by my side. His death was all a dream!"

"It was a fearful vision, dear Mary," said her sister, "and I do not wonder that it should make such a lasting and powerful impression upon your mind."

"It can never be eradicated from my memory, Laura," replied Mary; "and it has guided my conduct and restrained the expression of my feelings ever since. Whenever I feel disposed to reproach him, the warning which I received in that fearful dream comes fresh upon my memory; and though when I reflect upon the guilty life he is pursuing, it costs me many a pang of unspeakable anguish. I ever, on his return home, try to greet him with an affectionate smile of welcome, though, at the same time, my heart is full to bursting.'

"And did you make Edward acquainted with the particulars of your dream?" asked Laura.

"With part of it, I did," answered her sister.

"And yet it wrought no reformation in him?"

"Yes, for a short time it did, and fondly I hoped it would continue, but alas! I was doomed to disappointment. But I will not yet despair, my dear Laura, no—I will humbly put my trust in God, and endeavour to bear the heavy sorrows with which it is His will to afflict me, with fortitude and resignation; and oh, if I can by patience and submission at last bring my husband to repentance, what reason shall I not have to bless the hour when that fearful dream was presented to my disordered imagination?'

"Heaven help you, my dear sister," fervently ejaculated Laura, "and speedily restore you to happiness. But Edward still tarries; alas! I fear that he will again deceive you."

"Oh, no, I dare not entertain such a thought," replied Mary; "he will be here anon, my heart tells me that he will."

"God grant that your hopes may not be doomed to disappointment, Mary, and that this night may prove the prelude to your future peace of mind. I wish I could remain to keep you company, but I have already exceeded my time, and my mistress will begin to feel surprised at my delay. I will call to see you again as soon as possible; God bless you, and farewell."

"Bless you, my affectionate Laura!" responded Mary, embracing her tenderly; "and may you never experience the troubles that have fallen to the lot of your unfortunate sister."

Having kissed the children, Laura took her departure, and Mary was left in her loneliness again. Folding her children to her throbbing bosom, she knelt down, and earnestly supplicated the mercy of the Supreme. She then resumed her weary watching, and as the time flew rapidly away, and still there was not the least signs of her husband's return, the agony of her mind became insupportable, The two children had now fallen asleep, and placing them on the matress, she slowly quitted the room and descended the stairs, The front door was never closed, for persons passed in and out at all hours of the night. With a palpitating heart the wretched woman stepped into the dark and filthy alley and made her way to the end of it. She looked up and down the street upon which it opened, but only a few noisy revellers, or here and there a solitary pedestrian met her gaze, and fearful to leave her children for any length of time, she did not venture any further, but stood wringing her hands with the anguish of her feelings, and weeping bitterly.

"Oh, Edward!" she sighed, "you have again deceived me, and will not return to your miserable home until you have squandered the whole of that money which should procure us food. Alas! how soon have you forgotten the solemn promises you made me. The tempters have lured

THE WIFE'S DREAM.

you to their haunts of infamy again, and I shall not see you until you are infuriated with intoxicating drink. My God! my God! will nothing awaken you to a sense of the enormity of your conduct?"

She cast one more glance up the street, with the forlorn hope of seeing her husband coming, and then with a bursting heart she returned to the house, and retraced her steps to her lonely room. She sat herself down by the fire, unable to resume her work, and became the complete image of despair.

"He cannot love you, my little innocents," she sighed, looking with a melancholy expression of tenderness, "or he could never have the heart to act in the manner he is doing. He knows not that you have had anything in your lips to-day, and yet he can remain from home when he has or had the means of procuring you food. Oh, surely this is most cruel—most unnatural. Where are now all those bright visions of returning happiness which my imagination conjured up? Where are all the hopes that I suffered to take possession of my mind? Gone, gone, for ever; oh, Edward, your conduct will surely break my heart, and bring yourself to destruction; such a career of vice as this must terminate in something dreadful. Would that I could change your abandoned course of life, how willingly could I forgive the past, and what happiness might I anticipate for the future. But let me dry these tears, and banish these terrible emotions, and try to meet him on his return with calmness and without reproach. My dream! My dream! I can never forget its awful warning!"

She covered her face with her hands as she thus spoke, and shuddered with horror at the recollection; but in a moment afterwards nearly all traces of anguish had disappeared from her countenance, though her bosom was full almost to bursting. All was still in the house, save from the noise of some drunken brawler who staggered home to his wretched lodging; and everything was calculated to add to the melancholy of Mary's feelings. It was some time since the hour of midnight had struck, and the poor woman now became seriously alarmed, thinking that something had happened to her misguided husband. Had it not been for the fear of leaving her children, she would have gone forth in search of him; but as it was, she had no alternative but to wait with all the patience and fortitude she could summon to her aid the result of this awful night; but she could not do otherwise than anticipate the worst, and notwithstanding she was so anxious for it, she almost dreaded his return.

"He will be mad with drink when he comes home," she said, "and notwithstanding all my calmness and forbearance, I fully expect that murder will be perpetrated one of these nights. God help me! for I surely cannot endure this life much longer. My heart must break, and then what will become of my poor children?"

Again she offered up a prayer to Heaven, and endeavoured, but with little success, to become more calm. Another hour elapsed in this dismal manner, and still was the misguided Edward Langstone absent. It had been threatening all the evening, and to add to the dreariness of the hour, a violent storm now commenced, and the wind made every crazy timber and broken casement in the old house tremble again, whilst the rain soon made its way through the ceiling of the room. Mary listened not, however, to the howling storm, her whole attention was absorbed in endeavouring to catch the sound of her husband's approaching footsteps, and much did she fear the consequences of his being exposed to the inclemency of the weather, in the state he probably was at present. At length she heard the front door banged to with great violence, and then a stumbling footstep on the stairs, succeeded by several oaths uttered in a husky and incoherent voice.

"He has reached home at last," Mary ejaculated, "but, alas! in what a condition. God help me, and avert any evil that may threaten me or my children!"

She took the candlestick in her hand, and with trembling footsteps descended the stairs in order to assist him up. She peeped anxiously over the bannisters, and beheld him vainly endeavouring to ascend, for he was so frightfully intoxicated that he could not, and was every moment in danger of falling. Fearful that some accident would happen to him, the distracted woman hastened down the stairs, and grasping his arm with all the strength she could put forth, with the assistance of a man who lodged in the house, and who had fortunately just returned home, succeeded in getting him up stairs, and placing him in a chair, where he remained for a few minutes in a state of stupefaction, at intervals only stammering out some broken and incoherent sentences, no doubt imagining that he was still among his dissipated companions, at the scene of ruin and vice where the night's debauch had taken place.

"God help me and my poor children," sighed the unhappy wife to herself, as she viewed with mingled feelings of shame and pity, horror, and abject despair, the disgusting situation of her husband, and pictured to herself the misery that too evidently was in store for them. The fond and sanguine hopes with which his solemn promises throughout the week had inspired her, were now annihilated, and she had too much reason to fear that nothing whatever would reclaim him from that abandoned course of life into which he had been so unfortunately seduced.

Misery, starvation, shame, frowned hideously upon her, and her brain became distracted at the harrowing thought. However, she struggled hard with her feelings; and setting herself down by the side of the mattress on which her children were reposing, with an anxious and aching heart the wretched and devoted wife continued for some time to watch her misguided husband in silence.

CHAPTER II.

A WIFE'S FORBEARANCE.—THE DRUNKARD'S VISION.—A DEED OF BLOOD PREVENTED.

EDWARD LANGSTONE was still a young man not more than thirty years of age, and although the abandoned course of life he had for some time past led, had not failed to work its most terrible effects upon his person and his constitution, there were still the remains of a fine handsome man, the ruins of " one of the noblest works of God;" and when in his sober moments, his manners and conversation evinced a mind formed in the noblest mould, and which was calculated to excite respect and admiration, and to diffuse pleasure to all around him. He was the only son of humble but honest parents, who had taken the greatest pains in the moral culture of his mind, and little anticipated that their care and affectionate attention would at any time be so shamefully abused. His father was a poor village schoolmaster, a man of considerable acquirements and unblemished integrity ; but to whom fortune had been most niggardly in her gifts; however, he struggled on with patience and perseverance, and the urbanity and strict probity of his conduct obtained for him the respect and esteem of all who knew him ; and he was enabled by his own frugality, and the assistance of his more fortunate neighbours, to apprentice his son at the proper age to an excellent trade, by which he would have the means of obtaining a comfortable and respectable livelihood. Edward Langstone passed through his apprenticeship with the utmost integrity, and was highly esteemed by his master and all who knew him, and having acquired a superior knowledge of his business, it was fondly hoped by his parents that he was destined to attain a respectable position in society, and to be a comfort to them in their declining years. But, alas! how fatally were those hopes destined to be disappointed. The superior manners, and the manly qualities of Edward Langstone, rendered his society welcome wherever he went ; and the accomplishments of his mind and the attractions of his person made him an especial favourite among the fair sex ; but there was one who had been the companion of his boyish days, and to whom his heart was most fervently devoted. This was Mary Maysdale, who resided with her parents, who were likewise in humble circumstances, in the same village, and who had from the earliest period of childhood looked upon Edward with an affection which must increase with years, but which time could never subdue. Mary Maysdale was the village pride, and possessed of every charm, personal and intrinsic, which can render woman enchanting. Gay and artless she knew no care, nor did her gentle bosom harbour a single thought which the most pure and holy need be ashamed to acknowledge. Her parents felt proud of her, and she was beloved and admired wherever she went. No village festival could be considered complete without Mary Maysdale and her younger sister, the lively and amiable Laura, were present. Many advantageous offers were made for Mary's hand, but she respectfully declined them all; her heart was indissolubly fixed on Edward Langstone, and her parents loved her too fondly, and entertained too high an opinion of the man of her choice, to seek to bias her inclinations. Edward's term of apprenticeship having expired, the day of their nuptials was fixed, and solemnized with every demonstration of joy, and with the brightest and most sanguine anticipations of future happiness. For some time nothing occurred to interrupt their felicity; their affection towards each other increased every day. Two lovely children blessed their union, and they were looked upon as the happiest couple for miles around that part of the country. But this state of peace was not destined to continue ; Death suddenly laid his ruthless hand upon Mary's father ; and by an almost unparalleled calamity, Edward was deprived of both his parents within a few days of each other, only a month or two afterwards. This terrible affliction threw a gloom over the prospects of Edward Langstone and his wife, and rendered them for some time inconsolable. But their troubles were not fated to end there. Edward's employer fell into difficulties and became bankrupt, and he was thrown out of work at the most inauspicious season of the year, and at a time when an universal panic prevailed in the country. Edward, by his habits of industry and frugality, had saved a few pounds, but that, even with the greatest prudence, could not be expected to last long, especially as Mrs. Maysdale, who was now afflicted with blindness, and Laura, were entirely dependent upon them for support. To obtain employment Edward found it quite impossible in the country ; his money was almost exhausted, and he had no other alternative than to try his fortune in London. The thoughts, however, of being compelled to leave their native village caused Edward and his wife many a pang of poignant regret, and some sad misgivings and forebodings cameover the mind of Mary, which she found it utterly impossible to banish. Besides there was Mrs. Maysdale and Laura to provide for, and that involved them in a difficulty which they knew not how to surmount. Their friends and neighbours deeply sympathized with them in their misfortunes, and were willing to render them all the assistance in their power. Laura was introduced to a situation in London, and her mother, by the influence of some kind friends, was admitted into one of the alms-houses for aged widows, situated a few miles from town. It was a melancholy day for Edward Langstone and his beloved Mary, when they quitted their native village, and were compelled to separate from their old friends and dear associations, and to enter upon a scene so strange to them, and where they feared that the noise and bustle of a London life would so ill accord with their tastes and wishes; but still they endeavoured to encourage the hope that it would only be for a season, and that they might shortly be enabled to return to those scenes to which they were naturally so fondly attached. Edward had not been many days in London when he procured employment in a first-rate establishment, and being, as we have before said, an excellent workman, it was likely to be a constancy, for he quickly ingratiated himself in the favour of his master, by his abilities as a mechanic, his modest and unassuming behaviour, and the steadiness of his habits. For some months everything went on well and prosperous, and the happiness of Edward and his wife remained uninterrupted. Alas! it was not fated to last much longer—a heavy cloud obscured the horizon of their peace, which for some time impending o'er them, at length burst, and plunged poor Mary into further misery and despair, and her misguided partner, he whom she loved with all the strength of woman's most ardent affection and devotion, into shame and ruin. Suddenly Mary beheld a most strange and melancholy change in the manners and habits of her husband, which excited the utmost alarm in her breast. He did not seem to take that pleasure in her society and that of their children, which he formerly used to do: when at home he was sullen, restless, and thoughtful; several nights in the week he would not return home till a late hour, and then his countenance was flushed, his eyes inflamed, and many other symptoms too painfully appeared to show that he was labouring under the baneful effects of intoxication. What agony of mind did this alarming discovery cost his unfortunate wife; how many were the bitter tears she secretly shed, and how fervently did she pray to Heaven to snatch him from the path of destruction into which he had been too evidently lured by some evil advisers. But in vain she questioned him as to the cause of this fearful change, and in the gentlest accents expostulated with him on the madness and danger of his conduct; she could only elicit some harsh reply from him, which served alone to add to the anguish of her misery and despair. That home that had once been so happy and cheerful, had now become wretched and neglected; and the love which Edward had formerly evinced towards her, had given place to a morose and selfish feeling, and the comforts of his own fireside, and the smiles of his amiable wife and innocent children, seemed to have become hateful to him. He scarcely ever returned home till midnight, and then in a state of madness from the intoxicating poison; he became careless about his personal appearance, neglected his employment, and many were the Saturday nights he returned home minus every farthing of his wages. Had it not been for the united assistance which the affectionate Laura was enabled to afford, Mary and her children must frequently have starved, and as it was they were often without a meal. How Mary was enabled to find fortitude to support this cruel and unexpected fate was marvellous; but for some time she did so without a murmur, and in the hope that Heaven would yet open the eyes of her husband to the folly and guilt of his conduct. His master repeatedly expostulated with him on the madness of his conduct, and the ruin it must ultimately bring upon his head if he persisted in it: and had it not been for his peculiar skill as a workman, and the sake of his wife and children, he would have been compelled to have discharged him from his employment, but still he hoped that time would convince him of the folly and vice of his proceedings, and restore him once more to his former state of respectability.

Need we attempt to describe the sufferings of Mary?—the many sleepless hours she passed in her dreary watchings for the return of her husband; the scalding tears she shed when he was away, and the terrible thoughts and apprehensions that haunted and disturbed her brain during his absence? We are certain that we need not, for where is there the reader who is not insensible to every proper feeling, who cannot imagine them? Nothing but ruin and the most squalid poverty stared her in the face; debt accumulated upon debt, until their credit was entirely gone; every article of furniture with which their once comfortable home was supplied, was gone, sold to procure them the bare necessaries of life; nearly every article of wearing apparel was sold or pledged for the same purpose, and they were at length driven into the wretched tenement, to herd among the most depraved of society, where they have been introduced to the reader at the commencement of our narrative. But still nothing could arouse Edward

Langstone from the fatal dream (if so we may term it) which he had suffered to take possession of his senses; the demon had obtained too fast hold of him to suffer him to escape, and the destruction of himself and family seemed to be inevitable. The patience of the devoted wife at length became exhausted; could she hear her poor children crying for food, and she unable to contribute to their wants, without a murmur; could she behold the disgusting conduct of her husband, his brutal neglect of her and their offspring, without complaining? Oh, no, human nature had been tried beyond its utmost limits of endurance, and in the bitterness of her soul she cursed the very hour in which she had become his wife, and felt that she could not much longer endure so unmerited and unnatural a fate. The poignant anguish of her soul now found vent in words, and bitterly would she reproach him for the inhumanity of his conduct; but this only served to exasperate him, and many and alarming were the quarrels which ensued between them, and in which, frenzied with drink, the wretched man even dared to raise his hand against that gentle and affectionate being that had endured so much for his sake, and whom he had vowed to love and cherish through life. It was a dreary night that Mary was seated in her miserable room, watching by the dim light of a fast expiring candle the return of her profligate husband. Neither herself nor her children had tasted food during the day, and the helpless little ones had cried themselves to sleep. The madness of despair and agony was upon the wretched mother's heart—she could find no relief in tears. Terrible thoughts, thoughts such as she had never experienced before, crowded upon her burning brain, and a feeling, almost amounting to hatred towards the author of her misery, took possession of her bosom. Strange and ghastly phantoms seemed to flit before her eyes, to point derisively at the pale faces of her innocent children, and to mock her sufferings. She could endure no more; she started up in a state of horror, and gazed around her, scarcely conscious of where she was, and not knowing what to do. Her feelings wound up to madness in the bitterness of her anguish, she cursed her husband, prayed to see him no more, and wished that he were dead. A sudden stupor came upon her senses, her brain reeled, she staggered to a seat, on which she sank, and covered her face with her hands. Sleep gradually stole upon her eyelids, and it was then that the remarkable dream occurred to her imagination, which has been described in the first chapter of our tale, and which worked such a wonderful change in the unfortunate woman's mind. Nor was it without its due effect on Edward himself; for a time he was awakened to a full sense of the cruelty and guilt of his conduct, and the fatal consequences of which it must ultimately be productive. He felt the bitterest remorse for, and disgust at the infamous course he had been so long pursuing, he implored the forgiveness of his wife, and promised in future to reform, and to become the same dutiful and affectionate husband he formerly used to be. Need we say with what feelings of delight and gratitude Mary listened to him? How fondly she embraced him, and how fervently she prayed to Heaven to give him resolution to adhere to the promises he made? That night was one of the happiest she had experienced for many a day, and hope again reanimated her so long suffering bosom. For two or three weeks Edward Langstone kept his word, kept steadily to his employment, returned home immediately after the labour of the day was ended, and seemed to strive by every means in his power to make atonement for the guilty past. Many little comforts were restored to their home, the affectionate wife and her children were again well fed and better clothed, and they hoped in the course of a few weeks to be able to remove from their present wretched room to a more comfortable dwelling. With what cheerful smiles and looks of affection did Mary now ever welcome home to his humble hearth and blazing fire her late truant husband, and how grateful did she feel to Omnipotence for the happy and permanent change which she hoped had come over him. But alas! another, and a fatal change was destined shortly to take place. This happy respite from misery was not fated to last long. Edward again neglected his work, and absented himself till a late hour almost every night from home, and never returned without being in a disgusting state of inebriation. The temptors had again obtained their baneful and accursed influence over him, and it appeared that the wretched man was lost for ever. But remembering the fearful warning of her dream, although her heart was full to bursting, poor Mary never uttered a word of complaint of murmur or reproach to him. She sought to persuade him by the gentler means, and ever greeted him with the most affectionate smiles, when alone offering up her fervent prayers to the Supreme, to remove the destructive mist from before his eyes, and to awaken him to a full sense of the destructive course he was pursuing. Having now given these necessary explanations, we will return to that portion of our tale from which we have thus slightly digressed. Edward Langstone continued for some time muttering drowsy sentences to himself, singing broken snatches of bacchanalian songs, and evidently quite uncertain of where he was, or that his unfortunate wife was present. Mary was afraid to interrupt him, but continued seated by the side of her sleeping children, watching him with a bursting heart, and eyes blood-shot with the intense anguish of her feelings.

"Heaven in mercy look down upon us!" she murmured to herself! "and release us from the horrors of our situation. Oh, Edward! how fearfully art thou changed from what thou once used to be! What madness has taken possession of thy brain, what demoniacal spell has come upon thee? Who are the wretches that have tempted thee to this? May the curses of an injured wife and her poor helpless bereaved children descend upon them."

Edward had now sunk into a doze, which, however, did not seem likely to last long, and Mary advancing cautiously towards him, eagerly examined the contents of his pockets. Her worst fears were realized—she could find only a few coppers.

"All gone," she sighed, "another night of wilful waste and disgusting dissipation. Oh, Heaven! when will this cease? Will nothing recall him to his senses, and the enormity of his present conduct? Alas, alas, how soon has he broken the solemn promises he this week made me. If it had not been for poor Laura, we should have been without a morsel of food to eat. Father of Mercy again, I implore Thee to look down with pity on us!"

Overcome by the power of her feelings, she was unable to restrain her fears, and once more resumed her seat by the side of her children. Suddenly, however, her husband awoke, and she hastily approached him, and placing her hand upon his arm, looked persuasively up in his face, in her gentlest accents, and without anything which could be at all construed into the shadow of a reproach, she said—

"Dear Edward, it is very late, and you will catch cold by sleeping here. Come, come, let us retire to rest."

"Re—re—retire to rest?" stammered out her husband, "who talks of rest, when the night is not half over? Let's have another song; my friend Jack Clinton will oblige with the next. Jack is a cap—capital fellow. Landlord, fill these glasses, and—and——"

> "We won't go home till morning,
> We——"

"Dear Edward," interrupted Mary, "I beg you cease this riotous and unseemly noise. It is now Sunday morning—alas! a sorry Sunday for me and our poor little ones. But I will not reproach you, poor misguided man," she added, in an under tone to herself, "though Heaven knows I have sufficient cause to do so. Do you know where you are? Who it is that addresses you?"

"Wh—wh—what?" again stammered out the profligate, looking up at her with a stupid and drowsy expression. "Ah! Mary, my lass, is that you? Here I am, you see—confound it, don't look so sad and cross; what if I have spent all my money? There's more where that came from. I—I have had a glorious night of it; such merry dogs! Who cares? Where's Jack Clinton, my old particular? Capital fellow Jack, though he was once a lover of your's, Mary, and I believe you had a sneaking regard for him."

"Hold Edward!" exclaimed the disgusted woman, blushes of shame crimsoning her cheeks "what cruel and unjust words are these? But you know not what you say, and I forgive you. Oh, would that you had never known the villain Clinton, for it is he, I am certain, who has been the cause of your ruin."

"There, no preaching, Mary," said her husband in a surly tone, "I'm not in the humour to listen to it. Let's have some more brandy."

"Alas!" sighed Mary, "your brain is already maddened with the pernicious and accursed drink. Would that there was a law to punish the sordid wretches who amass large fortunes on the misery of their fellow creatures, by vending the deadly poison."

"Oh, grumbling as usual, I suppose, because I have no money to give you. What's the use of a man living, if he cannot enjoy himself now and then?"

"And can you call that enjoyment which sinks the man below the level of the beast?" demanded Mary—"call you that enjoyment which entails misery, shame, and starvation upon the wretched mother and her helpless little ones? Nay, Edward, do not frown, I mean not to reproach you, but I would startle you from your present unfortunate and destructive course, ere it is too late; I would recall to your memory the many hours of happiness we passed together in the days of our youth; the felicity that attended our union far away from these dens of vice and dissipation; contrast the pictures, and reason must tell you, which is the one in which true happiness is predominant."

"Bah!" cried Edward, impatiently, though the observations of his wife seemed to sober him a little, and to make some impression upon his half stultified mind; "I am not now in the vein to contrast the pictures to which you have alluded; my throat is parched, have you nothing better to offer me than dry lectures?"

"Here is some supper," replied his wife, placing before him the remains of the provisions Laura had brought them, and of which herself and children had so sparingly partook; "eat Edward, and then let us retire to bed, and God grant that a night's rest will prepare you for better thoughts."

"Ah!" he cried, suddenly turning round upon her, and eyeing her with a suspicious look;

" how is this ?—It does not seem to matter much my spending my wages, you have always got money ; how did you procure this?"

" By the kindness of my poor sister," answered Mary, " who has been here this evening, and, Heaven bless her, brought us sufficient to stay the cravings of hunger for one more day."

What selfish wretches does debauchery make of us. Edward Langstone never stopped to inquire whether his wife or their children had partaken of the humble meal, but set to and devoured all that was left most greedily.

" Ah !" he said, when he had concluded, " Laura is a very good girl; a fine wench, a hand-some wench, and such is the opinion of my friend Captain Braghall. A splendid fellow that Captain Braghall; spends a mint of money, and is deucedly fond of Laura."

" Edward," said his wife, with a look of disgust, " can you give utterance to observations such as these when speaking of my sister, Laura ?"

" To be sure I can," he replied, " and why not ?—Captain Braghall, as I said before, is a fine fellow, a handsome fellow, a rich fellow ;—I must introduce him to you one of these days —you will, you must be delighted with each other's company. He has taken a great fancy to Laura, and has solicited and obtained my promise to intercede with her for him. Laura has the chance of becoming a lady, and she is foolish if she reject it ; besides, consider the pecuniary advantages we might realize by bringing about the completion of his wishes."

The indignation which swelled the bosom of Mary, as her husband thus expressed himself, was almost too powerful for utterance.

" Good God !" she cried, " can this be that same Edward Langstone whom I ever believed to be the very soul of honour and virtue, and to whom I have not only sacrificed my whole affections but my happiness ?—I cannot believe the evidence of my senses ; some wild delusion must have taken possession of my brain ! Oh, Edward !—Edward ! reflect, I implore you, upon the cruel and unnatural words to which you have just given utterance, and you must shudder with shame and horror at the bare thought."

" Shudder with horror; ha ! ha ! ha !" laughed the profligate, " not I ; I am not such a squeamish fool as you seem to take me for ; and I have too great a fancy for the good things of this life, to reject in a hurry the propositions which my friend Captain Braghall has made to me."

" Edward," said Mrs. Langstone, " I cannot longer listen to language such as this. My dear sister is good and innocent, and we should be monsters indeed were we to expose her to such a fate as that to which you have alluded. Can you have become so callous to every sense of shame as to be ready to accept the wages of guilt, even at the sacrifice of the honour and happiness of that relative who should be so dear to you ?—Oh, monstrous ! But I will believe only that you speak under the influence of the intoxicating drink ; that you know not what you say."

" But indeed I do," was the cool reply.

" Then may Heaven pardon you !" gasped forth Mary, " and restore you to reason and justice. Oh, what a heartless villain must this Captain Braghall be."

" A heartless villain !" repeated Langstone, " for loving a pretty girl, eh ? Psha ! what nonsense is this."

" Alas !" sighed his wife, " I see it is useless to attempt to argue with you in your present state of mind. Come, come, dear Edward, once more let me seek to prevail upon you to retire to rest."

" Go to rest yourself," he replied sullenly, " I shall do very well where I am. I wish I was once more amongst my gay companions ; choice spirits they are ; especially Jack Clinton and Captain Braghall."

Mary turned away despairingly to conceal her tears, and watched her misguided husband with the most intense anxiety and anguish of spirit. The levity of his manners, and the reckless observations he had made use of respecting Captain Braghall and her sister Laura, greatly shocked her, and created the utmost alarm in her bosom. Never could she have believed that Edward could become so entirely degraded and lost to every feeling of shame, and she felt that it was necessary to put Laura on her guard without delay, or there was no knowing the danger into which she might be plunged, and from which it might be difficult, if not impossible, to ex-tricate her. Although her husband was not acquainted with the fact, Mary had heard sufficient of the character of the young libertine, Captain Braghall, to fill her with loathing and disgust ; but little did she imagine that he was one of the associates of Edward, and knowing that the captain had plenty of money at his command, she shuddered when she thought of the tempta-tions into which he might lead her husband in order to promote his own infamous designs. Captain Braghall was related to the family with whom Laura was living, and was a frequent visitor at the house, although his dissipated manners, and the abandoned society with which he was in the habit of associating, rendered him by no means a welcome guest. It was there that he had first beheld Laura, and the numerous charms she possessed immediately made a powerful impression upon him, and he longed to add her to the list of the numerous innocent beings who had already fallen victims to his infamous designs. Deprived of his parents when he had scarcely attained his majority, and becoming the uncontrolled master of a splendid fortune, he gave unlimited indulgence to his wild and dissipated propensities, and in order to gratify his guilty wishes, he did not hesitate to associate with even the very refuse of society, and to enter freely as " hail fellow, well met," into all their blackguard scenes of debauchery. He was the presiding genius of all their drunken revelries, and squandering his money extravagantly amongst them, he was considered by these worthies to be a very excellent sort of a fellow indeed. Knowing the re lationship in which Edward Langstone stood to Laura Maysdale, Captain Braghall did not fail to cultivate his friendship by every means in his power, for he hoped by so doing he should find in him a ready and powerful instrument to work out his designs ; but the character of this gentle-man will be fully explained in the course of our narrative. But what shocked poor Mary even more than all was the brutal and disgusting allusions her husband had made to herself and the man Clinton ; and she could scarcely persuade herself that such observations could have passed his lips. Clinton was a native of the same village in which Edward Langstone and his wife were born, and he had formerly made advances towards the affections of Mary, which knowing his real character she had peremptorily rejected with disgust. This, she had no doubt, had ex-cited in his breast a feeling of revenge, and she always avoided him in future as much as possi-ble, with a sentiment of dread and suspicion. Unfortunately it so happened that Clinton was working at the same establishment at which Edward obtained employment on coming to London, and it was to him that Mary justly attributed her husband's ruin. He, no doubt, was the tempter, who in a spirit of revenge, had first lured him astray, and who took a diabolical delight in seeing the misery he had brought upon his once happy home. All these painful thoughts rushed in rapid succession upon the mind of the faithful and unhappy wife as she still sat watch-ing with aching eyes her wretched husband, and feared for the present again to address him. The terror of her feelings every moment increased, and it was not without the greatest difficulty that she was enabled to keep her emotions within the bounds of restraint.

"Lost ! lost !" s'   ttered to herself, " the tempter has too well succeeded, and nothing, I fear, will reclaim m,   aded husband•from his guilty ways. Oh, Edward, Edward, whom I have ever, whom I still so fondly love ; for whose sake there is no misery, no privation that I would not endure without a murmur, that I should ever come to this ! What fatal madness has seized upon your brain, and rendered you insensible to the duties you owe your wife and helpless offspring ? Can you behold them steeped in the very depths of misery, of destitution, without one pang of remorse, when you know that you are the cause of all, and that you have it in your power to render them the happiest and most contented of human beings ? Alas ! alas ! my heart will break !"

At that moment, seeing that her husband was about to repose his head upon the table and to resign himself to sleep, she started up and again approaching him, laid her hand upon his arm.

"Dear Edward," she again said, in the same gentle accents, " again I beseech you to retire to bed, and Heaven in its mercy will, I trust, make to-morrow the precursor of a happy change. Come, come, we will talk no more to-night upon subjects that must be so painful and so disagree-able to us both, you shall not hear me give utterance again to a single word that can cause you the least vexation."

"Woman !" replied Edward, sternly, " will you cease to annoy me, or is it your wish to drive me again from the house, to which I was a cursed fool to return at all to-night ? But I have no doubt I can soon find some of my companions again, although I have spent all my money, I know I shall want for nothing."

"No, no, Edward," said his alarmed wife, " not for the world would I have you leave me in your present state, and at this unseasonable hour. Oh, if you could only know the dreadful anguish I endure when you are absent from home ; the terrible anxiety of mind I suffer lest some harm should have befallen you, the agony of my weary watchings, you would surely pity me and——"

" Cease !" interrupted Edward fiercely, " and reserve your canting lectures for those to whom they may be more palatable. Retire to rest with your brats, and leave me to myself."

The wretched woman again turned away from him with looks of horror and despair, and re-suming her seat by the side of her children, convulsive sobs heaved her bosom. Edward Lang-stone dropped his head upon the table, and he was soon buried in a sound sleep, from which his wife saw that it would be useless and dangerous to attempt to arouse him. But still she struggled against her own fatigue, and she continued for some time to watch him with bitter feelings of the most poignant regret, and to meditate upon the black and harrowing prospect of the future which was presented in such fearful characters to her mind's eye. The storm continued to rage without, and added to the horror of her feelings ; and as she gazed upon the pale faces of her children, and pictured to herself the wretched fate which seemed to be in store for them, the most terrible thoughts crowded upon her brain, and drove her to a state bordering upon madness. The fire in the grate had now expired, and all was cold and cheerless. Notwithstanding all her efforts, the power of sleep stole so irresistibly on her senses that she was unable to conquer its influence, and once more offering up a brief but fervent prayer to Heaven, she threw herself by the side of her children, and cuddling the youngest to her throbbing bosom, at length sank into a disturbed slumber. Edward Langstone, however, slept not calmly ;— no ; he frequently started as if in agony, and broken unintelligible words would escape his lips, whilst large drops of perspiration stood upon his forehead, and plainly showed the excitement under which his imagination laboured. Yes, the drunkard dreamt, and fearful was the vision which presented itself to his imagination. Again he was in his native village, in his happy dwelling, with his wife and little ones smiling around him. A plentiful meal was on the table, and everything bespoke comfort, cheerfulness, and content. The very cat who purred upon the hearth seemed to partake of the general happiness, and Carlo, the faithful dog, who had been so old a servant, wagged his tail in perfect enjoyment It was a beautiful summer evening, and the sleeper imagined that he had just returned home from his daily labour, and light and cheerful of heart he felt. The village bells were ringing forth their most joyous peal ; the balmy air, fragrant with the breath of myriads of flowers, was wafted refreshingly in at the open casement, the different gossips were seated on the benches of their cottage door, while the younger members of the community of both sexes were engaged in various healthy and innocent sports upon the green. It was such a scene that the eye could not help gazing upon with feelings of transport, one that the soul might delight to revel in, and never wish to wander from the contemplation of. But suddenly the scene and the situation of the dreamer and his family were changed ; they had quitted their happy home ; they had left the rural scenes of the country far behind them, and were on their road to London ; the smoke of which soon obscured the horizon, and all the noise and bustle which constantly prevails in the busy metropolis, smote their ears. Edward imagined that they looked back with feelings of regret upon the scenes they had quitted, but not without hope for the future. And now on were in the midst of the vast capital, and gazed with wonder at the novelties which met their sight, on every side, and which increased at every step they took. And now they found themselves once more the inmates of a happy dwelling, with every comfort around them, and imagined that content and peace were the inmates of his breast, and that health and happiness beamed in the faces of his wife and children. But suddenly a heavy gloom seemed to obscure his senses ; a dense darkness fell upon all around, he heard strange mutterings and grumblings in his ears ; his wife and children appeared gradually to fade from his sight and then the tumult of noisy revelry night he heard, and the atmosphere he breathed was hot and suffocating. He rubbed his eyes, and beheld through the cloud of smoke which filled the place, that he was sitting in a large gloomy looking room, filled with an heterogeneous congregation of individuals, smoking and drinking, and all evidently labouring under the greatest excitement from the effects of the deep potations of which they had partaken. The pots and glasses rattled on the tables ; the rude laugh, the drunken song, the ribald jest, and the reckless oath, all intermingled with each other, and caused a medley of confused sounds which set the senses reeling. Edward imagined that he felt sick at heart, and disgusted with the scene. He tried to rise from his seat, and quit the place, but he had not the power to do so, he seemed to be rivetted to the spot. A tumbler of the intoxicating drink was offered to him by one of the persons present. At first he rejected it, and requested to be permitted to retire, but the only reply he received was the jeers and taunts of the abandoned wretches in whose company he so strangely found himself, and, wrought up to a state of desperation, he seized upon the proffered glass and drained it to the very dregs. A sensation quite new to him came over him, another, and another glass of the poisonous liquor he quaffed, and all thoughts of his wife and children vanished from his brain. A spell seemed to seize upon his faculties ; he joined freely in the scene of debauchery, until his senses reeled, and in the excitement of the moment he awoke. He rubbed his eyes, and endeavoured to arouse himself to a state of consciousness, but in vain, and again he slept, and once more his busy imagination was at work, and conjured up fresh subjects of torture for his distracted brain. The situation in which he now fancied himself to be, was most awful. He was seated on the dirty floor of a miserable apartment, which contained not the smallest article of furniture. There was not a spark of fire in the rusty grate, and the wind blew keenly in at the broken casement, freezing the very blood within his veins, for he had nothing but filthy rags to shield him from the inclemency of the weather, and his feet were entirely bare. He felt the pangs of hunger gnawing at his vitals, and his throat was parched with a burning thirst. He looked around him in the agony of despair, and in one corner of the room he saw his wife lying upon the bare boards apparently dying, whilst the emaciated forms of their children were huddled round her, and crying aloud for food!—He tried to move towards them, but could not: he seemed afraid to approach them, for bitter reproach was visible in their pallid countenances, and curses seemed to falter on their lips. Oh, the maddening agony of that moment; all the torments of perdition could not surpass it. How awful was the change that had now fallen upon his unfortunate wife. Where were those roseate smiles of health and happiness that once animated her beauteous countenance, and rendered her an object of esteem and admiration to all who knew her?—Want and misery were stamped upon every feature; the traces of a broken heart were visible in every lineament. The graces of her form had vanished, and in their place emaciation and deformity held predominance. The light which formerly sparkled in her eyes was dimmed, and the film of death seemed fast gathering before them.

" Wretch!" the voice of some invisible being seemed to thunder in his ears, " behold the work of thine hands; go seek thy abandoned associates, revel in riot and debauchery; quaff again the maddening draught, and exult in the good it has already accomplished. Let the toast pass merrily round—hurrah! for the workhouse and the jail; the tap-room and the charnel-house!—the memory of the starved wife and her innocent offspring! Heartless profligate! this is thy lesson!"

The dreamer's brain seemed to be on fire. The countenances of his wife and children grew more ghastly; unearthly voices muttered in his ears, urging him on to deeds of horror, and he started on his feet with a shriek of terror! His whole frame was convulsed; his eyes seemed ready to start from their sockets, and the perspiration poured down his face in torrents. The candle was nearly exhausted, and shed but a faint and sickly light around the dismal apartment. The eyes of Edward Langstone wandered to his wife and children, and their ghastly countenances seemed almost to realise the circumstances of his dream.

" By every power human and divine, this shall never be!" he cried; "behold my wife and children perish of want, and myself reduced to beggary and the scorn and contumely of the world? Away with the thought! I cannot release myself from the spell which binds me to my fate; it is I who have brought them to their present state of misery, and my hand shall now release them from their sufferings."

Madness was upon the wretched man's brain. He looked around the room, fearful lest some one might be observing him, and then snatching up a knife from the table, he advanced towards the mattress on which his wife and children were unconsciously sleeping. He stooped down and gazed earnestly upon them, and his hand faltered.

" Coward!" he cried, " why do I hesitate? They sleep; let it be succeeded by the ever-lasting sleep of death!"

WROUGHT up to a pitch of frenzy, the guilty man was about to put his horrible crime into execution; the knife was already upon his wife's throat, when she suddenly started up with a wild scream, and grasping his arm with the strength of despair, arrested him in his deadly purpose.

" Horror! horror!" she shrieked, when she beheld the wildness of his looks, and saw the knife glittering in his hand; "Edward! husband! what would you do?"

" Release you and our children from your misery, since I cannot escape from the power of the demon spell which holds its influence over me!" replied the distracted man.

" Merciful God!" cried the terror-stricken Mary, " would you commit murder?"

" Fate threatens you with a still more horrible death," replied her husband, "and I will not shrink from the deed! You supplicate in vain! A maddening demon urges me on, and this moment you die!"

" Mercy! mercy! Edward!" again shrieked the unhappy woman; "spare me—spare our little ones!"

He attempted to release his arm from her hold, but she struggled with almost super-human strength, and screamed aloud for help. The two eldest children, aroused by the noise of the struggle, clung to their mother, and added their cries to her's, but the monstrous determination of Edward Langstone seemed to be unshaken, and the fate of Mary and her children seemed to be inevitable, when at that critical moment a hasty footstep was heard ascending the stairs, and the door being burst open, one of the lodgers, a powerful man, rushed into the room, and darting suddenly upon Edward, wrested the knife from his hand, at the same time hurling him to the other side of the room. Mary sank on her knees exhausted, and clasping her hands vehemently together, looked imploringly at her husband, but without being able to utter a word,

CHAPTER III.

THE REMONSTRANCE.—THE ABRUPT DEPARTURE OF EDWARD LANGSTONE.—ANOTHER DAY
OF ANGUISH AND SUSPENSE.—THE FRUITLESS SEARCH.—THE VILLAIN CLINTON.

"WHY, Ned Langstone," demanded the man, "what is the meaning of all this? Are you drunk or mad? Would you commit murder?"

"What business have you to interfere?" cried Langstone, fiercely, "leave the room."

"Not I, indeed," returned the man—"at least not till I see everything safe; I own I am not one of the most respectable individuals in the world, circumstances will not let me, but I am not quite so bad as to stand by and see murder committed. I should only be doing my duty by placing you in the safe custody of the police, and I fancy you would find yourself in rather an awkward situation when placed before the magistrate."

"Oh, no, no, no, not for the world!" ejaculated Mary, "I forgive him; he must have been mad at the time; he knew not what he was doing. My dear Edward, compose yourself, and say that these dreadful thoughts are banished from your brain."

"You have got a wife of ten thousand, Ned Langstone," said the man, "and should prize her as the apple of your eye."

"Will you quit the room?" again demanded Langstone, sternly.

"Not while I see you in this state of excitement, you may depend upon it," replied the other. "I am not going to suffer murder to be committed while I can prevent it."

"Then I must leave this place, or I cannot be answerable for the consequences," remarked Edward.

"Oh, no, for the love of Heaven, do not leave me thus," implored Mary; "whither would you go? What desperate purpose have you in contemplation? You will but again fly to the accursed drink, and maddened by its dreadful, its pernicious influence, be tempted to commit some dreadful act. Oh, do not, I beseech you, turn a deaf ear to my supplications and advice. I freely forgive you all that has happened, and never more shall the horrors of this night pass my lips. Say you will not go, and leave me in terrible doubt and suspense."

"You supplicate in vain," returned her husband; I shall go mad again if I remain here."

"Where do you intend to go, Edward?" eagerly asked his wife.

"Ask me not," he replied, "for I do not think proper to satisfy you. My brain is burning; my throat is parched; I must rid myself of these feelings, which are worse than the tortures of perdition."

"And you would fly to that which will only serve to increase them," ejaculated Mary;— "will nothing arouse you from this terrible infatuation?"

"No whining, maudlin arguments such as those you use," said Edward; "but enough of this; I am master of my own actions, I believe, and will not be thwarted in my purpose."

"Oh, forbear! forbear!"

A half muttered oath escaped the misguided man's lips, as he tore himself away from the frantic hold of his wife, and snatching up his hat, rushed hurriedly from the room.

"O follow him! follow him, I beg of you, and see whither he goes," supplicated Mrs. Langstone, appealing to the man, and tears streaming from her eyes; "in his present excited state of mind what may he not be tempted to do?"

"I will do as you wish, my good woman," replied the man; but I think it would have been much better, both for his own sake and yours, to have given him in charge."

Mary shuddered at the thought, and unable to return any answer, the man quitted the room. Again did Mary sink upon her knees in an agony of grief, and with clasped hands supplicated the merciful interposition of the Almighty. The horrors of that night were such as she had never thought to experience, and the blood froze in her veins as she reflected upon them, and the narrow escape which herself and her children had had from the murderous intentions of her husband. In a few minutes the man returned, and Mary eagerly inquired of him what success he had met with.

"I could see nothing of him," answered the man, "when I got into the street; and I cannot imagine where he could have vanished so suddenly."

"Alas! alas!" sighed our heroine, "how agonizing is this. The most dreadful apprehensions fill my bosom; oh, Edward, how can you thus delight to torture me? Do you not know any of the places he is in the habit of frequenting?"

"No, Mrs. Langstone," replied the person whom she interrogated; for you know I am no companion of your husband's; he does not think my society good enough for him, I suppose, and I am by no means solicitous for his friendship. I am but a poor, ignorant fellow, I know, but I sincerely pity you and your children, indeed I do, and hope that happier days are in store for you."

Mrs. Langstone thanked him for the good feelings he expressed towards her, and he quitted the room, promising again to come to her assistance, if she should require it. The anguish of Mary's mind increased every moment, and various were the conjectures she formed as to the intentions of her husband, but apprehensions of the most powerful and unconquerable nature distracted her bosom. To compose herself again to sleep would be impossible, and she did not make the attempt, though the children had again sunk to repose. In this manner she sat for some time, when feeling intensely cold, she arose, and rekindling the fire, its glowing coals soon imparted a somewhat more cheerful aspect to the wretched room. The storm had now ceased, and daylight was just beginning to dawn, but the storm that raged in the breast of the unhappy wife remained unabated, and forebodings of the most alarming description continued to district her brain. Oh, that her sister were present that she might impart to her her sorrows. and endeavour to receive consolation from her lips, for the loneliness of her situation was almost insupportable ; but there was no chance of her seeing her again before Monday at the earliest, and in the meantime what might not have happened to her and her children. She shuddered at the thought, and tears came to her relief. In what a terrible state of suspense did she listen for the return of her husband, and wonder what had become of him ; then when she reflected on the desperate and horrible attempt he had made upon the life of herself and her offspring, and the probability that he would still persist in his hideous design, she trembled so violently that she could scarcely support herself, and she could not help dreading his return home, convinced as she felt that he would again fly to the intoxicating drink, until he had worked himself up to a pitch of the most ungovernable fury, and then what might not the consequences be?

" Heaven protect us, my poor innocent children," she ejaculated, "and reclaim your misguided father from his present profligate course. Alas ! what a fatal influence have his villanous associates obtained over him, and from which it seems, he has not the power to escape. Oh, fatal and accursed was the hour which compelled us to leave our native village, where for so many years naught but happiness smiled around us. The temptations of this giddy metropolis, where vice abounds to entrap the unwary and the inexperienced, have worked my unfortunate husband's ruin, starvation hourly stares us in the face, and unless Providence mercifully interposes to save us we are irretrievably lost. I can scarce believe in the reality of our misery. At times I would fain persuade myself that it is all a frightful dream ; but, alas, that is impossible. It is not likely that Edward's employer will much longer put up with his intemperance, and neglect of his duty, and should he be thrown destitute and characterless upon the world, what will then become of us? I tremble with terror at the thought, for, urged by his guilty companions, and the desperation of his circumstances, he would then be plunged still deeper into crime, and an ignominious end would probably be the climax of his mad career. Oh, God, avert the realization of that awful foreboding, and rather let us perish altogether in the midst of our misery !"

Convulsive sobs choked her further utterance, and she remained for some minutes silent, and lost to everything but the agony of her own thoughts. Tediously the dreary hours passed away without anything occurring to ease the anguish and suspense of Mary's mind. It was now broad daylight—it was Sunday ; alas, what a sad one to the deeply wronged mother and her helpless children. The miserable room seemed to wear a more than usually dismal aspect to Mary's imagination, and the noise and laughter which proceeded from the different lodgers in the crazy house, sounded like bitter mockery to her ears. She had no heart, no spirit for anything ; the remorseless hand of fate had crushed her every hope, and life had become an insupportable burthen to her ; she wept over her poor children, who were now awake, and marked with the most unspeakable anguish the paleness of their looks ; but at length she aroused herself, and prepared for them their frugal morning meal, which the kindness of Laura had supplied them with ; and of which they partook heartily, whilst the hapless mother sat down and watched them with an aching heart, marvelling to herself how long it might be ere every means would be exhausted of supplying them with their wants. Taste of the smallest portion of the meal she could not, for her heart was too full, and the agony of her mind was so great that she almost sunk under it. What an awful time of suffering and suspense was the Sabbath morning, when the mind should be at rest from the cares and anxieties of labour, to poor Mary Langstone ; and as the hours passed away, and still her husband came not, her apprehensions increased. Sometimes the dreadful idea flashed upon her brain, that her husband had in the frenzy of mind in which he had quitted her, committed suicide, and then all the horrors of her dream recurred to her memory, and the judgment of heaven, for the wish she had so hastily uttered seemed to have descended upon her.

"Oh, merciful God !" she ejaculated, "pardon me, I beseech Thee, for that wish, so thoughtlessly uttered, and save my misguided husband from the perpetration of any rash and fatal act. With all his faults, he still possesses my fondest love, and would he but reform, how great would be my happiness. Alas, Edward, madness must assuredly have seized upon your brain, or you could never act in the manner you are now doing."

Then all the horrors of the night rushed with tenfold force upon her memory; again she thought she beheld her husband standing over her, with the deadly knife in his hand, his eyes blood-shot with the power of his passions and the ferocity of his inhuman determination, and the blood seemed nearly stagnate in her veins. It was a frightful picture, and yet in vain she sought to withdraw her mind from the contemplation of it; but still how grateful was she to Providence, who had preserved herself and her tender offspring from so fearful and untimely a fate. Heavily and drearily the morning wore on; still Mary continued to listen with the most breathless attention to catch the slightest sound which might indicate the return of her husband, and still was she doomed to bitter disappointment. She sat at the casement and looked into the dreary and filthy alley in which their miserable habitation was situated, in the hope of beholding him approach, but, alas! he came not, and the intensity of her despair became the more sickening and insupportable. To remain where she was became intolerable; she fancied that she could, if she went forth, succeed in discovering what had become of him, and yet she did not like to take her children, destitute, and nearly naked as they were, into the bleak air of that cheerless morning, and she feared to leave them behind her. What would she not have given, if she had but the means, to have seen her sister, that she might make her acquainted with her dreadful situation, and obtain her assistance in her terrible emergency? Eleven o'clock, twelve o'clock arrived, and still no relief to her anxiety; still Edward was absent, and she was left to form the most terrible conjectures as to what had become of him. She prepared the humble meal which Laura had brought her on the Saturday evening, and endeavoured again to encourage the hope that he would shortly arrive in a better state of mind to partake of it; but still bitter disappointment was her only reward, and her heart sunk under the weight of agony and suspense.

"Wretched man!" she cried at last, in the insupportable anguish of her despair; "you have been driven to the perpetration of some fatal crime, and the misery and destruction engendered in your improvidence is now, alas, I fear, consummated! My God! it would be a mercy to us, wert Thou to release us from our present sufferings, and those which too evidently are in store for us, by immediate death."

"Mother, dear mother," said the poor boy, who was the eldest of her children, looking up expressively in her face, "do not cry—oh, do not cry, or me and Nelly will cry too; for it makes us cry to see you do so. We are not hungry now, and will not ask you for any more, that we will not; aunt Laura is coming by-and-by, father too will be here, and we shall be so happy. Do not cry, dear mother, do not cry."

The distressed mother clasped her beauteous boy to her throbbing bosom, and the convulsive emotions which agitated it, for some moments deprived her of utterance.

"Edward!—Edward!—misguided husband," she sobbed at length, "could you witness such a scene as this in your moments of reason, and when away from the wretches who have plunged you into the vortex of guilt, surely, surely, it must, it would work a reformation in your wandering mind. Alas! alas! what can have rendered you so callous to the welfare of your wife and children? How can you have permitted the demon of intoxication thus to stifle all the noble and generous feelings of your nature? Oh, that fate should ever have driven us from our dear native village into the contaminating atmosphere of this vicious town; would to heaven that we had never been compelled to quit those rural, those happy scenes, where temptation was unknown, where content and peace ever reigned predominant and unlimited. With what melancholy feelings of delight do I recall to my memory those sunny hours of bliss; hours, I fear, alas! never fated to return. The rural cot, so clean and well furnished, the honeysuckle climbing the casement, the cheerful fire blazing on the hearth to welcome my then fond husband from the toils of the day; the affectionate smiles with which he ever greeted me; the village festival, of which we were always the welcome and happy guests; the merry dance; the mirthful jest; the healthy laugh; the smiling faces that ever beamed around us; the contented looks of our venerable friends, as they sat at their cottage doors, enjoying the contemplations of those innocent sports in which they were too old to mingle, but which in the reminiscences of their youthful days made them young again in heart. Oh, Edward! such moments as those must surely be banished entirely from your memory, or the frightful contrast now presented must awaken you to sense and rectitude."

She was interrupted by hearing a gentle knock at the room door, and before she could open it, Stephen Gadsby, the man who had been the fortunate means of preventing Edward Langstone from the perpetration of the horrible crime he had contemplated, entered the room.

"I beg your pardon, Mrs. Langstone," he said, in tones of the utmost respect, "for intruding upon you, but I could not help just stepping in to inquire how you and your poor children are this morning?"

"Alas! replied Mary, "wretched enough; how can we be otherwise under all the circumstances of our hard fate?"

"You must endeavour to bear up, Mrs. Langstone," remarked the poor fellow, "and times will yet be better with you. I am but an ignorant fellow, and know I have much to answer for; would that I could escape from my present course of life, but that is impossible; I am one of the wretched straws, uncared for and unpitied, who have been thrown upon the ocean of life to sink or to float, and I suppose I must be content to buffet with the tempest in the best way I can. My betters tell me that I have no business here, and perhaps I have not, but then I often wonder how it was that I was permitted to become one of the living creatures of this world at all. However, I will say no more upon that subject; this is the world and the other's the country, and I suppose everything will be reckoned up square and fair at last. I am very sorry, though, to see you in such trouble, indeed I am, and I only wish it was in my power to assist you."

"My good friend," said Mrs. Langstone, in tones which spoke the sincerity of her feelings, "I owe you an everlasting debt of gratitude for your kind and merciful interference last night; to you myself and poor children are indebted for the preservation of our lives, and my misguided husband from the perpetration of a crime, the very thoughts of which fills my breast with horror."

"O do not mention it, Mrs. Langstone, I beg of you," answered Gadsby; "I am too glad to think I was at hand, and that I had the opportunity of doing at least one good act in my life."

"But you will not mention the circumstance to any one?" said Mary, eagerly.

"Oh, no," returned Stephen, "since it is your wish; but your husband is still away, I see."

"Alas, he is," replied Mary; "would to Heaven that I knew where he was. Have you no idea, Mr. Gadsby, of the places he resorts to?"

"I have not indeed, ma'am," answered Stephen; "as I said last night, your husband is too proud to consider me worthy of his company; however, if you wish it, I will endeavour to find him out."

"Oh," exclaimed Mary, "how much you will oblige me by so doing. And should you fortunately meet with him, quarrel not with him, I implore you, nor taunt him with the occurrences of last night, but do your best to persuade him to return home, and to assure him that all shall be forgotten by me."

"You may depend upon me, Mrs. Langstone," replied Gadsby, "and I only hope that my efforts may be crowned with success."

"God bless you," said the anxious and grateful wife.

"God bless us all," returned Stephen, with a peculiar expression of countenance, but which showed the honest and fervent character of the feelings that were struggling in his uncultivated breast, "though that is a prayer that I do not often know how to utter; thanks to my betters for the *larning* they have given to me. I will be off immediately, missus; only keep up your spirits while I am gone, and I shouldn't at all wonder but I am successful."

Thus saying, Stephen Gadsby quitted the room, and after his observations, expressed even in the coarse and simple way they were, Mary did indeed feel a slight ray of hope and comfort dawn upon her heart, and she endeavoured to wait calmly and patiently the result. Two—three hours elapsed, the dinner remained untouched, except by the children, but still neither Edward or the man who had gone in search of him returned. The afternoon wore away, and evening set in dark, cheerless, and miserable, but still they were both absent. The patience of Mary was completely exhausted, and she traversed the room in a state of mind bordering upon madness. Despair seemed to be conveyed to her senses in every gust of the wind that howled so mournfully. At times she was driven to such a pitch of excitement that she was half tempted to rush from the house, to brave all the horrors of the night, and to trust to Providence to discover what had become of her husband, but some instinctive power arrested her in her purpose, and sinking in her chair, she hugged her infant still closer to her breast, and gave herself up entirely to despair.

"He will never return," she sobbed; "the demon which has taken possession of his b ain, has driven him to some act of desperation, and I feel that all the horrors of my fate are rapidly approaching to a crisis. And yet what did I say to urge him to such a course? Did I greet him with harsh words and bitter reproaches, although I had such ample cause to do so? Oh, no; Heaven can bear witness that I did not. Then, why—oh why, the horrible crime that he meditated, and which he was so narrowly prevented from perpetrating? My blood freezes at the thought! Oh, God! in mercy I beseech Thee, with all his faults, to preserve and restore to me my unfortunate husband?"

She opened the door, and listened with the most breathless and agonising impatience, but not a sound was heard either in the house or alley. Fate seemed to have conspired against her, and she even began to entertain some fearful misgivings as to the honesty and sincerity of Stephen Gadsby's intentions; but she reproached herself immediately afterwards for encouraging such thoughts, and again endeavoured to tranquillize her feelings, and to wait patiently the issue of events. This, however, was an arduous task, and one not easy of accomplishment. Ten o'clock tolled from the steeple of a church in the vicinity, and then the sufferings and suspense of the wretched and neglected wife became intolerable. The children were again fast asleep, and, wound up to a pitch very little short of madness, she was about to rush from the house, and to wander, she knew not whither, when the sounds of approaching footsteps met her ears, and she advanced hastily to the door, which she opened, and Stephen Gadsby presented himself. Being alone, the heart of Mary sank within her, and she could not articulate a syllable. Gadsby walked into the room, and his looks showed plainly how much he commiserated with her.

"Ah, missus," he observed, "I have had rather a hard day's work of it; but I should not complain if my efforts had only been crowned with a little better success."

"Then you have not seen him?" gasped forth Mary, with a look of despair.

"No, Mrs. Langstone," replied Gadsby, "I have neither seen him or been able to gain the least intelligence of him, though I have searched every nook and corner that I could think on, where I was likely to find him. I was in hopes that he might have returned home before now."

"Alas, alas!" groaned Mary, "he will never return again!"

"Nay, say not so, missus," said Stephen soothingly; "he must be a worse man than I even take him for, if he could thus desert his wife and his little ones. Cheer up—cheer up, and all will be well by-and-by."

"Never, never, again," sighed Mary, stung by remorse ; "he has, I fear, laid violent hands on himself, and if so, the cup of my misery and despair is filled to the brim."

"Oh, no, missus," returned Gadsby, "you must not give way to such thoughts as them. Ned Langstone is too good a judge, mark my words, to be tired of his life just yet. He has got amongst some of his old companions, no doubt, and they, seeing the state of mind he was in, will not suffer him to leave them."

"I cannot endure this state of torturing suspense any longer!" ejaculated Mary; "the most horrible certainty is preferable to it. I will myself go forth and endeavour to find him, and Providence will, I trust, in mercy guide my footsteps to where he is."

"No, Mrs. Langstone," said Gadsby, "you must not do this; it would be madness for you to attempt it; what better success could you hope to meet with than I have done? Besides, remember the lateness of the hour, and the danger which——"

"Oh, I care not," interrupted Mary; "I will brave everything; I cannot remain here in this awful state of doubt and anxiety."

"You cannot think of leaving your children, Mrs. Langstone," suggested Stephen Gadsby ; 'let me advise you to become calm, and not to entertain such apprehensions, for, depend upon it, they will be entirely groundless. Your husband will return shortly, mark my words if he don't ; and should he return in the same state that he was in last night, which I hope he will not, if you should require my assistance, I shall be on the listen, and will take good care that no harm shall come to you."

Mrs. Langstone looked at the poor fellow gratefully, but she could not return any answer, for her heart was too full, and having once more sought to inspire her with hope that her husband would shortly return home, he wished her good night, and retired from the room. For several minutes after his departure, Mary remained in a state of almost utter unconsciousness, but at length she started to her feet, and clasping her aching temples, she gazed wildly and distractedly round her as she exclaimed—

"Still away! still leaving me in this horrible state of agony and suspense! Oh, Edward, this is monstrous; I could never, even after all your cruel treatment, have believed you capable of such refined inhumanity. What have I done to deserve this? Heaven knows that I have ever been a devoted and dutiful wife to you, and would you but abandon your evil ways, not a murmur of reproach towards you should escape my lips. God! God! look down with pity upon me and my poor helpless innocents, and save their wretched father from the perpetration of any rash act."

Scalding tears streamed down her cheeks as she gave utterance to these melancholy words, and she rocked herself to and fro' in her chair, almost bereft of reason. The night wind howled dismally ; the silence of the dead, but for its melancholy wailings, would have reigned on everything around, and the hour itself (for it was now near midnight) was sufficient to excite feeling of awe in a bosom less agitated than Mary's ; but nothing came to relieve her—no sound announced her husband's approach, and the terrors of her mind gained strength every moment. Her disordered imagination was busy at work, and conjured up the most frightful apprehensions. The wild and excited state of mind in which he had quitted her, served to increase those fears, and she tried in vain to obtain the least tranquillity. One o'clock—two o'clock—three o'clock ! and still he came not, and she gave him up in despair. Even at that hour, while her children were sleeping, she was half resolved to rush from the house, and to go in search of him, but reason at length convinced her of the danger and fruitlessness of such a step, and she abandoned the idea in despair. She continued her dreary watch till daylight entered the gloomy precincts of her miserable chamber, but no thought of sleep entered her mind. Let whatever might be the consequences, she resolved to wander forth that day and endeavour to ascertain the worst. She could endure the agonising suspense no longer, and determined that nothing should dissuade her from the purpose, for she felt her errand was one of life or death. She had scarcely formed these resolutions, when Stephen Gadsby again knocked at her room door, and was immediately admitted,

"I am sorry, Mrs. Langstone," he observed, "to find that your husband has not yet returned, and he certainly has disgraced himself by such cruel and unnatural conduct. But keep up your spirits, and no doubt he will ere long be brought to his senses."

"Alas! alas!" sighed Mary, "something dreadful must have happened to him, or he never could have had the heart to absent himself thus."

"As for not having the heart, missus," returned Gadsby, "I cannot say much about that, after his behaviour to you on the Saturday night. However, I would still advise you to bear up with patience, and all may not turn out so bad as you now imagine."

"Oh, God!" ejaculated Mrs. Langstone, "what cause is there for me to hope? But I cannot stay here, in this dreadful state of uncertainty, indeed I cannot. Something tells me that if I go forth, I shall find him, or, at any rate, ascertain what has become of him. It is my duty to do so, and nothing shall persuade me from it."

"Very well, missus," said Stephen; "I would not for the world seek to persuade you from anything which may be likely to gratify your hopes, but remember your children."

"You have moved to me by your late conduct that you possess a kind heart," replied Mary, eagerly, "and I feel convinced that you and your wife will see that no harm comes to my two eldest children during my absence—the infant, of course, I must take with me."

"Aye, that we will, most readily," said Stephen Gadsby, "and I only hope that you may meet with success. Come, youngsters, I and my missus will take charge of you while your mother is away, and you will find that though I am a rough and ignorant sort of a fellow, I am not yet quite destitute of every kind of feeling.

"Oh, thanks, thanks," fervently cried Mary;—"Heaven will reward you for this. Come, my dear children, entrust yourselves to this good man; I will soon return. I go to bring your father."

The children sobbed, but Mary kissed them fondly, and resigning them to the care of Stephen Gadsby, she clasped her infant to her breast, and with a mental prayer to Heaven for success, she quitted the house, and entered upon the cold and cheerless streets. She had wandered for some distance before she had even made up her mind whither to direct her steps, when she stopped in her progress, and endeavoured to collect her thoughts. She was almost a stranger to the neighbourhood, for it was seldom that she quitted her wretched abode, and everything appeared strange to her. She had not the least idea of the places where her husband frequented, for he had taken good care to conceal them from her, and it was now that she felt the utter hopelessness of her expedition. The persons who passed her looked upon her with vulgar curiosity, and to her imagination seemed to mock her sufferings. Several times she was subjected to the most rude and insulting remarks, which, however, served to arouse her into action, and she proceeded on her way, though perfectly at a loss whither to direct her course. She glanced eagerly and anxiously towards every public-house she passed on her way, with the hope of seeing him whom she sought, and the different haggard wretches who were staggering senselessly from them, even at that early hour of the morning, excited in her bosom feelings of the utmost disgust and horror. She did not venture to look into them, for she felt convinced that she would meet with nothing but insult if she did so, and she walked on with a heavy and despairing heart. A day of fruitless toil and anxiety was this to Mary Langstone; numerous were the station-houses and hospitals she visited, but not the slightest intelligence could she gain of her husband, and when the shadows of evening began to fall around, worn out with fatigue, footsore, and heart-broken, she once more turned her steps towards her dreary home. It was a bitter cold night, and the snow was descending in large flakes. The covering of Mary was scanty, and her limbs were almost paralyzed with the intensity of the weather. All was dreary and dark before her, dismal as her own hard fate; but she thought not of that; her mind was too much absorbed by her anxiety for her husband. She pressed her infant closer to her breast to shelter it as much as possible from the cold, and weeping bitterly, she proceeded on her way. A stranger to the locality, she knew not which way to go, and coming upon a man turning abruptly round the corner of a street, she ventured to inquire of him. How startled and astonished was she, when, on hearing the sound of her voice, he mentioned her name, and looking up, by the light of a gas-lamp near which they were standing, she was filled with greater amazement than ever, and shrank back with terror when she recognised in the man whom she had accosted, the villain Clinton. She could not repress a faint cry of alarm, and endeavoured to rush past him, but he detained her.

"What, Mary," said Clinton, in a tone of vulgar familiarity, "would you shy an old acquaintance and in this manner? Come, come, this is too bad, and I must not allow it. It is a long time since we have met before, and now I am so fortunate I must have a little conversation with you."

Mary looked anxiously around her, but there was no one near to whom she could appeal for help; it was also in a lonely and unfrequented part of the neighbourhood in which they were standing, and her heart sank within her with terror.

"Unhand me, Clinton," she exclaimed, endeavouring to release herself in vain from his hold; "or my cries shall alarm the neighbourhood. Wretch! destroyer of my husband and my peace of mind, are you not satisfied yet with the fiendish work you have accomplished?"

"Nay," returned Clinton, coolly, "these are harsh words, methinks, to use to such an old particular as I am. However, I will not be offended with you; no doubt the conduct of your husband gives you plenty of cause for anger; as for my being his destroyer, that is all fudge, though I must say that if you had acted wisely you would at this time have been the wife of a much better man."

"Clinton," gasped forth Mary, "if you possess one spark of manly feeling, you will not detain me from my wretched home, where I have left my helpless children to seek my misguided husband, that husband brought to shame, to guilt, and degradation by the abominable artifices of yourself and your dissolute companions."

"Nay," replied Clinton, "there you wrong me, for surely I am not your husband's keeper. Indeed I have often regretted that he should act in the way he has done towards you, and have not only remonstrated with him, but given him good advice. Mary Langstone, my language when first addressing you might have seemed too familiar, and tinctured with a little tone of levity, but indeed it was not so intended. I pity you from my very soul, and, however much you may have heard prejudicial to my character, I would willingly render you any service that lies in my power. Nay, think not this is a mere empty boast, for the purpose of taking any advantage of your credulity, or that I have any bad feeling rankling in my breast because you thought proper to prefer Ned Langstone to me."

"Let me go, Clinton, I beseech you," said Mrs. Langstone, "I bear you no ill-will, whatever may have been your faults, nor any of my fellow creatures, Heaven knows, but I am weary, heart-sore, in a fruitless search after my misguided husband, and am anxious to return to my poor famishing children. Oh, do not detain me, I implore you."

"Poor woman," replied the crafty villain, in a tone of affected compassion, and releasing his hold of her, "I will not. But do not be too hasty, Mrs. Langstone; I would serve you if I could, in any way, indeed I would, notwithstanding the bad opinion you entertain of me. It is true that I have been your husband's companion accidentally on two or three of his drunken freaks, but I have never tempted him, but, on the contrary, have always endeavoured to persuade him to return home, and even now methinks I could assist you in your present difficulty."

This was spoken in such an apparent tone of sincerity that the unfortunate woman was taken completely off her guard.

"Mr. Clinton," she ejaculated, "do you really mean what you say? Are you not indeed attempting to deceive me?"

"By all my hopes I am not," replied the consummate scoundrel, "it is a late hour of the evening for you to be out, and I see you are in a terrible state of agitation. I say again that I pity you, and that with all my heart. Ned Langstone ought to be ashamed of himself, that he ought."

Had not poor Mary have been in the dreadful state of excitement she was, nearly bereft of her senses, she must have noticed the tone of sarcasm in which the villain uttered these words, but she did not, and she therefore said eagerly—

"If I have wronged you, Mr. Clinton, by any observations I have made use of, I am sorry for it, and hope you will excuse me, considering the agitated state of mind under which I am naturally labouring. My unfortunate husband has been absent from our wretched home ever since an early hour yesterday morning; I understood from him that he had been with you and Captain Braghall, and he left me in a most excited state."

"Why," returned Clinton, "if I were to say that I did not see him and the captain on Saturday evening after we left our employment, I should be telling a falsehood, however, I did not remain with him, but, on the contrary, endeavoured to the best of my abilities to persuade him to return home."

"Oh, tell me, know you where he is now?"

"Why I think I can form a pretty shrewd guess; and if you will only entrust yourself under my protection, I have very little doubt that I can lead you to him."

"Is it far from here?" anxiously asked Mrs. Langstone.

"Only a few minutes' walk."

"Mr. Clinton, by all your hopes here and hereafter, you are not deceiving me?"

"I can say no more than I have," replied the villain, with apparent sincerity, "and if you still doubt me, go your way, I will not attempt to detain you."

"I will trust you," said Mary, "and if you are a man you will take compassion on the desolate situation of me and my helpless little ones."

"This way, then," said Clinton, exulting to himself on the success of his plot, "and fear not, we shall soon be there."

Mary wrapped her shawl still closer around the form of the infant at her breast, and followed with trembling footsteps, looking up with despairing eyes into the dark and cheerless night, and noticing not (for her mind was too busily occupied) the few straggling passengers they met with on their way. They passed through some of the most miserable and obscure streets, which appeared to be entirely uncared for and unwatched, the individuals they met being of the most wretched class, and whose very aspects were sufficient to inspire disgust. Mary could not help a feeling of dread and misgiving stealing over her, and she again inquired of Clinton if they had much further to go.

"No," he answered, "we shall be there in a few minutes; do not be alarmed."

"This is a lonely spot," remarked Mary, shuddering. "Clinton, as a man, I again beseech you to inform me if you can accomplish what you have professed, or if you mean anything wrong?"

"I can say no more than I have done already," answered Clinton; "come, come, why should you doubt me?"

Mary offered up a mental prayer to Heaven for protection, and once more pressing her infant fondly to her breast, she followed her conductor with a palpitating heart. The idea of meeting her husband, and of being able to persuade him to return home with her, superseded every other, and inspired her with a feeling of fortitude, which, under the circumstances, was rather extraordinary. They now entered a dark alley, at the end of which a dim light was emitted from a dirty lamp, and which faintly disclosed an old-fashioned public-house, of the lowest and most forbidding possible aspect.

"That is the house," said Clinton, "and I have not the least doubt that we shall find him we seek there."

Mrs. Langstone hesitated, and looked at the house with a shudder of suspicion.

"Oh, it is impossible," she said, "that my husband can have become so abandoned and so totally lost to every feeling of self-respect as to resort to such a den as that."

"Have his habits of late, then, rendered it so improbable?" demanded Clinton, in rather sarcastic tones.

"Alas, no!" sighed Mary. "unhappy man. But I dare not venture into that place, its very aspect bespeaks crime and treachery."

"Nonsense," replied Clinton, "your fears are groundless; are you not under my protection? No one there shall dare to insult you. Come, come, we delay time, and it is now getting late."

"Heaven help me!" ejaculated Mrs. Langstone, fervently, and she then suffered herself to be led by Clinton, scarcely conscious of what she did, towards the house.

The blinds were all drawn close, and not a sound proceeded from it.

"There is no one here," said Mary, "you must be mistaken in the house."

"Mistaken!" repeated Clinton, "when I have been here so frequently; ridiculous. The guests are all at the back of the house or up stairs. There, do not be alarmed; I warrant we shall find your husband here."

Reluctantly Mrs. Langstone yielded, and opening the door, Clinton led her in and closed it carefully after him. A feeling of dread came over the mind of Mary at the gloomy and smoky aspect of the bar; while the atmosphere of the place was nauseous and oppressive. A solitary gas-light glimmered in the bar, and only served to cast a more sickly hue upon all around. There was no person present, but Mary could hear the muttering of several voices which seemed to proceed from the back of the premises, and once more her courage forsook her, and she regretted deeply that she had so easily been persuaded to accompany Clinton, who it was more than probable had some sinister design in view.

"The very sight of this place inspires me with terror," she said; "it is impossible that my unfortunate husband can resort to such an awful den as this. Suffer me to depart, Clinton; I was wrong in trusting to you at all; I dare not proceed any further."

"How silly you talk, Mrs. Langstone," said the villain, laying hold of her arm in a manner which plainly showed that he was determined not to be foiled in his purpose, whatever it might be; "what have you to fear? To be sure, this is not one of the most inviting looking places in the world, but if we find the object of our search here, and can persuade him to return home with you, your wishes will be obtained. What ho! my noble tap-tub! where the devil have you hid yourself? A pretty fellow you are to attend upon your customers."

"Is that you, Clinton?" demanded a coarse vulgar looking man, with extremely dirty face and hands, and an apron that had evidently not been in the washing-tub for some time—making his appearance from a side door. He started on seeing Mary, and he and Clinton changed significant glances with each other, which she did not observe.

"What may be your pleasure?" he added in a kind of mock politeness; "what can I do to serve you and this good woman? In course you will take some refreshments?"

"Yes," replied Clinton, "two glasses of your best brandy, and be quick about it, for our time is precious."

"Oh, none for me," said Mary, with a shudder of repugnance.

"Nonsense," returned Clinton, "I'm sure you must require something after your long walk, and to revive your spirits. Let me prevail upon you."

"Oh, not for the world, cried Mary, "the bare mention of the destructive drink inspires me with feelings of disgust and horror. Clinton, I do fear again you have deceived me, and that you intend me some harm. Let me go; let me return to my poor children."

"In a few minutes," said the villain; "how can you be so mistrustful, when I wish to render you a service? Is Mr. Langstone in the house?" he added, addressing himself to the landlord.

"He is, and has been here all day," was the reply, "although I did all I could to persuade him to return home; he is fast asleep up stairs."

"I must see him," said Clinton, "this is his wife, and I have promised her to try to find him out."

"And very kind of you," said the landlord; "well, you will find him, as I said before, in one of the rooms up stairs."

"I will remain below," remarked Mrs. Langstone, still doubting, and looking anxiously forward to the door.

"No, no," replied Clinton, "that would not have the desired effect, for when your husband beholds you he will be more likely to be roused to his senses, and to yield to your exhortations and persuasions."

There was something so reasonable in this, and it was spoken with such apparent sincerity, that Mary could not offer any further resistance, and the landlord handing him a candle, and mentioned the particular room in which they would find Langstone, Clinton led the way up a dark old-fashioned staircase, Mrs. Langstone timidly following him. He stopped at a door on the second story, and turning to Mary, said—

"This the room, and your anxieties will soon be at an end."

She still hesitated, and was almost induced to make a precipitate retreat; but the villian Clinton, taking advantage of her confusion, suddenly grasped her arm, and hastily opening the door, thrust her into the room, following himself, and locking the door after him. Poor Mary looked despairing and terrified around the room, but there was no one in it but themselves, and her worst fears were then confirmed—the heartless villain had betrayed her, and she was in that lonely and infamous place entirely at his mercy. She uttered a loud shriek of terror, and sunk with despairing and supplicating looks at his feet.

CHAPTER VI.

THE BASE ATTEMPT OF CLINTON.—THE INTERRUPTION.—THE NARROW ESCAPE.—THE WRETCHED WIFE'S DESPAIR, AND CONTEMPLATED SUICIDE.

"MARY LANGSTONE," said the ruffian, "at length fortune has placed you in my power, and this night shall fully repay me for all the scorn and hatred I have experienced from you. I thought the time would come when I should have the means of accomplishing my purpose, and I waited for it patiently. It is useless for you to raise any alarm, for there is no one near to hear you, who would be inclined to render you any assistance. Do you remember the time when you so insultingly rejected me, for that man who has proved so good and amiable a husband to you? Oh, you made an admirable choice, and are now reaping the full blessings of it."

"Mercy! mercy! Clinton," sobbed the distracted Mrs. Langstone, "you cannot surely contemplate so monstrous a crime, which cannot fail to bring down upon your head the most terrible vengeance of Heaven and the law. Think of my deplorable situation, and that of my poor innocent children, and have pity on me. Oh, reflect, reflect, before you proceed to such dreadful extremities; suffer me to depart uninjured from this place, and I promise you, faithfully promise you, nay, I am ready to be bound by the most solemn oath, never to reveal to any one what has already this night happened."

"Oh, no," replied Clinton, with a determined look, "believe me, I am not going to trust to you. Since I have proceeded thus far, I am resolved not to stop until I have fully accomplished my purpose. Besides, you are in distress, you are on the very verge of starvation, both yourself and children, and you might, if you only act in accordance with my wishes, find that I could be a friend to you. It is quite evident that if your husband ever loved you, he cares nothing about you now, and therefore I do not see but that you would greatly better yourself by the change."

"Shameless wretch!" exclaimed the disgusted and indignant woman, rising to her feet, "to dare to insult my ears by such a horrible, such a revolting proposal. Again I command you to suffer me to depart, or my cries for help shall arouse the whole neighbourhood, and must surely bring some persons to my assistance."

"Indeed," answered Clinton, with a look of triumph, "but you will find yourself mistaken. As for the law, I entertain no fear of that; I am not without every means of eluding its vigilance. If you think that Ned Langstone remains virtuously faithful to you, you wofully deceive yourself. No, no, Ned has plenty of kind females who furnish him with the supplies, when his own exchequer is exhausted."

"Base calumniator!" cried the blushing woman, "I will not believe you. With all my misguided husband's faults, I will never believe that he could so degrade himself. But I talk to a man who is callous to every feeling of humanity and integrity. Forbear! or you will have bitter cause to regret this brutal outrage. What have you ever witnessed in my conduct to raise such guilty thoughts and wishes in your breast?"

"It matters not," he returned, "I have presumed to entertain them, since you will have it so, and this night I am determined that they shall be realized. No more delay—you must, you shall yield, though I am placed in Newgate to-morrow for the deed."

Thus saying, he snatched the infant from her arms, and placing it on the floor, seized the hapless Mary in his embrace, and insulted her with his unlawful kisses.

"Oh, help! help! for the love of Heaven!" shrieked the terrified and distracted woman, struggling desperately to escape. "Monster! have you no feeling of pity. Help! help! help!"

"Cease your cries!" exclaimed the ruffian fiercely, and endeavouring to force her towards an inner room. "Since I have ventured so far, I will not be foiled."

Again Mrs. Langstone struggled violently, and redoubled her cries for help, but her strength was almost exhausted, and the success of the villain in his atrocious designs seemed all but certain, when, just at that critical moment, a loud and confused noise was heard proceeding from below, and Clinton started and released his hold of Mary, who sank exhausted and insensible on the floor.

"D——n!" cried the ruffian," as he heard heavy footsteps hastily ascending the stairs; "who would ever have thought of this interruption? I shall be detected if I am not quick, but how can I escape? Ah, the window."

With the speed of an arrow he threw up the window, and emerging his body for a moment hung by the window cill, then dropping on to the roof of an old shed immediately beneath, he leapt from thence to the ground, and flying across the yard he made his escape by a back-door. It was the landlord and two or three of his guests, who had been alarmed by the cries of Mary, for the police seldom ventured into the alley where this house was situated, and fearful of the consequences which might ensue if the villain Clinton was permitted to accomplish his diabolical purpose, they thought it was best to rescue the unfortunate woman from his power. Bursting open the door, they rushed into the room, and raised the insensible form of Mary from the floor. They then looked round for Clinton, and beheld the open window.

"He is gone," said the worthy host, "most likely thinking that the Peelers were in the house. Damn him! I did not think he was going to act with such violence as this, or I would not have suffered him to come up stairs. He might have got me into a pretty hobble, and even now if it gets wind I may have to pay dearly for it. What is to be done with this woman?"

"Why all that can be done," suggested one of the men, "is to restore her to sensibility as quick as possible, and endeavour to persuade her to go quietly about her business, and to say no more about it."

"I only hope we may be able to do so so easily," said the landlord.

They now removed Mary and her child from the room, and conveyed them down stairs, where such remedies were applied as were likely to restore the unfortunate woman to sensibility, and at length their efforts were successful, and Mary, opening her eyes and beholding her situation, uttered a cry of horror.

"Do not be alarmed, my good woman," said the landlord in tones of affected kindness, "it it is all right now; Clinton has gone, and I am very sorry that anything of this kind should have happened; I am sure I would have prevented it had I been aware of it, and I really thought that your husband was still in the house. He must have departed very secretly. You had better take a little of something to revive you."

"No—no—not a drop," replied Mary, averting her gaze from the man's forbidding countenance with a feeling of disgust: "oh, God! that I should be thus brutally insulted. My poor infant!"

"It is here, my good woman," said the landlord, "quite safe."

"Do not detain me any longer," gasped forth Mrs. Langstone, "my weary limbs will yet carry me to my miserable home and starving children. Oh, Edward! Edward! you are the cause of all this!"

"We do not wish to detain you. Mrs. Langstone," observed the landlord, in winning accents of conciliation, "but I hope you will not say anything to any one about this unfortunate business; I can assure you that I am not to blame, though I may appear to be so."

"Let me go, I implore you," said Mary, "and I will promise you anything."

"Very good," returned the landlord; "I am satisfied, and you are at liberty to depart whenever you think proper. Do you know your way home?"

"Yes—yes," replied Mrs. Langstone, impatiently, "that is—I will find it."

"Good night," said the landlord opening the door, "you will not forget your promise?"

Mary did not stop to make any reply, but pressing her infant still closer to her bosom, she darted along the dismal alley as fast as her trembling limbs would carry her, and was soon again traversing the cheerless and almost deserted streets, in the most distracted state of mind, and bewildered as to the road she ought to pursue. What madness and despair were upon her brain when she thought of the diabolical assault which had been committed against her by the ruffian Clinton, but at the same time how grateful was she to Providence that she had been rescued at the very moment when her destruction seemed to be inevitable.

"Wretched, guilty husband!" she sighed, "how cruel are you thus to expose me to such dangers and sufferings as those! Will no power mercifully interpose to rescue you from your career of crime ere it is too late? Where are you now? Can you entirely have deserted me and your helpless children?"

Scalding tears chased each other down her pale cheeks, and, overcome by the power of her emotions, she was obliged to pause to recover herself, and to collect her bewildered thoughts. She gazed anxiously around her; the place was quite strange to her, and she saw no one of whom she might inquire her way. The time was getting late, and there were but few persons in the streets.

"Alas!" she cried, "when will the horrors of this night be at an end? My poor children, when shall I be restored to you?"

Again she walked on with a heavy heart, but she was so completely worn out with fatigue that she feared she should not be able to proceed much further, and every street she entered still appeared strange to her. At length she found herself on one of the bridges, and she was so fatigued and sick at heart, that she was compelled to rest herself in one of the recesses. Her infant was crying with the cold, and every piteous wail it uttered went like a dagger to her bosom. She looked down upon the dark river, and frightful thoughts again flashed upon her distracted brain.

"But a plunge," she muttered to herself, in a hoarse and hollow voice, still gazing upon the dark waters, "and all is over! Why should I continue to live to drag out this life of misery and hopelessness? Does not a spell seem to rest upon my fate, and to mark me for one of its most unfortunate victims? Have I not lost my husband's love, and do I not daily behold him hastening madly to ignominy and destruction? What is there to tempt me to live? To become a wretched outcast from the world and its enjoyments, and to see my children and myself become the scorn and neglect of our fellow creatures? Dreadful thoughts! Any fate is preferable to that. There is no one near to arrest my purpose; pardon me, oh, God! for that to which I am driven by the blackest despair!"

She looked fearfully around her, she frantically kissed the lips of her innocent babe—her brain seemed to whirl round, and she began to ascend the parapet of the bridge, intent on her awful purpose—when she was suddenly arrested by some person from behind, whom she had not seen approach, and turning round, she uttered a cry of astonishment when she beheld that it was Stephen Gadsby, whom Providence had mercifully sent to save her from the rash and fatal deed just at that critical moment.

"Why, good gracious! Mrs. Langstone," said Gadsby, "what were you going to do?"

"Oh, Gadsby," sobbed the heart-broken woman, "from what a fearful crime have you saved me! My God! and could I for a moment think to rush unbidden into Thy presence, and to leave my children unprotected and friendless behind me? Pardon me, I beseech Thee; for despair, I verily believe, has turned my brain!"

"Come, Mrs. Langstone," said Gadsby, kindly, "you must not encourage such dreadful thoughts as these, for times will mend with you before long. Where can you have been to this late hour? I have been everywhere in search of you, and it was accident entirely that so fortunately guided my footsteps hither."

"Alas! Mr. Gadsby," replied Mary, shuddering at the thought, "you can form no conception of the horrors I have endured this night, but I must not repeat them, I have made a promise not to do so, and Heaven knows what the dreadful consequences might be, if I were to break it. But my husband! oh what of him?"

"Why," replied Gadsby, "I am sorry to say that he had not returned when I left home and I was unable to hear anything of him in any of the houses I visited."

"Heaven save him," sighed Mary; "and my poor children?"

"Oh, I left them quite safe in the charge of my wife; but come, let us be going, for I am sure that you and your infant must be perishing with cold, and a long way from home."

"Alas!" sobbed Mary, "I am worn out with fatigue and agony of mind; I shall never be able to walk much further; what in the name of Heaven will become of me and my child?"

"It's lucky here is a cab coming;" said Gadsby, "and it is still more lucky that I have got money enough to pay the fare."

"Oh, my good man," returned Mary, "how grateful am I to you for this disinterested kindness. But you cannot afford it, and it would be wrong in me to take it, indeed it would."

"Oh, never mind that, Mrs. Langstone," said the poor fellow; "and I dare say I shall be none the poorer for it in the long run; so make your mind easy about that."

Mary could make no further reply, and the vehicle at that moment having arrived at the spot, and being empty, Gadsby hailed it, and having agreed with the driver about the fare, he handed in Mrs. Langstone and her infant, and mounting the box by the side of the cabman, it was driven off to the wretched neighbourhood in which they resided. Mary had now an opportunity of resting her weary limbs, but the anguish of her mind suffered no abatement, and she reflected with shuddering terror upon the dreadful crime she had been about to commit, and from which she was miraculously and providentially rescued by Gadsby. The horrors of the fearful situation in which she had been placed with the villain, Clinton and from which she had so narrowly escaped, also afforded her much food for torturing meditation, which was increased when she thought of the uncertain fate of her wretched and misguided husband. The terrible state of excitement in which he had quitted her, caused her to entertain the worst surmises, and suspense was, if possible, even more torturing than certainty. These conflicting thoughts occupied her mind until a cab stopped at the end of the alley in which she resided, and Gadsby supported her trembling limbs to the door and up the stairs to her own room, in which she found his wife kindly watching her sleeping children, but despair fell upon her heart when she found that her husband was still absent: and it being now nearly one o'clock, there was not much chance of his returning. The kind-hearted Laura had again been there during the day, and was greatly shocked when she heard what had taken place, and had left word that she would be sure to call upon her on the following day. She had brought with her another supply of provisions, part of which Mrs. Gadsby had cooked, and of which she prevailed upon Mary to partake, though it was with little appetite that she could do so, and Gadsby and his wife then wishing her good night, and proffering to render her any further assistance which she might require, and which lay in their humble power, quitted the room. Mrs. Langstone sank on her knees when they were gone, and remained for some time totally absorbed in the agony of her feelings, but quite exhausted at last, and giving up all hopes of her husband's return, she threw herself on the bed by the side of her tender offspring, and in a few minutes sleep overpowered her senses. Morning dawned and brought with it no relief, but their humble breakfast was scarcely dispatched when Laura Maysdale arrived. Mary threw herself into her affectionate sister's arms, and for some time wept bitterly. Laura could only mingle her tears with her sister's, and could not offer to her the least word of consolation.

"My dear Mary," she said at length, "how it tortures me to see you thus cruelly situated, and I have so little power to assist you. Your misguided husband is then still away? Alas! how callous must his heart have become to every feeling of affection to treat you and your poor children in this inhuman manner. But Providence will surely ere long bring him to his senses."

"Alas! I fear not," sighed Mary, " ere it is too late ; and hourly do I apprehend some terrible result. Oh, my dear sister, how can I repeat to you the terrors I last night experienced, the dangers from which I escaped, the awful crime which, in the despair of my heart, I was, tempted to commit, and from the perpetration of which Stephen Gadsby alone saved me."

" Your words fill me with amazement, Mary," said Laura ; " what mean you ? Urged into the perpetration of crime !—oh, you must surely be labouring under some unhappy delusion."

" Ah, no ! indeed I am not, Laura, and even now the recollection of it freezes the blood in my veins with horror. Had it not been for the accidental arrival of Stephen Gadsby at the spot at the very critical moment, you would never more have beheld me or my innocent infant alive."

" Dreadful thought !" ejaculated her sister ; " I can scarcely believe what I hear. May Heaven preserve you, dear Mary, for how little do you deserve to meet with so cruel a fate. But tell me all the fearful particulars."

" Listen, Laura, and you will then, I am sure, not wonder that my distracted feelings should bewilder my senses, and urge me on to acts of desperation which at any other time I should shrink from the bare contemplation of, with horror and dismay."

She then in as few words as possible related the particulars of her meeting with the villian Clinton, and the alarming scene which had taken place between them, and Laura listened to her with mingled feelings of the utmost astonishment, disgust, and commiseration.

" Gracious Heaven !" she ejaculated, " and is it to such dangers and insults as those, the misconduct of your husband exposes you, my poor sister ?—Will nothing awaken him to a sense of the enormity of the course he is pursuing ?"

" Alas ! alas ! I fear not," sobbed Mrs. Langstone ; " despair seizes on my brain, and my heart sickens at the thought. And perhaps I have acted wrong in revealing even to you those revolting facts."

" Oh, no, that is impossible;" answered Laura, " for to whom could you better confide them ?"

" Hear the conclusion of my fearful narrative," said Mary, after a brief pause, during which she had endeavoured to collect all her fortitude for the painful task she had imposed on herself. She then detailed all the facts of her contemplated act of self-destruction of herself and infant, and from which she had been so narrowly and so providentially rescued. Laura shuddered with terror as she proceeded, and when Mary had concluded she said—

" Oh, how grateful ought you to be to Providence, Mary, for interposing to save you from committing so rash and awful an act. I beseech you to endeavour to banish such dreadful and dangerous thoughts from your mind, and, notwithstanding the misery of your present situation, you will yet be restored again to happiness and prosperity."

Mrs. Langstone shook her head despairingly as she replied—

"What prospect is there, Laura, of your predictions being realized ? Consider the time Edward has been absent from his wretched home, and the horrible circumstances under which he left me; my heart forebodes the worst, and every hour I expect to hear some dreadful intelligence of him. How willingly could I pardon him all that has taken place, would he but return home and persevere in abandoning his evil ways. May Heaven in its mercy preserve you, my dear sister, from such a fate as mine, but you have your enemies, and even now they may be plotting against your future peace."

" What mean you, Mary ?" demanded her sister in accents of alarm.

"I almost fear to tell you, but it is necessary you should be on on your guard—Captain Braghall has dared to raise his guilty thoughts towards you, and fain would he work your destruction."

" He is a villain, I know," returned Laura, blushes of shame and disgust crimsoning her cheeks, " and I have ever avoided his presence as much as possible, but still he dare not attempt to injure me while I am under the protection of his relations, and I will continue to set him at defiance."

" He is one of the abandoned associates of my husband, and I fear that his temptations will plunge him still deeper into vice."

" Is it possible?"

" It is too true ; and oh, Laura, how it shocks me to have to tell you that he has not only expressed his approbation of the captain's designs, but I fear would only be too ready to aid him in any plot he might have in contemplation."

"Good God !" exclaimed the blushing damsel, her bosom swelling with indignation, "is it possible that Edward can indeed have become so degraded ? How have I deserved this at his hands ? But Heaven, for your sake and mine, my poor sister, will not suffer them to triumph. Come, come, endeavour to be composed, and you will yet find friends when you least expect it. It was an unfortunate day when you became his wife, and surely it would be better for you, than to have to endure his inhumanity, if he were no more.'

"My dream, Laura!" gasped forth Mary, with a shudder of horror, as the fearful reflection arose to her mind ; "remember that, and do not give utterance, I implore you, to such torturing observations. Oh, could I wish him to die in the midst of all his guilt? Can I forget the days of happiness we once passed together, when he was good, honourable, and affectionate? Can I forget that he is my husband, the father of my children? No, no, I cannot! My heart still clings to him, and yearns to lavish upon him all its youthful fondness. Still must I ever be the devoted wife towards him, though that heart should break in the hard struggle with my cruel destiny. I will myself struggle with all a mother's anxiety and perseverance for the support of my little ones, and Heaven, I will endeavour to hope, will give me strength and opportunity to accomplish the task, and to snatch my husband from that destruction on the brink of which he is now standing."

A ray of hope did animate the pale countenance of the unfortunate woman as she gave utterance to these words ; and Laura was so deeply affected, that for several minutes she could not return any answer. At length they both became somewhat more calm, and Laura having made everything as comfortable in the place as she could, remained with her sister to the last moment; and sought to impart to her all the hope and consolation in her power ; though she could not help fearing that from the long and continued absence of Edward, something of a fatal nature had happened to him. When Laura had departed, and as the time wore away without anything occurring to inspire her with hope, the spirits of Mary again drooped, and unable any longer to bear up against the terrible fatigues of body and mind she was enduring, she sunk on a seat, and gave way entirely to the intense agony of her thoughts.

CHAPTER VII.

THE DEN OF INFAMY.—THE CAROUSAL.—THE REVELATION.—THE MIDNIGHT ENCOUNTER.— CLINTON AND LANGSTONE.—BLOODSHED.

"Pass around the goblets bright,
    Mirth from drink we'll borrow,
What if our rhino's gone to-night,
    We will have more to-morrow.
Pass them round! pass them round,
    Bumpers we'll be quaffing,
Here let wit and mirth abound,
    Drinking! singing, laughing.
Then pass around the goblets bright,
    Mirth from drink we'll borrow;
What if our rhino's gone to-night,
    We will have more to-morrow!"

SUCH was the noisy ditty that was sung, in a thick hoarse voice, by a young man whose inflamed countenance showed plainly that he was a most zealous devotee to the intoxicating god, and it was chorussed by about twenty dissipated looking individuals, in tones that made the place re-echo again, and shook all the glasses and measures on the different tables. It was about eleven o'clock, but none of the company seemed the least disposed to break up their noisy revel, but on the contrary, seemed to have attained the summit of drunken enjoyment. It was a long room at the back of the premises of a notorious public-house situated in one of those numerous low localities with which the metropolis abounds, and was the resort of some of the most reckless ruffians that ever disgraced society. But the parties were all known to each other, and it would not have been safe for any stranger to attempt to intrude upon their midnight orgies. The wainscot was profusely decorated with numerous coarsely executed sporting pictures, and everything the room contained was in strict keeping with the character of the place and the persons who frequented it. At one of the tables a party was playing at cards, at another a few individuals were amusing themselves at dominoes, and all were enjoying themselves after their own peculiar fashion. Edward Langstone was sitting on one side of the fire-place, apart from the rest, his elbow resting on his knee and his chin upon his hand, and apparently wrapped in half drowsy sullen meditation. His dress was disordered, and his countenance showed the debauch in which he had been indulging, and the gloomy state of his mind at that moment. It was painful to see the fearful change that was wrought in that man who had once been a pattern for emulation, and who possessed the esteem of all who knew him.

"Why, Ned," said the young man who had sung the song with which we opened the present chapter, advancing towards him and clapping him on the shoulder, "what's the matter?—it seems to be low water mark; cheer up—never say die, my boy; what if you have exhausted the exchequer, there is plenty to drink, so what's the use of calling a committee of ways and means just yet?—Drink, drink!"

"I want no more," said Langstone; "I shall go home."

"Go home," repeated the other one; "well, that is a good one. You have been here ever since Sunday morning, and you may as well finish the week out now. You are in no condition to work."

"No, and if I could do it, I am afraid that this time I have offended my employers. I feel that I am a villain."

"I see how it is," remarked another of the men, "Ned is stung with remorse for his conduct on Saturday night. Why it was a a foolish piece of business, I must say; children are very expensive things, and curtail a man of many little enjoyments; but if I wanted to release myself from the burthen, I would never risk my neck to do so; there is a much more simple way of doing it than that, and a legal one, too."

"What do you mean?" demanded Edward, sternly.

"Why, haven't we a new Poor Law?" demanded the fellow; "you have only got to throw them on the parish, and they will take them off your hands, and farm them out to some *respectable* establishment, where pauper children are taken in and done for, at so much a head, and there is no fear of them troubling you or anybody else long."

As the man made use of this coarse and unfeeling joke, he laughed, winked his eye, and resumed his seat. Edward frowned and again made towards the door, but at that moment it was opened, and a tall, good-looking young man, attired in the very height of fashion, entered the room, and his presence was greeted with loud shouts of welcome, which he received with every mark of condescension. The new visitor was Captain Braghall, who immediately took his seat at the head of the principal table, and rang the bell for the waiter.

"We began to fear you wasn't coming, captain," observed the young man who has already been introduced to the reader, and who, it appeared, rejoiced in the name of the "Stunner;" "Ned Langstone, who is rather out of sorts to-night, was just talking about going."

"Nonsense!" said the captain, with an oath; "drink, Ned; I have a few words for your private ear before I go, and I cannot stay long, for I have got a little business to attend to. Fill your glasses, lads, and I will give you a toast; here's to Ned Langstone's sister-in-law, the pretty Laura Maysdale."

Langstone could not help frowning a little at the levity with which this was spoken, but the toast was done full honour to, and Edward drank with the rest.

"Another glass, Ned," said the captain, replenishing it as he spoke.

"I would rather decline, captain," he said, "I do not feel at all in the humour to drink to-night."

"Nonsense! it will revive your spirits. I will not be refused."

Edward reluctantly quaffed the contents of the glass, and then took his seat by the side of the captain, who continued to force upon him the intoxicating beverage, until he had got him into a frame of mind that would answer his purpose.

"My time is getting rather short," he said, looking at his watch, "let us retire to another room. I have a few words to say to you, Ned."

The waiter took up a candle, and conducted them to a private room, the door of which the captain closed cautiously.

"You are in a miserable plight, Ned," he said, after a pause.

"Miserable enough," coincided Langstone, "and all through my own folly."

"You have made such havoc with your constitution, that it will be some time ere you can recover yourself, or be in a fit condition to attend to your employment, if even you might feel so inclined."

"I know that too well," replied Edward.

"The place that you reside in is not fit for the kennel for a dog."

"D——n!"

"Nay, do not get out of temper; your wife and children are starving."

"Do you come here to taunt and mock me, captain?" demanded Langstone, fiercely.

"Not so."

"Then what do you mean by observations such as these? Why remind me of that of which I am too well aware?"

"You have the means to release yourself from those difficulties."

"In what way?"

"I will tell you," answered the captain, "if you will hear me patiently. You know that I have a very strong regard for Laura Maysdale. You have it in your power to assist me in my amour—are you willing to do so?"

"Why, captain," returned Langstone, after a pause, "that is a very delicate and difficult question to answer. I am already sufficiently steeped in vice, but I shudder at the thought of becoming such a heartless miscreant as that. Laura Maysdale is a good and virtuous girl, who has been an excellent friend to us, and can I repay her kindness by such base ingratitude as that which you propose? Indeed, I cannot make up my mind to do so."

"Do not decide too hastily, remember the advantages I hold out to you—you shall be released from your present misery, and placed in comfortable circumstances, and as a proof of my good intentions, I offer you twenty sovereigns this moment, by way of a commencement."

The sight of the gold, which Captain Braghall counted upon the table, was certainly a very tempting thing to a man in Langstone's wretched condition, and caused his mind to waver.

"But how can I forward the object you have in view?"

"I will tell you," answered his companion. "It must be well made known that the change in your circumstances is caused by me; that will naturally tend to alter the opinion of the credulous Laura as regards my character. She will view me with less suspicion, and a feeling of gratitude will probably spring up in her breast, of which I will not fail to take every advantage — leave the rest to my ingenuity and to chance. What think you of my plan?"

"Why, I think it might succeed," replied Langstone.

"Will you then agree to what I propose?"

Edward still hesitated, but again the sight of the gold tempted him, his brain was inflamed with the drink he had taken, and at that time it did not seem to him as though he should be so deeply implicated. The captain noticed his hesitation, and he took advantage of it.

"Come, what say you?" he demanded, "there is no time to lose, and I should think it scarcely requires a second consideration."

"I agree," replied Langstone, "but I may depend upon you fulfilling the promises you have made to me?"

"Why should you doubt my word, when so much depends upon my fidelity? Take up the gold, be circumspect, say not a word to any of the fellows in the other room, and all will be well."

"You may be certain that I shall be cautious on that subject, captain, for my own sake;" said Langstone.

"Good night, then," said the captain; "but stay, remain here for a few minutes till I have departed; I have my reasons for it."

Langstone returned no answer to this, and the captain quitted the room. The former sat down for a few minutes; and reflected seriously upon what he had done. He now almost regretted that he had entered into the agreement he had with Captain Braghall, and he could not but consider himself a villain, but the thought of the glowing promises that had been held out to him quieted his scruples, and placing the money in his pocket, he retired from the room, and he made his way to rejoin his companions, but resolved to depart home immediately. He had arrived at the door of the room in which they were congregated, and was about to open it, when hearing the name of his wife mentioned by the "Stunner," his curiosity was excited, and he stopped to listen.

"I tell you," he continued, "that I was informed by Clinton himself, that Ned Langstone's wife went of her own accord with him to the 'Black Bull,' where he gammoned her that she would find her husband; she afterwards turned squeamish, and raised such an outcry, that he was obliged to make his escape by a back window. There would be the devil to pay if this was to come to Ned's ears."

The feelings that agitated the breast of Langstone on hearing these observations may very easily be imagined; he burst open the door, and rushing into the room, seized the "Stunner" fiercely by the collar, while his features were distorted with rage.

"Tell me all, or damme, I will strangle you!" he cried; "what of my wife and the scoundrel Clinton?"

"Come—come, I say, hands off, Ned," said the "Stunner," almost choking; "this is not a very civil way to serve an old friend; I am not to blame; I had no hand in the business; I was merely repeating what I had been told."

"Do not trifle with me," said Langstone, impatiently, but somewhat relaxing his grasp; "what know you of this business?"

"Why, that Clinton accidentally met your wife on Monday night, when she was searching for you; that pretending you were at the 'Black Bull,' he persuaded her to accompany him there, where, I believe, he was a little out of order in his proceedings. That's all I can tell you, and Clinton, of course, is the only man from whom you have a right to seek an explanation."

"The cowardly miscreant!" cried the enraged man, "he shall pay dearly for this."

"You had better not be too hasty, Ned," said two or three of his associates.

"Do not attempt to detain me, any of you," cried Edward, furiously, "or it shall be worse for you."

Thus saying, he darted past them and rushed from the house, making his way towards the house where Mary had so narrow an escape. His brain was on fire, and he muttered curses and threats to himself as he proceeded, but took no notice of any person whom he passed. He had got to some distance when he was obliged to pause, panting for breath. He looked around him, and at that moment he beheld the shadow of a man approaching up the street. The man paused when he saw him, and seemed to be irresolute whether to advance or retreat; Langstone, however, thought he recognised a figure that was familiar to him, and darting precipitately forward, with a cry of exultation, he beheld by the light emitted from an adjacent lamp that it was the very man he sought. It was Clinton.

"Villain!" he cried, as he rushed upon him, "fate, then, has guided my footsteps to you, and I will have a terrible satisfaction for the wrong you have attempted to do me."

"Are you mad, Langstone?" demanded Clinton, struggling to release himself from his hold, "what mean you?"

"Cowardly wretch!" replied the former, striking him a violent blow in the face, "dare you ask me such a question? I have heard all, and thus I take my revenge."

He repeated the blow, at the same time shaking him violently.

"Perdition!" cried Clinton—"struck! Nay, then we will see whose fate it is to triumph"

They closed with each other on the moment, and being both powerful men, a violent struggle ensued, and for a few seconds it seemed doubtful which was likely to obtain the advantage; their feet coming in contact with a broken part of the kerb they fell heavily to the ground, but did not relinquish their hold of each other, but at length Clinton being the strongest man of the two, and Langstone being somewhat weakened by passion, he was placed undermost. A terrible thought now occurred to him; he got his hands at liberty, hastily drew a clasp knife from his pocket, and before Clinton had time to offer any resistance, he plunged it twice or three times into his body, and shaking the bleeding man from him, he started hastily to his feet, horrorstruck at what he had done. Clinton cried murder two or three times, and then all was silent.

"Good God! what have I done?" exclaimed the wretched Langstone, striking his forehead in agony; "I have become a murderer!"

At that moment he heard the clattering of several footsteps hastily approaching, and filled with the most indescribable terror, he rushed wildly from the spot, and made his way through the most lonely and unfrequented streets.

CHAPTER VIII.

THE MEETING BETWEEN EDWARD LANGSTONE AND HIS WIFE.—THE FEARFUL SCENE.—THE APPREHENSION.

ON he rushed, in a state of mind which no language could adequately pourtray, but at length he was compelled to stop, for the speed with which he had fled had completely exhausted him. The sounds of pursuit no longer met his ears, the streets were almost deserted, and his terror was somewhat abated.

"Is he indeed no more?" he reflected to himself, "or have I merely wounded him?"

He looking at his hands—they were covered with blood, and he shuddered with horror. For a few moments he hesitated whither to go.

"Can I dare meet my unfortunate wife," he said, "after this dreadful crime? But she must soon know the worst, and it matters not whither I go, for I cannot long remain concealed from justice: Wretch that I am, this completes my ruin and that of all connected with me."

At one time so great was his excitement that he was half inclined to lay violent hands upon himself, but some secret power arrested his deadly purpose, and again he hurried on, resolved to make his way home and brave the worst. Mary had retired to rest with her children, but fearful dreams disturbed her imagination, and she frequently started from her sleep, and could scarcely persuade herself that they were not realized. At length, finding that it was useless for her to attempt to go to sleep again, she arose and kindled a fire, and seating herself before it, her mind soon became occupied by the most gloomy meditations. Frightful presentiments of

something about to happen flashed upon her aching brain, and she frequently started as she imagined she heard strange mutterings in the air.   Once or twice she could have sworn that
she heard stealthy footsteps on the stairs, and she trembled with the power of her apprehensions.

"Unhappy husband!" she sighed, "where are you now?   Have you entirely deserted me
and your helpless offspring?   The whole appears to me like some frightful delusion of my
distempered brain.   It seems too horrible to be real; and yet, alas! too fearfully do I know
its truth.   Edward, you must be mad, or you could never act as you are now doing."

She was startled from these reflections by hearing the lower door closed with a hard bang,
and then a hasty and agitated footstep ascending the stairs, her heart palpitated violently, a
sickly sensation came over her, and her limbs trembled so excessively that it was with difficulty
she could support herself.   The footsteps came nearer and nearer, and then she could almost
imagine that she heard a moaning sound, as if proceeding from some person in great agony.
But she was not long kept in suspense; the person, whoever it was, stopped at the door,
and the wretched guilty Langstone, breathless with the haste he had made, and ghastly pale,
and trembling with the horror of his feelings, rushed into the room.   Mary uttered a mingled
cry of astonishment, delight, and alarm, and flying into his arms, could scarcely prevent herself from fainting.

"Husband—dear, but misguided husband!" she exclaimed; and have you, indeed, once more
returned to your distracted wife and helpless children?—But why those looks of horror?   What
has occurred to alarm you thus?—Tell me, I beseech you, and ease the terrible doubts which
agonise my mind."

"Touch me not," gasped forth her husband, shuddering; "do not come near me! for there is
contamination in my very touch!   Bolt the doors! do not let them come!   They will bear me
to gaol, to an ignominious death."

"Oh, Edward!" cried the distracted woman, "why do you rave thus frightfully?   There is
no one here to harm you.   Ah!" she shrieked, for the first time, observing the blood upon his
hands, and she sank on the floor perfectly inanimate.

Edward Langstone was petrified to the spot, and stood gazing at her in speechless horror,
unable to render the least assistance.   The two eldest children, aroused from their sleep, rushed
to the side of their mother, and their piteous cries resounded through the house.   Gadsby and
his wife, with two or three of the other lodgers, alarmed, rushed to the room, and were paralyzed
with amazement and terror at the scene which presented itself.

"Wretched man," said the former, "what have you now done?"

"Do not let them approach me," frantically supplicated Langstone, "I have not harmed her."

Before Gadsby could put another question, there was a loud knocking at the outer door,
which was instantly afterwards forced back on its hinges, and several persons were heard rushing
up the stairs.

"They come!" groaned Langstone, in accents of despair; "it is too late to escape now.   I
am lost!—lost!"

Before he could speak another word, several officers entered the room; and sinking back in
a chair, and covering his face with his hands in a state of the greatest agony, soon revealed
that he was the person they wanted.

"What is this unhappy man charged with?" asked Gadsby, eagerly.

"With a desperate attempt at murder," replied the principal officers, "upon a respectable
man, who has been removed to the hospital in a very precarious state."

"Ah!" exclaimed Langstone, suddenly starting to his feet, and appearing to be recalled to
new life, "he is not dead then!   A respectable man!   What a monstrous libel on the name.
Clinton is a villain, who has been one of my principal seducers from the paths of rectitude in
which I formerly walked, and who committed a gross outrage against my wife (yon poor injured
woman), for which I sought satisfaction, and had I really slain him on the spot, it would have
been no more than his atrocious crime merited.   Oh, God!—oh, God!   I have indeed been a
wretch, but she is innocent, pure as the angels in Heaven; do with me as you please. but for
the love of mercy visit not my crimes upon her head."

"The officers, who were men not so callous to the feelings of humanity as many who have
to perform their unthankful duties, were much impressed by the observations of the unhappy
man, and greatly moved by the melancholy scene which presented itself, and the wretched aspect
of everything around them, and they offered not to interrupt their prisoner for a few minutes.
Mrs. Langstone had been raised by the wife of Gadsby, and placed in a chair, who was endeavouring all in her power to restore her to sensibility, while the two children were still sobbing
at her side, rendering the spectacle one of the most melancholy that could be imagined.

"It is a sad business," said the principal officer, "but we have no alternative; it is our duty
to take you into custody on this charge.   I will not fail to represent the deplorable situation of

this poor woman and her children to the magistrates, and no doubt they will pay every humane attention to the case."

"Oh, God ! has it, then, come to this ?" groaned Langstone, striking his breast, and evincing all the symptoms of the most intense and maddening agony; "accursed demon of drink, how securely and terribly do you work your hellish purposes upon your wretched and deluded vic-

MRS. LANGSTONE LAMENTING THE DISSIPATION OF HER HUSBAND.

tims. This—this is, indeed, the PROFLIGATE'S FIRST FEARFUL LESSON ! Stephen Gadsby, you have proved yourself a sincere friend; you saved me from the perpetration of a horrible crime, when I was under the maddening influence of drink on Saturday night; can a wretched criminal like myself ask you to do him one more favour ?"

"What is it, Ned ?" asked the poor fellow to whom he had appealed, and who was deeply affected; "anything which lies in my power to serve you and your unfortunate wife and children, you may command."

"Thanks—thanks," said Langstone, "this is more than I deserve; but I ask it not for myself. You know the place where my poor wife's sister is residing?"

"I do," answered Gadsby.

"Will you let her know the awful business that has taken place as soon as possible, and break the intelligence to her as gently as you can?"

"I will, Ned; I will, indeed," replied Gadsby.

"Heaven bless you," returned Langstone, in a voice half choked with emotion, "if such a miserable wretch as me dare invoke its power."

He approached his insensible wife, with the intention of pressing one parting kiss on her pale lips, but as a sudden thought seemed to flash upon his distracted brain, he recoiled from her with a convulsive sensation of horror.

"No, no—I dare not!" he groaned; "I, the assassin of her and her helpless innocents, must not pollute her lips with my kisses. Lead me away from this maddening scene," he added, in a broken voice, turning to the officers, "I am ready to accompany you."

"Father—dear father!" sobbed the poor children, in a breath, and clinging to his knees, "you will not go—you will not leave us—and poor mother dying—and you have been so long away. Oh, do not—do not!"

"Oh, God!" groaned Langstone, "this is too much. My neglected children, do not fret, but—but—I can no more—officers, let us begone, or this scene of horror will drive me mad."

The children were, with difficulty, soothed into some degree of composure, and Edward Langstone resigned himself into the custody of the officers.

"It is an unpleasant duty we have to perform," said the sergeant of the police, "but before we leave this place we are compelled to search you."

The prisoner made no reply—in fact, he did not hear them, his mind was too much absorbed by his own miseries—and the sergeant proceeding with his search, soon discovered the twenty sovereigns which Langstone had received from Captain Braghall. Astonishment and suspicion was exhibited in every countenance, but the wretched prisoner appeared to be perfectly unconscious of the discovery which had been made, or what had been going forward, until he was aroused from his state of lethargy by the observations of the sergeant.

"This is a large sum of money," said the latter, "to be found upon a person in the distressed circumstances of the prisoner and his family."

"Ah?" cried Langstone, starting wildly, "has fate conspired against me altogether? What an accursed mischance is this! I am ruined—irretrievably ruined!"

"You are not compelled to answer our questions unless you think proper," remarked the sergeant, "but how do you account for the possession of this large sum of money?"

"No, no, I will not—I dare not," replied Langstone; "a curse more bitter than that which has already descended upon my head would surely follow the declaration, and let whatever may be the consequences, I will not make it; but I solemnly declare that the money is not the proceeds of any robbery."

"At any rate, it looks very suspicious," observed the sergeant; "but that you will have to explain in another place, and before those who are authorized to make the inquiry. It now becomes my painful duty to apprehend you on this very serious charge, though, in being compelled to do so, I sincerely pity your unfortunate wife and children."

"Heaven knows," ejaculated Langstone, in tones that sufficiently showed the anguish and remorse of his feelings, "they are to be pitied, whilst I am a wretch who should be despised and loathed by every one. Gadsby, I implore you to remember your promise; Laura Maysdale loves her unfortunate sister, and will render her all the assistance under her dreadful trial that is in her power. Officers, do your duty, I am ready to attend you."

He fixed one parting look of anguish on his wife and children, then turned away, with a shudder of horror, and resigned himself into the custody of those who were sent to apprehend him. He was removed from the house, and Gadsby and his wife were left alone in charge of the insensible wife and her tender offspring. This was indeed the profligate's first most bitter lesson, and pity it was that there should have been any necessity for his learning a second. Mrs. Gadsby and her husband still continued their humane efforts to restore Mrs. Langstone to sensibility, and, at length, they were rewarded by a deep sigh, but she was still in a state of unconsciousness. They removed her gently to the bed, where they had previously placed her children, and then consulted together what was best to be done under the peculiar and painful circumstances. In a short time afterwards, a medical man arrived who had been sent by the inspector from the station-house, and who immediately proceeded to apply such remedies as might restore the unfortunate woman to animation, although, from her emaciated condition, and long state of almost unprecedented suffering, he expressed great doubts as to the results of his efforts. To remove her from her present wretched abode in such a dangerous state, would, in all probability, be attended with the most fatal consequences, and, therefore, all that could be done was to ameliorate as much as possible the misery that prevailed around. What was to be dreaded more than all, was the effect which the knowledge of the awful situation of her husband might have upon her when she was restored to consciousness, and it was evident that the utmost caution must be used in imparting that dreadful intelligence to her, or the shock might be the cause of her immediate death.

"Poor creature!" said the doctor, who was a most humane man, "it is a pity that this deplorable case had not been made known to the proper authorities, when it is probable that a great portion of their miseries might have been prevented."

It was getting daylight, and notwithstanding the earliness of the hour, Stephen Gadsby took his departure to communicate to Laura, the fatal intelligence of what had taken place, although the task was one he did not feel himself very competent to perform. In the meantime, the wretched Langstone had been removed to the station-house, where the charge having been entered against him, he was locked up in a separate cell. How shall we seek to pourtray the state of the guilty man's mind when he was left alone to his own thoughts? Surely the torments of perdition could not be greater than those he then endured. All the vices of which he had been guilty rushed in terrible array before his appalled and distracted imagination, and almost overwhelmed him. He cast himself down on the cold stone bench of his cell, and clasping his aching temples, groaned aloud. No ray of hope or consolation could come to his relief; he was enclosed on every side by the blackest despair and misery. For himself, he was content to suffer; it was no more than the just penalty of his crimes; but how many innocent beings had his guilt involved? Was he not, in fact, the murderer of those whom it was his bounden duty to love, protect, and cherish? The thought was maddening, and fain would he have withdrawn himself from it, but he could not, and suddenly starting from his seat, he paced backwards and forwards, muttering incoherent sentences to himself, with all the air of a maniac. Had he possessed the means, it is certain he would at once have put an end to his existence, and as it was, he dashed himself several times so violently against the wall that he was almost deprived of consciousness.

"Wretch! guilty wretch that I have been," he at length groaned forth, "when I had every opportunity of moving in a respectable sphere of life, and of gaining the esteem and encouragement of my superiors, thus to become the degraded villain I am, and to plunge my devoted wife and children into almost inextricable ruin. What now but an ignominious fate awaits me? Who will stretch forth a helping hand to assist me out of my difficulties? Who will sympathise with me in the disgrace and infamy I have brought upon myself? I deserve all that I may meet with; the severest punishment cannot be too great for my crimes; but must the innocent suffer for my faults? Oh, surely Heaven, in its mercy, will not permit them to do so. What mad infatuation has led me on to this depth of degradation? Oh, Mary—patient, deeply wronged Mary, what an unfortunate hour was that for you in which you yielded to me your hand, in all the confidence of love. I never, never deserved to be the possessor of virtues such as yours. And yet I could be base miscreant sufficient to receive the first instalment last night of the price for your gentle and amiable sister's destruction. Oh, villain!—villain! My punishment for that atrocious compact has quickly, but justly, overtaken me. Braghall, insidious scoundrel, you are the fiend who has been destined to complete my shame, and bring me to destruction. May eternal curses light upon you, and blast all your guilty hopes. But yet, coward as I am, I dare not divulge the truth; I dare not acknowledge the extent of my infamy, and thus the heartless scoundrel will be suffered to escape the punishment that is due to him. Clinton, you deserve your fate, whatever it may be, but still, had it not been for my own baseness, you would never have had the opportunity of committing the daring and atrocious outrage which has led to the present horrors."

He paused, for his brain was giddy, the blood ran scalding hot through his veins, and large drops of perspiration stood upon his quivering temples. Again he sank down upon the stone bench, and for some time all his faculties forsook him. Again all the horrors of the past and future rushed with overwhelming force upon his tortured imagination, and he once more started up, and paced his cell in a state of mind which it would be utterly vain to attempt to depicture.

"MARY!" he cried, "you are lost to me for ever! We must never meet again;—I dare not encounter your distracted looks, for that would be worse to me than even ten thousand of the most horrible deaths. But to die the death of a dog!—to end a career, commenced in virtue and integrity, on a scaffold; to meet the execrations of an unfeeling multitude—to know that my bones will never rest in hallowed ground; that no tear will ever be shed to my memory; that my wretched offspring will be branded and reproached for their guilty father's crimes—that they will probably be scouted from all society as something loathsome and contagious; to feel that infamy is the only legacy I can bequeath them, and that curses instead of blessings must ever escape their lips when speaking of my name ; oh, surely these thoughts are too horrible for the human brain to sustain ! Wretched, wretched, man, why was I ever born ?—And yet to perish with all this enormous weight of guilt upon my conscience !—to be thus ushered into the presence of the Almighty Judge !—My soul recoils and shudders at the thought ; let me not die, let me not die, until I have had time to repent, and endeavour to make some atonement for the awful crimes I have committed !"

The violence of his agony choked his further utterance, and he sank into a state of apathy, which, happily for himself, for some time afforded him a respite from his anguish. Stephen Gadsby on arriving at the house in which Laura Maysdale resided, walked for a few minutes backwards and forwards in front of it, undetermined in what manner it was best to act. He did not like his errand, for it was a most painful one, such a one as he had never had to perform before, and, in fact, he was not very proficient in such matters. He knew not how to break such dreadful intelligence to the sister of the unfortunate Mrs. Langstone, but there was no time to be lost, and he therefore put the boldest heart he could upon the subject and rang the area bell. Laura shortly made her appearance, and on beholding Gadsby, she turned ghastly pale, trembled violently, and gasped for breath.

"My God!" she ejaculated at last, "Mr. Gadsby, what has brought you here, and at this early hour of the morning? Something serious must have happened, I feel certain—my poor sister——"

"Compose yourself, my good young woman," said Gadsby," I am sorry to be the messenger of bad news to you; your sister is very ill, and needs your presence immediately."

"She is not dead—oh, tell me, she is not dead?" cried Laura, scarcely able to support herself.

"No, miss," answered Stephen, "but I left her very ill and insensible, and I do not wonder at it, poor woman ; her husband——"

"Ah ! what of him ?"

"He is accused of a very serious offence, and is now in prison ; they say he has so seriously wounded that rascally fellow, Clinton, that he is not expected to recover."

"My God! my God !" exclaimed the deeply agitated Laura, " and has it then at last come to this ?—My unfortunate sister !"

She covered her face with her hands, and convulsive sobs escaped her bosom.

"Do not take on so, miss," said Gadsby, "for perhaps it may not turn out so bad as it is expected, after all. Can you accompany me?"

"Oh, yes, yes," replied Laura, struggling with her feelings, although she was almost ready to sink ; "I will lose not a moment ; only wait until I have made my mistress acquainted with what has happened, and obtained her permission."

She then hastened up stairs to the chamber of her mistress as fast as her trembling limbs would permit her, and in as few words as possible made her acquainted with what had happened. The good lady was very much shocked when she heard it, for she was much attached to Laura, and had frequently heard her speak of her sister in the highest terms of affectionate praise.

"Unfortunate woman !" she said, "why did you not make me more fully acquainted with her wretched circumstances before, Laura?—But go to her immediately, do not lose a moment, and you can command my assistance in any way."

Laura returned her grateful thanks with tears in her eyes, and then hurrying to her own room and hastily putting on her bonnet and shawl, she soon rejoined Stephen Gadsby, and they quitted the house together. They hired a cab from the nearest rank, and were driven off rapidly to the melancholy scene of their destination. On their way. Gadsby made his fair companion acquainted with such of the sad particulars as he knew, and Laura listened to him with feelings of the deepest anguish.

"Alas ! alas !" she sighed, "I shudder to think what will be the dreadful termination of this affair. My poor sister will never be able to survive the shock, and then what is to become of her helpless children."

"Nay, cheer up, Miss Laura," said Gadsby, "and do not encourage such sad thoughts as these. To be sure, things look bad enough at present, but I have yet hopes that they will turn out better than we have a right now to expect."

"That misguided man," said Laura, "in what an awful situation has he placed himself. Should this man Clinton die, the law will convict him of murder, and nothing whatever can save him from an ignominious death. The thought is horrible, and my blood freezes as I think of it."

Stephen Gadsby knew not how to console her, and he therefore remained silent, and the vehicle in a short time stopped at the end of the alley in which the hapless heroine of our story resided. With a heavy heart Laura entered the house, and in a few moments afterwards she was kneeling by the bedside of her unfortunate sister, who was still lying in a state of unconsciousness, though the doctor said that she had revived for a brief interval, though not to be able to speak or to recognize any one. In that state she remained throughout the day, and Laura continued to watch her with the most intense anxiety; but towards evening her breathing became more free, and the hopes of her sister somewhat revived. In the course of the day Gadsby made inquiries respecting Langstone, and learnt that he had undergone an examination before the magistrates and was remanded to a future day. He also ascertained that Clinton was still living, but was in a most dangerous state. It also appeared that when he was discovered bleeding on the ground by the police, he for a minute or two revived sufficiently to inform them by whom he had been wounded, and to give them Langstone's address, which was the cause of his being so speedily apprehended. But we must now hasten to give some further particulars with which the reader will be interested.

CHAPTER IX.

CAPTAIN BRAGHALL'S ALARM.—THE DEN OF INFAMY AGAIN.—THE AFFECTING SCENE BETWEEN MARY AND HER HUSBAND IN PRISON.

CAPTAIN BRAGHALL, on leaving Langstone on the fatal night that they met at the infamous place of their usual resort, retired towards his home, exulting in the success that his guilty schemes had met with so far, and forming fresh plans for the future.

"That twenty pounds has sold him," he soliloquized, "and made him my future slave. The glowing picture I drew of his miseries, and the flattering promises I held out to him, overcame all his scruples, and I have not the least doubt of finding in him an able instrument. Laura Maysdale is a prize well worth contending for; I have set my mind on her, and notwithstanding the repugnance she now feels towards me, it is strange to me if she escape me. There is something to me particularly agreeable in that thought, and which urges me on to persevere. I have had many amours in my time, and have never suffered a defeat yet, and it strikes me that I shall be equally successful on this occasion."

In this agreeable state of mind he reached his lodgings, but it was some time before he retired to rest, but set concocting his plans for the future. He did not arise until a late hour the next day, as was his custom, and he then dressed himself and departed to the house where he had been the previous night with the hope of again meeting with Edward Langstone, being in utter ignorance of what had taken place. He found the usual persons assembled there, but was disappointed at not seeing Langstone. They were all busily engaged in conversation on his entrance, but they ceased when he made his appearance and greeted him with their usual familiarity.

"This is a sad affair, captain," remarked the Stunner, "of course you have heard of it?"

"No, I have not," replied Braghall, "what is it?"

"Ned Langstone."

"What of him?" demanded the captain; "I do not see him here."

"No," returned the Stunner, "and what's more, you are not likely to do for some time."

"What do you mean?" demanded the captain impatiently, and with some misgiving.

"Why, he is in limbo, that's all."

The captain started, and exhibited no little alarm.

"Yes, he is quodded safe enough," added the Stunner, "and it's a chance if it doesn't go hard with him."

"Is this possible?"

"It is true."

"What has he been doing?"

"Why, stabbed Clinton in two or three places, and almost killed him," was the reply.

"D——n!" exclaimed the captain, "how did this happen? I left him here last night."

"That is very true, captain, but it occurred after that. I was relating what had occurred between Clinton and Mrs. Langstone, the other night, at the Black Bull, when it seems he overheard me, and rushed in like a madman. He quitted the house in a great rage."

"And what then?"

"Why, it seems that he made his way towards the Black Bull, when some devil's chance threw Clinton in his way; they quarrelled, as you may be sure, and in the struggle which ensued, Langstone drew a knife, stabbed Clinton in two or three places, and left him for dead. He was apprehended a short time afterwards, and this morning he underwent an examination before the magistrates, and is remanded."

The captain again muttered several oaths to himself and paced the room in a disordered manner.

"Yes, it is a bad job," remarked the Stunner, "and what is more, that is not the worst of it."

"What more have you got to tell me?" asked Braghall, eagerly.

"Why, it is suspected that Langstone has also committed a robbery."

"What cause have they to suspect that?"

"Why, on searching him twenty sovereigns were found on his person."

The captain exhibited some confusion, but he quickly recovered himself and demanded—

"Twenty sovereigns, say you? Did he account for the possession of them?"

"No, he refused."

"That is fortunate," muttered Braghall, aside, "it is probable I may yet depend on him."

"But," continued the Stunner, "hew could he account for the possession of them without committing himself? Where could he get twenty sovereigns without committing a robbery?"

"Very true," coincided the captain carelessly.

"And yet he pretended here last night that he was quite cleaned out."

"Well, I am sorry for poor Ned," said the captain, "and must do all in my power to get him out of the scrape."

"I'm sure you will, captain," said the Stunner, "he is not a bad sort of fellow, and we have passed many a cheerful hour in his company."

"Very true; but where is Clinton?"

"In the hospital."

"And you say he is very dangerously wounded?"

"So much so that it is thought almost impossible for him to recover."

"That is a bad job, for should he die, I am afraid that neither money nor influence can save Langstone."

"No, it will go very hard with him," said the Stunner, "but I know you will exert yourself to the utmost, captain."

"You may depend upon that," replied Braghall. "But I must go and inquire further into this unfortunate affair."

He then quitted the house.

"What a cursed misfortune is this," he said, as he proceeded on his way, "it will retard the accomplishment of my designs to an indefinite period, and it is not at all unlikely that I may lose the services of Langstone altogether. I wish that fellow Clinton had been at the devil before he did anything to excite the wrath of Langstone. However, the latter has acted faithfully in refusing to account for the possession of the gold, and should he continue firm—but I have confidence in him. But then there is another danger to be apprehended—should Clinton have strength he may say something that might implicate me, and notwithstanding my position in society, and the influence I possess, I might find it a difficult task to extricate myself, and at any rate a stigma would be cast upon my character ever afterwards. It is a confounded unfortunate affair altogether, and mingled doubts and apprehensions torment my mind. Langstone must, however, be saved at any cost. Would that I could have a private interview with him; but that is hopeless, and there is nothing else for me to do than to try to devise some scheme by which he may be rescued from his present perilous situation. It is doubly annoying that it should have occurred just now, when my plot promised to proceed so successfully, and I had secured the aid of Langstone. Now it will be retarded for an uncertain period, though I am fully determined that Laura Maysdale shall not escape me. Let me but be cautious and play my cards carefully and the game is mine. I do not doubt that I shall yet be able to insinuate myself into the good graces of her and her sister, by the affected sympathy I shall evince in their misfortune and the situation of Langstone. They will be taken off their guard, and ultimate success will be mine. I must also see this fellow, Clinton, and endeavour to extort some promise from him which may be of service to me in the working out of my designs. He is an arrant rascal, and it strikes me that he could not make a very respectable appearance in a court of justice. He has, I know, been playing rather a criminal and dangerous game of late, and he might happen to be wanted. I must endeavour to ascertain the truth of my suspicions, and should they be confirmed, I may, by intimidation or promises of reward silence him, and persuade him to become *non est inventus*. Oh, I do not yet despair of being able to get Ned Langstone out of his present dilemma, black as matters notwithstanding are against him."

Thus did the worthy Captain Braghall seek to console himself; and as there was no time, he considered, to be lost, he determined at once to go to the hospital to which Clinton had been conveyed in order to ascertain his exact situation. Mrs. Langstone still remained in the same deplorable situation, totally unconscious of everything around her, and her affectionate sister watched her and attended to the wants of the poor children with the most painful and anxious solicitude. She almost dreaded her restoration to sensibility, for how could they break the whole of the dreadful truth to her? The shock would surely be too great for her strength to bear up against, reduced as she was by long and almost unexampled suffering; and should she sink under it, in what a melancholy situation would her helpless children be placed. The good doctor paid the most unremitting attention to his unfortunate patient, and he expressed his opinion, that notwithstanding the severity of the affliction, and the emaciated condition of Mrs. Langstone, she might, by proper care and the gentle offices of Laura, yet be restored to convalescence, and find fortitude to bear up against the terrible misfortune. It had been resolved, as soon as she was in a fit state, to remove her to a more comfortable lodging, and they entertained strong hopes that that might, in some measure, tend towards her recovery, though of course everything depended upon the ultimate fate of her misguided husband. In the course of that wretched day, the kind mistress of Laura called at the miserable abode of the sufferer, and she was deeply moved at the scene which presented itself to her eyes. The fortune of this lady and her husband, as has been before stated, was only limited, but they were truly benevolent, and many were the acts of charity they in secret performed, and they took the greatest delight in doing all the good in their power.

"Poor thing," said this excellent lady, "how terribly must she have suffered; alas! her wretched husband must have much to answer for. Let everything that kindness can suggest be done for her and her helpless children, Laura, and I will be answerable for whatever expense may be incurred. Do not leave her for a moment, until she has recovered; she will much need your affectionate attention and consolation."

Laura returned thanks with tears in her eyes, and her mistress having presented her with some money, in order to procure any immediate necessaries that might be required, left the house. In the meantime, Captain Braghall had made his way to the hospital, and found on his arrival there that Clinton was still alive, but in an insensible state, so that, of course, he was doomed for the present to be disappointed in his hopes; the medical gentlemen, however, assured him that, although the wounds he had received were of a very serious nature, they did not consider that they would prove mortal; but a few hours would probably afford them an opportunity of forming a more positive opinion. With this answer the captain was compelled to be satisfied, although he could not help entertaining many doubts and apprehensions. Towards the morning of the following day, Mary Langstone gave the first symptoms of returning life by breathing a deep sigh, and the doctor having applied a reviving cordial to her lips, she breathed more freely, and presently opened her eyes, but started with bewildered amazement on beholding her sister and her medical attendant hanging over her. She pressed her delicate hands upon her aching forehead, and tried to collect her scattered thoughts, but all was at present dark and impenetrable to her distracted mind. Laura embraced her affectionately, and whilst the tears gushed to her expressive and beautiful eyes, she ejaculated in a voice of the most intense emotion.

"Thank God! thank God! my beloved sister, you are again restored to life; and may He, in His infinite mercy, give you fortitude to support your dreadful trials."

"Laura here?" gasped forth the unfortunate woman, in a faint voice; "what means this? What has happened? Strange terrors flush upon my distracted imagination! Keep me not in suspense, but let me know the full extent of my misery at once."

"Dear Mary," replied Laura, in her most gentle accents, "I beseech you to endeavour to compose the agony of your mind, and not to urge me to answer questions till you are in a more fit state to be made acquainted with all the particulars. Come, come, let me prevail upon you, for the sake of your poor children."

"You torture me!" groaned Mary, "this mystery is worse than death. Laura, Laura, if you really love me, and pity me, you will not hesitate for a moment to remove the awful doubts that rack my brain."

"Alas! alas!" sighed Laura, "what is to be done? Merciful Heaven direct me how to act."

"My good woman," said the doctor, soothingly, "I must join my entreaties to those of your sister, and desire you to endeavour to restrain your impatience until you are in a more fit condition to be informed of what has taken place. I will not be answerable for the consequences if you give way to this state of excitement."

"You mock me," cried the wretched woman, with increased and insupportable agitation, "ah! the dreadful truth now flashes upon my recollection like a thunderbolt! Where is he? Where is my unfortunate husband?"

How agonizing was that question to poor Laura! she looked anxiously and piteously at the doctor, but could return no answer.

"Ah!" cried Mary in accents of frenzied wildness, and her bosom heaving with anguish, "I remember all now, and it is useless for you to seek to conceal the frightful trouble from me.

Even now his ghastly looks, as he accused himself of murder are present to my imagination; again the terrible words he spoke in his agony of remorse and horror vibrate in my ears! There was blood upon his hands too! It was no dream! No vision of my disordered imagination! Oh, horror! horror!—husband, wretched husband, the measure of thy crimes is full at last!"

Overpowered by the violence of her feelings, she uttered a faint shriek, and again became insensible.

"Alas! alas!" sighed Laura, "this will prove my poor sister's death blow! In the name of Heaven, what is to be done?"

"Do not give way to despair, my good girl," said the worthy doctor, "and all will yet be well, I trust. The fatal truth must be broken to her as gently as possible, and I hope that she will be able to support it with more fortitude than we now anticipate."

Laura sighed and shook her head disconsolately and doubtfully, but she returned no answer, and the doctor applied himself to the restoration of his suffering patient to consciousness; however she remained in a state of stupor, and Laura continued to watch her pale and careworn countenance with the utmost anxiety and solicitude. There was another subject which greatly racked the mind of poor Laura, and that was in what manner the dreadful intelligence was to be broken to their aged mother. She feared that the terrible shock would be too great for her enfeebled strength to support, and her mind was bewildered and distracted, not knowing how to act.

"My God," she reflected, "miserable man, how frightful are the results of your guilty career. How bitter must be the feelings of remorse which now torture your brain! Could nothing snatch you from the fearful course you have been so long pursuing, until it was too late? Surely the murderous influence of an accursed drink must have maddened your brain; you must have become totally insensible to all those feelings of virtue and integrity which formerly inhabited your breast, or you never could have acted in the manner you have done. Alas! my poor sister, how little have you deserved such a fate as this, and what is now to become of you and your helpless children? Never, never, can you survive your husband's ignominy, and I fear, alas! that nothing can save him from the punishment attendant on the dreadful crime he has committed. My blood freezes with horror at the thought."

Scalding tears chased each other down her cheeks as these thoughts occurred to her, and she tried in vain to compose herself, and to encourage the hope that all would yet terminate more fortunately than they apprehended. There was no change in the condition of Mary during the day, but she lay calmly, and did not seem to be suffering any pain. Laura never left her bedside for a moment unless it was to attend to the necessities of the children, and watched her with all that intensity of sympathy which the power of her affections engendered in her breast. We must now return to the wretched Edward Langstone, who in his gloomy cell gave himself up to the most frenzied feelings of remorse and despair. After his first examination before the magistrates, his misery, if possible, increased, and he raved with all the fury of a madman. He had obstinately refused to endeavour to account for the large sum of money that had been found in his possession, and that made his guilt appear the more heinous, as it seemed but too probable that he had added robbery to his other crime. But no, let whatever might be the consequence, he was fully resolved that nothing should induce him to acknowledge the truth, for by so doing, must he not confess himself to be a villain of the blackest dye; and never could he encounter the bitter reproaches which the amiable Laura and his wife must heap upon him! What a fearful alteration had only a few hours made in his appearance. His eyes were sunk and bloodshot; his face pale and ghastly as that of a corpse, and his lips livid and quivering. Twenty years seemed added to his age during that brief period. It was quite appalling to look upon him, and in spite of the heavy weight of guilt which was attached to him, it was impossible that any one could have helped gazing with pity upon him in his present abject and degraded situation. He threw himself on a seat, and rocked his body to and fro in the anguish of his feelings. He imagined he saw the pale and careworn faces of his wife and children gazing at him with looks of the most melancholy reproach, and then all the horrors of his dream rushed upon his recollection, and drove him to a state of complete frenzy.

"And that vision will be realised," groaned the wretched man, beating his breast, and the blood rushing to his brain; "yes, I see it all now, when it is too late to avoid it. Monster that I have been, what tortures can be too severe for me? Am I not the murderer of one of the most devoted of women, and of my unfortunate and innocent offspring? I am!—I am! and the retribution of offended Heaven has at last overtaken me for my abominable crimes! But must they suffer for my villany? Will not the Almighty, who knows their innocence, interpose to save them? On my guilty head let the wrath of offended Heaven alone descend. I deserve no mercy, no pity, but deserve to perish amidst the execrations of my fellow-creatures. I have outraged every feeling of humanity; mocked at virtue and integrity; I have turned a deaf ear to the remonstrances and supplications of that unfortunate being whom I at the altar swore to love and cherish. I have become a disgusting miscreant, and justice demands the penalty of my crime."

"Alas!" he added, after a pause, "with what powerful, what overwhelming effect do the reminiscences of my youthful days rush upon my recollection. Days when I was good, honourable, and happy—when the bare contemplation of such crimes as those of which I have been guilty would have smote my heart with horror; and when I possessed

MR. LANSGTONE'S DISTRESSED HOME

the esteem and friendship of all who knew me. No care ever then beset my mind, but everything around me was smiling and cheerful. Then had I nothing to reproach myself with, and I could set the world of calumny at defiance. Then could I boldly aspire to the love of Mary, and knew myself to be worthy of her numerous and unassuming virtues. What demon spell could have wrought such a fearful change in me? I shall go mad! I shall go mad! And what must be now the sufferings of my wretched wife and children, when they anticipate the ignominious fate which is too certainly in store for me? The thought is too much for human nature to support. Would that I were dead, or that I had never been born. But to perish upon the public scaffold, without one to pity me; to die the death of the most guilty criminal, when I might have continued to live universally respected, and seen my wife and children smiling happily around me! Oh, surely, this is torture the most exquisite!"

He was interrupted by the opening of the door of the cell in which he was confined, and one of the turnkeys made his appearance.

"A person who calls himself Captain Braghall, has obtained permission to see you," said the man, "and he is now waiting outside."

The prisoner started at the mention of that name, and exhibited much emotion.

"No, no," he said hastily, "I cannot see him at present, tell him I cannot, my mind is too greatly agitated to permit me to see him. Some other time, and probably I may, but not now, not now!"

"Ah, very well," said the turnkey, "you know best, though he says he is inclined to be a friend to you, knowing your wife and family, and you will stand much in need of a friend to help you out of your present difficulty."

"A friend!" repeated Langstone, with a shudder, but he quickly recollected himself and added, "I am grateful to any one who may feel disposed to assist me, out of compassion for my wife and children, but I cannot see any one just now."

"As you please," said the turnkey, "it is no business of mine."

He then quitted him, and Langstone was once more left to the anguish of his own thoughts.

"Braghall," he muttered to himself, "and can you have the effrontery to visit in his dungeon the poor wretch whom you and others have tempted to crime? Had I not listened to your voice on that fatal night, and remained at that den of vice from which I have to date the principal cause of my ruin, this might not have happened. Friend!—oh, villain! villain! and yet I dare not reveal the truth, though justice demands that I should do so, in order that the innocent Laura should be protected from his guilty designs. But surely Heaven will watch over the poor girl's safety, and not permit him to triumph over one so pure and innocent."

Thus did the unfortunate prisoner continue to distract himself with the most painful thoughts, and nought came to the relief of his black despair. He scarcely dared to raise his thoughts to his unhappy wife, and yet how anxious was he to know the real state of her present situation; and when he remembered the deplorable condition in which he left her on his apprehension, the terrible idea flashed upon his brain that the shock had been too much for her, and that she was no more. But surely that would even be a happy release from her present dreadful sufferings, and so truly wretched as were the future prospects of herself and children in the world. How anxious was he to see her once again, to assure her of his remorse; and yet he dreaded to meet her. Of what avail was his repentance when it was too late, and after the misery and destruction he had brought upon her? Had he listened to her gentle persuasions, he would never have been placed in the dreadful situation he now was; and how could he, guilty miscreant as he was, and after the brutal manner in which he had behaved to her, dare to ask forgiveness of her? Could she look upon him with any other feelings than those of horror and disgust? Must she not bitterly upbraid him for the shame and misery he had brought upon himself and their tender offspring; and how dared he to encounter her reproaches?—No, no, death was even less terrible to his imagination than to meet again the mournful glances of that innocent being whom he had so deeply, so irretrievably injured. These wild thoughts gained strength every moment; and the unfortunate man in vain sought to obtain the least consolation or hope. If he had had the means in his possession he would not have hesitated to have put a period to his existence, and thus have rushed unbidden, and with all his sins upon his head, into the presence of his Maker; but, at length, completely exhausted with the terrible weight of his thoughts, he threw himself on his mattress, and for some time his senses were wrapped in a complete state of stupor. Captain Braghall received Langstone's refusal to see him with no very great satisfaction, and he walked slowly away from the jail, muttering curses to himself, and endeavouring to form various projects by which he might be likely to accomplish his wishes.

"Why should he object to see me?" he said, "when he knows that I have the power to assist him in his present dangerous situation, and that I am sure to exert myself to the utmost for my own sake? Has the fool turned compunctious, I wonder; if so, there may be some danger to be apprehended, and I should be placed in rather a disagreeable situation. I must ascertain the truth or fallacy of that idea, and act accordingly. If he only remains firm, and refuses to divulge how he became possessed of the gold, I am all right, and it shall be no fault of mine if I do not get him out of his present dilemma; but if he acts on the contrary, I must do the best I can to protect myself, and he must take the consequences of his folly. In spite of everything, I am determined that my designs against Laura Maysdale shall succeed, and this delay, only adds to my resolution.   As for Clinton, should he recover, I have no doubt that I can purchase his silence and co-operations, and that once obtained, all no doubt will go on as well as I could wish."

Thus saying, he walked on towards the hospital, where he learnt that the wounded man was progressing as well as could be expected, but that he was not yet in a fit condition to be spoken to.   With this answer Braghall was forced to be satisfied, and not feeling inclined to return to his lodgings just then, he departed to the house where he was in the habit of meeting his dissolute companions.

"Glad to see you, captain," said the Stunner, "we began to fear that you intended to desert us after this unlucky affair of Ned Langstone and Jack Clinton."

"Oh, no," said the captain, "I shall not desert you yet awhile, and I do not know but that I may require your services by and by."

"Anything particular, captain?" asked the Stunner.

"Yes, yes," was the reply, "but we will talk more upon that subject at some future time."

"Very good, captain," returned the Stunner, "and I need not assure you, I believe, that you will find us all most ready to render you any assistance in power.   Jack Clinton is still alive, I understand?"

"He is," answered Braghall, "and is likely to recover."

"It will be a good job for Ned Langstone if he does," said the Stunner, "for it may save his neck from the halter; though it strikes me that Clinton would not cut a very good appearance in the witness box.   Langstone's possessing that twenty sovereigns, and refusing to say how he came by them, looks very suspicious, though; although I never suspected Ned had pluck enough to commit a robbery; Jack Clinton, I rather imagine, would not stand quite so particular."

"Ah!" said Braghall, eagerly catching at the Stunner's observations; "know you anything particular respecting Clinton?"

The Stunner seemed to think he had said almost too much, and he therefore wished to correct himself.

"Why—no—not exactly, captain," he faltered out.

"Of course you do not—what a fool you are," said another of the company, who was called Dick Hemlock; "what should you know; and what has Jack's business to do with you?—He is no churl, and when he has got money, is never afraid to spend it."

"Very true, Dick," coincided the worthy Stunner; "it was merely a slip of the tongue, and I did not know what I was talking about exactly at the moment."

"Well," remarked the captain, carelessly, though he saw plainly that the Stunner knew more than he thought prudent to divulge, "I do not wish to be inquisitive, and it is no business of mine, though I must say it is a fortunate job for Langstone that the rather questionable character of his prosecutor is not at all unlikely to go considerably in his favour."

"Aye, there I agree with you, captain," said the Stunner, "and I wish poor Ned may get off easy with all my heart.   He received great provocation from Clinton, I must confess, and I don't know but that I might have been urged to do the same under the circumstances."

"To be sure," said Braghall; "it is only natural that any man should be excited; though it is a pity you let him hear anything about the matter."

"Why, how was I to know that he was listening?" demanded the Stunner.

"Well, it would have been more prudent of you to have refrained from broaching the subject until after Langstone had quitted the house."

"Well, perhaps it would, captain; but have you seen anything of Ned since he has been in prison?"

"I obtained an order from the magistrates to visit him, this day," replied Braghall, "but he refused to see me."

"What could be his motive for that?"

"I know not.   His mind was too much agitated; that was the excuse he made."

"Why, I should say it is not in a very happy condition just now," observed the Stunner; "but you will not fail to do all you can for him, captain?"

"Oh, you may depend upon that," replied Braghall; "I am sorry for his situation, and pity his wife and children."

"Humph!" returned the Stunner, with a half satirical laugh; "I have not the least doubt you do, captain; though, for all the good they have experienced from him for some time past, they will not much miss him, I imagine."

"Well, I don't know much about that," said Braghall; "we are none of us perfect, and I suppose I have got my faults as well as other men.   Good night; if there is a possibility of saving him I will do so."

"Good night, captain," said the Stunner, "and I hope you may be successful."

Braghall then quitted the society of the worthy gentlemen, and bent his steps towards home.

"What a confounded fool you was, Stunner," observed Dick Hemlock, " to suffer your tongue to run so fast. You almost disclosed the secret, and we might then have found ourselves no better off than Ned Langstone."

"Well, well," replied the Stunner, " I own I was rather off my guard, but I will be more cautious in future."

" You had better."

" But hark ye, Dick ; I am not exactly satisfied with the conduct of the captain."

" Why not ?"

" There is something more between him and Langstone than we are aware of," replied the Stunner.

"What do you suspect ?" said Hemlock.

" It was rather strange that he should so earnestly request a private interview with Ned on the night when those events took place."

" I cannot exactly make out the twenty sovereigns found upon Ned ; I am certain that he never had the courage to commit a highway robbery, and you know as well as me, that he had not a fraction when the captain came in."

" Then do you suspect that he received the money from Braghall ?"

" Why, there are more unlikely things than that," answered the Stunner.

" Well, it does not seem very probable to me," remarked Hemlock ; "what should the captain give him such a large sum of money for ?"

" Why, he might require his services."

"In what way ?"

" You are aware that the captain is anxious to get possession of the person of Laura Maysdale, the handsome sister of Ned's wife ?"

" True ; but Langstone would never agree to assist him in a plot against his own sister-in-law."

" I do not know that ; money is a very tempting thing, and when a man gets once broken up, he is not very particular what he does."

" That's right," said Hemlock ; " but we must not lose sight of Braghall, for he says that he will require our services, and no doubt he will well reward us."

"Certainly ; we have always found him extremely liberal. But this little affair of ours and Clinton's ; what think you of it ?"

" Oh, it is all right enough, if you only keep your own counsel," answered Hemlock.

" I am half afraid of Clinton, lest he should in the excitement of his illness divulge all."

"Oh, there is no fear of him," said Hemlock. " He is is always on his guard."

" But we cannot be so confident as to what he may divulge in the delirium of pain ; and that might lead to the most dangerous and unpleasant results," said the Stunner.

" Well, it is no use unnecessarily alarming ourselves with such apprehensions as these," returned his companion ; " for it is my opinion that there is not the least ground for them. If we only keep our own counsel, depend upon it there is no fear of Clinton betraying us."

" Well, I hope not. It is unfortunate that this affair between Jack Clinton and Ned Langstone ever took place at all. Clinton will make but a sorry figure as prosecutor at the Old Bailey, and some awkward facts might be elicited, especially if it should so happen that Jack should have some friends at court. It would be much better if the business could be arranged, and Clinton got out of the way."

" Why, that's true," coincided Hemlock, " but there is no chance of that ; they have got him fast enough, and he must prosecute. You may depend upon it they will not lose sight of him."

" It's a d—d bad job," remarked the Stunner, " and I am still in doubt and anxiety as to what will be the end of it ; I pity Ned from my very soul."

"Aye, so do I," replied Hemlock, "for the case is a very bad one, and so large a sum of money being found upon him, makes it a great deal worse. But Braghall will not fail to do all he can for him, I should think ?"

" Oh, he will be sure to do that, for you may depend upon it that he has a much greater interest in Ned Langstone's restoration to liberty, than we are at present at all aware of."

" That is my opinion also ; and we must use our utmost endeavours to find out what that particular interest is."

" True," said the Stunner ; and having come to that determination, the two worthies rejoined their abandoned companions.

The hints and insinuations so thoughtlessly thrown out by the Stunner, had, as has been before stated, not been lost upon the captain; he saw that his suspicions as regarded Clinton were not wholly unfounded, and that if he could by any means elicit the truth, he might by persuasions and threats win him over to his purpose, and contrive, by getting him out of the way, to obtain the acquittal of Edward Langstone; and then he entertained very little doubt of the ultimate success of his designs against the beauteous and innocent Laura Marsdale. Vanity was one of the principal characteristics of Captain Braghall; and he had the baseness and presumption to think that Laura ought to feel highly flattered by the sentiments he entertained towards her. Long nursed in the school of vice, the heartless libertine had become entirely callous to every manly and proper feeling, and looked upon beauty and innocence as his lawful prey. The idea of matrimony was repugnant to his depraved taste, and he thought it would be quite sufficient time for him to settle down in the sober Benedict when all his profligate and abandoned pleasures were exhausted. But in order that he might be enabled to accomplish his present designs, it was indispensably necessary he should play the hypocrite—a task for which nature had completely fitted him in every sense of the word. Could he deceive Laura and her unfortunate sister by appearing to sympathise with them in their sorrows, his success, he considered, would be all but certain, and it would be impossible for Laura to escape him, especially if Langstone should be restored to liberty, and would still consent to co-operate with him in the accomplishment of his wishes. He resolved to obtain an interview with Mrs. Langstone at the earliest opportunity, and set about the commencement of his guilty plot. On his way home, he had to pass by the wretched alley where Edward Langstone and his unfortunate wife had for so many months resided, and he hesitated, whilst a variety of feelings entered his breast. He knew that Laura was staying with her sister, and he was half inclined to obtrude himself upon her presence; but he quickly abandoned the thought, for he knew that it would only be attended with the worst consequences, and might be the cause of frustrating his wishes. However, he was determined to address a letter in a day or two to Mrs. Langstone as a preliminary step to the furtherance of his plot; and he flattered himself that, with the promises of assistance which he would hold out, he should be able to dissipate the prejudices which her and Laura entertained against him, and thus render his triumph certain. He walked on and made his way to his lodgings, where his mind was occupied for some hours before he retired to bed in maturing his plans. Two days elapsed without anything particular taking place; the wounded man progressed favourably, and he was now pronounced out of danger. Braghall, on hearing this, again visited him at the hospital, and was permitted by the authorities to have a private interview with him. Clinton exhibited some degree of surprise and excitement on beholding him, but he seemed to entertain some suspicion as to his motives in appearing to possess so much anxiety for his recovery, and was determined to act with caution, in order that he might the better be able to elicit from him the truth. The captain inquired in a friendly manner after his health, to which Clinton replied in a sullen tone, that he was quite as well as could be expected, and added—

"To what may I attribute the honour of this visit, Captain Braghall?"

"To a wish to serve you, if I possibly can in any way," replied Braghall.

"Indeed," said Clinton, in a half sneering tone; "that is very kind of you; and, of course, if you have no other motive than my welfare at heart, I am sure I should feel very much obliged to you."

"This is a bad job, Clinton; and poor Ned Langstone——"

"Ah!" cried the guilty man, fiercely, "he is safe enough in limbo now, I know, and he will have to pay dearly for the daring outrage he committed upon me. Jack Clinton will have his revenge, and he cannot help himself."

"Clinton," said the captain, "do not be too hasty, but reflect maturely upon what you would do. If you have no pity for the unfortunate Langstone, you should at least have some consideration for his innocent wife and children."

"Psha!" replied the hardened villain, in ironical accents, "how long have you turned moralist, Captain Braghall?"

"These observations are uncalled for, Clinton," returned the captain, "you were the first aggressor, you know that, by the attempt you made upon Langstone's wife, and you must admit that he received the greatest provocation for what he has done. Come, come, you must think better of this, and let us see whether matters cannot be arranged in a satisfactory manner. It may not be too late to save Langstone, although you will be compelled to prosecute, if you cannot be got out of the way; it would be no very difficult job to prove an a'ibi, and you would find me very willing to reward you handsomely for such a service."

"Humph!" said Clinton, "you seem to take a particular interest in the fate of Ned Langstone, captain."

"I confess I do, and I do not despair of being able to persuade you to accede to my wishes."

"You had better not be too sanguine in that respect, Captain Braghall."

"What is the use of your remaining thus obstinate? Besides, you yourself might not cut a very respectable appearance in a court of justice; are you certain that your hands are quite clean?"

Clinton exhibited some confusion, but he quickly recovered himself, and fixing upon the captain a penetrating look, he said—

"You, at any rate, know nothing that can criminate me, I presume, captain?"

"Perhaps not," replied the latter; "however, if you are wise you will think seriously on what I have said, and not act rashly."

"Well, well," said Clinton, impatiently, "I am in no humour at present to talk further upon this subject. I know not why I should show any mercy or forbearance towards the man who has severely injured me. It was no fault of his that he did not murder me ; besides, the law now has him in its clutches, and must take its course. I have no power to help him, if even I were so inclined."

"But I tell you again that you have," said Braghall; "however, I will give you time to reflect upon what I have proposed, and call upon you again in a day or two, not doubting that you will see the policy of ultimately yielding to my wishes."

"I can hold out no such hopes to you, captain," said Clinton, "but I am too weak from the injuries I have received to undergo the fatigue of farther conversation. Good day."

Captain Braghall, finding that it was quite useless at present to attempt to make any impression on him, took his leave, and retired from the hospital, requesting that every attention should be paid to him, in order to his recovery being as speedy as possible.

"Clinton's obstinacy annoys me," muttered the captain to himself as he walked on his way home; "so powerful and inexorable is the feeling of revenge he entertains towards Langstone, that I fear I shall find it rather a difficult task to get him to comply with my wishes; however, I must persevere, for Langstone must be saved at all hazards and at any cost. Could I discover any particular crime of which Clinton has been guilty, the tables might possibly be turned against him, and all might terminate as I wish it to do. I must again endeavour to prevail on Langstone to see me, for until I have had an interview with him I cannot feel exactly satisfied what his future conduct may be. I understand that he is stung with remorse, and that may be fraught with no inconsiderable danger. It is a confounded unfortunate affair altogether, and I wish Clinton had been at the devil ere he committed the outrage against Langstone's wife; or, at any rate, that the circumstance should ever have come to his knowledge."

Occupied with these thoughts, he reached his home, where we will leave him, and return once more to the miserable abode of the suffering Mary Langstone. Her recovery was slow but gradual, and at length she was restored to perfect consciousness, but likewise to a full knowledge of the horrors of her situation. All the dreadful events of the night on which her wretched husband had been apprehended, flashed upon her memory with overwhelming force, and she felt convinced that he was the inmate of a prison on some terrible charge. In tones of the bitterest agony she implored her sister and the doctor, no longer to conceal the fearful truth from her, but to let her know the worst at once, for suspense was far more torturing than the most horrible certainty, and she trusted that Providence would give her fortitude to support the intelligence, however awful it might be.

"For the love of Heaven, dear Laura," implored the distracted woman, "do not any longer refuse to comply with my demands; your looks convince me of the worst, then why should you hesitate to reveal it to me? I remember his ghastly looks; his wild and fearful observations; I saw the blood upon his hands, and my appalled soul convinces me that he is charged with some horrible crime, and that the irretrievable ruin I have so long anticipated has at last overtaken us. God of Heaven, help us! Sister, beloved sister, again I supplicate you to make me at once acquainted with what has happened."

It was indeed a painful task, and poor Laura shrunk from it, and looked appealingly at the doctor for assistance. They saw, however, that it would be impossible to evade the questions of the suffering woman any longer, and they therefore, by degrees, broke the dreadful truth to her in as gentle accents as possible. With looks of the utmost horror, Mary Langstone listened to them, and when they had concluded, she uttered a wild cry of anguish and despair, and covering her face with her hands, as if she would shut out some frightful object, too hideous and appalling for observation, she sunk back in her chair almost inanimate. Convulsive sobs escaped her bosom, but no tears came to her relief, and she was completely insensible to the kind soothings of Laura and the doctor. At length she became somewhat more tranquil, and she looked up, the very image of despair.

"My worst, my most terrible fears are realised," she said, in a voice half choked with anguish; "the ruin I have so long anticipated is at last consummated, and he to whom I have so long been devoted, is now the inmate of a felon's cell, with nothing but the prospect of a gnominious fate before him. Oh, God!—oh, God! give me strength, I beseech Thee, to support this dreadful blow, for the sake of my poor innocent children—oh, Clinton, heartless villain! It is you who have been the cause of all this; but would to Heaven. that any other hand than that of my wretched husband had inflicted the punishment you so richly merited. But is this the only crime the misguided Edward has committed? How came so large a sum of money in his possession? I shudder at the thought, and horror and despair gather still closer around me. But I must see him. Surely he will not, cannot refuse to yield, to my earnest supplications, but will reveal to me the whole truth."

In this state of agony the much injured wife continued for some time, and not one ray of consolation or of hope could her affectionate sister succeed in imparting to her. In fact, she was at a loss for words to do so, and she could only trust to Providence to support her throughout this, the most fearful trial she had ever experienced in her unfortunate life. Towards the evening the violence of her grief had in some measure abated, and she was enabled to listen more calmly to the advice and tender soothings of Laura.

"But are there no means of saving him?" she cried; "must he suffer for such a wretch as Clinton, who has been the principal cause of his disgrace and ruin? Oh, surely the provocation he received, and the base character of his prosecutor, will be taken into the merciful consideration of his judges, and they may be induced to deal at least leniently with him."

"Yes, dear Mary," replied Laura, "I do indeed hope so, and that those hopes will not be disappointed. Clinton has proved himself to be a miscreant of the deepest dye, and is more worthy of being placed in the situation of your unfortunate husband than he is. But cheer up, Mary, for dismal as your prospects are at present, the Almighty is too merciful to suffer the innocent to become altogether the victims of guilt. Retribution will ere long overtake this wretch Clinton, and all those who have been instrumental in bringing this misery upon you."

"My poor husband," sighed Mary, "has been guilty, very guilty, I admit, but can I forget that he was once good and honourable? Can I banish from my memory those happy scenes of domestic bliss we once enjoyed together? Oh, no, no! even now, with all his faults, notwithstanding all the ill-usage and cruel neglect I have experienced from him, my heart clings to him with all the strength of its first devotion. God knows the feelings of remorse, I am convinced he is now enduring, must be a sufficient, a terrible punishment for all he has been guilty of. Would to Heaven that I might be permitted to share with him the horrors of his incarceration, that I might endeavour to impart consolation to his lacerated mind, and raise his heavily oppressed spirits to hope. Surely, if he is permitted this time to escape, he will be aroused from the frightful spell which so long held dominion over his senses, and by his future conduct make atonement for the many errors he has, through the temptations of others, so unfortunately committed."

"Yes, Mary," replied Laura, "I cannot believe that he would do otherwise, and God grant that he may be afforded the opportunity; he has been taught a terrible lesson, and it cannot, it will not be lost upon him. Be comforted, my sister; you have still friends who are able and willing to assist you. My kind mistress deeply sympathises in your misfortunes, and has desired that everything shall be done for the comfort of yourself and your poor children. As soon as you are able, you are to be removed from this wretched abode to a place where you may at least partake of a portion of your former domestic happiness."

Tears of gratitude started to the poor woman's eyes, and her heart was too full for some moments to give utterance to her feelings.

"May Heaven bless the benevolent lady for this!" she at last ejaculated; "God will surely reward her for her goodness to the wretched mother and her helpless children. Kneel with me, dear Laura, and invoke His merciful interposition for my unfortunate misguided husband."

Laura complied, and they joined their earnest prayers together, the two eldest children also sinking on their knees, and clasping their little hands together, repeating the solemn words to which their mother and aunt gave utterance. It was a most affecting and impressive scene, and the good doctor was much moved, and turned away his head in order to conceal his emotion. Having given some necessary instructions to Laura, he retired, and the two amiable sisters were left alone. During the remainder of the evening Mrs. Langstone continued more calm, than under the terrible circumstances could have been expected, and at length, by the persuasions of Laura, she was prevailed upon to retire to bed, and, notwithstanding the fearful agony of mind she must have been enduring, Laura had the happiness and satisfaction to see her drop off into a calm sleep; but she still continued to watch her with the greatest anxiety, for fear that any unfavourable change might suddenly come over her. The whole of the dreadful truth was disclosed to her, and Laura felt herself relieved from an almost insupportable weight. In the morning, when Mrs. Langstone awoke, which she did not do till the sun was stealing into the gloomy apartment, she was much better, and a faint smile of resignation even animated her pale careworn features.

"Laura," she said, "I have had such delightful visions, and I feel my breast inspired with the hope that they will be realised."

"Oh, my dear Mary," replied her sister, "how happy am I to hear you talk thus. God grant that your expectations may be fulfilled, and that the dark clouds of adversity that have so long obscured your destiny, are about to be dispersed, and that that happiness, that unbounded happiness which is so justly your portion, is about to be restored to you."

"I dreamt," said Mary, "that I was once more in my dear native village, surrounded by my husband and my children. He was again good, affectionate, and prosperous, and all the sufferings and fatal errors of the past were forgotten. No anxiety filled our bosoms; the very heavens seemed to smile upon us, and the air we breathed to impart a healthy and cheerful tone to our senses. Sincere friends, with smiling, joyous faces, flocked to our humble dwelling to greet and welcome us. The simple jest, the jocund laugh, once more passed freely round, and all were bent on contributing to each other's happiness. Oh, it was a delightful scene; will it, will it, indeed ever be realised?"

"It will, Mary, it will, depend upon it." said Laura, "it comes to you from Heaven to raise you from despair, and you must not, you cannot disregard it. Your troubles will soon be at an end, and the frightful past will, I trust, be for ever buried in oblivion."

"Oh, may such happy visions haunt the slumbers of my unfortunate husband," sighed Mrs. Langstone, "and give him fortitude to bear up against the horrors of his present situation. But I must see him—I shall go mad if I am not permitted to behold him, and to endeavour to impart to him some ray of consolation. They will not refuse me this, dear Laura, will they?"

"They will not, Mary," replied her sister, "but let me persuade you to defer the melancholy interview for a day or two, until you have gained more strength, and then I will accompany you"

"Oh, why should I delay? Every moment that I do so appears to me to be an age, and what must be the agony of suspense and horror that Edward is placed in? But is the villain Clinton pronounced out of danger?"

"He is, Mary."

"Thank Heaven for that!" fervently ejaculated Mrs. Langstone, "for had he died of the wounds which were inflicted on him, the fate of Edward would have been inevitable."

She was interruped by a knock at the room door, and Stephen Gadsby entered, bearing in his hand a letter addressed to Mrs. Langstone, which he said the postman had just delivered.

"A letter!" said Mary, trembling, as some misgiving crossed her mind; "a letter addressed to me? Who can this be from?—I know not the writing of the superscription, and I almost fear to open it. Look at it, dear Laura—I cannot."

Laura took the letter from the hand of her sister; but she had no sooner glanced at the address than she turned ghastly pale.

"What is the matter, Laura?" eagerly demanded Mary, "you seem alarmed. What occasions this?"

"It is in the handwriting of Captain Braghall," replied Laura.

"Captain Braghall!" repeated Mrs. Langstone, with a look of the most unspeakable astonishment.

"Yes; I knew his handwriting well, for I have had frequent opportunities of seeing it."

"What can be the meaning of his writing to me?" said Mary; "surely it cannot be to insult me in my misfortunes!"

"Oh, no," said Laura, "bad as I know him to be, he can never be such a heartless villain as to do that."

"Read the letter, my dear sister, for I cannot."

Laura broke the seal with a trembling hand, and complied with her sister's request. It ran as follows:

"UNFORTUNATE MADAM,

"I trust you will pardon me for my apparent boldness in writing to you, well aware as I am of the indifferent opinion you entertain of my character, and the general motives which prompt my conduct. If I can in some measure do away with that unfortunate prejudice, I shall feel but too happy. I freely admit that I have my errors, and that I have also, in moments of thoughtlessness, tempted him to acts of folly and intemperance, which I now sincerely regret. However, allow me to assure you that I deeply feel for his present deplorable situation, and commiserate with you in the terrible misfortunes you have so unmeritedly experienced. I would make some atonement for any injuries I have inflicted

LAGNSTONE'S RETURN HOME AFTER HIS ATTACK ON CLINTON.

on you, and think I cannot better do so than by devoting all my influence and my means towards restoring your husband to liberty, in which efforts I possess the most sanguine hopes that I shall be successful. I have already given instructions to the most able counsel to defend him, and I do hope that you will not reject the further services of, yours, most obediently,

"EVELYN BRAGHALL.

"P.S. If I receive no answer to the contrary, I will do myself the honour to call upon you, when I can explain further.—E. B."

The astonishment of Mrs. Langstone on the perusal of this letter may easily be conceived.

"Can he, indeed, be sincere?" she ejaculated.

"I scarcely know what to think," replied Laura, "but he must be a villain indeed to trifle with your feelings, and to seek to deceive you under the fearful circumstances in which you are placed.'

"How would you advise me to act?"

"It requires a little time to consider," answered her sister, "I know that the captain possesses great influence, and if he is only sincere in what he professes to do, he might be able to accomplish much."

"Oh!" exclaimed Mary, energetically, "I must not heedlessly reject any chance that is likely to rescue my unfortunate husband from his present awful situation. There is a certain candour about the letter which inspires me with some degree of confidence, and yet, when I remember that the captain was one of the principal parties who tempted Edward to crime, I hesitate."

"At any rate, I think it would be advisable not to refuse him the interview he seeks," remarked Laura, "although I confess that I feel some repugnance at meeting him, especially after the diabolical designs that I am aware he had against me."

"If he attempts to deceive us," said Mary, "for the purpose of forwarding some base design, he must be a miscreant indeed. But no, I cannot, dare not believe so, and were I to reject the offers he makes with so much apparent sincerity, and thus deprive my unfortunate husband of the least chance of being rescued from the dreadful fate with which he is at present threatened, could I ever forgive myself?"

"Heaven forbid, my dear sister," said Laura, "that I should advise you to do so, but an idea occurs to me of which I think you will approve."

"Name it, Laura," said Mrs. Langstone, eagerly.

"I will write to my mistress," replied Laura, "making her acquainted with what has happened, and ask her advice upon the subject."

"Ah! an excellent idea," said Mrs Langstone, "do so, dear Laura, and I will be guided entirely by her opinion."

Laura immediately seated herself at the table, and addressed a respectful note to her mistress, in which she explained every particular contained in the letter of Captain Braghall, and requested her advice upon the subject. With this Stephen Gadsby was despatched, and, in an hour or so, returned with the reply, which was to the effect that, in the opinion of the mistress of Laura, there could be no objection to the meeting taking place between the captain and Mrs. Langstone, as she had seen him on the subject, and her impression was that he was sincere; but still she would advise Laura not to be present at that interview.

"A prudent suggestion," observed Laura, at the same time a blush suffused her cheeks; "but still, my dear Mary, I must be close at hand, so that I may interpose should the captain attempt to play us falsely."

"Dear Laura," replied her sister, "I commend you for your precaution, and cannot, of course, raise any objection to what you propose; but still I cannot believe that any man, who could write as Captain Braghall has done to me, would become the abominable miscreant to take advantage of our present miseries to further any sinister designs he might have in contemplation. If he is sincere in his present professions, and by any means can save my poor husband from the terrible fate which now seems to be impending over him, not only can I freely forgive the past, but my heart must ever throb with gratitude towards him for the inestimable service he will have rendered me in restoring to me my Edward, cleansed from his impurities—the same dear Edward Langstone as when I first knew him. Almighty God! hear my humble prayer, and grant in Thine infinite mercy that such may be the result of my fervent hopes!"

Overpowered by her feelings, she threw herself, sobbing, into her sister's arms, and for a few minutes they were so completely absorbed by emotion that they could neither of them give utterance to a syllable. Stephen Gadsby had all this time stood in a humble attitude by the room door, and so completely moved was the poor fellow by the scene between the two sisters, and so great was the interest which the misfortunes of Mrs. Langstone had excited in his uncultivated breast, that, although he felt delicacy ought to have prompted him to retire, he could not; and when they had a little recovered from their emotion, he advanced a few paces towards them, and said—

"I hope you will pardon me, ladies—I am but a poor ignorant fellow, and no better than I should be, as I have told you before, Mrs. Langstone, but still I would serve you if I could, indeed I would."

"My good friend," said Mary, gratefully extending her hand to him, "why this ceremony in addressing a poor helpless creature like me, who is already indebted to you so much? Do I not owe to you my own life and that of my children? Did you not save my husband and myself from the perpetration of a horrible crime, and——"

"Nay, Mrs. Langstone," interrupted Gadsby, "say no more about that, for I am only too happy to think I was permitted to perform one or two good acts in the course of my useless life. However, what I wished to say was this—p'rhaps you will excuse me if I am too bold—I have no great opinion of this gent, Captain Braghall, as he is called, and though I would advise you to grant him the meeting he asks, and to accept of all the assistance it may be in his power to render your unfortunate husband, still I would advise you also to have some friend on whom you think you can depend, to be in hearing, so that he might take notes (don't they call 'em?) of what takes place, and mayhap he might be found a useful witness on some future occasion."

The suggestion of Gadsby immediately vividly impressed itself upon the minds of Mrs. Langstone and her sister, and the former eagerly replied—

"Thanks, thanks, Mr. Gadsby, for what you have advised; *you* are that *friend* in whose sincerity I know I can confide."

"Thank you, Mrs. Langstone," said Stephen, "for the compliment you pay me, which is more than I deserve, though I am sure that I would serve you in any way I could; however, that's nothing to do with it. I do not wish to be a spy upon your affairs, but somehow it strikes me that this young spark is a snake in the grass after all, and I wish to discover whether I am correct or not, if I can. I have heard something within the last few hours which excites my suspicions, and if they prove to be correct, your husband shall be saved, or my name's not Stephy Gadsby."

"Oh, God!" exclaimed Mrs. Langstone, in an agony of feeling which is perfectly indescribable. "Oh tell me how?"

"Pardon me, Mrs. Langstone," replied Gadsby, "I think it will be better to say no more upon that subject for the present, but, if you will only trust to me, I will not deceive you, and I hope that all will answer my expectations. What I propose is, that I should be secreted in an adjoining room to that in which the interview takes place, so that I may have an opportunity of overhearing the conversation; not that I wish to make any other use of it than to serve you and your husband. Will you trust me?"

"My kind friend," said Mary, "I should be most uncharitable and ungrateful were I not to do so."

"Enough," said Stephen, "then that business is settled; I have arranged all my plans, and all that I want to know is, when you propose that the interview shall take place."

"The sooner the better," answered Mrs. Langstone, "for there is no time to lose. Heaven send that it may be the means of restoring my unhappy husband to his liberty."

"Then," said Gadsby, "let it be to-morrow; if Miss Laura will only write a letter to the captain, making the appointment, I will convey it to him directly."

This was agreed upon, and Stephen gladly retired from the room, apparently with much satisfaction.

"The proposition of this man appears to be a reasonable one," remarked Laura, when he had quitted the room; "think you we can depend upon him?"

"Oh, yes," answered her sister, "I believe him to be honest in his intentions; after his conduct towards me, would it not be most uncharitable for me to think otherwise?—Oh, Laura, hope begins to revive in my bosom."

"Thank God for that, my dear sister; still cherish that hope, and I feel confident that it is not doomed to be disappointed. Gadsby has evidently acquired some knowledge of importance, and I trust that we may be able to turn it to the best advantage. I will write the letter."

She did so, and Stephen Gadsby returning to the room, it was delivered to his charge, and he immediately took his departure to the residence of Captain Braghall.

CHAPTER X.

THE LIBERTINE AND HIS EXPECTED DUPE.—STEPHEN GADSBY HAS AN EAR AND AN EYE TO BUSINESS.

WHAT information the poor fellow Gadsby had obtained which caused him to make the arrangements that have been described in the previous chapter, it would not be prudent to disclose at the present stage of our story, but certainly, if an opinion might be formed from the manner in which he chuckled to himself as he proceeded on his way with the letter to the lodgings of Captain Braghall, it was something important, and appeared to afford him the most infinite gratification.

"Yes," he said, as he hurried along, "I think I am down upon the d—d scoundrel this time, and if I can only succeed in doing this one good action, I shall be a happier man than I have been for many a day. Poor creatures—poor creatures; but we are all poor creatures, when left to ourselves, our own bad passions, and mayhap our own misfortunes. I wish I'd had th' luck to have been made a *scholard*, for then, mayhap, I should have been able to have said what I *think* in such sort of talk as my betters would have listened to me with something more than th' respect they pay to th' snarlin' of a mongrel cur. But what am I grumbling about ?—I'm only one of the *mobility*, and ought to be thankful to th' *'stockrasy* that they allow me to breathe at all. Ha! ha!"

There was an expression in the countenance of poor Stephen Gadsby as he made use of these observations, which showed that, although he bore the outward appearance of a ruffian, he possessed the innate feelings of a *man*; happy would it be for mankind in general, if those who have the good fortune to present a better exterior, could lay claim to the same qualities of mind.

"I shall have them! I shall have them!" he continued, after a pause: "I know I shall have them, if they do not look sharp; and only let me have them, see what I will do with them, the d—d scoundrels! I'm no better than I ought to be—I know I'm not; but whose fault is it? Not mine, I think, because I know I did not make myself, and I never was lucky enough to have any one to fashion or form me—(I wonder where I picked up those hard words ?) but there's something tells me I ought to be better, and I like the idea so well that I will be so, if I possibly can. Yes, I'm down upon ye, my nabs, I'm down upon you this time; Stephy Gadsby, you vagabond, only let fortin give you a chance of doing this one good turn; of bowling out these scamps, and easing the mind of that poor creatur', Mrs. Langstone, and you will be enabled to make out your will, turn over your *defects* to your *executioners*, and, knowing that you have saved a foolish man from a shameful death, and returned him to his poor wife and little ones, a good man, I hope, you may then stand some chance of dying in peace with all mankind."

There was pure nature in every word that the illiterate Stephen Gadsby thus, in the fulness of his heart and his hopes, gave utterance to; in fact, the reader will not need to be told, from even the faint portraiture, or rather inkling we have at present given of his character, that he was a rough diamond—one that might have shone brilliantly had some friendly hand snatched him in time from the mire of obscurity in which it was his lot to be plunged. But, if ever there was a happy individual, it was Stephen Gadsby at that moment when he thought that he was on the road to detect villany, and to render an essential benefit to his unfortunate fellow creatures. And as these thoughts continued to occupy his mind, he still laughed and chuckled in very glee as he proceeded to the lodgings of the worthy and respectable Captain Braghall. He arrived there at last, but would not be satisfied unless he saw the captain himself, and delivered the letter into his own hands. Braghall had been waiting most anxiously to know the result of his stratagem, and therefore it was not with a little pleasure and courtesy that he received Stephen Gadsby when he knew the purport of his errand, and especially when he saw that the letter he brought with him was in the handwriting of her to whom he had dared to raise his thoughts, and whose destruction ne at that moment contemplated. Gadsby eyed him with a peculiar look while he greedily devoured the contents of the letter, and it was evident that something was passing in his mind, and confirmed him in the suspicions which we cannot explain at present. Braghall could not conceal his feelings of exultation, but, of course, he had not the slightest suspicion that the simple looking being before him took the least notice of them, and Stephen Gadsby chuckled more and more to himself. At length Captain Braghall concluded the letter, and turning to Gadsby with a bland countenance, he said—

"Ah—ah! very good! very good! I will be sure to be punctual, you will tell the ladies. You acted perfectly right, my good man, in not delivering this letter into any other person's hands than my own; here is a sovereign for you. By the bye, have I not had the pleasure of seeing you before ?"

"Praps you might, sir," replied Gadsby, carelessly, "but I cannot call to my mind when I had that honour. I'm not wery familiar with the nobs."

"Ha! ha! ha!" laughed the captain, jocosely; "a man of retired habits, I see."

"No, sir," returned Stephen drily, "that's just what I want to be."

"Ha! ha!—very good, very good," graciously smiled Captain Braghall; "you're a shrewd fellow; a clever fellow, I see. You'll take a glass of wine ?"

"Thank ye, sir, though that's a medicine I haven't had many opportunities of testing my constitution with."

"Ha! ha! very good! ver—y good!" said the captain; "then suppose we test it on this one occasion ?"

"Very good," replied Stephen Gadsby, rather satirically.

The wine was brought forward and Gadsby was desired to help himself, and then Braghall added as a sudden thought seemed to occur to him—

"By-the-bye, I think I may as well return an answer to this letter. I trust that Mrs. Langstone is improving in health?"

This he affected to speak in a tone of seriousness, but Gadsby was not to be deceived, though, of course, he concealed his real thoughts from the villain in whose presence he stood, and in reply to his question said—

"Why, sir, poor Mrs. Langstone is going on quite as well as could have been expected."

"I'm glad to hear it," said Braghall; "I will not detain you many minutes, my good fellow, and while I am absent I hope you will enjoy yourself."

Gadsby bowed, and the captain then retired from the room to write the letter.

"I guessed right," muttered Gadsby to himself, when he was alone; "he is an infernal villain, and this is all some plot to mislead and betray Mrs. Langstone and her sister; but you must look very sharp, or I might chance to spoil your plans, poor devil as I am."

He was interrupted in the midst of his soliloquy by the return of Braghall, who presenting him the note, dismissed him, and Gadsby hurried on his way back, still chuckling with inward exultation at the discovery he imagined he had made, and the designs which were in his own mind to detect villany and to serve the innocent.

"By Jupiter!" cried Captain Braghall, when Gadsby was gone, "this has more than answered my most sanguine anticipations. I triumph! I triumph! 'tis a glorious triumph!— A reply to my letter, and written by Laura too;—oh, that is indeed much more than I ever expected, and if I do not take every advantage of the opportunity thus afforded me, my name's not Braghall. Exquisite thought! Oh, Laura, coy and scornful beauty, little do you suspect the plot that is laid against you, and from which it is now impossible for you to escape. You are a prize worth contending for, and I must and will win you by some means or other. That is a strange sort of fellow who brought the note," he added, after a pause; "I do not half like him. I must have a keen eye upon him. The answers he returned to several of my questions were anything but satisfactory, but if I allow myself to be duped by *him*, it will be my own fault. To-morrow, then, I shall have the felicity of once more seeing Laura Maysdale, and of conversing with her as a friend; of enlisting her esteem, from the notion that I so deeply sympathize with the misfortunes of the family. But I must be cautious how I act, or I may betray myself. I think I gammoned the old lady, my aunt, pretty well, or it is not at all unlikely that this interview would have been refused. She is quite in ecstacies! She thinks me a reformed character, and will be an excellent instrument to work out my plans. Ha! ha! —Oh, Braghall, oh, Braghall, it begins to strike me most forcibly that you are a d——d clever fellow!"

Thus gratifying himself in the hope of the success of his diabolical designs, the libertine rubbed his hands, and laughed in downright glee.

"Yes, yes," he said, "she is mine certainly; that is a settled fact, and nothing, I think, can alter it."

Leaving Captain Braghall to exult in his imaginary success, we will now pursue the footsteps of Stephen Gadsby, who having performed his office so well, and feeling a little exhausted by the over exertion he had made, dropped into a public-house on his road for the purpose of having a pint of porter and collecting his thoughts previous to his return home. Gadsby was, as he depictured himself, only "a poor devil," and it must therefore not be expected that he selected a first-rate tavern or hotel in which to refresh himself; in fact, the very house he happened to drop into was one of the lowest of the very lowest dens, which are as plentiful in the metropolis as mushrooms. A cluster of drunken individuals were at the bar drinking, and who appeared to lodge and *gin* there; if they *boarded* as well, it must certainly be when they could not keep their "perpendicular," but Stephen took no notice of them, and hastening into the tap-room, where there was no person at that time, he called for the refreshment he required, and seating himself in a retired corner of the room, re-discussed in his own mind what had transpired between himself and Captain Braghall at their recent interview. The longer he thought of it, the more he congratulated himself on the success of his plans, and the depth of his penetration.

"Ha! ha!" he laughed, "I certainly have got you this time, Mr. Braghall, and it strikes me rather forcibly that I shall spoil your sport. What a d——d scoundrel you must be to plot anything wrong against those who are so deeply plunged in misery already."

He became silent, for at that moment two individuals entered the room, who did not observe him, and retired into another box; but Gadsby had an idea, as soon as he noticed their ill-favoured countenances, that he had seen them somewhere before, and he determined to watch them, and to listen to any conversation that might take place between them. It was the Stunner and Dick Hemlock, and having been served with what they wanted to drink, they commenced talking, in low tones at first, Stephen Gadsby drawing himself into the smallest possible space in the corner where he sat, and listening attentively.

"Fifty pounds reward, and a description of our persons!" said the Stunner; "that is very awkward."

"D—d unfortunate," replied Hemlock.

"And Jack Clinton does not appear to be recognised in the transaction," remarked the Stunner.

"No, he does not," was the reply.

"What is to be done?"

"I don't know; we must take our chance, I suppose, and bounce it out as well as we can."

"We shall find that rather a queer job, I am afraid. I think we had better emigrate."

"Nonsense!"

"Well, perhaps it might be as well to save the money, for it is not at all unlikely that we shall be sent out at government expense," said the Stunner, with a rueful laugh.

"Psha!" replied Hemlock, "keep up your pluck, you are quaking upon the business?"

"I think it is almost time."

"Not a bit of it, they have got to find us."

"And I think this little picture is not at all unlikely to do that kindness for us," returned the Stunner, pulling a piece of printed paper from his pocket, which he read in the following words:—

"BURGLARY AND ATTEMPTED MURDER.—FIFTY POUNDS REWARD.

"Whereas the house of Christopher Hastings, Esq., merchant, of Cornhill, and the county of Surrey, was on the night of the seventeenth of October last burglariously broken into and entered by three men armed with bludgeons, who all attacked the aforesaid gentleman and his housekeeper in the most brutal manner, and afterwards plundered the house of property to a considerable amount, as specified below. Two of the ruffians were distinctly seen, and their persons thus described: one a man of apparently about thirty-five years of age, tall and bony figure, with a scar over his right eye. Dark complexion and large bushy whiskers—"

"That's my portrait," observed the Stunner, "as correct as any artist could have painted it; now for your's, Dick."

"'The other was a square built man, about the same age, with repulsive features, and blind of the left eye. This is, and cetera and cetera—' There, what do you think of that, Dick, for a fancy sketch?"

"D—n them!" said Hemlock, "they have indeed been too particular; and to leave Jack Clinton out of it altogether."

"Yes, that's the misfortune," said the Stunner; "and you see there is a free pardon promised to the other man if he will give such information as will lead to the apprehension and conviction of his accomplices. What if Clinton were to turn snitch?"

"Oh, I do not think he would do that."

"I am not quite so satisfied on that point," said the Stunner.

"Why, it would be rather bad policy for him to do so till after the trial of Ned Langstone, at any rate," observed the villain Hemlock.

"Very true; but I should like to see him upon the subject, if there be an opportunity; for if he becomes acquainted with this, fear might induce him to betray us to save himself."

"And yet he did the principal part of the business."

"Yes, but he was not recognized."

"Exactly so; however we have only to keep our own counsel, and we may yet be able to give them the go-by. You were too fast the other night in throwing out the hints you did to Captain Braghall."

"Well, I know I was, and I have admitted it, but it's no use talking about that now; it was only a slip of the tongue, and I don't suppose he understood it."

"That I doubt very much," said Hemlock, "for I noticed the avidity with which he cross-questioned you, and you know, for the purpose of furthering his designs against Laura Maysdale, he would be glad to elicit anything that might lead to the restoration of Langstone's liberty."

"That's true," coincided the Stunner; "and do you not think it would be as well for us to see the captain upon the subject, and explaining to him all the business, obtain his patronage and assistance in our difficulties?"

"Why," answered Hemlock, "I scarcely know what to say upon that point."

"You know," remarked the other, "that he is most anxious to find something out against Clinton, so that he may intimidate him against presecuting Langstone, and this would be rich food for him."

"Yes, it might be so," returned Hemlock, "but we must talk about that another time. Come, let us depart."

They finished their drink and took their departure accordingly, little suspecting that their conversation had been overheard by one so deeply interested in it.

"So, so," said Gadsby, when they were gone, "I am down upon you too, my covies. A pretty pair of rascals; how fortunate that I should drop into the very place to hear all I wanted to learn. Oh, oh, Captain Braghall, it strikes me that you will be disappointed this time, and that the worthy Jack Clinton and his respectable colleagues will find themselves in a bit of a fix. Fifty pounds reward! That is mine, safe!—Oh, this is a glorious day's work; there is nothing like doing a good action. Stephen Gadsby has always an eye and an ear to business. Poor Mrs. Langstone, I have news for you that will cheer your heart, I think."

The poor fellow having thus expressed his feelings, hastily arose from his seat, and quitted the place, making his way with all possible expedition towards the residence of those who were so anxiously awaiting his return.

CHAPTER XI.

THE INTERVIEW BETWEEN BRAGHALL AND MRS. LANGSTONE. — THE MEETING IN THE PRISON.

PERFECTLY satisfied with the knowledge he had so accidentally and fortunately obtained, Stephen Gadsby with elated spirits hurried on his way, still chuckling and exulting to himself, to think that he should have been enabled so easily to defeat the secret designs of the young libertine, Captain Braghall; but more than all, that the information he had gathered from the villanous Hemlock and his companion's conference would be the means of serving those in whom he now felt so deep an interest; and probably of restoring the misguided and unfortunate Edward Langstone to liberty. The poor fellow really felt happier than he had done for many a day, and all the natural good qualities of the heart expanded at the idea of being made the humble instrument of benefitting his fellow-creatures, and thus making some little atonement for the many errors he had in the course of his chequered life committed. He determined, however, to keep the knowledge he had obtained for the present confined to his own breast, and to allow Braghall to proceed in his designs, in fancied security, thinking, that by adopting that course, he would be the more likely to bring his own plans to a more triumphant conclusion, and to render the escape of the villains from justice impossible.

"Oh, yes," he said; "I am down upon you, my fine fellows, and if I do not spoil your sport, it will be strange to me. What I have heard is no more than I expected; but only to think that lucky accident should put me in possession of the very particulars I was so anxious to obtain. Methinks, Mr. Clinton, that you will make rather an awkward appearance in the witness box of the Old Bailey. I must see you, however, and kindly intimate to you the position in which you are placed, and then, if you are not a greater fool than I take you to be, you will see the prudence of being found missing as soon as convenient. Let me but be enabled to accomplish these, my honest intentions, and Stephen Gadsby will be the happiest fellow living."

By the time he had arrived at the conclusion of this soliloquy, he found himself at home, and immediately repaired to the room of Mrs. Langstone. She and her sister arose eagerly at his entrance, and inquired what had been the result of his errand.

"Oh, most successful, Mrs. Langstone," replied Gadsby; "gloriously successful; much better than I expected; ha! ha! I am down upon 'em!—I'm down upon 'em!—ha! ha!"

"What mean you, Mr. Gadsby?" demanded Mary, anxiously.

"Don't ask me, Mrs. Langstone," said Stephen; "I would willingly banish your suspense, but I think it would not be prudent to explain more at present. Let it suffice that certain matters have come to my knowledge by a lucky chance, which, if I am not much mistaken, will be the means of rescuing your husband from the fate with which he is at present threatened. I have discovered——"

"What! what!" eagerly interrupted Mrs. Langstone and her sister in a breath.

"That Captain Braghall is an arrant villain," answered Gadsby; "but that I knew before."

"Oh, Mr. Gadsby!" ejaculated the anxious wife; "do you indeed think there is any hope for my unfortunate husband?"

"I do, Mrs. Langstone," returned Stephen; "indeed I do, or, believe me, I would not make the assertions that I have done, believe me, I would not. Keep up your spirits, and take my word for it, your troubles will soon be at an end, and your husband once more restored to you, a better man, I hope, than he has been for some time past."

Mrs. Langstone clasped her hands vehemently together, and raising her eyes towards Heaven, mentally returned her grateful thanks, whilst Laura's feelings may be better imagined than described, and she joined her sister in her prayer of gratitude to the Almighty.

"But will you not explain more fully, Mr. Gadsby," said Mrs. Langstone, "what has excited those hopes in your breast?"

"Pardon me, ma'am," returned Stephen, "but I do not think it would be exactly prudent to do so at present; but I will not keep you in suspense many days—and of this rest assured, that I have heard sufficient of the fellow Clinton, to render his prosecution of your husband a decided failure."

"Oh, God!" exclaimed Mrs. Langstone, tears rushing to her eyes; "can this indeed be true, and is there still hope for you, my unfortunate husband?"

"There is indeed, Mrs. Langstone," said Gadsby; "but compose yourself, and receive this respectable captain without any apparent suspicion of the integrity of his intentions."

"You saw him, then?" said Mary.

"Oh, yes," answered Gadsby, "and I can assure you that our interview was a most interesting one, and a most profitable one to me. He little thought, I dare say, that a poor simple fellow like me was so much on the alert to frustrate his designs. I am only a rough uncultivated fellow, Mrs. Langstone, and I have not been one of the most respectable, which, perhaps, I need not tell you, but indeed I have a wish to serve you, and to prove that I am anxious to become a better man if I can."

"My good man," said Mary, "why should you talk to me in this strain, so deprecatory to yourself? You have been to me one of my best friends in my misfortunes, and I owe you a debt of gratitude which I can never repay. Would to Heaven that every one possessed as good a heart as that which throbs in your bosom, there would then be not so much misery in the world as there is at present."

"You flatter me, Mrs. Langstone, more than I deserve,' returned Gadsby; "but I do hope that the time will come when I shall not be altogether unworthy of such compliments. Perhaps, if I had had any one to care for me in my childhood, and to teach me better, I should not have been the poor devil I now am. But we'll say no more on that subject."

He then detailed what had taken place at the interview between him and Braghall, but made no mention of what he had overheard in the public-house into which he had by a most fortunate accident dropped. Mrs. Langstone and her sister listened to him with the greatest attention, and nothing could exceed their indignation and disgust as the real character and motives of Captain Braghall were clearly revealed to them. Gadsby presented them the note which he had received from the captain, the contents of which breathed the same tone as his former letter, and in the most fulsome language, which it required very little wisdom to penetrate, returned his thanks for the condescension of Mrs. Langstone and her sister in granting him the interview which he had requested.

"Oh, how can I see the hypocrite," said Mary, "when I know the villany of his intentions?"

"But for the sake of your husband, Mrs. Langstone, you must,' replied Stephen; "th re can be no harm in receiving the assistance he offers, though there would be great danger in making him aware of your suspicions. Depend upon it, his evil designs will recoil upon himself."

"I do believe that they will," remarked Laura, "and t ink that what you propose, Mr. Gadsby, is nothing more than what is just and reasonable."

"I'm much obliged to you, miss," said Gadsby. "Heaven forbid that I should propose anything that is wrong to those whom I wish to serve."

"Then you advise me to receive the captain with the same respect as if I believed in the sincerity and integrity of his intentions?" said Mrs. Langstone.

"Certainly," answered Gadsby, "for by so doing you will best forward the designs we have all in view, and from what has this day come to my knowledge I have not the least fear of the results."

"Oh, Mr. Gadsby," said Mary, "what you have said does indeed inspire me with hope. Oh, Edward, if it should be the merciful will of Heaven to rescue you from your present perilous situation, my gratitude will know no bounds, and I shall be one of the happiest of human beings, burying in oblivion the dreadful, the gloomy past. A terrible lesson have you been taught, my husband; God send it may not be lost upon you."

"But you will grant me the request I made this morning, Mrs. Langstone," said Gadsby, "namely, to be in an adjoining room when the interview with you and Captain Braghall takes place? It is no feeling of idle curiosity which prompts me to wish to be a listener, but it is necessary to the furtherance of my designs that I should become acquainted with all I can."

"I place every confidence in you, Mr. Gadsby," replied Mr. Langstone, "and will leave you to act entirely as you think proper."

"Thank you, ma'am," said Gadsby, "and you will find that I will not abuse your confidence

EDWARD LANGSTONE IN PRISON.

Everything I have promised I will perform; and should I succeed, I shall consider myself but too well rewarded for any trouble to which I may be put. The world shall yet see that Stephen Gadsby is not exactly the heartless rascal he has hitherto been looked upon. Keep up your spirits, Mrs. Langstone, and mark my words, you shall yet be restored to happiness."

Mrs. Langstone again heartily expressed her thanks to the honest fellow, and once more assured him of her confidence in the integrity of his intentions.

"But would you not advise me to make my unfortunate husband acquainted with my suspicions?" she asked.

"Not for the present," replied Gadsby, "for it might be the means of preventing the accomplishment of our wishes. You may, however, hold out the strongest hopes to him, and that will afford him some consolation. Oh, Mrs. Langstone, I have heard something this day which will strike confusion into the minds of your enemies, and bring them to that shame and ignominy to which they think to consign your husband. Stephy Gadsby may be a fool, but still he has sometimes an eye and ear to business, and so some of them may find to their cost."

"Mr. Gadsby," said Mary, "your words have re-animated my bosom with hope, and I feel myself totally incapable of returning my acknowledgments in language such as I ought to do."

"Do not mention it, Mrs. Langstone," said Stephen ; "I have done no more than my duty, and require no thanks, indeed I do not ; I only hope that I may be able to accomplish what I wish, and I have, at present, every reason to believe that I shall not be disappointed. But I am intruding upon you ; I wish you good day, and you shall find me ever most ready to render you all the assistance in my power."

With these words Stephen Gadsby quitted the room, well satisfied with the adventures of the day, and sanguine in his expectations of the future.

"Yes, yes," he said, "I cannot fail, I have got the rascals secure, if I only play my cards well. This is the best day's work I have ever done, and I feel quite a different man. Oh, what a pleasure and satisfaction there is in performing a good action. I have imparted comfort and hope to this poor woman, and Heaven knows how much she stood in need of them."

And Stephen Gadsby was indeed a happy man, and determined from that time to lead a different course of life to what he had hitherto done.

"What can be the information which makes him so sanguine?" said Mrs. Langstone, when he had quitted the room.

"I cannot form the least conjecture," replied Laura, "but I place the utmost reliance upon what he says, and I feel confident that you will yet be restored to happiness, my dear sister, and see your husband once more placed in that respectable position in society from which he should never have strayed."

"God grant that your predictions may be faithful," dear Laura, said her sister, "how grateful shall I ever be to the Almighty for this mercy. Oh, Edward, surely if you are rescued from your present terrible and disgraceful situation, you will never again plunge into that vortex of vice and folly which has ever been accompanied by so many horrors."

"Oh, no," ejaculated Laura, "he must indeed be abandoned, callous to every sense of virtue, gratitude, or humanity, could he do so? But do not torture your mind, Mary, with any such apprehensions, which I trust will turn out fallacious."

Mary clasped her hands, and raised her eyes devoutly towards Heaven, as she said—

"All merciful God, grant that such hopes may be realized, and I shall be sufficiently repaid for all the troubles it has been my hard lot to endure. But I must see my unhappy husband, and endeavour to console him in his confinement."

"Defer your melancholy visit till the day after to-morrow, and I will then accompany you," said Laura.

"Be it so," returned Mrs. Langstone ; "and in the meantime may Heaven inspire his bosom with fortitude and resignation. Oh, Laura, how shall I ever be able to support the interview——"

"You must endeavour to exert yourself for the occasion, Mary," replied her sister, "though I know that the trial will be a severe one."

"Alas ! it will indeed. But the money that was found upon him ; that fills my mind with the most terrible doubts and apprehensions."

"I trust that they will prove groundless, and that Edward will be able to give a satisfactory account of it."

"How can he do so? And has he not refused, which imparts a stronger colour to the suspicions entertained against him? He could never have become honestly possessed of the money, and my heart sinks with despair when I think of it."

"Do not give way to such sad thoughts, my sister, for, notwithstanding everything at present looks so suspicious against your unfortunate husband, I trust that he will be able to exculpate himself. To you he will, at any rate, explain everything, and remove the doubts and fears which at present distract your mind."

"May he be able to do so satisfactorily," said Mrs. Langstone, fervently, "for if he cannot, in spite of all that Stephen Gadsby said to the contrary, I feel confident that his fate is inevitable. My God ! how I shudder when I think of it."

Laura sought to compose her, and to banish such apprehensions from her mind, and she at last succeeded much better than might have been expected.

"But this interview with Captain Braghall," she said ; "I half dread it, and wish it could be avoided."

"You have nothing to fear, my dear sister," replied Laura ; "if you only follow the advice of Gadsby and do not suffer him to imagine for a moment that you entertain the least suspicion of his designs. In fact, if he only performs what he promises, he may be the principal cause of restoring your husband to liberty."

"I will do as you advise, Laura, and put my trust in Heaven for success," said Mrs. Langstone; "surely it will not desert me at such a solemn and trying occasion."

"It will not, dear Mary, depend upon it;—continue to encourage such thoughts, and all will be well. I will be within hearing, and should I see any necessity for it, I will immediately make my appearance, notwithstanding the disgust and repugnance I feel towards the unprincipled libertine, who would fain bring about my destruction. No doubt he is priding himself on the success of his plot, and in the thought of seeing me, but he will find himself most bitterly mistaken. Stephen Gadsby is a shrewd man, and no doubt he will not deceive our expectations, if we only put our trust in him."

"I do believe him to be sincere," remarked Mrs. Langstone; "and I should be most ungrateful did I not put every confidence in him, after the services he has rendered me. To him I am indebted for the preservation of my own life and that of my children; and it was him who saved my unhappy husband from the perpetration of a crime which I cannot think upon without feelings of the most unspeakable horror. Oh, God! the fearful events of that night can never, surely, be effaced from my memory."

"Do not give way to such thoughts, Mary," said her sister, "for they only serve to distract your mind."

Mrs. Langstone sighed, and the conversation for the present dropped; but they looked forward to the following day with no little anxiety. Captain Braghall in the meantime was congratulating himself on the fancied success of his nefarious designs, and the gratification that was in store for him from his interview with Mrs. Langstone and her beauteous sister, and he awaited the arrival of the following day with the greatest impatience.

"They have caught the bait I threw out for them," he said, "and it is strange to me if they can escape me. No doubt that Laura will by and by think me a most amiable being, and reproach herself for the prejudice she formerly entertained towards me. Ha! ha! ha!—this is a clever scheme, and must succeed. I must, however, contrive to quiet that fellow, Clinton, somehow or the other, or he might be the means of spoiling everything. My first interview with him did not make a very favourable impression upon him, but I must try what effect a second will have. He knows the value of money, and by that means I think I shall be able to secure him; besides, it strikes me that it would not be altogether safe for him to make his appearance in a court of justice, and should that turn out to be true, he will the more readily accede to my wishes. Let me only get Langstone out of the present danger in which he is placed, and my triumph over the girl Laura is certain. The thought is delightful, and the longer I dwell upon it the more determined do I become. She will have no suspicion of me, and will, therefore, the more easily fall into my snares."

Thus he continued to meditate after the departure of Stephen Gadsby, and every moment he became more sanguine in his expectations; but how different would have been his feelings had he been aware of the knowledge which Gadsby had obtained in so singular a manner, and the use he was determined to make of it. The next morning came, and Mrs. Langstone and her sister had scarcely finished their breakfast when Stephen entered the room and informed them that the captain had arrived and was waiting below. Mary trembled.

"Be firm, Mrs. Langstone," said Gadsby, "remember the advice I gave you, and all will be well. Do not let him have the least reason to think that you suspect the integrity of his intentions. Shall I tell him to come up?"

"Yes, yes," answered Mrs. Langstone, "I am now prepared to meet him. Laura, you will, of course, retire."

"Yes," said Gadsby, "and so will I in a minute, into the next room, where I can hear all that passes."

He made his exit as he thus spoke, and Laura having embraced her sister, also quitted the room, and had scarcely done so when the captain knocked at the room door, and was desired by Mrs. Langstone in a faint voice to walk in. He did so, and looked much disappointed when he saw that Laura was not there, which Mrs. Langstone did not fail to perceive, although she affected not to notice it, and greeted him with a respectful curtsey.

"Mrs. Langstone," he said, "I appear before you under rather embarrassing circumstances, when I remember the prejudice you probably entertained against me. But I hope you will try to view me now as a friend who is anxious to serve you, and who sincerely and deeply sympathises with you in your misfortunes."

"I feel obliged to you, sir, for your sympathy and the promises you have made me," replied Mrs. Langstone, "and if I can indeed be the means of rescuing my unfortunate husband from his present terrible situation, my heart must ever throb with gratitude towards you."

"I will use my best endeavours to do so, Mrs. Langstone," replied Braghall, "and I entertain the most sanguine hopes that I shall be successful.   I possess considerable influence, and I' am ready to go to any expense to accomplish my wishes.   Your husband received great provocation I know; Clinton is a villain, and I think that his character will go a great way to prejudice the mind of the jury against him, which will be all in the favour of Mr. Langstone; a for the money which I understand was found upon him, I have but little doubt but I shall be able to account for that."

"Oh, sir," said Mrs. Langstone, eagerly, "can you indeed do that?   You are not flattering me with false hopes?"

"I should be ashamed of myself if I could thus cruelly trifle with your feelings, Mrs. Langstone," replied the captain.

"Do you, then, believe that my husband came honestly by the money?" asked Mary.

"I do."

"God grant that you may be able to prove that," said Mrs. Langstone, "but it was a large sum, and when I remember that my husband was completely penniless when he left me, I know not what to think."

"There are more ways of obtaining money than by thieving," said Braghall, "gambling, for instance."

"Oh, how could he gamble without money?" demanded Mary.

"Might he not find a friend who would not object to lend him a trifle, myself for instance?"

"Ah!" cried Mrs. Langstone, "there is some truth in that.   Edward could never become a robber; my heart convinces me he could not."

"I do not believe he could," said the captain, "so make your mind easy upon that point.   As I told you in the letter I sent to you, I have already given instructions to one of our most eminent counsel to defend him, and I have not the least doubt that his eloquence will not be lost upon the jury."

Mrs. Langstone again expressed her thanks, and she began to think that Gadsby was mistaken, and that the captain was really sincere in what he proposed to do.   Braghall noticed the impression he had made, and he exulted in his imagined triumph.

"Then," he observed, "may I flatter myself with the hope that you will trust to me, and accept of my services as an atonement for the past?"

"Oh, sir," replied Mary, "if you do but what you promise, I shall be for ever indebted to you.   Should I be deprived, by the stern hand of the law, of my unfortunate and misguided husband, what would become of me and my poor children?"

"Make your mind easy, Mrs. Langstone," said the captain, "for I repeat that there shall be no means left untried to save him, and I feel satisfied that my wishes will not be disappointed. Will you permit me to call upon you again?"

Mrs. Langstone replied in the affirmative, and the captain having forced some money upon her, took his leave, very well satisfied with the success of his schemes, though he was not a little disappointed at not having seen Laura, who he strongly suspected had purposely kept out of the way.   As soon as he was gone, Gadsby and Laura re-entered the apartment, they having overheard all that had passed.

"What is your opinion now, Mr. Gadsby?" asked Mrs. Langstone.

"Why," replied Stephen, "the same as it was before, that the captain is an arrant villain."

"Then you do not indeed believe he is sincere in the promises he has held out?"

"Why, I don't doubt that he will do all that he has said," returned Gadsby, "to answer some secret purpose of his own, but out of no good feeling towards you, Mrs. Langstone."

"That's exactly my opinion," said Laura.

"I have heard quite enough to convince me of that," said Gadsby.

"But," said Mrs. Langstone, "do you not think that what he said in respect to the money which was found in the possession of my unfortunate husband possesses some degree of reason, and is worthy of serious consideration?"

"A mere juggle, Mrs. Langstone, depend on it," remarked Gadsby; "got up for the purpose of misleading you, and forwarding his own guilty designs.   Place no reliance upon such assertions, for they are false as they are base.   Pardon me; indeed I would advise you for the best, at least so far as a poor ignorant fellow like myself can do; and I would serve you also."

"My good friend," said Mrs. Langstone, "you have done so already, and believe me, I am not unmindful of it, and only wish that it was in my power to reward you."

"Reward me, Mrs. Langstone," said the poor fellow; "what have I done that should deserve it?   Hows'ever, if you please, we will talk no farther upon that subject.   Mark my words, this Captain Braghall is a bad man, and only pretends to be now your friend, and to sympathise with your husband in the bad fortune which has overtaken him, so that he may, by chance the sooner and the readier put his plans into operation.   What say you, Miss Maysdale?"

"I perfectly agree with all that you have said, Mr. Gadsby," replied Laura, "and we must be upon our guard, or God knows what may be the consequences."

"I will be guided by you, my dear sister, and our kind friend here," said Mary, "and may Heaven bless you for the sympathy you evince in our misfortunes."

"I have heard a great deal, Mrs. Langstone," remarked Stephen, "as I told you before; a great deal more than I think it would be prudent to disclose at present; but you will excuse my being so *close*, and keeping you in suspense; it is all for the best, and so, it strikes me, the captain will find out to his great disappointment. I am only a poor foolish sort of a chap, but I think I am a match for him, with all his education and experience. Ned Langstone shall be rescued from his present situation, and have an opportunity afforded him of becoming a better man than unfortunately he has been for some time past."

Mrs. Langstone could only express her gratitude to Stephen by her looks, and Laura perfectly coincided in all that he had said, and mentally thanked Heaven for raising them up such an honest and sincere friend in the midst of their difficulties. She took precisely the same view of Braghall's motives as Gadsby did, and the longer she reflected upon all the circumstances, the more she became disgusted with his abandoned and degraded character; the conversation that had passed between him and her sister completely corroborated the hints which Stephen had thrown out, and she shuddered with disgust and indignation to think that any man could thus take advantage of the misfortunes of his fellow-creatures to forward his own sinister designs.

"But it will all recoil upon himself, my dear Mary," she remarked; "and depend upon it, he will be severely punished for the base part he is at present acting, whilst all his deep-laid and diabolical plans will be rendered abortive."

"Very true, Miss Laura," said Gadsby, "that is my opinion, and if you only knew all that I do, you would say that I had very good reason for being so confident. Clinton appear in a court of justice as a prosecutor, the scoundrel!—I should like to catch him at it. He is much more likely to figure there as a criminal; and perhaps it may not be long before he does. Keep up your spirits, Mrs. Langstone; do not let Captain Braghall have the least cause to suppose that you suspect the honesty of his motives, and all will be well. Ha! ha! ha! Stephy Gadsby is down upon the rascals. Oh, what a very fortunate job it was, that you entrusted me with that note to the captain, or we might have all remained in ignorance of that which I know now. I am a happy fellow, to be made the humble instrument of so much good as I expect to do. Keep up your sprits, Mrs. Langstone and Miss Laura, and God bless you both."

Thus exulting in himself, the poor fellow rubbed his hands, snapped his fingers, winked first his right eye and then his left, laughed outright, and exhibited many other eccentric demonstrations, peculiar to the consciousness of being about to perform a good action.

"Only to think," he continued, after a pause, "that this young gentleman, at the very time when he flatters himself that he is in the right road to triumph in his base and secret designs, should be taking such pains to defeat himself, and also to serve you, Mrs. Langstone, and your unfortunate husband, against his will. Ha! ha! ha! he little suspects that I have discovered him to be the associate of thieves and housebreakers!"

"Thieves and housebreakers!" reiterated Mary and her sister, in a breath.

"Bah!" ejaculated Gadsby; "I have said too much; I have suffered my tongue to outrun my prudence. However, I trust you will take no notice of it, and a short time will prove to you, no doubt, whether I am right or wrong. Do not forget what I have said, I beg of you, Mrs. Langstone, and if you can take the word of a poor devil like myself, depend upon it, I will not attempt to deceive you."

"I do not believe you will," returned Mrs. Langstone, "but why all this mystery?"

"Do not ask me for the present, ma'am," replied Stephen Gadsby, "but rest assured that I act, as far as my simple judgment will allow me to do, for the best."

"I place every confidence in you," said Mary, "and will not fail to act as you advise."

"Very good, ma'am; but you will not reveal to your poor husband, when you see him, what has passed between us?"

"I will not," answered Mrs. Langstone, "but may I not hold out to him some hope?"

"Oh, yes," returned Gadsby, "every hope. I have told you so before, and it will be most strange to me if those hopes are doomed to be disappointed. Good day, Mrs. Langstone, good day, Miss Laura, I have a little business to attend to, and no doubt you can dispense with my presence for the present. Rest satisfied that I shall have a keen eye to your interests."

The two sisters once more returned their thanks to the honest-hearted fellow, and he then took his departure from the room, and shortly afterwards quitted the house.

"What can be the information Stephen Gadsby has obtained, and which he keeps so secret?" said Mary, after he was gone.

"I know not, I cannot form the least conjecture, but depend upon it, it is something of importance. and it has inspired me with fresh hopes," replied Laura.

"He appears to be sincere in what he says. I think we may trust him," observed Mrs. Langstone.

"Trust him, oh, yes ; I feel certain that an honest heart throbs within his breast, underneath a rough exterior. I cannot but agree with all his opinions as to the real motives of Captain Braghall, and I consider that we should follow his advice to the very letter."

"What a heartless villain must this young man be to contemplate any base designs against those who are already plunged in so much misery."

"He is indeed, Mary, I am convinced of that; but I firmly believe, as Stephen Gadsby does, that his nefarious designs will recoil on himself, and that the time is not far distant when you will be restored to happiness."

Mrs. Langstone clasped her hands and raised her eyes devoutly towards Heaven as she ejaculated—

"God grant that those predictions may be verified !—how grateful must I ever be. And, oh, my unfortunate husband, should it be the will of the Almighty that you should be released from your present awful situation, I trust that the terrible lesson you have received will prove a salutary warning to you, and that you will never more be tempted to wander from those paths of rectitude in which you once so happily trod.'

"He must, indeed, be abandoned, dear Mary," remarked her sister, "if he did. But I entertain no such apprehensions, and would fain banish them from your mind."

"I will, indeed, endeavour to encourage hope," said Mrs. Langstone, "the bright hope that we shall again be participators in that domestic bliss which it was once our happy lot to enjoy, until the demon of folly and dissipation stepped in to interrupt it. But can that be true which Gadsby stated, namely, that Captain Braghall is the associate of thieves and housebreakers?"

"It is a startling accusation," replied Laura, " but after the conduct of the captain, I can scarcely doubt it."

"My God !" exclaimed the horror-struck Mrs. Langstone, "and Edward was one of those associates ! My heart misgives me !"

"Be firm, Mary, and do not form too hasty a judgment. With all your husband's faults, I cannot believe him to have become so entirely insensible to every feeling of virtue as to turn the plunderer of his fellow creatures."

"But the money found upon him," said Mary, with a shudder.

"Wait patiently, my dear sister, and I trust that all that will be yet satisfactorily explained."

"His hesitation to account for its possession adds to my terrors,". said Mrs. Langstone.

"To you, he must, he will explain everything."

"Braghall declared that he should be enabled to prove that he came honestly by it."

"I know he did, and no doubt he knows more about it than he chooses to disclose to you at present."

"And yet if Edward came honestly by it, why should he hesitate to speak the truth?" demanded Mrs. Langstone, in an agitated voice.

"No doubt he has good reasons for his singular conduct, which will shortly come out," returned Laura. "Do not alarm yourself unnecessarily, Mary, but put your trust in Providence. I feel confident that we have an honest and sincere friend in Stephen Gadsby, and that something which we little expect will transpire shortly. It is evident, from the observations of Gadsby, that he has ascertained something respecting the villain Clinton of the utmost importance, and which may serve to counteract his designs, and go all in the favour of Edward."

"And do you indeed think so, my beloved sister ?" said Mrs. Langstone, eagerly.

"I do," replied Laura, " and nothing can banish the impression from my mind."

"What consolation is there in those words : yes, I will indeed endeavour to be calm, and to place reliance on the goodness and mercy of that Supreme Being, who never forsakes the unfortunate in the hour of their tribulation. But I must see my poor husband to-morrow, and may Heaven give me fortitude to support the melancholy interview."

"I am afraid, Mary," said Laura, "that you have not yet sufficiently recovered to undergo such a painful trial."

"Oh! yes, yes," returned her sister, "I feel that I shall have power to struggle against my feelings, and that I ought no longer to delay. Will not my wretched husband think that I have entirely abandoned him, and left him to his fate, if I were to do so ? He would, he must ; and, therefore, I am determined to banish all such thoughts from his distracted mind ; to prove to him that I am the same devoted, affectionate wife that I have ever been to him, and to endeavour to impart to him some consolation in the awful situation in which he is placed. Oh! if I can but raise his thoughts to hope and confidence, how happy, in the midst of all my abject misery, shall I be."

"I cannot but applaud your affectionate anxiety, Mary," observed Laura, "and may your efforts be attended with the best results. I will accompany you."

"Thanks, thanks, my kind sister," said Mrs. Langstone, "I shall much need the attention and advice of so beloved, so sincere a friend as you; and my poor Edward, too, oh! how much must he benefit by your soothing admonitions?"

Having come to this conclusion, the two sisters sat down more calmly to discuss their plans. Thus occupied, we will leave them for the present, and follow the footsteps of Stephen Gadsby, who felt himself perfectly satisfied with the events of the last few hours, and the opportunity it afforded him of rendering essential services to those whose misfortunes he so sincerely pitied.

"Poor things!" he soliloquised, as he hurried along; "they are in great trouble, sure enough, and if I can only succeed in serving them, I shall consider myself to be one of the most fortunate fellows in existence. But there is not much fear of that; oh, no; I have learnt too much for the infernal rascals, and I will not fail to make good use of it. They little suspect what is brooding, and when they do know the truth, I rather imagine it will come upon them like a thunderbolt. I have only to play my cards well, and I fancy that there is not much of the greenhorn about Stephen Gadsby. I must see what I can do with this fellow Clinton, though, and I do not much apprehend failing in that respect, for it strikes me rather forcibly that I have got him pretty securely in my power."

With these observations, he moved on towards the hospital where Clinton was lying, resolved to elicit as much as he possibly could from him, in order that he might put it to the purpose he wished. It was not long before he arrived at the place of his destination, and he found no difficulty in gaining admittance to the ward in which Clinton was, who stared at him with some amazement and confusion, and with looks not very expressive of a welcome, when Stephen walked up to his bedside.

"What is your business with me?" he demanded abruptly, "I do not remember ever to have seen you before."

"No," answered Gadsby, coolly, and with a satirical smile, "I do not recollect that you ever had that honour."

Clinton frowned, and eyed Stephen impatiently and suspiciously.

"Come, come," he said, sternly and anxiously, "this is not the time or the place to trifle."

"That is decidedly my opinion," returned Stephen, with the same imperturbable coolness.

"What is your business?"

"That you shall know presently."

"The sooner the better; I am not in a fit state to bear the infliction of a long conversation."

"Very good. Your name is Clinton?"

"It is."

"Commonly called Jack Clinton?"

The latter again frowned; but, affecting to smile good humouredly, he said—

"You are rather familiar, methinks, for a first introduction."

"Well, perhaps I am," returned Gadsby, "but it is a habit of mine."

"Perhaps you will furnish me with your name?" said Clinton.

"I dare say you will know it by and by," replied Gadsby, "but that is of no importance just now."

"I should feel obliged to you by being as explicit as possible."

"All in good time, master; I believe you know one Ned Langstone?"

"Why put such a question to me?" demanded Clinton, savagely, "were it not for that d—d rascal, I should not have been here."

"As for his being a d—d rascal," retorted Gadsby, "I do not know so much about that; however, if he is, I believe he has been made so by scoundrels worse than himself."

"Begone," said Clinton, fiercely, "how dare you, a complete stranger to me, come here to insult and mock me?"

"I do not come here to mock you, master," replied Stephen, in the same cool and collected manner, "but upon the most important business."

'Why do you not name it then, at once?" said Clinton.

"I am just coming to it, master," returned Gadsby, "do you intend to prosecute Ned Langstone for this unfortunate affair?"

"Prosecute him; yes, hang him, if I can," answered Clinton bitterly.

" Had you not better pause before you come to such a decision ?"

" Pause ! why should I ?"

"There are many reasons why you should do so. Have you no pity for his poor wife and helpless children ?"

" And who are you that presume to put such questions to me ?"

" I have before told you you shall know that by and by. Do you happen to know two worthy and respectable gentlemen, one called the Stunner, and the other Dick Hemlock ?"

Clinton turned pale, his lips quivered, and he fixed upon Stephen Gadsby a more penetrating look, as he demanded,—

" Why do you ask me that question ?"

" Do you know them ?" asked Stephen, determinedly.

Clinton still hesitated, but at last he said, sternly—

" Supposing I should, what then ?"

" Oh, perhaps, you are the best judge of that. You do know them ?"

" I have been in their company, I believe."

" I believe you have," returned Gadsby with a satirical grin.

" Why do you put such questions to me, and what authority have you to do so ?"

" Well, perhaps I have none, but it is a whim of mine, and perhaps when you and I are better acquainted, you will not be much disposed to despise it. I cannot resist the temptation to put another question to you."

" What is it ?" asked Clinton, in a faltering voice, and looking at Gadsby still more suspiciously.

" There is no one at hand to overhear me, I believe," said the latter, " for that might not be exactly convenient."

" No, no," replied Clinton, impatiently, " speak on."

" Did you ever hear of an individual called Sir Christopher Hastings ?" demanded Stephen, in a low tone.

Clinton started at the mention of that name, and he could not conceal his alarm and confusion.

" No—n—o—ye—yes," he stammered out ; " why do you put that question ?"

" Three fellows committed a burglary in that gentleman's town house, a short time since," said Gadsby, " and a reward is offered for their apprehension."

Clinton trembled violently with the consciousness of guilt, and he stared upon Gadsby perfectly aghast. However, he made a violent effort to recover himself, and then he said—

" And what has that to do with me ?"

" A good deal, I rather imagine ; the three burglars are known."

" Ah !--to whom ?"

" To myself."

" Liar !" cried the agitated Clinton.

" Well, but," returned Gadsby, coolly, " it strikes me rather forcibly that I can convince you they are ; but for fear you should any longer remain in doubt, I will tell you : their names are Dick Hemlock, the Stunner, and——"

" And who else ?" interrupted Clinton, in eager, but almost breathless accents.

" Jack Clinton !" replied Stephen, placing his lips to his ear.

Clinton turned as pale as a corpse, and no person could have entertained the least doubt of his guilt who gazed upon his countenance at the moment. Gadsby marked it with the utmost satisfaction.

" 'Tis false !" Clinton said at length, recovering himself a little ; " how learnt you this ?"

" From the lips of Hemlock and his companions themselves. I have sufficient proof that you are the men, and, therefore, it is useless for you to deny it. I happened fortunately to be sitting in the taproom of a public-house which those two worthy gentlemen entered ; they did not observe me, I listened to their conversation, and overheard all the particulars of the burglary."

" D—n !" cried Clinton, thrown completely off his guard, " that this should occur at such a time. The fools to go blabbing in a public taproom about the affair !".

" Oh, you do not deny it, then ?" said Gadsby, with a look of triumph ; Clinton returned no answer, but for the moment he covered his face with the bed clothes, and groaned.

' Who are you? I again dem   he at length said, in a faint voice.'

" A friend of the unfortunate Mrs. Langstone and her children, I hope," said Gadsby.

" What is your purpose in coming to me ?"

" Merely to make you acquainted with what I have just now stated to you, and to ask you whether you think it would be safe or prudent to appear as the prosecutor of Ned Langstone."

" Will you betray us ?"

LAURA LANGSTON ATTENDING HER SICK SISTER.

"There may be a way for you to escape," replied Gadsby, "and, perhaps, there is no occasion
me to point out to you the means. I wish you good day, I will call upon you again."

"Stay! stay!" cried the alarmed Clinton, "do not leave me thus, let us come to a prope
derstanding."

"No," said Gadsby, who felt the greatest delight in torturing the villain, "you are not yet in
it state to hold a lengthened conversation; I will give you a day to reflect on what I have
d, and make up your mind as to the course it would be most wise for you to pursue. Good
y."

And without uttering another syllable, Stephen Gadsby walked out of the ward, exulting in
? uccess of his scheme.

"All goes on as well as I could wish," he said, as he proceeded on his way from the hospital,
have this fellow completely in my power, and Ned Langstone is safe, or I am much mistaken

You are a lucky fellow after all, Stephy, and I congratulate you. Clinton must either make his exit as soon as he is able, from the country, or else stand his trial for this robbery, in which case there can be little or no doubt of his conviction. I think I can form a pretty shrewd guess as to which alternative you will choose, and without a prosecutor it is impossible that Langstone can be put upon his trial. Stephy Gadsby, this is one of the most fortunate jobs that ever occurred to you, and I never felt so much satisfaction at heart."

Turning round the corner of a street, he perceived two men walking at rather a rapid pace some distance before him, and whose persons he immediately recognized. It was the Stunner and Dick Hemlock.

"Ah!" muttered Gadsby to himself, "I am very happy to see you again, my worthy gentlemen; I must watch your movements, and probably I shall be able to ascertain where to find you, should I ever require you."

Chuckling at this idea, he followed them slowly at a distance, but taking good care to keep them in sight, and after they had traversed several streets and bye-lanes, he saw them enter the house which has already been described as their infamous haunt, and that of their abandoned companions. He walked up close to it, inspected it narrowly, and noticed particularly the sign.

"All right!" he said, "I cannot forget this place, at any rate. No doubt this is their rendezvous, the place from which poor Ned Langstone may date his ruin, and I dare say a very nice respectable crib it is. All right, I say again; I shouldn't at all wonder but I have to wait upon you in a short time, my fine fellows. It's lucky that I know where to find you."

He had a good mind to enter the house, but upon second consideration, he thought perhaps that it would not be safe or prudent for him to do so, and he therefore turned his steps towards home. The alarm and excitement which the visit of Stephen Gadsby, and the disclosures he had made, had caused Clinton, was most excessive, and it was some time before he could at all recover himself again to the least composure.

"By h—ll!" he cried, fiercely, "I am ruined, and all through the carelessness and imprudence of those two felows, my colleagues. Fool that I was to have anything to do with them. I must allow Langstone to escape, for I dare not appear in a court of justice after what has come to light, and, perhaps, even before I can have an opportunity to effect my escape, the officers may be here to apprehend me on this serious charge; and what dependence can I place upon the silence of this man, who is a complete stranger to me?—I liked not the sarcastic observations he made use of, and the threats he held out to me; besides, it is not likely that he can withstand the temptation of the reward which is offered for our detection. In whatever form I view it, the danger of my situation appears the more imminent, and unless I can by some means or other win the favour of this unknown man, I am ruined. I wonder who he is? He is evidently a crafty fellow, and I am afraid I shall find him an awkward customer to deal with. Curses light upon this misfortune, and the idiots who should so imprudently have discussed the business in the place in which they did. It will prevent the gratification of my revenge against Langstone, and probably place my own liberty, if not my life, in jeopardy. The idea tortures me. Would that I could see this man again, and ascertain who he is; then, perhaps, with the assistance of Captain Braghall, who is deeply interested in the affair, we might probably come to some satisfactory understanding. Ned Langstone, you have escaped me this time, but only let me get out of this scrape, and I will yet have my revenge; nor shall your wife escape me, either."

Thus did the villain continue to soliloquize at different intervals throughout the night, and he had but little rest; and the excitement which his unexpected interview with Gadsby had caused, tended to retard the progress of his recovery, and thus added to the danger of his situation. The morning came, and found him very little more composed, but still he had the precaution not to let slip any observation which might commit him in the eyes of those who attended upon him.

"To be thus confined at such a critical moment as this," he said, when there was no one near to hear him, "it is doubly torturing; for were it not so, I might still set the law at defiance, and yet have the opportunity of gratifying my revenge against those who have excited my hatred. But I will not despair; by some means or other, I have no doubt, I shall be enabled to escape the difficulties by which I am at present surrounded."

He was interrupted in the midst of this soliloquy by the entrance of the very man on whom his thoughts had been fixed, and whom he was so anxious to see, Captain Braghall, who, walking up to his bedside, inquired anxiously after his health.

"I feel myself much the same as when I saw you last, captain," replied Clinton, "but I am glad you have come, for I felt anxious to see you."

"Indeed!" returned Braghall, unable to conceal his satisfaction, "have you reflected seriously upon what I suggested to you on our last interview?"

"I have," answered Clinton.

"And are you prepared to yield to my wishes?" asked the captain.

"If you will fulfil the promises you then made me, I am."

"You are willing to fly from this part of the country, and thus to abandon the prosecution of Langstone?"

"If I have the opportunity and the means afforded me, I am," returned Clinton.

"Enough," said the captain, "I will take good care that you shall have the means and the opportunity you require. You have come to a wise determination, Clinton, and you will have no cause to regret it. I will supply you with money, and methinks that will be much better and more safe for you than appearing in a court of justice."

"Ah!" ejaculated the alarmed Clinton, taken off his guard by those observations, "have you heard anything?"

"What mean you?" demanded Braghall, eagerly.

"Nothing—nothing," replied Clinton, recollecting himself, "I merely thought——"

He hesitated, and Braghall fixed upon him a penetrating look as he observed—

"You cannot conceal from me, Clinton, that there is something more labouring in your breast than you think proper to disclose. I strongly suspect——"

"What?" interrupted Clinton.

"That you have been engaged in certain criminal transactions which might render your appearance in a court of justice not only imprudent, but extremely dangerous."

"And what are your reasons for suspecting this?" said Clinton.

"They are many; and why, since we now so well understand each other, do you object to confide in me?"

"If I were certain that you would not take advantage of it, I would."

"I pledge you my word that I will not; nor shall anything you may reveal in the least alter the determination I have come to."

"Enough, captain," said Clinton; "on that assurance, knowing you to be a gentleman of the strictest honour and most unimpeachable integrity, I will rely."

Captain Braghall did not halt like the sarcastic tone in which Clinton spoke this, but anxious to hear what he had to divulge, as he knew it was likely to forward his own nefarious designs, he merely laughed good humouredly, and requested Clinton to proceed. The latter looked around the ward, to satisfy himself that there was no one near who was likely to overhear him, and then said—

"Come nearer, captain; I believe I need scarcely remind you that this is only for your own private ear."

"True," coincided Braghall, doing as Clinton had requested him.

"The patients on either side of us," said Clinton, in a low voice, "are suffering too much to pay any attention to what we are saying. Listen."

Braghall did, attentively and eagerly, while Clinton related the particulars of what had transpired at the interview between him and Stephen Gadsby, and when Clinton had concluded, he could scarcely conceal the satisfaction which the discovery had offered him.

"And do you admit the truth of this?" he eagerly demanded.

"Since I have said so much, perhaps foolishly, it would be useless for me to deny it," replied Clinton.

"Good!" cried the captain, in a tone of exultation.

"What is good?" demanded Clinton, sternly.

"Why—why—but no matter. Ha! ha! Jack, you have been a daring fellow, and it would have been still more daring of you had you appeared as the prosecutor of poor Ned Langstone."

"You seem to chuckle, captain, at what I have confessed to you," said Clinton, fixing upon him a looks of suspicion.

"No, I do not."

"I begin to doubt you."

"Psha! there is no necessity for that; what you have told me will only render me the more anxious for your safety. But who the deuce can this fellow be who has taken the trouble to call upon you?"

"I cannot form the least conjecture."

"And he refused to state to you his name?"

"He did."

"Have you no recollection of ever having seen him before?"

" Not the least."

" It is strange, and you do not know when he will call again ?"

" I do not," answered Clinton, " he declined to tell me, and left abruptly. I cannot consider myself safe for even a moment, notwithstanding the assurances you have given me, while that man, a perfect stranger to me, possesses the knowledge he does."

" Oh, do not alarm yourself," remarked Captain Braghall, " for it would seem, from what he stated to you, that his silence is to be bought upon certain conditions, similar to those I have proposed to you, and with which you will, of course, comply."

" But what dependence can I place upon him ? He is evidently in the most humble circumstances, and therefore the reward which is offered will be an inducement to him to betray me."

" Nonsense !" returned Braghall, " have I not the means of doubling the reward ? I must manage somehow to be here on the day that he calls again, and then, no doubt, everything will be arranged satisfactorily. Describe him to me more minutely."

Clinton did so, and the description immediately struck the captain.

" By Jupiter !" he cried, " it is the very portrait of the man who brought me the letter from Laura Maysdale. Large features ?"

" Yes."

" Dark complexion, bushy whiskers, and a mole upon the left cheek ?"

Clinton replied in the affirmative.

" Wearing a velveteen jacket, corduroy knee-breeches, and ankle-jacks ?"

" Yes," answered Clinton.

" The very same," said Braghall, " there can be no mistake about it. This is a fortunate circumstance, a devilish fortunate circumstance. Make your mind perfectly easy, Clinton; I will see this fellow, and all will be well. Nothing could have happened luckier. We now perfectly understand each other ?"

" I believe so," returned Clinton.

" That is right," observed Braghall. " When do you expect you shall be able to leave the hospital ?"

" In a few days, I hope."

" When Langstone will be again examined before the magistrates, and you will be expected to appear and give evidence against him ?"

" True."

" But it must so be contrived that you shall be far away from London at that time, eh ?"

" I hope to be so, captain, and if you only fulfil your promises, I shall."

" You may depend upon me," said Braghall, " I have too much interest at stake to deceive you. I will supply you with a sufficient sum of money to provide for your present necessities, and I will continue to be a friend to you."

" Thank you, captain."

" Why, Clinton, my boy, you will become quite a reformed character. Where do you think of settling yourself ?"

" I have not made up my mind yet."

" It must be in some distant and retired part of the country, where you are not known."

" Very true."

" And you must change your name, too."

" Certainly, or I should soon be discovered. But have you yet seen Langstone ?"

" I have not, but I have had an interview with his wife, and placed his case in the hands of an eminent lawyer, so that if even you had appeared against him, I doubt much if you would have succeeded in obtaining a conviction against him."

" Perhaps not," returned Clinton, " but I will not disguise from you the fact that I bear him the same hatred that ever I did."

" I have no doubt of it," said Braghall, " but that is a matter entirely between yourselves, and I dare say that some day or other you will have an opportunity of settling your differences."

" I hope so," said Clinton, with a fierce look, " he must not be permitted to triumph altogether."

" Why, as for that matter, I think the triumph so far has been all on your own side; Langstone has been sufficiently punished by the imprisonment he has suffered, and the terrible anxiety of mind he must have endured."

" Oh, not half enough for me," said the villain; " has he not nearly murdered me, and are the bodily sufferings I have undergone not to be taken into account at all ?"

" Well, well," said Braghall, " there may be something in that to be sure, but it is no use thinking anything about that at present. I must now leave you."

"When shall I see you again, captain?"

"Probably to-morrow."

"Let it be as soon as possible, for I shall be in a state of the greatest suspense till this business is settled."

"I will not fail, for my own sake, to complete it as soon as possible," replied Braghall.

"And you think you know the man who called upon me?"

"I am almost positive of it."

"And if your suspicions are correct, do you consider that I have anything to apprehend from him?"

"Nothing whatever."

"You will endeavour to ascertain whether you are right in your conjectures as soon as possible?"

"I will, and I have no doubt I shall be successful," replied Braghall; "keep up your spirits, remain firm in the resolution you have formed, and take my word for it that this business will be settled as well as we could either of us wish."

"I am satisfied, captain, for I do not think you would deceive me."

"Certainly I would not, for by so doing I might frustrate my own plans."

"Which are——"

"Oh, pardon me, my good fellow, those I think are best confined to my own breast. They do not concern you in the least."

"Well, I have no wish to be inquisitive, captain," said Clinton, with a look of dissatisfaction; "but I thought that you might, perhaps, not have had any objection to become a little more communicative upon that subject, as we understand each other so well, and probably I might be of some assistance to you."

"Oh, no, circumstances would not permit you to be so," returned the captain; "you forget that you must leave this part of the country as soon as possible, and that it would not be safe for you to be mixed up in any stratagem in which you might stand the chance of being discovered."

"True," coincided Clinton; "I did not think of that, I am obliged to you for your precaution, and am prepared to follow your advice in every respect."

"If you do that you will have nothing to fear," said Braghall; "good day. You will shortly see me again, when I hope to have good news to communicate to you."

With these words Captain Braghall quitted the hospital, and left the guilty Clinton to his own reflections, which, as may be supposed, were of the most conflicting nature.

"Have I acted right in divulging what I have to Braghall, and in yielding to his wishes?" he said; "I think I have, for it is better to secure him as a friend than as an enemy, and I have no doubt that he has the power to perform all that he has promised; but still I shall not rest satisfied until I have seen this man again, and learnt more about him. Should he prove to be the party that the captain suspects him to be (and there appears to be little doubt that he is), I am safe. But still it is most provoking to think that Langstone will be allowed to escape, after all that I have suffered from him. No matter, the time will yet come when I shall have an opportunity of gratifying my revenge against him, and it shall be no less terrible than it is certain. Mary Langstone, too, you have escaped me once, but you shall not always do so. I will yet give you bitter cause to repent having so scornfully repelled me for that man whose wretched wife you now are. Oh, it affords me the most unspeakable satisfaction to think upon the miseries your marriage has brought upon you, and the degradation into which your husband is plunged. It is I who have been his principal tempter to crime, and I will not rest until I have worked his complete destruction."

Thus did the heartless miscreant exult to himself, and pant for the opportunity to put his diabolical threats into execution. Captain Braghall on leaving the hospital, as he proceeded on his way home, exulted in the success of his schemes, and encouraged the most sanguine anticipations of the future.

"All goes on better than even I ever expected," he said; "Clinton is now completely in my power, and he dare not refuse to submit to anything I may demand of him. Oh, this is indeed a lucky discovery, and one that I will not fail to take advantage of. Laura Maysdale is as safely mine as if she was now in my power, and that thought is sufficient to make me one of the happiest men alive. Little do her and her sister suspect my real designs, and if Langstone does not betray me, which for his own safety, I do not think he would be fool enough to do, they will never know them until it is too late to frustrate them. I must see this man, however, and purchase his silence. I have little or no doubt, from the description which Clinton gave of him, that he is the same fellow who brought me a letter from Laura. A shrewd rascal that, and one whom I might find useful if I could only win him to my purpose. However, I don't think there would be much difficulty in doing that, for money will accomplish almost anything, as I have often enough experienced. I wish that Clinton would recover speedily, for I cannot consider my plans exactly certain of success while he remains in the country. There will be some difficulty in getting him away from the hospital, however, and preventing his appearing before the magistrates on the re-examination of Langstone. I must consider how it will be best to accomplish that; but I have no doubt I shall be able to do it with my usual skill."

He had just arrived at this satisfactory point, when suddenly turning the corner of a street, he, to his no small amazement and satisfaction, beheld Stephen Gadsby advancing towards him. Gadsby recognised him at the same moment, and stopping, took off his hat and bowed respectfully. Captain Braghall approached him familiarly, and smiled good humouredly.

"Good morning, my fine fellow," he said, "I am glad to see you."

"I am sure you do a poor fellow like me a great honour," replied Gadsby.

"Not at all, not at all," returned the captain, in the same tone of familiarity; "taking your walks, eh?"

"Yes, your honour," answered Gadsby, "but upon business."

"Ah! I see. But how is poor Mrs. Langstone and her amiable sister?"

"Much the same as usual, sir."

"Are they at home?" asked the captain.

"No, poor creatures," replied Stephen, "they have gone upon a melancholy duty this morning."

"What is that?" demanded Braghall.

"To visit the unfortunate Mr. Langstone in prison."

"Ah! that will be a severe trial for them. The meeting must be one of the most melancholy description."

"It must indeed, sir," coincided Gadsby, "but I must be going, sir. Good day."

"Stay, stay," said Braghall, placing his hand upon his arm, "I want to have a few words with you."

"With me, sir?"

"Yes; I will not detain you many minutes. Let us retire into this alley, where we are not so likely to be observed."

Gadsby complied, wondering what it could be that the captain had to say to him.

"You appear to be a shrewd, honest fellow," he commenced.

"Oh, you flatter me, sir," replied Gadsby.

"No, indeed, I do not. I have taken quite a fancy to you; you do not seem to be any too well off."

"You may say that, sir; but I don't know but I am quite as well off as I deserve to be."

"Let me see, your name is—is——"

"Stephen Gadsby, your honour," added the latter.

"Ah!" said the captain, "Stephen Gadsby, that's it; I recollect now. You visited the rascal Clinton in the hospital yesterday, I understand?"

Stephen looked surprised, and hesitated.

"How do you know that, sir?" he asked, looking at the captain suspiciously.

"Clinton himself told me so," said Braghall; "I have but just left him."

"But how could he do that?" asked Gadsby, "when I refused to tell him my name?"

"True, but I was quite satisfied, from the description he gave, that it was you. Was I mistaken?"

"No, your honour, you was not; it was me sure enough," answered Stephen.

"Ah! I thought so."

"But did he tell you what passed between us?"

"Every word. It is a fortunate thing that you have made this discovery, Mr. Gadsby, and I commend you for the manner in which you have acted; but do you mean to betray Clinton into the hands of justice?"

"Why, sir, would it not be a shame to let such a scoundrel escape?"

"True," replied the captain, "but still I have been thinking that it would save a deal o trouble, and render the preservation of Langstone more certain, if Clinton were suffered to escape and to leave the country altogether."

"Why, those are the very terms I proposed to him, sir," said Gadsby.

"We accept them," answered Braghall.

"Then," returned Gadsby, "that settles the business; but do you think he is sincere?"

"Certainly I do," said the captain; "he must be mad to attempt to act differently. Do you agree to those terms?"

"Yes," replied Stephen, "I would do anything to restore the unfortunate Ned Langstone to his suffering wife and family, and I hope he may come out of prison a better man."

"Well said, my friend," remarked Braghall; "then in this matter we may be supposed to act together?"

"Yes, your honour," returned Gadsby.

"You will not say anything about the discovery you have made, unless necessity should compel you?"

"I will not, sir."

"And, as for the reward, if you only act faithfully, as you have promised, I will double it."

"Oh, thank you, sir," said Stephen Gadsby; "why that will make my fortune at once. I'm sure it is very kind of you to take such an interest in the misfortunes of this poor family."

Stephen Gadsby said this in a half sarcastic tone, for he saw through the motives of the captain, and he was determined to watch him narrowly, and to thwart his designs, if possible. Braghall, however, took no notice of him, and observed—

"As for that, Mr. Gadsby, we will say no more about it; I shall consider myself amply rewarded should I succeed in rescuing Mr. Langstone from the fate with which he is at present threatened, for the sake of his wife and family, and I think there is every prospect now of my wishes being realised."

"I sincerely hope they may, sir," said Gadsby; "and I should think, if Langstone does regain his liberty, he will have been taught such a lesson as he will never forget, and that in future he will be an honest, steady, industrious man, and an affectionate husband."

"I heartily respond to that wish, Mr. Gadsby," said the captain.

"I'm sure there cannot be a better woman, or a more faithful and devoted wife in the world than Mrs. Langstone," said Stephen, warmly, "and Ned ought to be proud of her, and be stung with the bitterest feelings of remorse for the sufferings he has inflicted on her."

"True, Mr. Gadsby," said Braghall, "I perfectly agree in your sensible and humane observations."

"Poor woman," continued Gadsby, "I wonder how she has been enabled to support her many severe trials with the fortitude she has done. But, excuse me, sir, I must be going."

"Very well, Mr. Gadsby," replied the captain, affably, "I will not detain you. I shall see you again shortly, I hope. Call upon me at my lodgings at any time; it is necessary that we should meet as frequently as possible till this business is settled."

"Very good, sir," said Gadsby, "I will attend to what you say."

"And mind, be cautious, for on that all depends."

"You may trust to me, sir," replied Stephen.

"Present my compliments to Mrs. Langstone and her sister, and tell them I will do myself the honour to call upon them to-morrow, if it is agreeable."

"I will do so, sir. Good day."

"Good day, Mr. Gadsby," reiterated the captain, placing some money in his hand, and they then separated."

"So," said Gadsby to himself, when the captain was gone, "you think you can deceive me, my fine fellow, do you? But I will keep a strict watch upon your actions, and if I do not frustrate your designs, my name is not Stephy Gadsby. The villain Clinton is secured; myself and the captain have him in our power; he must yield to all our demands, and therefore the acquittal of Ned Langstone is certain. For the sake of his poor wife and children, I hope he may, and that he may sincerely repent of his past conduct, and endeavour to make all the atonement in his power. The captain has promised to double the reward—good; and after Clinton is safely out of the way, I can then give the necessary information respecting his companions in the robbery, and thus secure the reward also. It strikes me, that as well as doing my duty, I shall make a very good thing of it. Oh, there is nothing like being honest, after all."

With these agreeable thoughts he proceeded to the place of his destination, resolving to pay another visit to Clinton on the following day in order that he might judge for himself how far the statements of Captain Braghall were true, though he entertained very little doubt that they were. Captain Braghall felt very well satisfied with what had passed between him and Gadsby at their last interview; he did not for a moment imagine that he suspected his real designs, and he had no doubt that he should find in him a very useful fellow, and one who might greatly aid him in his plans, notwithstanding the friendship he professed for Mrs. Langstone and her sister.

"But should Langstone change his mind," he said, "and refuse to assist me in my designs, I shall find myself rather awkwardly situated, and shall not know how to act. But he will not be able to resist the temptation of my gold, and I will therefore not give way to any such ideas. Laura Maysdale must be mine at all hazards, and I will spare no expense to obtain the gratification of my desires. The more I think of her the more anxious do I become to possess her, and should anything occur to prevent me from doing so, it would be the greatest disappointment I could experience."

But we will leave the libertine Braghall to his guilty reflections, and follow the devoted wife and her sister to the prison in which the unfortunate Langstone was confined. Need we describe the terrible weight of care and anxiety which pressed upon her mind, but she struggled with her feelings as much as she could, and endeavoured to wait with fortitude the melancholy interview which was about to take place, in which she was greatly assisted by the soothing advice and gentle admonitions of her sister. Her heart, however, sank within her, and a deadly sickness came over her, when they came in sight of the prison, and she was compelled to pause and to lean upon the arm of Laura for support, or she must have sunk to the earth.

"Oh, God!" she cried, "that I should ever be put to such a trial as this. Give me strength, I beseech Thee; and may my unhappy husband be enabled to undergo the painful meeting with fortitude."

"Courage, dear Mary," said her sister, "and it will soon be over. Remember, how much depends on you, and how greatly your unfortunate husband stands in need of consolation in his terrible situation."

"Yes, Laura," returned Mrs. Langstone, recovering herself; "for my poor husband's sake, I will be firm, and endeavour to inspire him with hope. Come, let us no longer delay."

They approached the prison and were admitted. Langstone was sitting in a melancholy attitude in his dungeon, his mind filled with the most distracting thoughts and apprehensions, and without the least ray of hope to relieve his misery. He felt that he was justly punished for the crimes he had committed, but when he reflected upon the disgrace and anguish into which he had plunged his affectionate wife and helpless children, he was driven to a state almost bordering upon madness.

"What a heartless villain I have been," he cried, "thus to abuse the devoted affection of one so good, so gentle, so amiable. Why did Fate ever bring us together? I was never worthy of her; I must have been a scoundrel at heart, or I could never have acted in the manner I have, my good and kind wife, towards thee. Mary, Mary, I must never behold you again, the sight of you would drive me mad; my presence would contaminate you. And what is now to become of you and our poor children?—Who will pity you, and hold out to you the hand of friendship? There is nothing but misery and starvation in the world for you, and all this I have brought upon you by my accursed crimes. Even should I escape the danger which at present threatens me, what means have I of redeeming my character?—I am ruined, lost for ever. All respectable persons will despise me—shun me as something hateful; and unable to procure employment, what is to become of me and those dear innocent beings on whom I have inflicted so much misery? Terrible thought! how does it distract me."

He was interrupted in the midst of these reflections by the entrance of one of the turnkeys, and he started on beholding him, and looked at him anxiously, for a presentiment crossed his mind that he had something particular to communicate.

"Two females desire to see you," said the man.

"Two females!" repeated Langstone, turning very pale; "it must be them! Oh, God!—what shall I do?—I cannot, dare not see them!"

"What, not see your own wife?" said the turnkey; "for such, one of them states herself to be."

Langstone groaned, but returned no answer, and the turnkey having quitted the cell, in a few moments returned, conducting in the unfortunate Mrs. Langstone and her sister. She no sooner fixed her eyes on the haggard and care-worn features of her husband, than she uttered a loud scream, and sunk almost senseless in his arms, whilst Laura stood by and watched the affecting scene, with tearful eyes.

"Husband! dear, but unfortunate husband," at length sobbed forth Mary, looking up with an expression of the deepest anguish in his face, and the tears streaming in torrents from her eyes, "that we should ever meet thus. Oh, God! oh, God! look down with mercy and compassion upon us!"

"Mary! Mary!" ejaculated Langstone, in a hoarse-broken voice, "I cannot bear this! I shall go mad! Leave me, for I tremble with horror in your presence. I am not worthy of your pity; I have been to you and my children a heartless villain, and I deserve to suffer."

"No, no, Edward," cried his wife, "talk not thus; do not recall the dreadful past, and thus so bitterly reproach yourself. Oh, how freely do I forgive you everything, and still does my

CAPTAIN BRAGHALL'S INTERVIEW WITH CLINTON IN THE HOSPITAL.

throb with the fondest, the most unbounded affection towards you. To save you, I would ongly sacrifice my own life, and—"

Cease, cease, Mary, for the love of mercy, cease!" interrupted the wretched man, in ts of the greatest agony, "every word you utter goes like a dagger to my heart ; they drive me mad ! I could better bear your reproaches than this. I am a wretch, totally rthy of your love and sympathy."

Oh, no," sobbed Mrs. Langstone, " say not so. Oh, think you that anything can ever the sentiments I have always entertained towards you, or that I will now abandon in the midst of your trouble ? By Heaven ! never ! I should be unworthy the name woman if I could. Dearest, unfortunate husband, our trials have been great, but the ghty is good and merciful, and gloomy and fearful as our prospects at present are, er days will yet dawn upon us. Courage, courage, my husband, the utmost exertions are being made in your behalf, and I have every reason to hope that they will be crowned with success."

"Who is there that will interest themselves for a poor guilty wretch like me?" said Langstone.

"I tell you no more than the truth, Edward," answered his wife, "but I am not permitted to reveal more to you. The villain Clinton is fast recovering, and but a few days probably will elapse before everything will be decided according to my most anxious wishes and expectations."

"Oh, Mary," said her husband, "I dare not encourage such hopes, and yet for the sake of you and our helpless little ones, I fain would. Alas! I have by my accursed folly brought disgrace and ruin upon you, and I must be an object of abhorrence in the eyes of every well disposed person. Should I even by some fortunate accident escape the fate with which I am at present threatened, how can I again venture to show my face in society? Who will employ me? Who will again place confidence in me?"

"Banish such torturing thoughts from your mind, Edward," replied Mrs. Langstone, "and hope for the best. Something assures me that we shall never be suffered by an all merciful Providence to be sacrificed thus, and that we shall again be restored to happiness. Let the same hopes inspire your breast, and look forward to the future with the brightest anticipations."

"Yes, Mr. Langstone," said Laura, who had hitherto remained silent, " let not the observations of poor Mary be lost upon you, for indeed she speaks the truth. You still have friends, who will not fail to assist you all that lies in their power, and the sufferings of the past may well be forgotten in the happiness of the future."

"Ah! Laura here too?" said Langstone, in a faltering voice, as though he recognized her for the first time, "oh, this is still more torturing."

"Mr. Langstone," said Laura, "if you have ever injured me by thought or deed, which I do not believe you have, I freely, sincerely forgive you."

"Forgive me!" replied Langstone, with a shudder; "oh, this is too much. I do not deserve it; do not look upon me, do not speak to me, for if you knew all, you must view me with disgust and horror."

"Oh, Edward!" ejaculated Mary, "what mean those fearful words?"

"Do not ask me," he groaned, at the same time averting his gaze from Laura; "I dare not answer you; but, oh, I feel myself, more than ever, a most despicable villain, and that I deserve to suffer all that may befall me. Leave me, Mary, I implore you, leave me to my own remorseful thoughts, for I cannot any longer endure this torturing interview."

"Leave you," sighed Mary, embracing him with the most ardent affection, "oh, how can I leave you while you are in this state of mind? Why do you look upon me with such an expression of horror?"

"Because," replied the wretched man, "I witness in that pale countenance, in those haggard and careworn features, the terrible effects of my guilt, and conscience tells me that I am a villain, a monster!"

"Oh, no, no," replied Mrs. Langstone, vehemently, "you too cruelly reproach yourself, indeed you do. You have erred, greatly erred, but you now repent, and Heaven will pardon you for all that you have done."

"But can repentance recall the past, Mary?" sighed her husband; "will repentance restore you and your poor children to that happiness of which I have so mercilessly, so recklessly deprived you?"

"Oh, yes," answered Mrs. Langstone, eagerly, "it will, it will, and we shall yet again be happy."

"Happy!" he repeated, "alas! happiness will never again be my lot."

"Why give way to such feelings of despair, Edward? I tell you again, that everything that can be done to save you, will be put in practice, and that I have every reason to look with confidence to success. But there is one question, and an important one it is, that I would ask you, and surely you will not, cannot refuse to answer me."

"What mean you, Mary?" demanded her husband, in a faint voice.

"There is no one to overhear us?" said Mary, looking round, and finding that the turnkey had respectfully retired from the cell during the interview; "oh, Edward, did you but know the dreadful anxiety of mind I am enduring, you would not hesitate a moment."

"What is the question you would ask?" said Langstone.

"The large sum of money that was found upon you when you were apprehended, oh, tell me how did that come into your possession?"

Langstone started and trembled violently, although he had naturally expected that his wife would put such a question to him.

"Do not ask me," he gasped forth shuddering; "I dare not answer you."

"My God!" cried the alarmed Mary, "why should you hesitate? Surely you have not—I cannot finish the sentence."

"No—no," replied Langstone, "the money was not the proceeds of a robbery; I solemnly swear it was not; but—but——"

"But what, Edward? Oh, ease my doubts, I earnestly supplicate you."

"I cannot," he answered; "the words would choke me. Urge me not, for that secret must never pass my lips. Would to God, that I had never received the hated gold."

"Oh, why should you hesitate to reveal the truth to me?"

"Because by so doing I must become hateful in your eyes."

"Never! never! What horrible mystery is this?"

"Time may unravel everything, but I can never repeat it. Spare me, Mary, for your questions torture me."

"Alas!" sighed Mrs. Langstone, "what fearful doubts does this create in my mind."

"Mary," said her husband, solemnly, "once more I assure you that I am no robber; but I cannot, dare not give you any further explanation."

"But should you not consent to account for the possession of the money," said Mrs. Langstone, "even though you should be acquitted on the charge brought against you by the villain Clinton, may you not be detained on suspicion of having committed a robbery?"

"And what right have they to detain me?" demanded Langstone; "what proof can they have that I came not honestly by the money? Banish your fears, Mary, on that point, and rest assured that the possession of the gold will not involve me in any difficulty."

"God grant that it may not," ejaculated Mary.

"Dear Mary!" said her husband, "if such I may still dare to call you, let this painful interview terminate, for I cannot any longer endure it. Heaven bless you, my much wronged wife, and restore you to that happiness of which your guilty and misguided husband has so cruelly deprived you."

"Alas! alas!" sighed Mrs. Langstone, still clinging to him with the utmost intensity of anguish, "and must we indeed part? must I leave you in this awful place, and with no one to impart to you one word of consolation? God of Heaven, give me strength to support this dreadful trial with becoming fortitude."

Langstone could make no reply, for his emotions were too great for utterance, but he pressed the form of his unfortunate and suffering wife to his bosom, and she sobbed and wept bitterly, as if her heart would break. Again and again they embraced, when the turnkey re-entering the cell, they tore themselves asunder, and Mrs. Langstone resigning herself to the care of her sister, and scarcely conscious of what she was doing, was conducted by her from the cell. On reaching the outside of the prison, Laura hired a cab, and assisting Mary into it, she followed herself, and they were driven off to their residence.

CHAPTER XII.

THE DISAPPEARANCE OF CLINTON.—THE RE-EXAMINATION OF LANGSTONE, AND HIS DISCHARGE.—HAPPIER DAYS BEGIN TO DAWN.

FOR some minutes after Mrs. Langstone and her sister had quitted the cell, Langstone stood with his eyes fixed upon the door, in a state of stupefaction, but suddenly awakened to consciousness, he sunk down on a seat, and gave free vent to the torturing emotions which had been so long struggling in his breast. But still he felt a great relief now that the long-dreaded interview was over.

"Heaven watch over her," he ejaculated, "and shield her from all future danger. Alas! what a terrible fate is hers, and of which I alone am the guilty cause. How could she ever find strength to support it with the fortitude and resignation she has done? But what could have made her so sanguine in her hopes? Who is it that can have interested himself in my favour in the manner she stated? Have I still friends left? How little do I deserve this, yet, oh, God! for her sake, how grateful am I to Thee for it. Should I once more be restored to liberty, how zealously will I endeavour to redeem my lost character, and make atonement for the past by my future conduct. But can I ever disclose my villanous arrangements with Braghall? And how shall I escape from his trammels? That thought tortures me; but let whatever may be the consequences, I am determined that the captain shall never triumph in his atrocious designs against the innocent and amiable Laura. Oh, what a miscreant I must be ever to enter into his monstrous plans, and how much must Mary and Laura despise and loathe me should they ever become acquainted with it; but they must do so sooner or later, and that thought fills my mind with terror. The villain Clinton is fast recovering they say, and I shall therefore soon know my fate; but will he have the boldness to appear against me, and surely the jury will take into consideration the provocation I received, and deal mercifully with me! Yes, yes, I will endeavour to wait patiently the issue of this terrible affair, and put my trust in the mercy of Providence."

He became more calm as these thoughts occurred to his mind, and looked forward to the day of his re-examination before the magistrates with more confidence and hope. As they proceeded on their way home, Mrs. Langstone gave vent to the feelings which her interview with her unfortunate husband had excited in her bosom, but still she encouraged the most sanguine hopes of his speedy restoration to liberty, and that the many troubles it had been their hard lot to experience were nearly at an end.

"Surely," she said, "the dreadful situation in which the errors of my misguided husband have involved him, will prove a salutary lesson to him, and his future conduct will be such as to redeem his character, and render us again happy and respected."

"Oh, yes," answered Laura, "there can be no doubt of that; his penitence is evidently sincere."

"God grant that it may be," said Mrs. Langstone; "alas! he has been most fearfully punished already for the errors he has committed, but why does he refuse to explain the mystery of the money that was found upon him, even to me?"

"I cannot form the slightest conjecture as to his reasons for so doing," replied Laura.

"And you noticed his emotion when I put the question to him?"

"I did."

"There must be something of an important nature connected with that money," said Mrs. Langstone, "which I find it impossible to penetrate; however, he has solemnly declared that he came by it honestly, and that has removed a weight of care and anxiety from my mind. Unfortunate, but still beloved Edward, oh, may our troubles soon be at an end."

"I trust, my dear Mary, that they will," said her sister, "and that it may never again be your fate to experience such heavy and unmerited trials and afflictions as those you have undergone. I see the dawning of happier days approaching, and when you will be enabled to look back upon the gloomy past with little of sorrow and regret."

"Thank you for those observations, my sister," ejaculated Mrs. Langstone, "they inspire me with fresh courage."

They had now arrived at home, and they had scarcely seated themselves, when Stephen Gadsby knocked at the door. The poor fellow had made up his mind to make them acquainted with all he knew, for he did not see the use of any longer concealing it from them, and he knew it would be a great relief to the mind of Mrs. Langstone, for whom he felt the greatest respect, and in whose misfortunes he so deeply sympathized. He inquired most anxiously after the situation of Edward Langstone, and they gave him a brief account of what had taken place at the interview, with which he seemed very well satisfied, although the refusal of Langstone to account for the possession of the money, even to his wife, caused him some surprise, and puzzled him greatly.

"However, Mrs. Langstone," he observed, "I have no doubt that everything will be cleared up satisfactorily at last."

"I hope it may," said Mary, fervently, "but have you anything to communicate to us, Mr. Gadsby?"

"Oh, yes, a great deal, ma'am," answered Stephen, "and something that I think will afford your satisfaction, and increase your hopes."

Mrs. Langstone and her sister looked anxious, so he no longer kept them in suspense, but related to them all the particulars of the important discovery he had made respecting Clinton.

"Ah!" ejaculated Mary, "this is indeed a most fortunate discovery, and will surely prevent Clinton from having the daring to appear against my husband."

"He would find himself in the wrong box, ma'am, if he did so," replied Gadsby, "but I have secured him from doing that."

"How so?" asked Mrs. Langstone.

Gadsby then detailed the other particulars with which the reader has been made acquainted, and Mrs. Langstone and Laura were even more satisfied than before.

"You have acted most prudently, Mr. Gadsby," said the former, "and I owe you a debt of gratitude for the trouble you have taken, and the sympathy you evince in our misfortunes, which I can never repay."

"Oh, do not mention that, Mrs. Langstone," returned Stephen, "for I'm sure I only feel too happy to think I have been enabled to do what I have. Clinton will not appear before the magistrates, and therefore, you see, the charge against your husband must fall to the ground."

"Great God! I thank Thee for this!" cried Mrs. Langstone, fervently, and raising her hands and eyes towards Heaven.

"But, of course, I need not remind you, Mrs. Langstone," remarked Gadsby, "that the utmost secrecy is absolutely necessary."

"Certainly," said Mary, "there is no fear of our divulging anything, when we have so much at stake. But is Clinton recovering?"

"Rapidly," answered Stephen, "and there is no doubt he will be able to leave the hospital in a few days, when he must be hurried out of London as quickly as possible."

"Think you he is to be depended upon?"

"Yes, and simply because he is in a fix; he is not such a fool as to prefer transportation or the gallows to liberty. I intend to visit him again to-morrow, when I shall finally settle the business with him."

"But do you still entertain the same opinion of the motives of Captain Braghall?" asked Mrs. Langstone.

"I do," replied Gadsby; "he is a designing villain, take my word for it; but we shall find him useful in this business, and, as the saying goes, we must sometimes hold a candle to the devil."

"And he intends to visit us again to-morrow?" said Mrs. Langstone.

"So he desired me to tell you; so that you must be on your guard, and not let him know that you are acquainted with what I have told you."

"I will attend to your advice, Mr. Gadsby. Oh, my unfortunate husband, your troubles, I trust, are almost at an end, and you will shortly be restored to my arms."

"Yes, Mrs. Langstone," remarked Stephen, "I hope he may; and that his conduct will in future be such as to do himself and you honour. You will pardon me for my boldness, ma'am, I am but a simple, plain-spoken fellow, but I mean sincerely what I say."

"I am convinced you do, Mr. Gadsby," said Mary, "and I return my sincere thanks to the Almighty for raising me up such a warm and disinterested friend as you."

"And I am no less grateful, Mrs. Langstone, to think that I have been enabled to perform one or two good actions, which I hope will be received as some atonement for the many bad ones I have committed."

With these words, Stephen Gadsby took his leave.

"What an excellent heart does this poor fellow possess," said Laura, when Stephen had made his exit.

"He does indeed," coincided her sister, "would to Heaven that all mankind were like him, there would then not be so much crime and misery in the world as there is at present. I wish that it was in my power to reward him as he merits, but I have nothing more to bestow upon him than my warmest gratitude."

"Which, my dear Mary," said Laura, "as he says, and I believe sincerely, is all he seeks. But what an extraordinary tale is this he has been telling us. Thank God! if all succeeds according to his expectations, a very few days will restore your husband to your arms, and happiness will again be your's."

Mrs. Langstone clasped her hands vehemently together, and raising her eyes towards Heaven, she ejaculated in accents of the most impressive solemnity—

"Almighty God, in Thine infinite mercy, I most humbly but earnestly beseech Thee to realize these hopes; to rescue my unfortunate husband from his present perilous and degrading situation; to work a reformation in his heart, and to afford him an opportunity of once more possessing and deserving the respect and esteem of his fellow creatures. Let the guilty past be a warning to him, and his future course of life be such as to do him honour and confer happiness in all around him."

Fervently did Laura respond to this prayer, and for some time the affectionate sisters sat in silence, totally absorbed in their own feelings.

"But," said Mrs. Langstone, after awhile, "should anything occur to prevent the escape of Clinton, may not Edward still be placed in the most imminent danger?"

"Do not alarm yourself, Mary," replied Laura, "for depend upon it that Captain Braghall and Stephen Gadsby will take good care that their plans succeed, and Clinton, knowing the penalty which hangs over his head if he does not comply with their demands, will be only too happy to have an opportunity of escaping from the danger. Fear not, all will go as well as we could wish it, and only a few short days will suffice to remove the terrible suspense and anxiety which you have with such exemplary fortitude so long endured. But when will you quit this wretched abode, and retire to the comfortable lodgings which I have through the kindness of my benevolent and amiable mistress procured for you?"

"In a day or two, my dear Laura," replied her sister, "when my mind becomes a little more settled and collected. Oh, how shall I ever know how to repay the kindness of that excellent lady, your mistress? In a day or two!—and should it be the will of Heaven to restore my poor husband to liberty, what tenfold happiness will it afford me to be enabled to receive him in a home partaking so largely of our former comforts. But I wish this second interview with Captain Braghall could be avoided."

"It cannot, Mary, without exciting his suspicions, which might tend to injure, if not to frustrate our hopes."

"I believe that Braghall is a villain, as Stephen Gadsby has pronounced him, and it is revolting to my feelings to act the hypocrite."

"Stern necessity compels you to mask your real thoughts and feelings, Mary," replied her sister, "and however repugnant it may be, and is, I know, to your feelings, for the sake of your unfortunate husband, you must submit. All will turn out for the best depend upon it, and ample justice be rendered to those who merit it."

"God grant that it may," returned Mrs. Langstone, energetically. "But I will follow your advice, dear Laura, and endeavour to meet the captain firmly."

"Well said, sister," observed Laura, "and depend on it, you will have no cause to repent it. Keep up your spirits, and mark my words, the time will come, and that shortly too, when the black clouds that have so long obscured the sunshine of your destiny, will be dispersed, and peace and tranquillity will bless your future days."

Mrs. Langstone threw herself on Laura's bosom, and whilst tears of gratitude and affection started to her eyes, she ejaculated.

"Oh, my beloved sister, what would have become of me and my poor children if it had not been for you? We must have perished. You have been my gentle soother and friend in all the terrible afflictions with which it has been the will of Heaven to visit me. Bless you—bless you, dear Laura, and may it never be your fate to be exposed to the bitter miseries it has been my hard lot to experience. But I will not murmur; God is good, and in Him will I put my trust."

The two sisters embraced each other in the most affectionate manner, mingled their tears together, and sobs for some time choked their utterance.

"Dear Mary," at length said Laura, "what sweet, what delicious satisfaction it affords me to think that I have been enabled to render you the humble assistance I have. But why remind me of that which was no more than my duty? Can I ever forget the affection you have shown towards me, even from my earliest days of childhood? Can I ever forget when you, as my eldest sister, nursed me and caressed me with the same fond care as if you had been my mother? How you taught my infant tongue to perfect its innocent prattle; how you led me through the green fields and verdant meadows, entering joyously with me into all my childish sports, and culling for me the prettiest and sweetest wild flowers; how, if I had ever committed myself, you interceded for me with our parents for forgiveness, and——"

"Oh, cease—cease, dearest Laura," interrupted Mrs. Langstone, her bosom swelling with emotion; "recall not those blissful scenes of our childhood, never more to return, for they do but make the present appear more dismal. Ah! they were indeed happy days; could we always experience the sunshine of our youth, when guilt is unknown to us, when care or anxiety are strangers to our breast, what a family of happy and congenial spirits should we indeed be. But the Supreme wisely ordains that we should taste of the bitter cup of sorrow, so that we should be enabled more fully to appreciate the innumerable blessings he has so bountifully lavished upon all his creatures."

"True—true, Mary, and therefore should we learn to submit patiently to those sorrows it may be our lot to have to undergo. But we will drop this subject, since it seems to afford you pain. Throughout your whole life there is nothing, I am sure, that you can have to reproach yourself with; you have been a dutiful daughter; pure and innocent when single, a devoted and affectionate wife, a fond mother, and a loving sister, and for this Heaven will yet reward you with the choicest of its blessings."

Mrs. Langstone could make no reply to this affectionate speech, for her heart was too full, and she continued locked in her sister's embrace for several minutes. Having somewhat recovered themselves, they changed the topic of conversation, and calmly discussed their future plans, the observations of her sister inspiring Mrs. Langstone with the brightest hopes, and serving to tranquillise her spirits. At the time he had fixed, Stephen Gadsby again visited the hospital, in order to make his final arrangements with the villain Clinton, and was glad to see him so far recovered that he looked quite a different man to what he did when he had seen him before. On beholding Gadsby, Clinton appeared to be somewhat abashed and confused, and averted his gaze from him, but he quickly recovered his usual self-possession, and beckoning Stephen to his bedside, he said in low tones—

"I am glad to see you again."

"I dare say you are," replied Gadsby, significantly.

"Do not speak loud," said Clinton, "for it would be dangerous for us to be overheard."

"It might to *you*," returned Stephen, drily, but at the same time scarcely raising his voice beyond a whisper—"how do you feel yourself now?"

"Much better."

"I am gratified to hear that."

"No doubt you are," replied Clinton, biting his lips. You have come upon business?"

"What else do you suppose should have brought me hither?" demanded Stephen.

"Well, well! I have seen Captain Braghall."

"I know it."

"You are acquainted with the captain?"

"I am."

"Your name is Stephen Gadsby?"

"So I have always understood it to be."

"And why could you not have told me that when you first visited me?"

"Because I did not think it prudent to do so," answered Gadsby. "You made the captain acquainted with all that occurred between us at that interview?"

"I did."

"And you admitted the truth of my statement?"

"Yes," answered Clinton, in a tremulous voice, and fixing upon his interrogator a penetrating and suspicious look.

"You acknowledge, then, that I did not accuse you wrongfully?"

"Why need you ask such a question? Let us proceed to business at once, and be as brief as possible."

"That is my wish."

"Have you seen the captain since he visited me?"

"I have."

"And he told you the arrangements we had come to?"

"He did."

"And do you agree with those arrangements?" eagerly asked Clinton.

"Certainly," replied Gadsby, "they are the same that I proposed to you myself."

"Very true; but you were a stranger to me then."

"And now," returned Stephen, with a sarcastic smile, "it seems we are better acquainted."

Clinton frowned.

"Gadsby," he said, after a pause, "may I depend upon you?"

"Whilst you faithfully adhere to the promises you have made, but as sure as you attempt to deceive me, I will immediately hand you over to——"

"Hush! hush!" interrupted Clinton, with a look of alarm, "I am ready to do all you wish."

"Enough, then there the business ends."

"I hope so."

"You may rest assured it will, if you only keep your word; all depends upon yourself."

"Why do you take such an interest in this affair?"

"Because I pity and respect Mrs. Langstone and her children, and consider that her husband would not have become the abandoned and profligate scoundrel that he unfortunately has been, had it not been for such villains as yourself."

Clinton winced under this, and once more frowned and bit his lips, but finding he had no common man to deal with, he stifled his rage as well as he could, and with a forced smile said—

"You are not very complimentary, Mr. Gadsby."

"I never flatter any one," was the laconic reply.

"So it appears, but may I ask you one question?"

"Name it," said Stephen.

"You say that there is a handsome reward offered for the apprehension of—of—the—the—those burglars?"

"There is."

"And you have the means of earning it ?"

"Certainly ; do you doubt it ?"

"No—no ; but you do not appear to be very rich."

"As poor as a union pauper," replied Gadsby, with a smile.

"Then how is it you can resist the reward ?" inquired Clinton.

"That I do not choose to explain."

"You are a strange fellow."

"Very likely. But you say you agree to the terms that have been proposed by myself and Captain Braghall ?"

"I do," answered Clinton, in a faltering voice.

"That is enough," said Gadsby, "and I think you are remarkably wise for so doing. When do you expect to leave here ?"

"In a day or two."

"The captain and you have arranged how you shall meet ?"

"We have."

"And you will be ready then to make your exit to some distant and obscure part of the country as soon as possible ?"

Clinton answered in the affirmative.

"Enough," said Gadsby, "I am satisfied, though perhaps your particular friends, the Stunner and Mister Richard Hemlock, may not be equally so."

"Ah !" said Clinton, with a look of alarm, "you know them, then ?"

"Why," replied Stephen, with a satirical laugh, "I certainly have had the extreme felicity of seeing their remarkably handsome phizogs, and perhaps may have the honour of becoming more intimately acquainted with them one of these days."

"Gadsby," said Clinton, gazing suspiciously at him, "you will not attempt to do anything until I am far away?"

"I have given you my word, and if you only keep your's, you will find that I will not break mine. Rest satisfied of that, now we seem to understand each other."

"I will depend on you."

"You had better do so, if you value your safety. You know the power I possess, and you may rest assured that I will not fail to exercise it should you attempt to deceive me."

"I will not."

"You must be mad if you did."

"Well, well," returned Clinton, in an agitated voice, "let what I have promised suffice. Have you anything else to demand of me ?"

"No."

"Then this meeting is at an end?"

"It is, good day." And with those words Stephen Gadsby abruptly walked away, leaving the villain Clinton in a state of rage, consternation, and disappointment.

"Confusion !" he muttered to himself, when Gadsby had retired ; "to be thus caught in my own trap, and at the very moment when I thought the gratification of my revenge was certain ; to be entrapped, too, by this beggarly, impudent hound, and not to be able to help myself—what a cursed fool I was ever to have anything to do with the Stunner and Dick Hemlock ; I might be sure that their folly would betray us. The confounded idiots, to go talking, too, of this business in a public house. Bah ! I could go mad with pure rage. But it is no use grunting now the job is done, and I must submit. But to think that Ned Langstone should be suffered to escape at the very time when I was flattering myself that I had him safe in my clutches. No matter, the time will yet come when I shall have an opportunity of gratifying my revenge, and they shall have reason to shudder at the name of Clinton."

Thus consoling himself, the ruffian sought to calm his feelings, but he had no small difficulty in doing so, and lay for some time muttering curses to himself. But as circumstances had arrived at the point they were, he was now most anxious to quit the hospital as soon as possible, for fear that anything should occur to discover that he was implicated in the burglary, and that he should fall into the hands of justice before he had an opportunity to effect his escape. There were other fears too, that crossed his mind, namely—that his associates in crime might be detected and apprehended, in which case he felt almost confident that they would not fail to betray him, and then his escaping from the strong arm of the law would be rendered all but impossible. Thus was the villain kept in a constant state of agony and suspense, and every moment of delay caused to his complying with the demands of Captain Braghall and Stephen Gadsby seemed fraught with danger the most imminent. When Stephen Gadsby had quitted the

STEPHEN GADSBY OVERHEARS THE HOUSEBREAKERS.

hospital, he made his way towards home, exulting in the success of his errand, and the tortue he had evidently inflicted on the ruffian Clinton.

"I have him entirely in my power," he said, "and poor Ned Langstone must escape. Oh, what a glorious satisfaction it is to me to think what happiness I shall thus be the humble means of imparting to that poor woman who has suffered so much. If there is so much pleasure to be derived from the performance of a good action, who would ever commit a bad one?"

He was startled from his reverie by some one giving him a hearty smack upon the shoulder, and turning round, he beheld Captain Braghall.

"Ah! my honest friend," said the captain in his blandest accents, "so we meet again; whither are you going in such haste?"

"I am going home, sir," replied Gadsby.

"And if it is not an impertinent question," said Braghall, "may I ask you whither you have been?"

"Oh. certainly, captain, merely to see our old friend."

"What the rascal Clinton?"

"The same, sir," replied Stephen, "and I find as you told me, that he is perfectly agreeable to do all we desire. Of course I did not fail to alarm him a little bit."

"Good, good—you acted perfectly right, Mr. Gadsby," said the captain; "and is he progressing favourably?"

Stephen answered in the affirmative, and he then detailed the particulars of the interview with which the reader has been already made acquainted.

"This looks well, Gadsby," observed Braghall; "our plans must succeed."

"*My* plans, I hope, will succeed," returned Stephen, significantly. The captain looked amazed and confused for a moment, but he turned it off into a good humoured laugh, and replied—

"Exactly so—Gadsby, your plans or mine, it is all one and the same thing, eh?"

Stephen returned no answer.

"What a gratification I am sure it will be to us both, Mr. Gadsby," continued the captain, after a pause, "to be the means of restoring poor Langstone to liberty, and thus mitigating the sufferings of that very excellent woman his wife."

"Ah, sir," replied Stephen, in the same significant tone, "I shall indeed be gratified. But I wish you good day, sir, for I must be going."

"Good day, Mr. Gadsby," said the captain, in the same affable manner, "I am sorry that I have detained you so long."

"Oh, do not mention it, sir," replied Stephen, "I am sure I ought to feel highly honoured and flattered to think that a gentleman like you will condescend to stop and speak to a poor fellow like myself in the open street."

"My good fellow," remarked Braghall, "you entertain by far too humble an opinion of yourself, indeed you do, but real talent is always modest. Here is a sovereign to drink my health."

"Thank you, sir," said Gadsby, making one of his best bows, but scarcely able to repress a laugh, "I am sure you are very kind."

"Oh, pray do not mention it, good day—my best compliments to all at home; good day—good day."

"Good day, sir," responded Gadsby, with another of his best bows, and he then turned on his heel and walked quickly away, laughing in his sleeve, yet filled with honest indignation at the base character and designs of the young libertine.

"I do not half like that fellow," muttered the captain to himself as he walked away, "there is something too pointed in many of his remarks, and there is a low cunning about him which half excites my suspicion. I must watch him narrowly, and if I discover that he is playing a false game with me, it will be strange to me if I do not have my revenge. However, I must be cautious not to offend him till I find my suspicions are confirmed, for he might prove a dangerous enemy."

Stephen Gadsby made the best of his way home, where he found Mrs. Langstone and her sister anxiously awaiting his return, and to whom he related all those particulars which we have transmitted to our pages. They both listened to him with the deepest attention and satisfaction, and when he had concluded Mrs. Langstone said—

"Thank Heaven, all promises to end favourably, and in a few days I trust that my unfortunate husband will be rescued from his present terrible situation, and have an opportunity offered him of redeeming the past."

"Oh, yes, Mrs. Langstone," observed Gadsby, "you may depend upon it that your husband will not be long where he is, for where there is no prosecutor, the prisoner must, of course, be discharged."

"Happy assurance!" ejaculated Mary, tears starting to her eyes, "but oh, Mr. Gadsby, to you and you alone shall I be indebted for the restoration of a beloved though misguided husband."

"Pray, Mrs. Langstone," said Stephen, "do not always be thanking me in such a manner, for it is more than I deserve, I am sure there is no one who would more readily or honestly serve you than I would, and it would afford me greater satisfaction to be able to do so than I can find words to express."

"I know it would, Mr. Gadsby," said Mrs. Langstone, "but do you think that the villain Clinton is to be depended on?"

"Were it under any other circumstances," replied Stephen, "he could not be, but he knows that it is neck or nothing with him, as the common saying is, and therefore, very much against his will, he is obliged to submit."

"And he considers that in a day or two he will be able to leave the hospital?" said Mrs. Langstone.

"He does," answered Gadsby, "and he is evidently nearly recovered."

"Then I shall not be kept much longer in suspense?"

"You will not, ma'am, depend on it."

"And you and Captain Braghall have made the necessary arrangements to secure him?"

"We have," answered Stephen; "we will never lose sight of him for a moment from the time he leaves the hospital till he is mounted on the coach to leave London, and I warrant me he will not be such a fool as to return in a hurry. The captain, with all his cunning, has made himself a very useful instrument to work out our designs and wishes. No doubt he is chuckling within himself on the certain success of his villanous plans, but Stephy Gadsby is down to him; Stephy Gadsby is down to him. Ha! ha! ha!"

"Oh, Mr. Gadsby," said Laura, "what a fortunate thing it is that you were enabled to gain the valuable information you have."

"Yes, miss, it was indeed a lucky accident, and I shall ever bless the day when you entrusted me to convey the letter to Captain Braghall—had it not been for that, we probably should never have known those interesting particulars relating to that most worthy individual Mr. Clinton."

"True," said Mrs. Langstone, "and I am most grateful to Providence for bringing it about. The captain will be here, I suppose, at the time he appointed?"

"Oh, yes, ma'am," replied Gadsby, "there is not the least doubt he will be punctual, and, of course, I need not advise you to be cautious how you receive him; for if once his suspicions should be aroused, all our hopes would probably be knocked on the head."

"I will follow your advice, Mr. Gadsby, to the very letter; I have too much at stake to commit myself by any act of imprudence or incautiousness."

"I do not believe you will, Mrs. Langstone," said Stephen, "but you will pardon me for making so bold as to say what I have done, since it is all from an anxiety for your good?"

"Oh, yes," replied Mrs. Langstone, "and most fervently do I thank you for the kind solicitude you evince towards us in our misfortunes."

"No more thanks, Mrs. Langstone, for somehow or other they do not seem to agree with my constitution; for I have done no more than what becomes every one to do towards his fellow-creatures, when they are oppressed by either misfortune or villany. Good day, ma'am; good day, miss; keep up your spirits, and if we do not triumph over your enemies, and speedily see your husband restored to liberty a reformed character, say my name's not Stephen Gadsby."

He then quitted the room, and left the sisters to themselves.

"Joy! joy! Mary," ejaculated Laura, when he was gone; "what Gadsby has just now told us confirms all my hopes, and there can be little or no doubt that Edward will shortly be restored to your arms, and that the happiness you once experienced will again be yours."

"My bosom is indeed animated with hope, dear Laura, after all that I have heard," replied Mrs. Langstone: "and something seems to tell me that I shall not be disappointed. My poor, misguided Edward, surely the terrible fate he will have escaped, must work a salutary effect upon his mind, not naturally vitiated; he will abandon the depraved wretches who have led him into such cruel and fatal errors, and once more turning to industrious pursuits, he will again establish himself in that respectable sphere of society he formerly occupied, and then, indeed, what happiness will be ours. The late interview we had with him convinces me that he is fully aroused to compunction, and that no temptation whatever can ever more lead him into the paths of error. God grant that my fond hopes may not be doomed to disappointment."

"And they will not, Mary, depend on it," said her sister; "the Almighty is too good, too merciful, to permit one who has never wilfully offended Him, to be put to any further trials beyond her strength to bear. Edward's natural good sense and integrity of principle will prevail over the fatal errors to which he has unfortunately for some time been the victim, and the bitter lesson he has been taught, will stimulate him to make all the atonement in his power for the miseries he has caused you and your children, and urge him on to redoubled exertions for your happiness and prosperity."

"Thanks, thanks, my affectionate Laura, for those words of consolation; they arouse all my energies into action, and I already feel as if I were another woman, and as if all the dreadful past was indeed but a DREAM!—Oh, how much am I indebted to that noble-hearted man, Mr. Gadsby, for the inestimable, the disinterested services he has rendered me, and it will be the happiest moment of my life, if it ever lies in my power to reward him as he merits."

"Heaven will reward him, Mary, for the many noble, generous, and humane acts he has performed," returned Laura. "But how fortunate you ought to consider yourself, that Providence rose you up such a zealous and warm-hearted friend in the midst of your difficulties."

"I am indeed, my dear sister, and surely Edward will profit by the example which is set him in this humble, but honest man."

"He will—he must," replied Laura; "oh, how many a noble heart throbs beneath a humble jacket; how many a generous spirit is left to perish in neglect and scorn, whilst the unprincipled wretch whom fortune has favoured with its choicest blessings, by a strange perversity of fate, is held up as a paragon of virtue, and by licence of their rank and station are permitted to carry on their vice with impunity, spreading misery and desolation around them."

"Very true, Laura," coincided her sister; "and of that, Captain Braghall is a powerful corroboration. If all be true that is reported of him, which I believe it is, how much human misery has he been the author of."

"I firmly believe him to be a villain," said Laura, emphatically.

"And yet he has dared to raise his thoughts to you, my gentle sister, and even now contemplates your destruction, should he have the opportunity."

"Too well I know it," replied Laura, crimson blushes suffusing her cheeks, and her fair bosom swelling with indignation; "but Providence will, I trust, protect me from his diabolical machinations, and make his wicked designs recoil upon himself."

"It will, Laura, and the time will come when he will be brought to a full sense of his own enormity, and all the pangs of remorse will sting his guilty soul. But we will drop this subject, Laura, so repulsive to our feelings; for should we dwell upon it, I am afraid that I shall not be able to meet him in the way that Stephen Gadsby has advised, and which prudence requires."

"Very true, Mary," coincided Laura, "and much, if not everything depends upon your doing that. As Mr. Gadsby has observed, Braghall will become a useful and unconscious instrument to work out our hopes and wishes; in fact, we could not do very well without him, and therefore the utmost care must be taken that he has no cause to imagine we suspect his real motives. How great will be his chagrin, confusion, and disappointment, when he is awakened to the truth, and finds that his diabolical plans are defeated."

"Very true," observed Mrs. Langstone; "but will he not be goaded on to revenge, and might he not be enabled, in secret, to work us some serious injury?"

"Do not alarm yourself that way, my dear sister, he will be afraid of being exposed, and held up to public odium, and, in all probability, will think it most advisable to abandon any guilty designs he might previously have had in contemplation. At any rate, he will not be mad enough to reveal to the world the part he has acted in the liberation of your husband, for that would not only expose him to the scorn and opprobrium of the world, but likewise to punishment."

"Your observations are reasonable and just, Laura," said her sister, "and I will therefore endeavour to banish from my mind all such apprehensions. I pray to Heaven that all may terminate as our sanguine hopes anticipate, and that no future troubles may beset us, for God knows, we have had our ample share of them."

The subject here dropped, and Laura sought to divert her sister's thoughts to other topics, in which she succeeded much better than could have been anticipated. Captain Braghall was punctual to the hour he had appointed, and was again vexed and disappointed to find that Laura was not there. He could scarcely conceal his chagrin, but quickly recovering his self-possession he assumed the same air of affability and sympathy he had done on the previous occasion, little suspecting that Mrs. Langstone so deeply penetrated his innermost thoughts and secret designs; but as what occurred at that interview differed very little from the preceding one, we will not tire the reader's patience by recapitulating the particulars of it; suffice it to say that Mrs. Langstone was more than ever convinced of the truth of Stephen Gadsby's surmises as to his real motives, and her disgust and indignation were so strongly excited, that it was not without the utmost difficulty she could stifle the expression of her feelings.

"I like not the proud and scornful beauty, Laura Maysdale, absenting herself from my presence," said Captain Braghall to himself, when he had quitted the house after this interview. "Can she have any suspicion of my designs?—If so, she has doubtless revealed them to her sister, and yet the reception I have met with on both occasions from the wife of Langstone contradicts that supposition. She appears to place the most implicit reliance on my promises and professions, which it is not likely she would do, were her mind prejudiced against me. No, no, I must not vex myself by such ideas, my plot has hitherto worked much better than I could expect, and I have very little or no doubt of its ultimate success. I will expend a fortune to obtain the realization of my hopes, and to force Laura to yield to my will. Gold, they say, will purchase anything, and I flatter myself that it will have the same talismanic effect in this case. Laura Maysdale—Laura Maysdale, you may think to escape me, but if money, ingenuity, stratagem, and determination do not fail, you will find yourself mistaken in this instance."

"So I say, captain," said a voice behind him, and turning sharply round he was rather startled on beholding that the words proceeded from that very respectable individual, the Stunner."

"So I say, captain," repeated the ruffian, "and I admire your pluck. There is nothing like securing a pretty girl on whom you have fixed your mind, as I have had the extreme felicity of doing frequently in my time, though I suppose it was all owing to the handsomeness of my face and person, and the irresistible accomplishments of my mind."

"What do you here?" demanded Braghall, sternly and abruptly.

"Why," replied the other, "mere accident brought me here, captain, and seeing you, I thought you would not shy an old pal. You have not honoured the crib with your presence lately."

"Begone, begone!" said Braghall; "I am in no humour to talk to you."

"Nay, now," said the Stunner, with a satirical grin, "this is not the sort of treatment that one gentleman should expect from another."

"What is it you want?"

"Nothing more than the pleasure of your society, captain."

"Here is money, take it, and leave me."

"Thank you, captain," said the ruffian, pocketing the cash; "but will you not accompany me to the crib?"

"No," answered Braghall, repulsively; "begone, I say!"

"Upon my word, captain, I cannot leave you thus."

"If you are wise you will, and make your way to the 'Crib,' as you call it, by all the least frequented alleys and streets you can find."

"What do you mean, captain?" asked the Stunner, in rather a faltering voice.

"Are you not afraid to be seen in the streets, especially in open daylight?"

"Afraid!"

"Yes, afraid."

"Afraid of what, captain?"

"That you might be recognised."

"As whom?"

"One of the fellows who plundered the house of Christopher Hastings, Esq., on the seventeenth of October last," replied Braghall.

The Stunner started, and turned very pale.

"How do you know this, captain?" he asked, in a tremulous voice.

"Are you not aware that there is a reward offered for your apprehension, as well as your colleagues in the burglary?"

"But how do you know that I was concerned in the robbery?"

"Oh," answered the captain, with a satirical laugh, "that's my portrait, as correct as an artist could paint it. Now for your's, Dick. Ha! ha! ha!"

The Stunner again started and trembled violently, as he exclaimed—

"D——n! how has this reached your ears?"

"No matter," replied the captain; "were they not your words in a certain public house, when you and your friend Hemlock were conversing together?"

"Ye—ye—yes," stammered out the Stunner, "but there was no one in the room but ourselves at the time."

"Then how could they come to my knowledge?" demanded Braghall.

"Jack Clinton was in the job as as well as me and Dick."

"I know it; but you have nothing to fear from him, if you do not betray yourselves."

"I cannot understand you, captain."

"In a few days he will be out of the way, and you will never see him again," replied the captain.

"It was an unfortunate job," said the Stunner, "but you will not betray us, captain, for old acquaintance sake?"

"Not if you do as I desire you; but if you do not, why you must e'en take the consequences."

"What would you have us do?"

"Keep yourselves concealed till after the affair has blown over; you must be mad if you do not follow my advice."

"We will do so, captain; but you will give me your word that you will not——"

"What I have said is enough," interrupted Braghall; "begone!"

"I will do so, captain," replied the Stunner, sneaking off, and turning into a bye street as quickly as possible, slouching his hat over his brows as well as he could, to conceal his features from recognition, and muttering curses to himself.

"It is all up with us!" said the Stunner; "I never expected this; who could have overheard the conversation that passed between myself and Dick Hemlock? There certainly was no one in the room but ourselves at the time, and yet the captain repeated the exact words I made use of. Well, this is a mystery; this is a go! What is to be done? I must see Dick directly, and consult with him."

He hurried on as fast as he could, looking every now and then cautiously behind him, as if he was fearful that he had been recognised, and that some one was in pursuit of him, until at last he arrived at the place of rendezvous, and entering the room in which the villains usually congregated, he flung himself on a seat completely exhausted, and wipe his face with his handkerchief.

"Why, what's the matter, Stunner?" demanded Dick Hemlock, who happened to be present; "you seem quite flurried."

"And well I may be, if you knew all," replied the Stunner.

"What do you mean?"

"I can't answer; I shall choke—give me a go of brandy, or I shall swown to a dead certainty!"

The brandy was given to him, which he swallowed at a gulp.

"There—you are better now," said Hemlock, "so explain yourself. Why you look as frightened as if it was hot-roll time and you was the first about to be served."

"Oh, Dick! Dick! such a go!"

"What's a go?"

"It's all U P."

"Why the devil don't you speak plain?" demanded Hemlock, impatiently.

"Dick," said the Stunner, "I must have a few words with you privately; let us retire."

They then quitted the room, and having entered another remote one, and locked the door, Hemlock said—

"Now then, perhaps you will be so condescending as to let me know what it is that has alarmed you thus."

"Oh, Dick," returned the Stunner, "I am afraid it is all over with us; they are down upon us as dead as a hammer."

Hemlock started, and looked as much alarmed as his companion.

"What," he said, "are the traps upon our scent?"

"I don't know that, but it is all known."

"Come—come, be quick."

"You remember the conversation we had at the Cock and Magpie, the other day?"

"Yes; well, and what of it?"

"It was all overheard."

"Nonsense!—how could that be, when there was no one present in the room but ourselves?" said Hemlock.

"So I thought, but there must have been, though we did not observe them. I tell you the very words I made use of were repeated to me not an hour ago."

"By whom?"

"Captain Braghall."

"The devil!—are you serious?"

"Indeed I am."

"You met the captain, then?"

"Of course I did," answered the Stunner, "or how could he have told me that?"

"No more hesitation," said Dick Hemlock, impatiently, "but tell me all about it."

The Stunner complied, and Hemlock listened to him with the greatest consternation.

"Curses light on it," he exclaimed, when the Stunner had concluded; "this is a d—d bad job; what would you advise us to do?"

"I don't know, but I think we had better vanish as soon as possible."

"No—no, I think we are safe enough here; the captain will not betray us?"

"He promised me not to do so," replied the Stunner, "but should Jack Clinton turn snitch, it would be all up with us."

"But you have told me that the captain promised he should be put out of the way as soon as he left the hospital, and that we should never see him again."

"True; but don't you see that Braghall holds us in his power, and that if we don't do exactly what he wishes, he may deliver us over to the hands of the law, whenever he pleases?"

"It is d—d provoking," said Hemlock. "I cannot imagine how the captain gained his information."

"Nor I," said the Stunner.

"It was a great piece of folly for us to broach the subject at all in a public-house where we were not known."

"It was so; but who would have thought that any one was listening to us?"

"Well, we must make the best we can of it," said Hemlock: "and after all, I do not think the captain will act unfairly towards us."

"Perhaps not; but I wish Jack Clinton was out of the way."

"We may depend upon Braghall's word," said Hemlock, "and, therefore, I think we may rest satisfied on that point. This is a scheme of the captain's to secure the discharge of Langstone."

"No doubt of it, and of course, after what he has heard, Clinton would not think it very advisable to appear against him."

"True," said Hemlock, "and therefore you see on that score we are safe. The affair is not so alarming, after all, and all that we have to do is to follow the captain's advice, and to keep out of the way as much as possible, until the affair has blown over, or if we do go out, it had better be only at night, and then in such disguises as it would be impossible for any person to recognize us."

"Well," said the Stunner, "I don't know but that you are right; however, I had much rather that it had not happened at all."

"And so had I, but we must be cautious not to drop the least hint of it to our companions."

"Ah! there it is again," said the Stunner, "how can we depend upon them? They will be sure to see the bills again giving a description of us, and the reward would be almost certain to tempt one of them to betray us."

"That is devilish awkward again," said Hemlock.

"I think," observed the Stunner, "that we had better make our exit from here as soon as possible, and go and ruralize in the country for awhile."

"Well, perhaps that would be as well," observed Hemlock, "but I think we had better see the captain first, and consult him on the subject. No doubt he will visit us again before long."

"I am quite agreeable to that arrangement," said the Stunner, "and we must try to gain from him how he obtained his information, for that might be of use to us afterwards."

"True; so that business is settled."

"It is."

"Then endeavour to compose yourself, especially when we are in the company of our associates, and we shall get over the job, never fear." gir,a

Having thus settled the business to their mutual satisfaction, the two worthy gentlemen rejoined their companions. The day after the last visit of Captain Braghall, Mrs. Langstone removed to the new apartments which Laura had taken for her, and which were furnished in a humble but comfortable manner; indeed the accommodation they displayed were such as Mary had not experienced for many a day, and on entering the room she could not help shedding tears.

"Oh, my dear sister," she cried, throwing herself sobbing on her neck, "how can I ever repay such unexampled goodness and consideration as this?"

"You have little, my dear sister, to thank me for," said Laura, "but my kind hearted and benevolent mistress, whom may Heaven reward for her generosity. Here I hope it may be your lot to enjoy many years of happiness, blest with the affections of your husband, and surrounded by the cheerful and contented smiles of your dear children."

"Thank you for that wish, my beloved sister," said Mrs. Langstone, "it fills my bosom with hope and gladness. Thank God that I have now a comfortable home to welcome my unfortunate Edward to, and to urge him on to fresh exertions to redeem those fatal errors of which he has unhappily been guilty. He will repent, I am convinced he will, and then indeed shall I have nothing else to wish for."

"Oh, yes, Mary, he must indeed be hardened in guilt did he not do so, when he reflects upon the terrible miseries his improvidence and dissolute habits caused you, and the narrow escape ne will have had of meeting with an ignominious fate. But I entertain no doubt of him, and I sincerely thank Heaven that happier days are dawning upon you."

Mary raised her eyes towards Heaven as her sister gave utterance to those observations, and offered up a fervent prayer of thanksgiving to the Supreme for the goodness He had shown in the midst of her tribulation.

"But Laura," said Mrs. Langstone, after a pause, and as a sudden thought seemed to occur to her, "I am encroaching too much upon the kindness of your excellent mistress. You have been with me a long time, and she must be put to great inconvenience by the loss of your services."

"Do not let that trouble you, Mary," replied her sister, "for she has given me permission to remain with you until the whole of this melancholy and unfortunate business is finally settled."

"Oh, how kind and considerate of her," said Mrs. Langstone, "and how I rejoice to think, Laura, I have found such generous friends, such a happy asylum."

"Yes, my dear sister," observed Laura, "I often return my heartfelt thanks to Heaven for thus providing for me, and never can I cease to feel the most unbounded gratitude to my bene-factors for their kindness."

"You would be unworthy of all esteem, my Laura, if you could; but I know too well that your gentle nature would recoil from such a feeling."

While this conversation was going forward the two eldest children were engaged in deep admiration of the new furniture, and the novelty of everything which met their gaze evidently excited their utmost wonder and delight. There was not an article in the room which escaped their attention, from the pictures and chimney ornaments down to the flowered carpet which covered the floor, and the hearth-rug before the fire-place, luxuries that were entirely new to them. They were in perfect extacies, and as Mrs. Langstone and her sister watched their antics, and saw their smiling faces, tears started to their eyes, and they were unable for some moments to give utterance to their feelings.

"Receive this, dear Mary," said Laura at length, "as a happy omen of the future, of the joys that are yet in store for you."

"I do, indeed," replied her sister, her bosom swelling with emotion, "and oh, may my fond hopes never more be doomed to be annihilated."

"They will not, Mary, I trust to God they will not," said Laura.

"Oh, Edward," sighed Mrs. Langstone, "what must be your feelings when you behold this; how bitterly will you reproach yourself for having by your errors for a time destroyed that happiness we once enjoyed; what a contrast, what a painful contrast must this scene present to your imagination, to the squalid misery and wretchedness you, by your acts of profligacy, brought upon us."

"Nay, Mary," interposed her sister, "you must not encourage such thoughts as these. They are opposed to your nature, I am certain."

"I was wrong, Laura, I was very—very wrong," ejaculated Mrs. Langstone, "but I scarcely knew what I was saying; Heaven forbid that I should ever remind my husband of his errors, or give utterance to a single word which might be construed into reproach; I will never allow the past to enter my thoughts, but it shall be my constant study to cheer him on to deeds of virtue and integrity for the future; my cheerful smiles shall ever welcome him from the toils of the day, and should cares beset his mind, mine shall be the voice that shall endeavour to sooth him into peace; such shall be the constant study of my life, and may Heaven aid me, as I trust it will, in my efforts."

"Spoken like my own sweet sister," cried Laura, throwing her fair arms affectionately round her neck; "spoken like my own sweet sister, and Heaven, in its infinite mercy, will realize all your hopes. You will see the glad time again when your greatest delight will be to welcome the tread of your husband's foot upon the stairs, and he will joyfully respond to all your feelings. You will see prosperity gathering around you, and no cares or anxieties corroding your breast: such are my hopes and anticipations, dear Mary, and I fear not that they will be realized."

"Dear girl," ejaculated Mrs. Langstone, whilst tears of affection and gratitude chased them-selves down her cheeks, "you have ever been—you are always my gentle soother under every affliction. God has been good indeed to send me such a sister and friend. But we will say no more this day, Laura, upon that subject; we will endeavour to imagine that our visions of future happiness are already realized, and be happy."

"We will, my sister," replied Laura; "and here is a scene that will still further stimulate us to do so. See how happy your little innocents are, Mary; and can you be otherwise than so, now that Heaven has brought your trials to an end, and that the clouds of adversity that have so long obscured the horizon of your peace are rapidly dispersing?"

"True, true, my Laura," said Mrs. Langstone; "but my poor husband—could he be made acquainted with the prospect we have now before us of his speedy restoration to society, what a relief would it be to the dreadful anguish of mind he must now be enduring?"

"Perhaps it would be better," suggested Laura, "that he should not; for should anything occur (which I trust to God there will not) to disappoint those hopes, the shock would be still more terrible for him to endure. But a day or two will decide everything, and I am sanguine in the idea that everything will turn out as we anticipate."

Mrs. Langstone could not but coincide with her sister's observations, and their humble meal

CAPTAIN BRAGHALL'S RECEPTION BY MARY.

having been prepared and got ready for them previous to their arrival, they sat themselves down to the table, and enjoyed it with a much better appetite than they had done for many weeks before. Bob and Nelly especially, although they were already full of the grandeur of their new *domicile*, did a most excellent part towards its consumption, and in the happiness of her offspring, the affectionate mother became comparatively happy too. The meal was scarcely over, when the landlady, a respectable, motherly, kind-hearted woman, made her appearance, and informed them that a person who called himself Stephen Gadsby was waiting below, and requested to see them.

"Show him up stairs, by all means, Mrs. Austin, if you please," said Laura, "he is our best earthly friend."

"Ah," replied Mrs. Austin, who was a simple unsophisticated little woman as one would wish to see, "I thought he must be a friend to his fellow-creatures, because he has such a good-humoured face; just like my old man, poor fellow. I will *escorch* him up directly."

But Mrs. Austin had no occasion to take upon herself that responsible office, for Stephen Gadsby was already standing at the door, cap in hand (for like many others he could not afford to sport a hat) with as much humility and respect, as if he were about to enter the presence of his sovereign. Mrs. Langstone and her sister arose and welcomed him cordially, and Mrs. Austin, who knew something of manners (although the lower orders are not alway allowed to do so), curtseyed and retired from the room. Poor Stephen Gadsby, who had previously most vigorously performed an operation on the mat of the door, to the imminent peril of causing a dissolution of partnership between the soles and upper-leathers of his boots, (which, truth to say, had been in a declining state for some time past), repaid the reception he met with in full, and accepting of the chair which Laura had handed him, he took a survey of the apartment, and everything it contained, with the most unmistakeable expression of satisfaction.

"Ah!" he said, "this looks something like; this is as it should be. Oh, I am so glad! What a palace, to be sure. I never thought it possible that there could be such things, but then you see I was dragged up in a cellar, where I saw nothing but darkness, fever, and the rats. Hows'ever, I suppose that was good enough for such as me. Well, this is handsome : I hope my boots won't hurt the carpet, Mrs. Langstone, because, if you think they will, I'll take 'em off. But I beg your pardon for what I have said, I am very glad to see you so comfortable, indeed I am.'

"Thank you, my good friend," replied Mrs. Langstone; "and, indeed, I am very glad to see you."

"Thank you, ma'am," said Stephen, in tones of the utmost respect, "I could not help calling to see you in your new lodgings, and I hope you will not think me rude in doing so."

"Mr. Gadsby," replied Mrs. Langstone, "after the services you have rendered me, you can never be an intruder. But do you bring us any news?"

"Yes, a little, ma'am," answered Stephen, "and such as I have no doubt, will afford you much satisfaction."

"What is it, Mr. Gadsby?" asked Laura, anxiously.

"Why, in the first place," replied Gadsby, "that most confirmed of scoundrels, Clinton, comes out of the hospital to-morrow."

"Ah!" ejaculated Mrs. Langtone and her sister, in a breath.

"The re-examination of your husband, Mrs. Langstone, is appointed for the day after to-morrow."

"Oh, God!" groaned Mary, shuddering.

"Do not alarm yourself, I beg, ma'am, for there is not the least necessity for it," observed Stephen.

"Tell me why?" asked the anxious wife.

"I will, ma'am," returned Gadsby, "you see that before that re-examination takes place, Clinton will be far enough away."

"Are you sure of that?"

"I am, or else I would not assert it."

"Have you seen Captain Braghall?" asked Laura.

"I have, miss," replied Gadsby, "and we have made such arrangements for the accommodation of that respectable gentleman, Clinton, that there is not the least fear of his being present to prefer any charge against Mr. Langstone."

"Oh, thank Heaven for that!" exclaimed Mrs. Langstone, fervently, and clasping her hands vehemently together.

"Yes, ma'am, so I say," remarked Gadsby, "though I have not been much accustomed to say my prayers; hows'ever, that has nothing to do with the business. I thought you might be anxious to hear this, and so I took the liberty of calling upon you."

"Oh, thanks, thanks," said Mary, "you have removed a load of anxiety from my breast, and how, how can I ever repay you?"

"By saying nothing more upon the subject, ma'am. Stephen Gadsby is poor enough, God knows, but he would not enrich himself by doing that which is his duty; if he could only be placed in a position (don't you call it?) to get an honest living by his own industry, it strikes me very forcibly that he would be as happy a fellow as any king that wears a crown. But that's no matter. Jack Clinton to-morrow, as I have said before, leaves the hospital; myself and the captain take charge of him with all due honours—the captain has very generously supplied me with a swell suit for the occasion—ha! ha! ha!—the idea of the poor devil of the rookeries and back-slums, Stephy Gadsby, appearing in the character of a nob! Ha! ha! ha!—but, as I said before, the captain and myself take charge of the scoundrel, and, escorting him to Braghall's lodgings, never lose sight of him, till he is mounted on the stage (it ought to be on the gallows), and far away from London, to which, if he values his life or his liberty, he will not be over anxious to return in a hurry."

" The plan is admirably arranged," said Laura, " and Heaven send that it may not be thwarted."

" Oh, there is no fear of that, miss," returned Gadsby, " I will take good care of that. Well, then, the day of re-examination comes : Mr. Langstone is *deranged* at the bar. ' Where's the *persecutor* ?' says the magistrate ; he is not to be found, and what must be the *verdict* ?— why, that the magistrate will turn round and say to Ned Langstone—' Pris'ner at the bar, you are honourably acquitted, without the slightest blemish on your character.' That's the way the business will end, depend on it."

In spite of the cares and anxieties which agitated their minds at that moment, Mrs. Langstone and her sister could not help smiling at the honest but simple manner in which poor Stephen Gadsby delivered himself.

" Yes, Mrs. Langstone," he continued, " that's the way it will be done, take my word for it, and the day after to-morrow, I think, I can promise you, will restore your husband to you, and I hope that you will have no further cause for trouble. That is all I have to say."

" Mr. Gadsby," said our heroine, " you have indeed proved yourself to be our most disinterested friend."

" Have I ?" said the poor fellow, his honest countenance glowing with pleasure, " then all I can say is, that I am a very happy man. Oh, I only wish I was a gentleman of fortune— and I have been told that I ought to be, if I had my rights—wouldn't I come out then in the right way. Hows'ever, there's no knowing what may turn up by and by; Stephy Gadsby has got his eyes open, though some folks may think he's asleep; but that's neither here nor there. Well, this is a snug place, and may you prosper in it, Mrs. Langstone, that's all the harm I can wish you."

Mrs. Langstone again returned her heartfelt thanks to her humble but sincere friend.

" But I have something more to tell you, Mrs. Langstone," he said, after a pause, " which no doubt you will be pleased to hear."

" What is it, my good friend ?" asked Mrs. Langstone, eagerly.

" Why," replied Gadsby, " this morning I visited your husband in prison."

" Ah !" ejaculated Mrs. Langstone, with much emotion, " and how did you find him ? Oh, tell me, I pray you."

" Do not agitate yourself, ma'am," returned Gadsby, " for indeed there is no occasion. I found him much more composed than I expected, and when I told him what was being done to restore him to liberty, his joy and thankfulness was such as a poor ignorant fellow like myself cannot properly describe."

" God bless you for this, Mr. Gadsby," said Mary, tears starting to her eyes, " my poor Edward !"

" I am sure, Mrs. Langstone," continued Stephen, " had you heard what he said to me, you would feel satisfied that if he once escapes from his present dilemma, he will never more act in the way he has done."

" Heaven grant that he may be able to keep in the same mind," said Mrs. Langstone.

" Oh, I'm sure he will," observed Gadsby. " He must indeed be a very bad man at heart, which I do not believe him to be, if he does not."

" And you told him all the particulars ?" said Mrs. Langstone.

" Yes, as far as I dare, ma'am," replied Stephen, " for you know there are listeners there, and it would not be prudent to say too much. To hear how he talked of you and your children, I'm sure it would have made any person's heart bleed."

Mrs. Langstone sighed, and was unable to make use of any observation.

" He desired me," continued Stephen Gadsby, " to assure you of his sincere penitence, and that if it is his fate to be rescued from his present difficulty, you will find that it will be his constant study to endeavour to make atonement for the past."

" Dear, unfortunate Edward," said the devoted wife, whilst tears still chased each other down her cheeks, " I do believe you, and Heaven knows with what transport I shall again receive you to my bosom, and try by every means in my power to convince you how anxious I am to bury the past in oblivion. Oh, how anxious am I for the time to arrive which will set all my doubts at rest, and restore my husband to that liberty of which, I trust to all-merciful Heaven, he will never more be deprived through any misconduct of his own. Mr. Gadsby, you have rendered me a great service, and removed a weight of care and anxiety from my mind by what you have now told me."

" I am very glad to hear it, Mrs. Langstone, that I have been enabled to do so," said Gadsby; ' indeed you may freely command me in anything that my humble means may be likely to serve you; and, if you will permit me, I will call upon you again to-morrow, when perhaps I may have something more of a satisfactory nature to communicate to you. Keep up your spirits, that's a good soul, and if I am not very much mistaken, only a few hours will elapse before you are made a happy woman. Good day, ma'am—good day, miss; and depend upon it, that you have a sincere friend in Stephen Gadsby."

"I know it, Mr. Gadsby," said Mary, extending her hand towards him; "I must indeed be ungrateful did I for a moment doubt it. Good day, my kind-hearted friend, and may God bless you."

Honest Stephen Gadsby waited to hear no more, but immediately made his exit, his bosom swelling with feelings of the utmost satisfaction at the consolation he had been enabled to impart to the afflicted wife.

"Excellent man," said Mary, when Stephen had taken his departure, "he is indeed an honour to his sex; what a pattern is he to many who move in the most elevated ranks of society, and pride themselves upon their superior virtues and education."

"True, my dear Mary," said her sister, "Stephen Gadsby is worthy of every respect and esteem, and I hope the time is not far distant when Heaven will reward him as his merits deserve."

"Most fervently do I respond to that wish, my affectionate Laura," said Mrs. Langstone, "and I feel confident that our wishes will be gratified. The day after to-morrow, then, if all terminates as Stephen Gadsby anticipates, I may hope to be enfolded once more to the bosom of my unfortunate husband."

"You may, Mary, and I feel satisfied that Providence is too kind and merciful to suffer you to be disappointed. The villain Clinton, as Gadsby has informed us, leaves the hospital to-morrow; he and Captain Braghall will take good care that he is far away from London before night, and then, as there will be no evidence against him, it follows as a matter of course, that your husband must be discharged."

"Blissful thought!" ejaculated Mrs. Langstone, tears of gratitude starting to her eyes: "but should Clinton deceive them?"

"He would not be mad enough to attempt to do so, when he knows the peril that is hanging over his head," answered Laura; "no, Mary, you must not entertain any apprehensions or misgivings of that kind, for I cannot see that there is the least occasion for them. Clinton will be ready enough to make his escape as soon as possible, unless he is resolved to precipitate that fate which his crimes have incurred. Stephen Gadsby and Captain Braghall hold him completely in their power, and he must submit to their demands, however much it may be, and will, no doubt, be against his inclination to do so."

Filled with these hopes and expectations, the remainder of the day was passed much more cheerfully than any that they had for a long time experienced. They retired to rest at an early hour, having first offered up their fervent prayers to the Supreme, and supplicated His future protection; and the slumbers of Mrs. Langstone being calm and refreshing, she arose on the following morning with increased spirits, and the smiles of peace and content which her many severe and almost insupportable trials had so long banished from her brow, once more animated her countenance, and added to the feelings of happiness and gratitude which filled the bosom of her affectionate sister. The afternoon had far advanced before Stephen Gadsby made his appearance, and they both eagerly inquired if he had any fresh news to impart to them.

"Yes," replied Stephen, "and such as I have no doubt will afford you much satisfaction."

"What is it, Mr. Gadsby?" anxiously asked Mrs. Langstone.

"Clinton has quitted the hospital," answered Gadsby.

"Ah!" ejaculated Mary and her sister, in a breath.

"Yes," returned Stephen, "and he was duly escorted from thence by myself and the captain, and he is now at the lodgings of the latter, until it is dark, when he will take his departure from London by the night coach, to a retired little village on the western coast, where we can at any time communicate with him, and know how he is going on, without any fear of a discovery, or his attempting to deceive us."

"Thank God for that!" ejaculated Mrs. Langstone, "then all goes on as well as we could wish or expect?"

"It does, ma'am," said Stephen, "nothing could go on better, and before this time to-morrow Mr. Langstone will be at liberty."

Mary clasped her hands vehemently together and raised her eyes towards Heaven in humble thanksgiving to the Almighty, whilst tears of joy and gratitude started to the eyes of the affectionate and deeply sympathising Laura.

"Mr. Gadsby, kind-hearted man," said Mrs. Langstone, in the warmth of her grateful feelings, "again must I express to you my unbounded thanks for the unexpected services you have rendered to me and mine. Indeed I cannot find language sufficiently powerful to convey to you an adequate idea of the sense I entertain for your noble and disinterested conduct, but——'

"Now, now, Mrs. Langstone," interrupted Gadsby, "if you will persist in lavishing upon me so many thanks, which I feel is much more than I deserve, I really cannot stand it, and I must retire; what I have done you are quite welcome to; I am very glad to think I have been enabled to do it, and all I can say is this, that if I can serve you in future in any way, you will find no man more ready or happy to do so than Stephen Gadsby."

Mrs. Langstone extended her hand to him, and returned no verbal answer, but her looks expressed even much more than words could have done.

"I thought," continued Stephen, after a pause, "that I would call according to promise, in order to banish the doubt and suspense that I knew you must naturally feel;—but my visit must only be a short one, for I promised to rejoin the captain as soon as possible, and I shall not rest satisfied until I have seen this rascal fairly out of London.

"But the captain," asked Mrs. Langstone;—"you still entertain the same opinion of him as you did, Mr. Gadsby?"

"Yes, ma'am," replied Stephen, "that is, that he is a villain, but we will say no more upon that subject, if you please; wait a little time longer, and you will find that he will fall into the very trap he has set for others. I think he has no suspicion that I can so thoroughly read his real motives, and if you will only place a firm reliance on me, you will, I flatter myself, find the all I have promised shall and will be fulfilled."

"And that confidence do I strictly place in you, Mr. Gadsby," said Mary, "and leave everything to your discretion."

"Thank you, ma'am," said Gadsby, and he then took his leave, and once more made his way to the lodgings of Captain Braghall, sanguine with hope as to the result of his anxious wishes.

"To-morrow," he soliloquized, as he walked along, "to morrow, and the whole of my efforts, I feel confident, will be crowned with success; poor Ned Langstone will be released from his present scrape, and his good wife be happier than she has been for many a day. The scoundrel, Clinton, too, will be far away from London, but as soon as he will be some of these days if he only meets with his just reward, which I trust he will, for it would be a great pity if such a dastardly and heartless villain as he is were allowed to escape the punishment that many a better man than himself has met before him. When he is disposed of, then you and I, my worthy Captain Braghall, will settle accounts, and it strikes me rather forcibly that you will find Stephen Gadsby much more than a match for you. What an arrant villain you must be to think to destroy the happiness of such an amiable young girl as Laura Maysdale. Bah!—how I do long to pay you out in the coin you deserve. But I have no doubt the time will arrive, and therefore I will endeavour to rest myself contented till then."

Thus talking to himself, honest Stephen Gadsby arrived at the house where Captain Braghall resided, and was immediately ushered into the apartment in which he and Clinton were seated together.

Braghall drew him aside on his entrance, and speaking in low tones, said—

"How now, my worthy friend: Gadsby, you have seen Mrs. Langstone, I suppose?"

"I have," answered Gadsby.

"And Laura Maysdale?"

"Yes."

"And she looks as beautiful as ever?"

"It is impossible that one so good and virtuous can ever look otherwise than beautiful," returned Stephen, significantly.

"True, true;" said the captain, rather confused; "she is a fine girl; worthy to be the wife of an emperor."

"Worthy to be the wife of a respectable and honourable man," retorted Gadsby, "whatever his rank in society; too good to become the victim of a villain."

"Humph!" ejaculated Braghall, fixing upon Stephen Gadsby a suspicious look, and wincing under his observations; "I declare you are a perfect moralist, Mr. Gadsby."

"Much obliged to you for the compliment, Captain Braghall," returned Stephen drily; "I suppose I was born so."

"Ha! ha!" laughed Braghall, but with a very bad grace, "very good—ve-ry good. But come, we will just take a glass or two of wine, and then our friend here, Mr. Clinton, having assumed the disguise, we will do ourselves the honour of escorting him to the coach office."

"I wish you a very pleasant journey, Mr. Clinton," said Gadsby, with a sarcastic smile; "I trust there will be no accidents on the road, no upsetting of the coach, no dislocating of necks, for that is very awkward and vexatious, when it comes before our natural time."

Clinton bit his lips, and muttered a curse to himself, but he saw it would be a losing game to endeavour to contend with such an antagonist as Stephen Gadsby, and he therefore stifled his rage as well as he could, and merely replied—

"I am happy to see you in such excellent spirits, Mr. Gadsby; I hope that you and I may have the pleasure of meeting each other under different circumstances."

"Thank you," was the laconic answer of Gadsby; "I hope we shall."

"Time wears apace," remarked Captain Braghall, who did not appear to be exactly comfortable at the sarcasms and insinuations of Stephen Gadsby, and wished to put an end to the conversation; "so we had better depart at once, I think, to the coach office."

"I am quite ready," said Gadsby, "and I suppose our friend, Mr. Clinton is the same? You have arranged everything with him, I presume, during my absence, captain?"

"Everything," replied the latter, "and Clinton is quite satisfied, I believe; are you not, Jack?"

"Perfectly so, captain," replied that worthy; "you have promised to communicate with me as soon as I am enabled to inform you where I have taken up my abode?"

"I will not fail to do so," returned Braghall, "and if you keep good faith with me and Gadsby on this occasion, you may have no cause to repent it."

"At any rate you have not much cause to fear me on that point, I should think," remarked Clinton, in accents of dissatisfaction; "you and Stephen Gadsby here, have told me true enough that I cannot help myself; curses light on the accident which has reduced me to such a position, and has thus rendered my plans of revenge against Ned Langstone abortive."

"And do you still cherish feelings of revenge against him?" demanded Gadsby.

"Why should I seek to conceal them?" returned the villain; "yes, I continue to hate him with a mortal hatred; and cheerless though my prospects are, I do not entirely despair that the time will yet come when I shall have an opportunity of gratifying my vengeance."

"Clinton," said Stephen Gadsby, with a look of the utmost contempt and abhorrence, "you are an arrant scoundrel."

Clinton bit his lips and frowned fiercely upon Stephen.

"Aye you may frown, my worthy hang-gallows," said Gadsby, scornfully, "I do not mince my words; . . . . a confirmed scoundrel, or you would never continue to harbour such thoughts as those, after the miseries and outrages you have inflicted upon society, particularly Mrs. Langstone and her unfortunate though misguided husband."

"'Tis well for you, Stephen Gadsby," retorted Clinton, "'tis well for you that you can exult now that you have me in your power; but the time was when you would not have dared to use such language as this to me."

"I would not have dared! Ha! ha! ha!—Stephen Gadsby was never yet afraid to speak his mind, especially to such a fellow as the housebreaker Clinton."

"By the infernal host, this is not to be borne," cried the latter, bursting with rage, and clenching his fists; "Stephen Gadsby, fallen as I at present am, we may yet meet again under different circumstances, when I trust I shall have the opportunity of seeking satisfaction for these insults."

"Psha! think you that I mind your threats a single straw?—No, I treat them as they deserve, with the utmost scorn and contempt."

"Come, come," interposed the captain, "there is quite enough of this altercation; I must say, my good friend, Gadsby, that you treat Clinton rather too severely, especially after he has yielded to our demands."

"From no good will of his own," returned Stephen, "as his own observations ought to convince us."

"Well, well," said Braghall, "that may be, but let us say no more upon the subject. Clinton will, I dare say, think better of this when he is away, and, if he only manages right, and adheres strictly to the promises he has made us all may yet be finally arranged to our mutual satisfaction."

"   hope it may," replied Gadsby, significantly, but of which the captain did not seem to take any notice.

"Come," said the captain, "the time has now arrived, are you ready to depart, Clinton?"

"I am," replied the latter, laconically and sullenly.

"'Tis well," observed Braghall, giving him a well filled purse, "then here is money for your present necessities, and I will forward you more when you require it. You will find this much better than remaining here to prosecute poor Ned Langstone."

"Yes," coincided Gadsby, with a sarcastic grin, "I should rather imagine he will, and far less dangerous too, as he must be aware by this time."

Clinton again frowned upon him, but returned no answer; and a vehicle having been summoned to the door, they all three stepped into it, and were driven off to the inn from whence the coach was to start. The captain and Gadsby conversed but little on the way, and Clinton maintained a dogged and sullen silence. In a short time they arrived at the inn, and found the coach just ready to start on its journey.

"You will not fail to write to me as soon as you are settled?" said Braghall, as Clinton stepped from the vehicle.

"You may be certain of that," answered the latter.

"And under an assumed name," suggested Gadsby, in a low voice, "in case the letter should miscarry."

"A prudent recommendation," remarked the captain; "you will attend to it, Clinton?"

"I will."

"And remember your promises, for on that your own safety, I need not remind you, depends."

"You need not," answered Clinton. "Is this all you have to say to me?"

"It is," said Braghall, "farewell."

"Farewell," repeated Clinton, in the same sullen tones that he had assumed all along, and taking his place in the coach, in a few seconds it was driven off, and soon rolled out of sight. The captain and Gadsby watched it until it was hidden from their view in the surrounding darkness, and then once more stepping into the vehicle which had brought them to the inn, they returned to the lodgings of Braghall.

"All is safe now," said the captain, as they proceeded on their way; "nothing could have been better conceived or executed, we have got rid of the rascal Clinton; he dare not return, and the discharge of Langstone is certain to take place."

"Yes," coincided Gadsby, "I do not think there can be much doubt of that, captain."

"Doubt!" reiterated the latter; "not the shadow of one; there is not one tittle of evidence against him, and it is therefore impossible for them to detain him."

"And most sincerely do I rejoice at the circumstance," remarked Stephen, "not only for the sake of Langstone, but more especially for his innocent and unfortunate wife and children."

"Very true, Stephen; you have been an excellent friend to them, and I honour you for it."

"You flatter me, captain," replied Gadsby, in half sarcastic tones; "and I only hope all those who profess themselves to be their friends, may prove themselves to be as sincere as I am."

"Very good, Stephen," returned his companion, though he somewhat winced under the promptness of his remarks; "I hope they may; but really you must pass an hour or two with me this evening, just to drink success to our future undertakings."

"Your honour is very condescending," said Gadsby, with an affectation of much humility.

"Oh, not at all," replied the captain; "your conduct in this business entitles you to my warmest friendship; besides, I have a few words to say to you of some importance, and do not think that they could be spoken at a more fitting opportunity."

"Very good, captain," replied Stephen, "I am at your service."

The cab now stopped at the door of Braghall's residence, and the captain and Gadsby having alighted, entered the house.

"Take a seat, Mr. Gadsby," observed the captain, politely, when they had entered his sitting-room; "take a seat, my good friend, and make yourself quite at home."

Stephen obeyed, and the captain having placed a couple of decanters on the table, containing wine and spirits, and charged their glasses, also sat down opposite to Gadsby.

"Success to all our future undertakings!" said Braghall, raising the glass to his lips.

Gadsby responded to the toast, although it was not with sincerity that he did so as regarded Braghall. The latter having replenished the glasses, said—

"And now, Gadsby, I will propose another toast, to which I think you will most heartily respond. Here's reformation to Edward Langstone, and future prosperity and happiness to himself, his wife, and family."

"I will drink that toast most cheerfully," said Stephen Gadsby, with all his heart; "here's reformation to Edward Langstone, and future prosperity and happiness to himself, his wife, and family. Ah, Captain Braghall," he continued, "Langstone must indeed be a villain at heart if he should again inflict such miseries as he has already done on those who ought to be so dear to him. But I do not believe he will; he has been taught too severe a lesson, I should think, already."

"I should imagine he had," returned Braghall; "but I have no fear for him as regards his future conduct."

"I hope there will be no occasion," said Gadsby. "Oh, there will not be, you may depend upon that; but we will say no more about that at present; I wish to talk to you upon another subject."

"Name it, captain," said Stephen.

"You recollect," observed Braghall, "that I promised to double the reward which is offered for the apprehension of Clinton and his colleagues, if you would give me all the information you could, and render me all the assistance in your power?"

"Very true, captain," replied Stephen, "and have I not kept my promise faithfully?"

"Why," returned Braghall, after a moment or two's hesitation, "I do not doubt that you have, and in that spirit of confidence, I now present you with a cheque for one half the money, the remainder to be paid at a future period, say two—three months.'

"Very good, captain," said Gadsby, carefully depositing the cheque in one of the side pockets of his jacket; "I am in no particular hurry for the remainder—when it suits your convenience, I'm sure it will suit me. I ought to be extremely obliged to you, Captain Braghall, for the *disinterested* friendship you have shown to me; such liberality—you will pardon a poor simple fellow like me, I dare say, captain, who cannot express himself in the fine words that you can?"

"You are a good fellow, a clever fellow, Gadsby," said the young libertine, "and I consider it one of the most fortunate occurrences that ever happened to me when I met with you."

"Why so, your honour?"

"Because—because—you—you—you see, our ideas so perfectly associate."

"Do they, captain?" asked Stephen, with a sly wink, which he meant not the captain to see, but which, however, he did, and did not like it, although he affected to appear that he had taken no notice of it.

"Yes," added Braghall, "they completely associate; and this is the reason why I took a fancy to you the first moment that I had the pleasure of meeting with you."

"How highly flattering, captain," said Stephen Gadsby, in the same satirical tones.

"Not at all," observed Braghall, evincing as much coolness and nonchalance as he possibly could; "by the by, I understand that the new apartments that have been so kindly taken for Mrs. Langstone and her family are extremely comfortable?"

"They are, Captain Braghall, thanks to the benevolence of your honour's excellent aunt.'

"Ah! ah! she is a good old sort of a lady; and I believe she has permitted Mrs. Langstone's sister, Laura Maysdale, to remain with her?"

"She has," answered Gadsby, "and without her, I don't know what would have become of the poor soul."

"Laura Maysdale is, I think, a good girl."

"Think!—d—e your honour, pardon me for swearing, she is one of the best and sweetest tempered young creatures that ever breathed."

"Rather beautiful, too," said the young libertine, carelessly, as though he had scarcely made up his mind to decide upon that critical point.

"Rather beautiful!" repeated honest Stephen Gadsby, energetically and pointedly, "I should say she is beautiful, and as innocent as she is beautiful, and he must be a d—d villain, and so Stephen Gadsby would not be afraid and ashamed to tell him, who would dare harbour a thought to her injury."

The captain, who felt confused and abashed at the warmth of Gadsby's manner, hastily arose from his chair, and took two or three rapid strides across the room; then he returned to Stephen, and with an affected smile of good humour, he observed—

"Why, I must confess, my good friend Gadsby, that you are quite a gallant."

"Your honour," returned Stephen, "I don't know much about that word gallant, because you see, I don't happen to be much of a "schollard," but if you mean that I admire and respect an innocent female, you are correct, and d—me, if I wouldn't stand up in her defence while there was a drop of blood left within my veins; that's what I say, and that's what I mean, too, Captain Braghall, whether it offends or pleases."

"It cannot offend me, Mr. Gadsby," said the captain, with some confusion; "of course, I cannot but agree in the sentiments you have expressed. Well spoken, Stephen, well spoken. I admire you for your manly feeling. We must yet become better acquainted, for I see you are a man exactly after my own heart."

"And not much of a compliment either," thought Stephen Gadsby, though, of course, he did not express himself so.

"You are very clever," remarked Braghall, after a pause.

"Your honour again flatters me," was the reply.

"No, indeed I do not," said the captain; "there is a shrewdness and foresight about you which is not often our fortune to meet with in individuals."

"I am happy to hear it, your honour, though I was not exactly aware of it before."

"Oh, yes, there is, and, as I said before, you and I must become better acquainted '

"I trust we shall, captain," replied Stephen Gadsby, drily.

"Should I require your private services on any future occasion, if I well remunerate you, will you render them me?"

A COLLOQUY BETWEEN CAPTAIN BRAGHALL AND HONEST STEPHEN GADSBY.

"Why, that depends entirely upon the nature of them," replied Gadsby.
"We will talk more upon that subject by and by."
"Very good, your honour."
"I have a wish to serve Edward Langstone and his family, and I have no doubt that in carrying out that object, you can greatly assist me."
"I am glad to hear that, Captain Braghall," said Stephen Gadsby.
"You will take another glass of wine before you go?"
"Thank you, sir, you are very kind."
"Of course you will be at the Police Court to-morrow?"
"Certainly."
"When we shall bring Langstone away triumphant."

"I hope so," answered Stephen ; "and what is more, I trust, a better man than he has been for some time past."

"No doubt of it, and I hope so," said Captain Braghall, affecting the amiable. "Of course, whatever takes place between you and myself is all secret ?"

"Oh, certainly," replied Gadsby.

"Enough, then ; I think I may depend on you."

"Of course you may, your honour," said Stephen Gadsby ; "but if you entertain any misgivings upon that subject, we may as well terminate our business, and there is no harm done, you know."

"Oh, no," returned Braghall, hastily, "there is no occasion for that ; I feel satisfied that I may place every confidence in you."

"Very good, Captain Braghall," returned Gadsby ; "have you anything more to say to me?"

"Not at present," replied the captain.

"Then I must wish you a very good night," said Stephen, rising from his seat and taking up his hat ; "I am much obliged to you, Captain Braghall, and I trust that you and others may find me a man not altogether unworthy of encouragement."

"Good night," responded the captain ; "I do not entertain any doubts of your strict integrity."

"And I think," said Stephen, as he retired, with a peculiar look, "that you will find yourself not altogether mistaken. Good night, captain, good night."

"A shrewd fellow, a remarkably shrewd fellow," said Braghall to himself, when Stephen Gadsby had taken his departure ; "and yet there are certain traits in his character I cannot exactly or satisfactorily fathom. Some observations which he made use of sounded anything but harmonious in my ears. I must be guarded with him, and watch him closely. But why should I entertain any doubts? All goes on as favourably as I could wish or expect. Clinton is removed far out of the way of danger, or of doing any harm.—Mrs. Langstone and her sister believe that I have been the principal cause of this ; the release of Edward Langstone has consequently been caused through my exertions, and when Langstone is again at liberty, I shall have a powerful auxiliary to aid me in my designs. They must succeed—I cannot think differently ; and notwithstanding all the obstacles that may and will, no doubt, be placed in my way, the beauteous Laura Maysdale shall, before many months, probably before many weeks have elapsed, be in my power. That thought gives me courage to pursue my plot with energy and perseverance, and by all my hopes, I will not falter until it is fully accomplished. Laura has hitherto, sedulously kept herself out of my way, but it strikes me, notwithstanding, that I shall see her to-morrow, and then will I feast my eyes upon her glowing charms, and picture to myself the blissful time when she shall be wholly, irrevocably mine."

Thus did the young libertine flatter himself with his guilty hopes, and every moment that intervened between the consummation of his wishes seemed to him to be an age. As Stephen Gadsby pursued his way towards home, he also soliloquised ; but very different were his thoughts to those which occupied the mind of Captain Braghall.

"I have managed this business," he said, "even much better than I expected. This worthy Captain Braghall imagines that he has not only a dupe, but a tool in me ; but how wofully will he find himself mistaken. Ha! ha! ha! Stephy Gadsby is always down to them—he is always down to the rascals. I have made a rare night's work of it ;—fifty pounds! Why, I am a perfect gentleman! What shall I do with it? I never even saw so much money in my life before ; fifty pounds! and the promise of another fifty if I only mind my P's and Q's! Why, I'm independent. Let me see, what shall I do with it? I will enter into business—take a chandler's-shop, which, with the assistance of a mangle, I think I and my old woman might be able to manage very well. Not a bad idea that! And who knows but that in time I might save a fortune. I have been told that I ought to be a great gentleman now, only somebody else has shuffled me out of that character. Well, that may be true or it may not, I can't say, but time will show, I suppose ; however, if ever I do have the good luck at any time to become a man of fortune, I hope that Providence will teach me how to make a good and proper use of it, that's all. I am heartily glad that that infernal rascal, Jack Clinton, is got rid of, that I am, and so will poor Mrs. Langstone be to hear it too, I know. If he had his deserts, he would now have been got off in a different and far readier manner. However, all in good time for that ; his day will arrive by and by, no doubt."

But notwithstanding all those reflections, and the conscientious goodness of his motives, Stephen Gadsby could not feel exactly satisfied with the part he had taken in the escape of Clinton. He was very well aware of the serious light in which the law would view the aiding of a criminal to escape from the hands of justice, and should it ever be discovered, himself and Captain Braghall would be placed in a very awkward and dangerous position ; but he endeavoured to console himself with the thought that he had done so from the best of principles, and that Providence, consequently, would not suffer him to fall a victim to the generosity and humanity of his feelings. As it was getting late, he thought of returning home, but knowing how anxious Mrs. Langstone and her sister would be to know whether Clinton had really taken his departure from London, he changed his mind, and made his way towards the lodgings of the former, in order that he might make them acquainted with all that had taken place. They received him with anxious looks, and eagerly enquired the particulars. He did not keep them a moment in suspense.

"All right, Mrs. Langstone," he said, "the rascal, Clinton, has taken his departure ; myself and Captain Braghall saw him safely in the coach, and no doubt he is many miles away from London by this time."

"Thank God for that!" ejaculated Mrs. Langstone, fervently clasping her hands together.

"So I say," observed Gadsby, "and were he to break his neck before he arrives at the termination of his journey, it would be all the better. He is one of the most hardened villains that ever I met with."

"So I believe," said Mary.

"And Captain Braghall is not much, if any better," observed Gadsby.

"I am afraid he is a bad man," said Laura.

"A bad man, miss," repeated Stephen, "I say again he is a heartless scoundrel, and that is not mincing the matter ; but I read him perfectly well, and it strikes me rather forcibly that he will find me a troublesome customer to deal with yet. However, he places every confidence in me, poor fool, and therefore shall I be the better enabled to defeat his plans."

"I trust you may, with all my heart," said Mrs. Langstone.

"I know I shall," returned the honest fellow ; "although I say it, that should'n't say it, there are very few that can get over Stephy Gadsby, when he is on the right scent. Ah, miss," he continued, addressing himself to Laura, "all his conduct, I am satisfied, from the observations he has made use of to me, has been prompted by the wicked designs he has against you."

Laura blushed and sighed, whilst her gentle bosom swelled with feelings of shame and resentment, and her sister replied—

"Right Mr. Gadsby, I do believe you are correct in your surmises, and what a base and unprincipled man he must be, that, under the mask of humanity and friendship, can harbour such diabolical designs."

"He is," said Gadsby, "but fear not ; they shall be defeated. He requires my future service—I understand him ; and no doubt he thinks that I will assist him in his plans. I will appear to do so, but you may be sure it will only be to bring shame and confusion upon him."

"Thank you for this, Mr. Gadsby," said Mrs. Langstone ; "I do not doubt that, with your assistance, we shall yet be able to defeat him."

"You may rest certain of that, Mrs. Langstone," replied Stephen ; "I have got the captain in such a fix that he will find it a very difficult, if not an impossible matter to extricate himself. However, this is matter for after consideration. Clinton, as I before said, is got out of the way ; he has taken his departure, and dare not again make his appearance, and therefore the, liberation of your husband to-morrow is certain."

Mary clasped her hands and raised her eyes gratefully towards Heaven as she piously and fervently ejaculated—

"Great God, for this receive my heartfelt thanks, and may the restoration of my unfortunate husband be the precursor of future peace and happiness to us all. Watch over him I humbly beseech Thee, and prevent him from again falling into those fatal errors which have been productive of so much misery, shame, care, and anxiety. Oh, may his future conduct be such as to make ample atonement for the past, and may the guilty tempter never again have power to influence his thoughts or actions."

In this simple but earnest prayer, Laura Maysdale and Stephen Gadsby ardently joined and a silence of some moments ensued, during which time they all endeavoured to compose their feelings.

"Nothing can be more promising than matters as they stand at present," at last observed Stephen Gadsby, "and you may safely entertain the most sanguine anticipations as to the result, without any fear of being disappointed. Long before this time to-morrow night Mr. Langstone will be once more restored to you, never again, I trust, to be separated from you."

"How grateful do I feel to you, Mr. Gadsby," said Mary, "for your kind and humane wishes ; you have proved to me one of my best earthly friends——"

"Pardon me, Mrs. Langstone," interrupted Stephen, "you already know my sentiments upon that subject, and therefore I will thank you to say no more about it. But I have something more to tell you of what took place between me and Captain Braghall, which I have no doubt will prove interesting to you."

He then related all the particulars of that interview, to which Mrs. Langstone and her sister listened with the deepest interest, but at the same time with the most unmitigated disgust; for it was quite evident from the observations of Bragball, what the villanous motives were that guided his conduct towards them; and while they despised him as a contemptible hypocrite, they also loathed and abhorred him as a heartless villain. But to honest Stephen Gadsby they felt an inexhaustible debt of gratitude for the knowledge he had, entirely by his own wit and ingenuity arrived at, and the valuable information he had thus been enabled to afford them, and to put them on their guard against the unprincipled man, who, under the mask of sympathy and friendship, sought to work them so much misery. They forbore, however, to express their thanks to Stephen, knowing how obnoxious they were to his feelings."

"Your estimate of the captain's character, and his secret designs, Mr. Gadsby," said Mrs Langstone, " was perfectly correct; there can be no doubt that he is an unprincipled, deep, designing villain."

"There can be no doubt of that, ma'am," said Stephen, "and I am only too happy to think that fortune made me acquainted with his secret schemes, and thus enabled me to put you on your guard against the snare he had laid to entrap you and Miss Laura. Deep as he fancies himself, it strikes me, as I have frequently said before, that he will find me more than a match for him. But all in good time, Mrs. Langstone; I must, in my turn, in order to work out my intentions, which Heaven knows are for the best, act the hypocrite, so that I may be able to frustrate him at every point. He has told me that he may require my future services, and I have agreed to render them to him. and I think you will perfectly understand me for having done so, for, don't you see, by that means, I shall not only become acquainted with all his secret thoughts, and be able to communicate them to you, but I shall likewise place him in your power, and enable you, when the proper time arrives, to hold him up to the world in his true colours, to his disgrace and confusion? Do you approve of my plans, Mrs. Langstone?"

"Perfectly so, my good friend," answered our heroine; "reason and every honourable motive must justify them; and the blessings of the unfortunate wife, and all those fondly connected with her, must and will pursue you for your generous, manly, and disinterested exertions in their behalf and the general cause of humanity. Would to Heaven that all the human race possessed the same noble feelings as the humble, unpretending Stephen Gadsby. Pardon me; I know you like not flattery, but I must indeed be an insensible being, could I refrain from expressing the incalculable obligations I am under to you."

"Well, Mrs. Langstone," replied Stephen, "I suppose I must let you have your way, since you seem determined to place so much value upon my simple services. I am but a poor illiterate man, but, thank God, He has given me the knowledge of right and wrong, and I trust that I shall now ever be able to pursue the former. The time was when I was an idle, reckless vagabond, for the way in which I had from infancy been buffeted about in the world, led me to suppose that no one cared for me, and that I, therefore, had no right to respect those laws of virtue and honour, in which no one had ever taken the pains to instruct me (oh, what a blessing is *eddication*)—but since I have witnessed the evil consequences which the errors of your poor husband, Mrs. Langstone, have produced, a new light has seemed to dawn upon me; I feel myself something more than a wretch without a soul; I—I—I cannot express myself as I ought, but I wish, oh, how I do wish that one of these days I may be worthy to be called a *man* !"

As the noble, but uneducated Stephen Gadsby gave utterance to these observations, every expression of his countenance spoke more eloquently than laugnage could have done, as to the sincerity of his feelings. A manly tear started to his eye, which he hastily dashed away. Mrs. Langstone and Laura were deeply affected by the simplicity, but energy of the poor fellow's remarks, and unable to return any immediate reply, a silence of several minutes ensued. Aristocratic and hereditary legislators! who boast so much of your wisdom, Christianity, and philanthrophy, this is not an exaggerated picture of one of the unfortunate children of poverty, whom you have, for want of education, consigned to crime and destruction. It is thus you obey the precepts of the Almighty Father of the whole human family who you profess to worship, but whose just laws you are hourly violating.

"But pardon me, Mrs. Langstone and Miss Laura," said Stephen Gadsby, after a pause, and having recovered himself from the excitement into which he had been thrown, by thoughts which had involuntarily suggested themselves to his mind: "pardon me for the strange observations I have made use of, and which had, perhaps, better not have been made at all; but singular thoughts do occur to me sometimes; I don't know how it is, but I cannot help giving utterance to them. Sometimes, do you know, I have the presumption to imagine that I was born to better things than it has been my lot to experience; but, however, that is neither here nor there I will say no more upon that subject. There is one thing I wish, notwithstanding, to state.'

', And what is that, Mr. Gadsby?" asked Mrs. Langstone.

"Why, ma'am," replied Stephen, "that I do not feel exactly satisfied in taking the money of Captain Braghall, which seems to my fancy very much like receiving the wages of guilt. But I will make no use of it at present, and perhaps, at some future time, I shall be able to see how it will be advisable to dispose of it."

"Very true," said Mrs. Langstone; "and indeed I should not let that trouble me at all; it will be no loss to Captain Braghall, and is nothing but a just reward to you, for the services you have rendered in the cause of suffering humanity."

"I will follow your advice, Mrs. Langstone," said Gadsby, "and by so doing I think I shall not be acting wrong."

"You will not, Stephen," said our heroine, "and I sincerely hope that this sum of money will be found sufficient to place you in that position of society, which, from your merits, you are entitled to."

"Thank you, ma'am," returned Gadsby, "all that I wish is, to have an opportunity of escaping from the vagabond life I have so long been leading, and to get my living by my own honesty and industry."

"And fear not but Heaven will assist you in your praiseworthy efforts, Mr. Gadsby," observed Laura.

"Thank you, miss," he returned, "I trust it will. Oh, I do not despair, I still think the time will come when I shall be better off, and if it should ever be my good fortune to become so, depend upon it I shall not forget my old friends. But I am afraid I am intruding upon you too long, and will therefore now wish you a very good night."

"Good night, Mr. Gadsby," said Mary; "shall I see you to-morrow?"

"Yes, ma'am," replied Stephen, "I will take the liberty of coming here before I go to the court, and perhaps you will accompany me?"

"No, Mr. Gadsby," answered Mrs. Langstone, "I have been thinking that, perhaps, it would be better for me to remain at home, and to await the result; for my appearance might disconcert my unfortunate husband, and unfit him for the painful business he will have to undergo."

"Why that is very true," remarked Stephen, "and I think the resolution you have formed is a very prudent one. But you need entertain no apprehensions as to the result, I can confidently assure you. Your husband must be discharged; what is there to prevent it? Nothing; and it will be my pleasant task to conduct him home to this very pretty and comfortable place, which is prepared for his reception, and where, I hope, he will in future make himself and you happy, and become again a respectable man. I have but a plain way of expressing myself, but what I do say comes from my heart."

"I know it does, my kind friend," said Mary, gratefully; "and I must indeed be insensible, did I not properly estimate your generous and humane wishes. Good night."

"Good night," repeated Gadsby, and he took his departure.

"Excellent man," said Mrs. Langstone, when he was gone, "how worthy is he of a better fate than that which has hitherto fallen to his lot."

"True," coincided Laura, "and I have no doubt that Providence will not suffer him to go unrewarded. But cheer you, my dear sister, for I feel confident that your troubles are now at an end, and that many years of happiness are in store for you to recompense you for the dreary past."

"My hopes indeed revive," said Mrs. Langstone, "and a sweet confidence takes possession of my mind. God grant that I may not be doomed to disappointment, for that, I am satisfied, after the many severe trials I have experienced, is more, much more than I could find fortitude to support."

"Entertain no misgivings, Mary," observed her sister, "for I am convinced that they are groundless. All, at present, is proceeding much better than our most sanguine ideas anticipated. How different are now your prospects to what they were only a few days since."

"They are indeed, dear Laura, and never can I be sufficiently grateful to the Almighty for raising me up such kind and real friends in the midst of my difficulties, and when I thought that nothing whatever could interpose between me and the dreadful fate which threatened me. Had it not been for you, my beloved sister, myself and my helpless little ones must have perished long ere this."

"And should I not have been a wretch, unworthy of the name of woman, had I neglected to perform what I have done towards my suffering fellow creatures, but especially my only sister, from whom from the earliest days of my childhood I have ever experience such unbounded kindness and affection?—Thank me not, dear Mary, for doing only that which was my bounden duty, for it pains me."

Mrs. Langstone embraced the affectionate girl, and for a few moments sobs choked her utterance.

"Oh, God!" she ejaculated at length, "what a heavy weight of almost insupportable care and anguish is removed from my breast, only within the last few hours. It seems almost too blissful to be true, and I know not how to give adequate expression to the feelings which now animate my bosom. Dear Edward, and is thy restoration to liberty and my arms indeed so near at hand? Will that terrible fate which I thought too surely awaited you, be averted? and may I hope to see you again restored to that respectable station in society from which you have, by the guilty and fatal influence of others, so long unfortunately strayed? Will happiness and content once more smile upon us, and the brand of crime and infamy be removed from your brow, where once alone sat honour and virtue? Delightful thought! how my heart throbs with extacy as the blissful picture presents itself to my imagination."

"And it is no delusive vision, Mary," said her sister, "rest assured it is not. It will, I feel satisfied, be realized in every particular, and the All Merciful Father of us all will amply reward you for all the many sufferings it has been your hard lot to undergo."

"But what a villain must Braghall be," said Mrs. Langstone, after a pause, "to contemplate the atrocious designs he does against you."

"He must," said Laura, "but still I fear him not; I am armed so strong in virtue that I may set his guilty machinations at defiance. Providence will protect me from his power, and yet bring him to shame and remorse."

"It will, dear Laura, and your numerous virtues will meet with that reward they so richly merit. But to Stephen Gadsby, how greatly are we indebted for the exertions he has made to counteract the libertine's designs, and for the very valuable information he has been enabled to afford us."

"Oh, yes," warmly coincided Laura, "and I must indeed be ungrateful could I ever forget the services that kind-hearted, noble-minded man has rendered me. Humble though his station in society be, despised as he probably may be by his more fortunate fellow creatures, he is an honour to his sex, and well would it be for many were they to endeavour to emulate his virtues."

"True," said Mary; "but, alas! how few like him do we meet with in the world, and what little right had we to expect to find such principles and feelings in one who has all his life been treated as a complete outcast from society; riches may make men great, in the common acceptation of the word, but it is only virtue that can make them noble or worthy of respect. In honest Stephen Gadsby we view one of Nature's true noblemen, though his home is but a wretched hovel, unfit for human habitation, and his clothing is only composed of rags."

"You are right, my dear sister," said Laura, "and need I say how much I admire and applaud the sentiments to which you have just given utterance? But come, the night wears apace, and we had better seek repose."

Before they did so, however, they dropped on their knees and offered up a fervent prayer of thanksgiving to Heaven, and earnestly supplicated its future protection. And blissful were the visions that haunted the imagination of Mrs. Langstone that night, glowing with hope, and blissful promise for the future. Again she beheld her husband seated by his comfortable fireside, all traces of care and dissipation removed from his countenance, and in their place, smiles of health and happiness beaming on his manly brow. Once more their children gambolled in playful innocence around them; they gazed upon the green sunny fields from the window of their well-furnished apartment, and inhaled the perfume of the flowers with which their little and neatly arranged garden abounded. There were honest, hearty friends to greet them, too, with cheerful smiles, and words of kindness and respect; and not a pang they felt to disturb their peace, serenity, and content. Oh! what a blissful change was this, and well might the dreamer revel in the gladness of her heart. And happy was the effect that this vision had upon the spirits of poor Mary when she awoke. Hope and confidence animated her breast, and she felt, as it were, another being. And how delighted was Laura to behold the happy change which only a few short hours had wrought in the bosom of her so long suffering sister. She hailed it as the harbinger of future prosperity, and did all she could to continue her in the same state of mind. Mary related her dream to her, and dwelt on it with feelings of the most unbounded delight.

"Oh, dear Laura," she ejaculated, "what a different being do I feel since that blissful vision has occurred to my imagination; and something seems to assure me, and to inspire me with the hope that it will be realised."

"Continue to encourage that hope, Mary," returned her sister, "and rest satisfied that it will not be disappointed."

"I feel confident that it will not," said Mrs. Langstone with increased animation; "I have suffered severely, but never will I murmur at the past, if such happiness is in store for me."

"It is, dear Mary," replied Laura, "your self-devotion and resignation will meet their due reward; your troubles are now at an end."

With lighter hearts than had throbbed in their bosoms for many a day, they sat down to their morning repast, and it was scarcely concluded when a knock at the door announced the arrival of Stephen Gadsby, whom they hastened to welcome with their usual friendship and cordiality. Gadsby was attired in a new suit of clothes, and such was the alteration they made in his appearance, that had it not been for his smiling, good-humoured face, he could scarcely have been recognised as the same individual.

"Good morning, Mrs. Langstone," he said, "good morning—Miss Maysdale; I am glad to see you looking so cheerful, and this will be a *good* morning too, and such a one as you have not experienced for some time."

"Thank you, Mr. Gadsby," said Mrs. Langstone, "for those kind hopes and wishes. I feel indeed inspired with confidence, and God knows that it would break my heart if I should be doomed to be disappointed."

"Do not entertain such a thought," said Stephen, "for there is no fear as to what will be the result of this day. Keep up your spirits, Mrs. Langstone, and I promise that in a few hours your husband shall be restored to liberty."

"Oh, blissful thought!" ejaculated Mary, clasping her hands, and tears of joy rushing to her eyes; "dear Edward, with what anxiety do I wait to embrace and welcome you."

"Ah! Mrs. Langstone," observed Gadsby, "this has been a severe trial for you, and I wonder how you have found strength to support it; but you will be rewarded for all in the happiness of the future, or I am much mistaken. At any rate, such is the sincere wish of Stephen Gadsby."

Mrs. Langstone again returned her thanks, and the observations of Stephen Gadsby inspired her with fresh hope.

"But are you now going to the police office?" she inquired.

"Yes, ma'am," answered Stephen, "and I have no doubt that a couple of hours will settle the business."

"So soon," ejaculated Mrs. Langstone, an expression of joyful anticipation passing over her features."

"Yes, Mrs. Langstone," replied Gadsby, "as there are no witnesses to examine, and no prosecutor to make his appearance, it cannot last many minutes, and it will be impossible for the magistrates to detain your husband any longer in custody. That is as clear as the sun at noonday, and they must be very ignorant persons indeed who would attempt to dispute it.

"Thank God!" cried Mary, vehemently.

"Yes, Mrs. Langstone," resumed Gadsby, "rest assured that I would not flatter you with vain hopes for the world."

"I do believe you," said our heroine, "but have you seen Captain Braghall this morning?" Stephen replied in the negative.

"He will be at the court, of course?" said Mrs. Langstone.

"Certainly," replied Gadsby, "leave the worthy gentleman alone for that."

"And he will want to accompany you here, no doubt."

"He will, I dare say, but I will disapoint him if possible, for I well know how painful and embarrassing his presence would be to you on such an occasion."

"Oh," ejaculated Mary, "I could not look upon him without betraying my real feelings, but surely he will have the delicacy not to intrude himself upon me under such trying circumstances."

"As for his delicacy, Mrs. Langstone," returned Stephen, "I do not think that is a quality that he can boast of possessing; however, I will prevent him from coming if possible."

"Do that, my kind friend," said Mary, "and how greatly will you add to the numerous obligations I already owe you."

"You may depend upon me, ma'am," said Gadsby, "and therefore do not alarm yourself. Keep up your spirits, and in a short time you may expect me to return, accompanied by your husband."

"God grant that it may be so," ejaculated Mrs. Langstone, "oh, with what impatience shall I count the moments till your return."

"Take my word for it, Mrs. Langstone," said Stephen, "that I will be no longer than I can help. But I must be going, for the business of the court will commence presently. Farewell for the present, and hope for the best."

"Heaven bless you, kind-hearted man," said Mrs. Langstone fervently, and pressing his hand with a feeling of gratitude to which she found it impossible to give adequate expression Stephen Gadsby waited to hear no more, but bowing respectfully to her and Laura he quitted the room, and hastened on his important and humane errand. As soon as he was gone, Mrs. Langstone sunk on her knees, and earnestly supplicated the Almighty not to disappoint her anxious hopes, but to restore her unfortunate husband speedily to her arms; and in that prayer Laura most ardently joined.

"How terrible must be the doubt and suspense he is now suffering, when his fate hangs upon a thread," she ejaculated; "and should anything occur to disappoint the hopes we now entertain, his fortitude, his reason, must sink under the overwhelming blow."

"My dear sister," expostulated Laura, "why will you persist in torturing yourself with such groundless fears? All evidence of the offence with which Edward is charged is removed, and nothing can prevent his restoration to liberty. Pray compose yourself, and prepare for the trying and affecting meeting which will shortly take place. Remember your dream of last night, and be firm and confident. The dark clouds which have so long obscured the horizon of your happiness have nearly dispersed, and the moment of renewed prosperity is rapidly approaching. Come, come, Mary, smile again as you did a short time since."

Mrs. Langstone threw her arms affectionately around her sister's neck, but her emotions were too powerful to suffer her to speak. At length, however, she became more calm, and hope once more animated her bosom.

"I place the utmost reliance on the assurances and sanguine anticipations of Stephen Gadsby,' observed Laura, "for they are prompted by reason and truth, and so you must yourself acknowledge, Mary, when you calmly reflect."

"I do, I do," answered Mrs. Langstone; "but you will bear with my weakness, I am sure, dear Laura, knowing as you do the feelings that at present agitate my bosom."

"Oh, yes, Mary, indeed I do," said her sister, "but it will soon be over; the gloomy past will be forgotten, and the feelings of anguish it has so long been your hard lot to endure will give place to these of the most rapturous joy."

"I will endeavour to believe so," said Mary, "and in that hope find consolation for the heavy afflictions with which it has pleased the Almighty to visit me."

"Well spoken, my dear sister," returned Laura, "and amply will you be rewarded for your patience and resignation under troubles that were sufficient to crush the strongest spirit."

With such gentle words as these, did the affectionate Laura soothe the feelings of her sister; but as the time flew away, and the hour drew nigh at which the result of the important and painful event was expected to be made known to them, she found it impossible to control her suspense and agitation. The time that had elapsed since Stephen Gadsby had left them seemed an age, though it was little more than an hour, and again did the most torturing misgivings and forebodings take possession of Mary's mind, which her sister, notwithstanding her most strenuous efforts, found it impossible to dissipate.

"It is all over," she sighed; "the hopes we too fondly entertained are disappointed, and Stephen Gadsby is afraid to return to announce to me the fatal truth."

"For Heaven's sake, Mary," replied Laura, "do not give way to such dreadful thoughts as those, which are as unreasonable as I feel assured they are fallacious. Recollect, that the time is only short since Mr. Gadsby quitted us, and that it is utterly impossible for him to return so soon. You may, however, depend upon his promise—namely, that he will not keep you a moment longer in suspense than he can help."

At this moment the sound of carriage wheels were heard rattling over the stones along the street, and which seemed approaching the house in which the anxious wife resided. The sounds had almost an electrical effect upon her and Laura, and without being able to utter a syllable, they both simultaneously sprang to the window, just as a cabriolet stopped at the door. How the heart of poor Mary palpitated against her side as the driver alighted from his box, and approaching the door, raised his hand to the knocker, and struck what might have seemed to have been, to any thoughtful individual acquainted with the facts that have been detailed in this narrative, a peal of hope and consolation to the so long afflicted heart of our unfortunate heroine. Laura, too, was so deeply agitated, that she could not utter a sentence: but they were not long kept in suspense; the door was immediately opened by the good, kind landlady of the house, who has been already introduced to the reader, and from the vehicle first sprang Stephen Gadsby, who instantly assisted in alighting from it the careworn Edward Langtone, who, casting up his eyes towards the house, his countenance became fully revealed to his anxious wife and the affectionate Laura.

"He is saved!—he is rescued!" exclaimed Mary. "God of Heaven! for this, Thine infinite mercy, I thank Thee. Edward!—Edward! I——"

She could not finish the sentence; her emotions overpowered her, and she sank insensible in the arms of her sister, just as the room door was thrown open, and Edward Langstone, followed closely by Stephen Gadsby, entered the room.

"Mary—my wife—my devoted—my much-wronged wife!" cried Langstone, in a voice half stifled by the intensity of his feelings; and he snatched her inanimate form to his bosom, and wept like a child, whilst the humane Stephen stood by in silence, and watched all that took place with the deepest sympathy and the most lively interest.

STEPHEN GADSBY, MARY LANGSTONE AND LAURA, AT THE NEW HOUSE.

CHAPTER XIII.

THE RESTORATION.—INTERVIEW BETWEEN EDWARD LANGSTONE AND CAPTAIN BRAGHALL.—VILLANY DISAPPOINTED.

WITH what emotion, far more powerful than any language could do justice to in description, did the expatriated Edward Langstone press his still lovely and amiable wife to his bosom; and what tears of mingled rapture and remorse did he shed upon her pale cheeks. Feelings, such as he had not experienced for many a day, struggled in his breast, and to which he in vain tried to give vent. Again and again he pressed warm kisses of the most ardent affection upon her lips, and sought to restore her to sensibility by every affectionate means that his feelings could suggest at the moment. He seemed totally unconscious of the presence of any other persons but themselves, whilst Laura and Stephen Gadsby stood by, and gazed upon them with feelings of the deepest commiseration, but not for the world would they have attempted t⁰ interrupt him, well knowing how exquisite must be the unlimited indulgence of his emotions be to him at that moment.

" How beautiful still," at length sighed Edward Langstone, as he parted the glossy tresses that had flowed negligently on his wife's forehead ; " how beautiful still, notwithstanding all the care which my accursed guilt has implanted on her brow. Oh, wretch ! wretch ! that I have been, to cause such a wreck as this."

The two eldest children were clinging to his knees, and whilst tears of joy were streaming down their innocent cheeks, they looked up in his face, and sobbed in scarcely articulate sounds—

" Father, dear father ! oh, why have you been so long away ?"

He started, as if suddenly aroused from a dream, and fixing his eyes upon them with an intensity of expression, which no language could adequately pourtray, he ejaculated—

" My poor injured innocents, helpless victims of my villany ; and do you indeed recognise and welcome the misguided author of your being ? Oh, God ! oh, God ! this is too much !"

" Edward—brother," said Laura, as she gently took the insensible form of her sister from his arms, and placed her on the the sofa ; " be calm for the love of Heaven ! This is the hour of joy ; let the dreary and hateful past now for ever be buried in oblivion."

He started aghast at her voice, trembled convulsively in every limb, and staring at her for an instant with a wild and vacant expression, covered his face with his hands, and groaned aloud in the depth of his anguish and remorse.

" Edward," said Laura, in her sweetest and most soothing accents, and laying her fair hand gently on his ;—" why this emotion on beholding the sister of your wife, and one who would, Heaven knows, willingly lay down her own life to serve you or her?"

" I know it ; I know it," ejaculated Edward Langstone, in a hoarse voice, and still averting his look ; " and 'tis that which tortures me more than all. Do not touch me ; do not come near me ; do not speak to me ; for every word that you utter is a dagger to my heart. Oh, what a wretch, what a miserable, degraded, unprincipled wretch I am !"

" Edward," said the astonished Laura, " what means this violent emotion ? Why do you shrink thus appalled from the sister of your wife, who has ever been your friend and best wisher ?"

" Yes, there it is," gasped forth Langstone, with a shudder of horror and the most incontrollable compunction, " my friend, my well wisher, my sister ; oh, God ! and how have I repaid you ? By the basest ingratitude ; by conspiring against your future happiness ! Oh, villain ! villain !—I—I—shall choke !"

He sunk exhausted by the power of his emotions in a chair, and the agony of his feelings was quite distressing to behold. Stephen Gadsby, unwilling to be a witness to the scene which was likely to follow, and fearful of being considered intrusive and inquisitive, respectfully retired from the room. The observations of her brother-in-law had completely astonished Laura, and she was at a loss to understand them, but she did not attempt to interrupt him, and soothing the poor children, who were greatly alarmed by the scene which was so far beyond their innocent comprehension, she turned her whole attention towards the recovery of her sister. It was not long before Mary once more opened her eyes, and passing her fair hands across her brow as if she would bring her scattered thoughts together, she looked vacantly around the room. Laura was at her side in an instant, and endeavoured to draw her attention towards her, but Mrs. Langstone did not seem to recognise her, or any other individual in the room, and in wild accents she ejaculated—

" No—no—they would delude me with false hopes ; he is not here, I shall never behold him more. His terrible doom is sealed ; why then mock and torture me thus ? Surely I have suffered enough to satisfy the malice of the most deadly enemy. Oh, Edward, dear, dear Edward, why am I deprived of you ?"

" Mary," said Laura, laying her hand on her shoulder, and speaking in the most affectionate accents, " why these dismal ideas ? You are labouring under no delusion, happiness is in store for you, all is over now ; Edward is here—he is restored to you, never more to be separated from you until death."

" Edward ! dear, dear, Edward !" exclaimed Mrs. Langstone, aroused by her sister's observations, and rushing frantically towards her husband, and throwing her arms around his neck, " All Merciful God, Thou hast heard my prayers ; I once more embrace the partner of my soul, my whole affections the only solace of my life, and to Thee I bend the knee of humble, but earnest gratitude, and will no more murmur at the trials and sufferings of the past. Edward ! dear Edward !—do you not hear your own fond wife ? Oh, look up ! speak to me ! let me hear the tones of your voice, and render my happiness complete."

Edward Langstone did indeed look into the lovely countenance of his affectionate wife, she who had suffered so much for his sake, and through his improvidence and guilt, with an expression which spoke more, ay, much more than volumes could possibly have done; his whole soul was in his eyes; his heart palpitated against his side with an emotion as though it would burst its tenement; he tried to speak, but for a moment utterance was denied him, heavy sobs swelled his manly bosom, large tear-drops rolled down his cheeks, and, enfolding his wife in one fervent embrace, the whole torrent of his remorse and gratitude burst forth in one unrestrained display of feeling. Thus they continued locked in each other's arms for several minutes, and Laura stood by, and never for an instant attempted to interrupt the exquisite feelings she knew they must at that moment be experiencing, and in which she so warmly and sincerely participated.

"Oh, Mary, deeply injured wife," at last Edward Langstone found words to articulate; "and can you indeed thus receive and welcome the wretch who has caused you so much misery? Never did I feel the consciousness of the heartless villany of which I have been guilty more severely than I do at this moment. It is more than I can bear. I shudder to look into your careworn countenance, every lineament of which presents an appalling index to my enormous crimes, and makes me shrink within myself. Nay, twine not your arms so fondly around me, poor sufferer! you should rather shun me as you would one of the most loathsome things in creation. You should hate me, despise me. Methinks your hatred to me now would be even more welcome than the fondest love you could possibly lavish upon me."

"Edward, dear Edward," gasped forth the distracted wife, embracing him still more vehemently, but at the same time shuddering with horror at his wild observations, and the extreme agitation of his whole demeanour; "oh, forbear, I beseech you—what awful words are those to which you have just now given utterance? Have I not ever loved you? Has not my conduct proved it?—and the hard lesson it has been our lot to learn in the school of adversity, but makes me love you more. Away with the past—it has been only a frightful dream, to teach us how to appreciate as we ought to do the illimitable blessings which a beneficent Almighty has provided for the humblest of His creatures. Husband, beloved husband, you are restored to me, and, though the most abject poverty it may be our fate to have to encounter and endure, we will be happy and contented."

"Best of women!" exclaimed Edward, as he still pressed her to his heart with more than the warmth of their most youthful love; "thine immaculate—thine unexampled virtues have indeed aroused me from a frightful vision, and made me once more feel worthy of the name of man. Great God! hear the prayer of a repentant sinner, and give me power to make more than ample atonement for my past errors, and if ever I deviate from the feelings which now prompt me, may Thy heaviest curse descend upon my head and crush me. Oh, Mary, Mary, I cannot give expression to the feelings that now rush tumultuously through my bosom; it seems as though my heart would leap from my breast with extacy; the ponderous clouds which have so long obscured the horizon of my reason melt away like snow beneath the genial influence of the sun, and I feel as if I were another man, a being newly created and ordained for the noblest pursuits of nature. Oh, what a glorious change is this. Let us kneel, my Mary, and pour forth our humble thanks to that Supreme Being that has been the cause of this."

Devoutly and solemnly Mary, her husband, and Laura knelt down, and raised their hands and grateful eyes towards Heaven, and the two children involuntarily followed the pious example which was thus set them, and in the most plaintive and impressive accents lisped forth the words their parents uttered. It was a scene which must have moved the stoutest heart to witness, and which the painter would have delighted to sketch. It calmed their emotions—it tranquilized their feelings, and when they again arose from their knees, they felt more happy and confident than they had been for many months previously. They spoke not a word, for their hearts were too full of gratitude, but Edward and his wife, now seated side by side before the cheerful fire, and Laura bustling about to prepare the plentiful meal, which for so many months had been a stranger to Edward Langstone, they experienced all the happiness it had been their lot to enjoy ere misfortune had stepped in to interrupt it. Edward cast his eyes around the room, and the comforts it presented so strongly contrasted with the wretchedness and squalor in which he had left his wife and children, completely overpowered him, and, in spite of all his efforts to the contrary, he could not refrain from tears.

"Oh, what a change is this," he said, "and how totally unworthy do I feel myself of it. To whom are we indebted, Mary, for all this unexampled kindness.

"To our dear Laura and her benevolent mistress," answered our heroine.

"To Laura," said Langstone, in a faint voice, and once more averting his face, as a shuddering feeling of horror and remorse came over him; "oh, how little do I deserve this. Wretch, miscreant, villain, that I have been."

"Edward, dear Edward," said his wife, with looks of astonishment and alarm, "for Heaven's sake, what mean you?"

"Do not ask me, I implore you," groaned Edward Langstone, "for I dare not—cannot answer you. Oh, Mary, did you but know all, you would say that I have indeed been a villain, and in spite of the affection you now bear towards me, you must look upon me with disgust and detestation. Laura, too, how much must she despise me, if she knew the injury I have done her."

"Edward," said the generous-hearted Laura, "for God's sake do not torture and reproach yourself thus. You must be labouring under some fearful delusion, the effect of the suffering to which you have been lately subjected, for confident do I feel that you could never wilfully injure me by thought or deed."

"Oh, forbear, forbear," cried Mr. Langstone, striking his breast, "for this generous, this unmerited confidence is more torturing than all. I tell you again that I have acted with the basest ingratitude and the most dastardly and unnatural villany towards you, Laura; but I will repent, and try to make that reparation to you which justice demands. But advantage was taken of the wretched and degraded state to which I had reduced myself, and—"

He could not finish the sentence, but covering his face with his hands, groaned in the anguish of his remorse. Mary again threw her arms around his neck, and while she affectionately endeavoured to calm his feelings, she said—

"Edward, what words, what fearful words are those you utter? What do you thus accuse yourself?"

"Do not interrupt me, Mary," said her husband in reply, and with increased emotion, "for the words would choke me. Let it suffice that I speak the truth, and bitterly does my conscience reproach me for it. But I will yet cast away the damning stain, and release myself from the trammels in which in my moments of madness and guilt I supposed myself to be entrapped."

He was interrupted by a knock at the room-door, and Stephen Gadsby entered.

"I beg your pardon," said the simple, but noble-hearted fellow; "I beg your pardon for again obtruding myself upon you, but as I must be gone on a little business, I thought, perhaps, you would not think me too bold in just calling in to bid you good day, and to wish you future happiness."

"My generous-hearted friend," said Mrs. Langstone, "without whose aid, Heaven only knows what would have become of us, we owe you a debt of gratitude which no language can properly express, and which I fear we shall never have it in our power to repay. I pray you be seated, for we must not part thus."

Stephen took a seat accordingly, and he then said—

"Once more I must request you, Mrs. Langstone, not to thank me for having done no more than what was my duty. I am more than rewarded, indeed I am, by witnessing the present happy scene. Did I not tell you, Mrs. Langstone, that all my hopes would be realized, and that I should not return again to you without being accompanied by your husband? Oh, we came off most triumphantly, and I am so rejoiced at the circumstance, that I scarcely know how to contain myself."

Edward Langstone grasped his hand vehemently, and for some moments he could not give utterance to a syllable, but at length he said—

"Mr. Gadsby, excellent man; how can I sufficiently testify the gratitude I feel towards you? You saved me from the perpetration of a hideous crime, the bare contemplation of which chills my blood with horror. You rescued my unfortunate wife and her innocent offspring from an untimely fate. You have devoted your whole energies towards her protection since I have been separated from her; you sustained and encouraged her under her heavy afflictions. It is to you and you alone that I owe my restoration to liberty, and—"

"Now—now—now," interrupted the poor fellow, impatiently, "I must beg that you will cease, for, upon my soul, I cannot bear it; I am one of the worst fellows in the world to stand flattery, and I do believe that if there is one particular quality I possess more than another, it is a feeling of modesty which I was never able to conquer in my life. God bless you all. May you be as happy as the days are long in future, and I hope that you will not think Stephen Gadsby unworthy of your friendship."

"Our friendship," repeated Langstone, again shaking him cordially by the hand; "oh, that is by far too mild a term by which to express the feeling we must ever entertain towards you. Our most unbounded esteem must be your's. Oh, that I had followed your noble example, what months of misery and degredation would it have saved myself and those who are so dear to me."

"Well, let us drop the subject, Mr. Langstone," said Stephen Gadsby, "I am no better than I should be, I feel satisfied; but I hope to improve as I grow older. There is one thing, however, which I suppose I need not intimate to you."

"And what is that, my friend?" asked Mr. Langstone.

"Why that Captain Braghall is one of the most consummate hypocrites and scoundrels in existence," answered Stephen.

"He is," said Edward, "and yet to him I am partly indebted for my restoration to liberty."

"Ah, do not let that trouble you," observed Gadsby; "you are nothing indebted to him for the interest he has pretended to take in your fate, which I suppose you know. He imagines that it will serve to forward his guilty designs; but he will find himself mistaken. It strikes me that they will all recoil upon himself, and I will readily lend my hand to bring about such a desirable result."

Langstone shuddered and looked confused, for he felt certain that Stephen Gadsby perfectly penetrated Braghall's intentions, and he was fearful that he might have become acquainted with the guilty compact into which they had entered together, and if so, what a degraded miscreant must he appear in that honest-hearted man's eyes. Gadsby seemed to read his thoughts, and he therefore alluded no more to the subject at present, while in the presence of Mrs. Langstone and her sister.

"It was a good job, however," he said, after a pause, "that we prevailed upon him not to accompany us here, for I know that his company would have been anything but agreeable to Mrs. Langstone and Miss Laura."

"Very true," said Langstone, "and I am indebted to you for preventing him. But I fear that we shall find it rather a difficult matter to rid ourselves of him altogether."

"Oh, I do not fear anything of the sort," said Stephen; "if you only act with determination."

"You seem to possess great influence over him, Mr. Gadsby," said Langstone.

"Why I think I have obtained a little," replied Stephen, "and I will not fail to take advantage of it. You may be certain, Mr. Langstone, that Stephy Gadsby will always have his eyes open, and that they will have to rise very early in the morning—and then to come all the way by a special train—to take him in. Ha! ha! ha!—Come, come, my friend, let us have no more sad thoughts, but live in hopes that all your sorrows are at an end, and that henceforth your enjoyments will be as abundant as the misfortunes you have hitherto experienced."

It was not without much persuasion they prevailed upon Stephen to remain till the repast was over, so fearful was he that he might be intruding upon the privacy of Edward Langstone and his wife; but at length he took his leave, and promised to call upon them again on the following day, and in the meantime to endeavour to ascertain all he could as to the future designs of the villain Captain Braghall. When he had departed, Laura, who felt that her sister and her husband might have many things to communicate to each other which her presence might obstruct, retired from the room, taking the children with her, and for a time sought the worthy landlady of the house. When Edward Langstone and his affectionate wife were left alone, they again gave the most unrestrained indulgence to their feelings of delight and gratitude, in silence, and embraced each other with transport. All the sorrows of the past, in that moment of exquisite pleasure, were forgotten, and they were only conscious of their present happiness.

"Oh, Mary—beloved Mary!" at length said Edward, looking into her face with all that affection and admiration which had characterised his youthful love; "and you indeed forgive your truant husband for all the miseries he has caused you?—Do you believe his feelings are at length awakened to remorse, and that he is anxious by his future conduct to show that he would only be too happy to make to you all the reparation which is in his power?"

"Edward—dear Edward," replied his wife, while tears of the fondest love bedewed her cheek, "why thus address me? Can you doubt the rapture which at this moment is glowing in my bosom at your restoration to me—or the confidence that I feel in the continuance of the happiness it has pleased the Almighty to shower upon us?—It was not my Edward's heart that for a time committed itself, but a fearful dream that had obscured his reason, and made him the unfortunate victim of designing miscreants. Forgive you, my love—husband—oh! how sweet is the thought that prompts me to say I feel more joy now in your awakening from that frightful dream, than even I did in your brightest moments of reason. But we will forget the dismal past, and devote ourselves alone to the completion of the happiness of the future."

"Best of women," cried Edward, "my tongue cannot find words to speak the eloquence and gratitude of my heart. Wretch—wretch, then, must I have been ever to have caused you y single pang. Never did I feel my own self debasement and villany more than I do at the present moment."

"Edward!" gasped forth our heroine, gazing reproachfully in his face.

" Yes, yes," he said, " I was wrong and uncharitable to doubt you. Pardon me, Mary, for the events of the last few hours have so bewildered my brain with delight that I scarcely know what I say. Oh, Mary, you desire me to forget the past, but I cannot do so ; it is from these reminiscences that I derive at once my just punishment—nay shudder not, dearest—and my future hopes. It is from them that I feel that I am more likely to be stimulated once more to enter the path of rectitude and honour. The errors that I have committed present, from the miseries they were productive of, such a powerful contrast to the joys, the content, and respect which I experienced when pursuing a course of virtue, that I think I can never deviate from the latter, course again. Oh, who that has once been initiated into the awful school of vice, would not if the glorious opportunity were afforded them, throw aside the galling and degrading fetters that enslaved their reason, and burst once more into the golden sunshine of rectitude and a clear conscience ? Dear wife, what mingled thoughts of horror, remorse, self-reproach, and yet of happiness and hope have I not experienced since my separation from you. What opportunities have I had dearly purchased, of recalling to the recreant memory, life's chequered history. I have once trodden the flowery path of my youth, when a thought of wrong to human being had never gained an entrance to my breast, and you, my sweet, gentle Mary, were by my side, stimulating me by your own bright, yet unassuming example to deserve you. Oh, what moments of bliss were those, and how could I ever have become the madman to sacrifice them ? I have seen the same verdant pasture—the happy homes of our beloved parents ; seen your heavenly smiles—heard your jocund laugh ; seen your light and agile form bounding over the verdant hills of our native land ; I have heard the feathered warblers carolling their sweetest notes at early dawn, as if to cheer us on to love, and in unison with our feelings ; the honied perfume of innumerable flowers has come as fresh to my senses as it did in those halcyon days ; all this I have seen and heard in the gloomy precincts of my dungeon, and when the stigma of the felon was resting on my head, and——"

" Oh, Edward, dear Edward," interrupted his wife, throwing her fair arms around his neck, and sobbing upon his bosom ; " forbear, forbear, I supplicate you ; do not thus torture yourself by harrowing reflections."

" Mary—Mary," returned Edward Langstone, " you must, you will, I implore, suffer me to proceed. What I utter is but a confession of the soul, and which if kept locked within my own bosom, would but drive me to distraction. It is such reflections as these I have described that have aroused me to a full sense of the fatal errors I have committed, and which I trust will be the means of preventing me from again rushing into crime. Yes, my beloved Mary, all these thoughts have occurred to me, and then came the black — the disgusting contrast which was presented by my dereliction from the paths of virtue. Oh, how awful was it—how did I shudder when I reflected upon the misery which I had brought upon you and our poor children ; the patience and resignation with which you had borne my cruelty, and all the brutal words I had uttered to you. The pale and emaciated looks of you and my poor innocent, helpless offspring were ever present to my imagination ; they were the ghastly visions that haunted me sleeping. or waking, and aroused me slumbering conscience. I remembered the fearful night when I contemplated and attempted the innocent lives of you and them, and I thanked God, in the whole fulness of my heart, for having by His most merciful interposition prevented me from becoming so hideous a criminal. And then the frightful vision that occurred to me that night would return to me in the most vivid and impressive colours ; and the warning words of the invisible being ; they were these, Mary ; I have never ventured to repeat them to you before :—'Wretch ! behold the work of thine hands ; go seek thy abandoned associates ; revel in riot and debauchery ; quaff again the maddening draught, and exult in the good it has already accomplished. Let the toast pass merrily round—hurrah ! for the workhouse and the jail ; the tap-room and the charnel-house !— the memory of the starved wife and her innocent offspring ! Heartless profligate, this is thy lesson !' "

Mary turned ghastly pale, and trembled convulsively in every limb, but she could not utter a syllable in reply.

" Such were the terrible words, much wronged wife," continued Edward Langstone, " and though they were only delivered to me in a vision, I feel satisfied that it was the voice of Heaven which spoke, for how awfully have they been realized. It was those reminiscences, my Mary, that awakened me from my dream of guilt, and may they never be eradicated from my memory, for I trust that they will be the means of preventing me rom again plunging into the vortex of crime, from the consequences of which I have so narrowly escaped."

Mrs. Langstone could return no verbal answer, but her looks expressed much more than words could have conveyed. For a few moments they both remained silent ; but at the same time, they both gave free indulgence to their feelings.

" Let us divert our thoughts from such dismal scenes, Edward," at length said our heroine ;

" it has pleased Heaven to restore us to each other, and let us be grateful for it, and endeavour to look forward to the future with the brightest hopes."

"I would fain do so, Mary," replied her husband, "but, alas! how can I in future support you and our children? What is to become of us? Is not my reputation gone for ever?"

"No, no," said Mrs. Langstone, "you must not give way to such feelings of despair, Edward; that All-merciful Power that has rescued you from the fate which threatened you will not leave us to perish. You will again obtain employment; your late kind and humane employer will pardon your errors when he is convinced how sincerely penitent you are, and receive you once more into his service. We shall soon be able to recover ourselves, never fear, and something seems to assure me that we shall be happier, if possible, than we have ever been yet. But, dear Edward, there is one question I must put to you, which I trust you will not now object to answer me."

"What is it, Mary?" demanded her husband, in a faltering voice, and partly guessing to what she alluded.

"That money, Edward, which was found upon you, when you—when you was appre-hended?"

Langstone groaned, trembled, and covering his face with his hands, could return no answer.

"Why this extraordinary emotion, Edward?" interrogated his wife, eagerly; "what terrible secret is it, that you should hesitate to divulge it to me?"

"For the love of God, Mary, do not ask me," answered Langstone, with a shudder of horror, which he found it utterly impossible to repress.

"Your words fill me with dismay; oh, banish this horrible suspense."

"I dare not—I dare not."

"You dare not?"

"No; you must look upon me with disgust and abhorrence."

"Oh, never! never! Edward; why do me such an injustice?"

"Heaven forbid that I should, Mary; but were I to reveal the truth, which can never pass my lips, you must hate me."

"Impossible, dearest Edward," said his wife, with increased agitation and alarm; "oh, why give way to such terrible ideas? Surely you wrong yourself. But, for Heaven's sake, do not keep me any longer in this state of mystery and uncertainty. As you love me, remove all doubts from my mind. Why should you wish to have any secrets from me? Have I not ever shown myself to be worthy of your confidence; and in any troubles that may have afflicted you, have you not ever had my warmest sympathy, my best advice and consolation?"

"Oh, yes, yes," answered Edward; "but again I implore you, in this instance, not to urge me; very shame will not permit me to let the secret pass my lips."

"Very shame!" repeated Mary, fixing upon him a look which seemed as if it would penetrate his soul.

"I have spoken the truth," he replied, with a groan of anguish; "oh, pity and spare me, Mary."

"This is most torturing—it is insupportable," ejaculated the agitated woman; "your hesi-tation, and the emotion you evince do but serve to increase my fears, and to excite terrible sus-picions in my breast that I would fain reject."

"Oh, Mary, I am a wretch, but I dare not reveal to you the whole of my villany. The accursed gold!—would that I had never seen a coin of it!"

"Tell me," gasped forth Mrs. Langstone, "for the ambiguity of your words, in spite of my wishes to the contrary, arouse the most terrible apprehensions in my mind, and I shall go distracted unless my fearful misgivings are removed. To obtain possession of so large a sum of money, you could not—oh, surely you could not have been tempted into any act of dishonesty?"

"Oh, no—no—no; villain though he has been, Edward Langstone was never yet a thief!"

"Oh, thank God, for that assurance!" cried Mary, clasping her hands vehemently to-gether.

"The money was a gift," faltered out the unhappy man; "but—but—oh, I cannot. I can say no more."

"A gift!" repeated his wife, "oh, who could have been so generous?—and why should you hesitate to reveal the particulars of such disinterested benevolence?"

"Benevolence, Mary," groaned her husband with a shudder.

" Yes, surely it must be the greatest of benevolence in any one who could perform such an act towards one who was in such a state of misery and destitution."

" It was the act of the most atrocious villany, and I must ever despise and loathe myself for being made the dupe."

"Mystery upon mystery," said Mary, " will nothing induce you to explain yourself to me, your wife, your affectionate and devoted wife, who can never reproach you for the past, but is only anxious to ease your mind of any cares that may oppress it, and to afford you all the consolation in her power?"

" Not now—not now," answered Edward, " my mind is too bewildered and distracted but at a future time I may find courage to reveal the whole painful truth to you, dear Mary, and to appeal to your mercy and forbearance."

" My mercy, my forbearance, Edward?"

" Yes, yes, alas! I shall much need them both."

Mary looked at him imploringly, but he averted his gaze, and shuddered.

" And is this money still in your possession, Edward?" she eagerly demanded at last.

" It is," answered Langstone, " would to God that it had never been, I should not now have had so bitterly to reproach myself; Mary, I purchased the gold at the price of honour, by the sacrifice of every manly principle."

" Great Heaven!" exclaimed the astonished and terrified Mrs. Langstone, "what fearful words are these you say, Edward? Surely your mind must wander!"

" No, no, I speak the truth, the blush of shame and disgust mantle in my cheek while I recall the degrading fact. Oh, spare my feelings for the present, Mary, I entreat; for you can form no idea of the torture you are inflicting on me by urging these painful though natural questions."

" Alas! alas!" sighed Mary, looking at her husband with a mingled expression of pity and reproach, " your words alarm me much more than the truth, however terrible it might be, could possibly do. I fear our troubles are not yet at an end, when I would fain hope, now that you are restored to me, that future happiness is alone in store for us."

" No, no," said Edward, " for your sake, my much injured wife, I trust that Providence will avert any future evils that may threaten us. I know full well, how torturing it must be to you to be kept in this state of suspense; but indeed, at present, I cannot find courage sufficient to remove it. But the time will come, I hope, when I shall be enabled to do so, and then all may end well. I would not appropriate a single coin of this ill-gotten money to my own use for the world, for it would, I am certain, bring down upon my devoted head the bitterest curses of offended Heaven. No, I will not have it in my possession many hours longer; I will return it to the polluted source from which I obtained it, and brave the worst that can befall me in consequence."

" Oh, Edward," said the trembling Mrs. Langstone, " for Heaven's sake, do not do anything too precipitately, and which you may afterwards have cause to repent. Have you reflected well upon this?"

" I have, Mary," answered her husband, " and nothing can alter my determination. When the hated gold is out of my possession, my mind may become more at ease, and I may hope by remorse and sincere repentance to make atonement for the act of villany it tempted me to be guilty of."

" An act of villany, Edward?"

" Yes, and such an one as sinks me in shame and degradation to reflect upon it.

"I dare not believe you, Edward," said his wife, " indeed you must be accusing yourself wrongfully."

" Oh, no," replied Langstone, " would to Heaven that I were, what a weight of care would it remove from my conscience. But let me once more implore you to drop this torturing subject for the present, Mary; you would, I know, could you but form an adequate idea of the torture it is inflicting on me."

" I yield to your wishes, Edward," sighed Mrs. Langstone, " although the suspense in which I am thus kept, and the painful and, perhaps, erroneous ideas I am compelled to form, are almost insupportable."

" I know it, Mary, and I pity you from my very soul."

" But you promise me that you will at some future time, probably before long, reveal to me the whole truth?"

" I do, I do, though you despise me ever afterwards; let that satisfy you."

" You must form a most ungenerous opinion of me, dear Edward," said his wife in a tone of gentle reproach " if you imagine that, under any circumstances, I can ever love you less than I do now. Has my conduct towards you since I have been your wife ever given you cause to entertain any such thoughts?"

"No, no, my Mary, my all gentle Mary," replied Edward Langstone, embracing his beauteous and deeply attached wife with a feeling of the utmost devotion to her superior virtues; "you have been all too good for me;—you have patiently endured all my ruffianly and disgusting conduct; without a murmur you have submitted to that which would have driven, many women whose minds were not cast in the same noble mould as your own, to acts of violence desperation, and revenge. Pardon me for what I have said, I beseech you, for indeed my

THE "STUNNER'S" SOLILOQUY OVERHEARD BY CAPTAIN BRAGHALL.

tongue runs riot with my reason, and I scarcely know what I say. Oh, without your wise counsel, your gentle admonitions, (which, in my madness of dissipation I so cruelly, so brutally disregarded,) what would have become of me? Without that fortitude prompted by your innate virtues and heroic devotion, what must have been the fate of you, myself, and our innocent offspring? God of Heaven! what a wretch have I been thus to abuse the love and generosity of one of thy fairest creations! Mary, Mary, I never felt my self-degradation more than now

I never more despised or loathed myself for the sufferings I have caused you and our little nnocents. Miscreant, unprincipled scoundrel that I have been, I deserve not to live any longer to degrade or to contaminate the earth by my loathsome presence, and yet how unfit am I to die."

He turned away with a violent burst of emotion, covered his face with his hands, and convulsive sobs of the most extreme and harrowing remorse escaped his bosom. Mary threw her fair arms once more affectionately around his neck, and whilst the tears streamed fast from her eyes, in a voice which expressed all the strength of her woman's love for her unfortunate and misguided partner, she ejaculated—

"Oh, Edward! my husband, my beloved husband, I implore you to forbear these cruel upbraidings of yourself, every word of which is a dagger to the heart of her who, through ill or weal, must ever be the same Mary to you that you knew her in her days of childhood. Come, come, dear, calm your anguish; we will be happy, for we are restored to each other—a bright sunshine bursts upon our future prospects; the tempest of our sorrows has subsided, and Heaven, in its infinite mercy, will prevent its dreadful recurrence. It is past now, dear Edward, it is past now, never more to return. I feel a delicious confidence in that fact; a firm reliance in the goodness of that Supreme, who, though He may try us in the school of adversity, never leaves the humblest of His creatures who place their trust in Him, and sincerely repent of the errors they may have committed, to perish in despair. It was wrong of me to urge you in the way I have done; but I know, my husband, that you will make every allowance for my anxiety, and the wish that I must always have to be the participator in your cares, so that I may have the opportunity of rendering you my fondest advice, and imparting to you that sweet consolation which affection and reason might suggest. But we will banish this gloomy subject for the present. Come, come, my love, we should be ungrateful to that all—merciful Providence, who has thus raised us from the most abject misery, were we to murmur now. Discard every dismal thought from your mind—we will be happy now!"

Edward Langstone turned upon his lovely wife a look, which expressed more, far more than the most eloquent language could possibly have done; he could not speak, for his emotions were too powerful for utterance, but his looks sufficiently evinced the feelings that had taken possession of his bosom.

CHAPTER XIV.

EDWARD LANGSTONE'S INTERVIEW WITH BRAGHALL.— THE QUARREL.—BRAGHALL'S VOW OF VENGEANCE.

WE will not dwell upon the blissful scene which followed the restoration of the unfortunate Edward Langstone to liberty, for we feel assured that the reader will be able to form a pretty just conclusion of it. The following day their spirits were all greatly reanimated, and they could converse more calmly than they had previously done; but still Mary Langstone felt the most anxious wish to be made acquainted with all the particulars of the money which had been found in the possession of her husband, more especially after the reluctance which he felt to gratify her curiosity, and the strange hints he had thrown out; however she forbore to question him any further at present, trusting that in due time he would no longer hesitate to remove the doubt and anxiety which had naturally gained an ascendancy in her bosom. Laura Maysdale seeing them now restored to comparative happiness, and fearing that she had already too far intruded upon the kindness of her mistress, thought it would be prudent for her to return to her situation, especially as she would, as formerly, have plenty of opportunities of visiting them, and of rendering them all the assistance in her power. It was not without some misgivings, however, that she did so; for when she remembered the dark hints that had been thrown out by Langstone and Stephen Gadsby, and well convinced as she was of the base thoughts which Braghall presumed to entertain towards her, she could not help fearing that she might yet experience no inconsiderable degree of annoyance from him. However, she would be under the protection of her master and mistress, and she therefore tried to banish such apprehensions from her mind. Edward Langstone now determined to seek an interview with Captain Braghall, in order that he might at once relieve his mind from the weight of self-reproach and degradation which oppressed it, and returning the money by which the unprincipled libertine had thought to have purchased his assistance in his nefarious schemes, renounce all further connexion with him. He did not think it prudent to make Mary acquainted whither he was going, as her fears and suspicions would doubtless at once have been excited, but left her under the impression that he was going to seek for employment, and immediately made his way towards the dwelling of the captain. Braghall had been in a very unsettled state of mind ever since the liberation of Edward Langstone, and he was anxious, yet dreaded to visit them, much doubting the reception he should meet with from them. He had seen and heard quite enough to convince him that Langstone repented of the agreement he had entered into with him, and that he had little, if anything to expect from his assistance; besides, he felt satisfied, from the care she took to avoid his presence, that Laura was well aware of the guilty designs he entertained towards her, and that she would not fail to use every precaution to frustrate them. He was likewise not altogether satisfied with Stephen Gadsby, and was rather doubtful whether or not he might be depended upon; and he felt convinced that it would be necessary to keep a strict eye upon him.

"He is a crafty fellow, I am satisfied," he observed; "and I cannot exactly fathom him. But could I only be certain that I could depend upon him, I might find him a most useful fellow indeed. I must see promptly after this business, for delay might be fraught with danger. I suppose it would be madness for me to expect any assistance from Langstone now, since he has become so penitent; however, his tongue must be silenced, if possible; for if my designs should become known, not only would they be most effectually frustrated, but it would also bring down upon me the scorn and opprobrium of the world; and I should never again be able to show my face in society. But, notwithstanding all the numerous difficulties and obstacles thrown in my way, I am fully determined to persevere, and I entertain but little doubt that in the end I shall be triumphant. Laura Maysdale may imagine that I shall be abashed and diverted from my purpose by her scorn and the power of her virtue; but I flatter myself that she will find herself mistaken. But it is not a trifle that will deter me from putting into execution any design upon which I may have fixed my mind; and I dare say I shall yet find means to accomplish my wishes, when they are least prepared for it."

He was interrupted in the midst of this soliloquy by a knock at the room door, and a servant made her appearance, who informed him a person was waiting below in the hall, who desired to see him.

"Is it male or female?" asked Braghall.

"A male, sir," answered the servant.

"Any one that you have seen here before?"

"Not to my knowledge."

"Did he not state his name?" demanded the captain.

The servant replied in the negative.

"Humph!" muttered Braghall, "who can it be? However, it is not likely to be any one that I have any cause to dread; so you may show him up."

There was no occasion to do that, however, for Edward Langstone at that moment made his appearance at the door. The servant retired, and Braghall motioned our hero to enter the room, and closed the door after him.

"So it is you, Ned?" said the captain, with the greatest familiarity.

"It is," replied Langstone, unceremoniously, and fixed upon Braghall no very agreeable look.

"Be seated, my good fellow, and make yourself quite at home," said the libertine, in the same bland accents, "I am extremely glad to see you, indeed I am."

"No doubt you are," returned Langstone with a sarcastic and reproachful expression of countenance.

"Upon my soul I am, my dear fellow," said Braghall;" of course, you do not doubt me? But you must take a glass of wine with me."

"No, Captain Braghall," said Langstone, with a look which showed the sincerity of the observations to which he gave utterance, "I would not again taste the pernicious drink, from the accursed influence of which I have suffered so much degradation and misery, even for the wealth of nations. Tempt me not, captain, for already have I experienced sufficient to make me more cautious for the future."

"Well, well, I will not press you," said Braghall, with apparent indifference, "since that is your whim. I hope you may always be able to adhere to such excellent and praiseworthy determinations."

Edward Langstone fixed upon him a look of contempt as he replied—

"No doubt you do, Captain Braghall, but this is quite irrelevant to the subject. I wish to have a little serious conversation with you, for it is time you and I came to a proper understanding."

"Ah, certainly, my good friend, I am quite ready to listen to what you have to say; proceed, proceed."

"Your villanous designs are known," said Langstone, boldly, and with the most marked emphasis. Braghall, who was quite unprepared for such a salute as this, started, and bit his lips.

"Langstone," he said, haughtily, and his blood glowing with mortified pride, "this language from you, and addressed to me?"

"Even so, Captain Braghall," replied Edward Langstone, coolly; "the time is gone by for mincing the matter, and I shall speak plainly, perfectly indifferent as to whether I offend or please."

"By jupiter, man!" exclaimed Braghall, "But," he added, "you are excited, and I will take no farther notice of it."

"And what think you I should care if you did?" demanded our hero, scornfully. "I owe you no respect; on the contrary, I do not hesitate to tell you that I loathe and despise you Ay, to your face I tell you this."

Captain Braghall took two or three hasty strides across the room, and it was quite evident that he had the utmost difficulty in subduing his passion; however, his excitement made not the slightest impression upon Langstone, who had come with the full determination of speaking his mind, let whatever might be the consequences, and he was not easily to be intimidated from his purpose.

"By G—!" Braghall exclaimed at last, turning to Langstone, "such language as this is not to be borne, and is such as I never expected to hear from you. Is this the return you make to me for all the trouble I have taken to save you from the ignominious fate which would in all probability otherwise have attended you?"

"You do well to remind me of this, Captain Braghall," said Edward, "but what were the base, the atrocious motives which guided your conduct? Was it not with the hope of forwarding your own villanous designs against the innocent Laura Maysdale that you assumed the character of disinterested benevolence that you have done? But I withdraw myself from your detestable plot, into which I was tempted in a moment of madness and weakness by the offer of your gold! Take back the hated dross; I would not appropriate a farthing of it to my own use were it to save my life. It has been a curse to me ever since I accepted it from you. Take it, I say, and may we never meet again."

Thus saying, Edward Langstone dashed the purse containing the gold which he had received from the libertine upon the floor at his feet; and his whole demeanour was such as was calculated to make the most powerful impression. Braghall was for a few moments completely bewildered and confounded by the determination of Langstone, and the boldness of his words, to attempt to make any reply. His conscience, however, would not allow him to deny the truth and justice of all that he had said, and he therefore felt the more abashed, and found it utterly impossible for him to attempt to justify his own conduct. At length, once more turning towards Langstone, he said—

"Are you mad, Langstone, that you thus give utterance to such observations as those you have just now given utterance to? Psha! man, you cannot mean what you say. Take up the purse, and its contents shall be increased a hundred fold, if you do but promise me that you will never repeat this folly, but, on the contrary, will steadfastly adhere to our first compact."

"Wretch!" cried Edward Langstone, his eyes flashing with indignation; "are you a man? Although you bear the form, your conduct proves you not to be so!"

"Be calm—be calm," expostulated Braghall, by a powerful effort restraining the ebullitions of his own rage: "there still must be some misunderstanding, although you say to the contrary. I am willing to make every allowance for——"

"You willing, despicable scoundrel!" interrupted Langstone: "ay, you may frown. I heed not your wrath; it is I who should feel indignant. But this is a waste of time: now, mark my words, Captain Braghall, and repent ere it be too late."

"Repent!" repeated Braghall, with a look of contempt.

"Ay, repent," answered our hero; "and if you be wise, and would shun disgrace and ignominy, you will not scorn the advice I give, notwithstanding your wealth and station in society. You may threaten me by exposing the whole that has passed between us; but let me ask you, Captain Braghall, whether you imagine you can do so without holding yourself up to public odium? Will it not be seen who is the actual criminal? Will it not be shown who was the common associate of the very refuse and most abandoned of society? Reflect coolly upon these facts, Captain Braghall, and it strikes me that you have not yet become so callous as to obstinately persevere in your present course. I have applied opprobrious epithets to you, I admit; but have you not given me ample cause, and have you not provoked me to do so?— Does not your conduct justify my observations? It does, and I maintain it. I am a poor man; you are rich, and by your position in the world, and the advantages of superior education which you have received over me, you are supposed to be enabled to set me an example of probity, of morality, and honour, instead of seeking to corrupt and vitiate my principles—to take a mean advantage of my poverty, and render me the abandoned wretch that I have been, and make me the instrument to the perpetration of a crime, as hideous as it is unnatural and revolting. Take back the wages of guilt, I say; leave me to myself—let me resume the principles that were instilled into my breast from the earliest period of childhood; abandon your monstrous designs, which can only recoil upon yourself—repent, I again adjure you, and by looking back with horror upon the scenes of your past life, and, by making all the atonement you can to those whom you have so deeply wronged, endeavour to render yourself worthy the name of a MAN!"

This lecture was delivered with the most impressive energy, and Captain Braghall absolutely quailed beneath it. He had never before formed the slightest conception of the powers of that mind, which he had for a season subjugated to his own base purposes, and towards the ruin of which he had so largely contributed.

Braghall traversed the apartment with hasty strides, muttering sentences to himself. At length he turned to Edward Langstone (who, having given free vent to his honest feelings of indignation and shame, had calmly resumed his seat, resolved that this interview should not be brought to a termination until he had arrived at a fair and satisfactory conclusion, and insured the future protection of Laura), and said—

"Why all this violence, Mr. Langstone? You accuse me too severely."

"Accuse you too severely," said Edward Langstone, with a look of scorn; "oh, can you still be so hardened in iniquity as to have the effrontery to tell me this? Is is not your design to work the destruction of the innocent sister of my wife? Would you not make me your too in the consummation of that atrocious act? And yet you say I accuse you too severely! Oh, this is surely most monstrous, and only adds to your guilt. But beware how you try my patience too far, for you might have bitter cause to repent it. Look to it, Captain Braghall, ere it be too late."

"Ah!" exclaimed the exasperated libertine, unable to control his temper, "would you dare to threaten me?"

"Threaten you," retorted Edward Langstone, contemptuously, "what is there so alarming about Captain Braghall, that I should be afraid to threaten him when I have truth and justice on my side? But I merely warn you, I do not threaten you; again I tell you to look to it."

"This is more than can be endured," cried Captain Braghall, passionately.

"Be calm, be calm, sir, those bursts of passion will have not the least effect upon me, I assure you."

"Do you seek to insult me?" demanded Braghall.

"No, I merely demand justice, and that I am at all hazards determined to have."

"Had justice been rendered you," retorted the enraged Captain Braghall, "you would at this moment have been a convicted felon instead of at liberty. Who rescued you from the doom which otherwise awaited you?—and this is the grateful return you make for the services I have rendered you."

"By Heaven!" cried Langstone, "I would sooner have met the felon's fate than have become the degraded, the despicable wretch you wish me to be. The blood congeals in my veins when I think of it, and I consider myself one of the most contemptible of human beings in condescending to argue the disgusting point with you."

"Did you not bind yourself by a solemn oath to assist me in those plans which you so loudly now condemn?"

"In a moment of madness and dissipation, of which you, coward-like, took a mean advantage, I admit I did," replied Langstone. "May Heaven pardon me for the deed; but think you that an oath extorted from any one under such circumstances, by a heartless wretch, is at all binding in the sight of that all just Power above?"

"A wretch!" repeated Captain Braghall, unable any longer to restrain his resentment within the bounds of reason; "dare you, Edward Langstone, apply that gross epithet to me?"

"Ay," returned Langstone, rising with manly dignity, "and to any other individual who deserves it. Nay, sir, you may frown as you please, your looks or words will not intimidate me, for I know that I have truth and justice on my side, and I will set all your puny efforts at defiance."

"Will you recall your words?"

"No!"

"Quit the house immediately."

"Not on your imperious mandate," was the firm reply.

"Are you resolved to exasperate me to commit violence?"

"Edward Langstone, humble though he be, laughs to scorn any violence that such a man as Captain Braghall can use towards him," answered our hero, coolly, and folding his arms.

The rage of Braghall was aroused to the utmost pitch; he could endure no more; all the wild and bad passions of his nature rushed with maddening and ungovernable fury to his brain, and darting at Edward Langstone with a dreadful oath, he endeavoured to grasp him by the collar, in order to force him from the room, but before he could achieve his object he was stretched at full length upon the floor by a violent blow from the clenched fist of Langstone, and at the same moment several servants, both male and female, alarmed at the noise of the scuffle, hastened to the room, and gazed amazed at the unusual and unexpected scene which presented itself.

"What is the meaning of this?" demanded one of the men.

"The meaning of it is, that your master is a consummate villain, a cowardly ruffian,' answered Edward Langstone, firmly, "and that he has got no more than his deserts."

"Seize the ruffian," cried Captain Braghall, fiercely, and gathering himself up in the best manner he could, "do not suffer him to escape, he grossly insulted and assaulted me."

"At your peril any one attempt to lay a finger on me, or seek to obstruct my departure from hence. It is he who has insulted me, and it will be well for him if he does not yet have dearly to repent of it. He knows where I am to be found, should he require any further explanation. Captain Braghall, when next we meet, I trust you will have learnt reason and justice."

The determined air of Edward Langstone, and the reasonableness of his observations, completely awed the servants, and no one offering to prevent him, fixing a look of abhorrence, scorn, and defiance upon Captain Braghall, he took his departure abruptly from the house, leaving his defeated adversary foaming with rage.

"Leave the room!" he commanded furiously, addressing himself to the astonished and bewildered servants, when he could first recover the power of speech, "leave the room, I say."

The servants, well knowing the violence of his temper, immediately obeyed, and he was left to himself. For some moments he could only give vent to the most bitter maledictions, but at length, in a hoarse voice, he said—

"To be thus mocked at, reviled, defied, insulted, struck a degrading blow: it is more than human patience can endure. Why did I act with so much forbearance? Why did I thus tamely brook his taunts? And yet, have I not ample reason to fear? I feel that I have, much as I may endeavour to persuade myself to the contrary. But shall I allow myself to be so defeated? Shall I permit him to laugh at me, and to defeat all my plans? He has it in his power to expose the entire of my guilt to the world; but still, for his own sake, I do not think he will be bold enough to do that? What is to be done? Let me reflect coolly, but now, I am in no condition of mind to do that at present. But I will not suffer myself to be trampled over thus, he shall be made to repent all; and much as he may think to escape me, I will have a terrible revenge yet. Yes, by all my hopes, I will; and though he may put Laura Maysdale on her guard, and adopt every possible means to protect her, she shall not escape me. It is perhaps as well that she should be suffered to remain in fancied security for the present, until I have had more time to mature my plans; and also it is as well that Langstone has thus openly avowed to me his intentions, for I shall know better how to cope with him, and to consummate the deadly revenge he has by his threats aroused within my breast. Yes, for this, Edward Langstone, I will adopt such means as shall wring your very soul to madness. But he will not be bold enough to expose me to the world, since by doing so he will but likewise reveal his own guilt. Let me endeavour to be calm, and I may yet triumph when they least expect it."

Thus the libertine endeavoured to reassure himself, and quaffing off a glass of wine, tried to consider what was best next to be done. Should Langstone reveal to Laura all the particulars of the designs he had in contemplation against her, which he could have very little doubt he would if he had not even done so already, the result would be anything but agreeable to him, and he should never be able to bear up against the exposure; however, in spite of all, he determined to proceed with his plot, since he had already advanced so far, and he had no doubt that by perseverance he should be enabled to surmount all the difficulties that might be thrown in his way. He could not altogether place confidence in Stephen Gadsby, who was evidently the warm friend of Edward Langstone and his wife, and therefore it was not likely that he would aid him in his nefarious designs against Laura, in whose safety their happiness was too much involved.

"And yet," he remarked, after a pause, "his silence must be secured by some means or other, if even I cannot obtain his assistance in my plot. For should he divulge all he knows, I should certainly find myself placed in a more awkward position than I am at present. I must see him again without delay, and at once come to a final arrangement of my plans for the future."

Thus did Captain Braghall seek to console himself for the temporary disappointment he had received, and to buoy himself up with the hope of future success, notwithstanding the present obstacles there seemed to be towards the accomplishment of his wishes. At length he walked from the house, with the hope of being enabled to regain that equanimity which had been somewhat disturbed by the events of the last few hours. He longed to behold Laura Maysdale again, but he was fearful of visiting the house of her relatives, with whom she resided, strangely suspecting that they were made fully acquainted with his designs, and consequently the kind of reception he was likely to meet with. But still he nurtured the most diabolical feelings of revenge against Langstone, whose recent attack upon him had not only mortified his pride, but likewise convinced him he had no child to deal with, and that he must be cautious, or he would not only be defeated in his plans, but also be held up to the scorn, the derision, and contumely of the world. He had not proceeded far, buried in these guilty meditations, and scarcely conscious of whither he was going, when a stoppage in the crossing he was about to make, caused him look up, when he beheld Stephen Gadsby standing before him.

"Ah, Mr. Gadsby," he said, with an assumed air, "you are the very man I wished to see. I hope you are quite well."

"Very well, captain," answered Stephen, with his usual coolness; I trust you are the same?"

"Yes, yes, thank you, perfectly so," returned Braghall, hastily, and with some confusion "but were you going to call upon me?"

"No, captain," replied Stephen, "I was not about to do myself the honour."

"I wish to speak with you, Gadsby," said Braghall, after a moment or two's hesitation.

"Very good, your honour, I am at your service."

"Enough," observed the captain, "let us retire into some tavern, where we may converse without fear of interruption."

"Agreed, captain," said Stephen Gadsby; "and there is one over the way that appears as though it would suit our purpose exactly. Shall we go there?"

CHAPTER XV.

STEPHEN GADSBY OPENS HIS MIND.—RAGE OF CAPTAIN BRAGHALL.—HE BEGINS TO FIND THAT HE MUST FIGHT A DESPERATE GAME, AND RESOLVES ACCORDINGLY.

IT was several minutes after their entrance into the room before the captain ventured to break the silence, for he was, in fact, considerably at a loss to know how to begin; but he eyed the countenance of his companion narrowly, with the hope of being enabled to discover the thoughts that might be passing in his mind; but Stephen maintained his accustomed coolness, and there was nothing in the expression of his features from which he was at all likely to gather the smallest information.

"Mr. Gadsby," at length he said; "I think it is now quite time that you and I should properly understand each other."

"Very good, your honour," coincided Gadsby, "I am perfectly agreeable."

"You will recollect, Mr. Gadsby," resumed Braghall, after another brief pause, "that I intimated to you that I should be glad to avail myself of your services on a future occasion, and that you stated you were quite willing to render them."

"In anything honourable, captain," rejoined Stephen Gadsby, pointedly and emphatically. Braghall, evidently, by his looks, did not at all like this reply, but he endeavoured to conceal his real thoughts from Gadsby, and said—

"Well—well, of course I should not propose anything which can be at all detrimental to your interests."

"I thank you, captain; then pray, in what manner can I serve you?"

"You are aware of the gratuitous services I have rendered to Mr. Langstone and his family."

"Your honour has certainly contributed in a great measure towards the restoration of Mr. Langstone to liberty, and I hope, and do believe sincerely, that what he has himself suffered, and been the cause of others suffering, and the narrow escape he has had, will act as a warning to him in future. But I think I have also rendered my humble aid in this good cause."

"You have, Mr. Gadsby, and there is great credit due to you for it. But there may be such a thing as ingratitude from those you serve."

"I do not exactly understand you, captain; what I have done has been entirely dictated by my own heart, and from motives of humanity alone, and I have seen nothing yet in the conduct of Langstone and his amiable wife, to make me regret it."

"You misconstrue my meaning," said the captain, rather abashed and confused at the observations of Stephen; "Listen to me."

"I am all attention, Mr. Braghall."

"I have done many acts of kindness towards Mr. Langstone, of which you are probably not aware."

"Well, that may be, captain, and if you have done so disinterestedly, and with no sinister motives, your own conscience, I should think, would be a sufficient reward."

"Pshaw! this is wandering from the point," said Braghall impatiently.

"Well, it may be, and you must excuse me, Captain Braghall, if you are not more explicit," returned Stephen Gadsby.

"Well then," said," said Braghall, "in the first instance I I must inform you that the money which was found in the possession of Edward Langstone, and which has caused so much supicion and mystery, was a voluntary gift from me."

"Indeed!" said Gadsby, with affected surprise, "that was very kind of you; but why not have explained this before?"

"Because it would have been exceedingly inconvenient for me to have done so at the time," answered the captain.

"No doubt of it," thought Stephen Gadsby; but he did not venture to express himself, for he was anxious to elicit all he could from Braghall in order to forward his own designs, and to serve those in whose welfare he felt so deep an interest.

"Edward Langstone has called upon me this afternoon," continued Braghall after a pause.

"Indeed!" said Gadsby.

"Yes," replied the captain, "and indignantly returned the money."

"Surely he must have had some strong motives for doing so, captain," remarked Stephen "money is a very tempting thing, especially to a man in his circumstances."

"True; and he must have been mad for so doing," said Braghall; "but to come at once to the point on which I wish to consult you and retain your services."

"Well, captain, I am anxious to hear you, so speak without any reserve."

"I will; Laura Maysdale is a lovely girl."

"She is, and as virtuous and amiable as she is beauteous," replied Stephen Gadsby, vehemently, "and he must be a heartless scoundrel who would seek to harm her by word or deed."

"You are warm, Stephen Gadsby," said the libertine, gazing upon the honest fellow with no small degree of confusion.

"I speak the sincere sentiments of my mind, Captain Braghall, and I care not who hears them," retorted Stephen.

"Tut, tut, tut," ejaculated the former, impatiently; "a truce with this—it is quite irrelevant to the subject."

"It may be so in your opinion, but, pardon me, I must also be permitted to entertain mine. Will you be kind enough to explain your business with me, for I am rather in a hurry?"

"Briefly then," replied Captain Braghall, mustering all his determination and effrontery to his aid, "the charms of Laura Maysdale have captivated my senses, and I wish to possess her; but she is coy and scornful, and I see the utmost difficulty in obtaining the gratification of my desires. You possess great influence with the family, and might render me most essential assistance in the accomplishment of my wishes, for which I will not fail to reward you to your heart's content. You are poor, but I have it in my power to make you independent, and——"

"Hold! Captain Braghall," indignantly interrupted Stephen Gadsby, suddenly starting from his seat, and fixing upon the libertine a look of the utmost resentment and disgust; 'let me hear no more of this. What a heartless and unprincipled scoundrel you must take me for, to suppose for a moment that I would pander to your atrocious designs against an innocent girl! Oh, shame, shame on you—you that call yourself a gentleman, to entertain such monstrous ideas! Ah, you may frown; I heed not your wrath, for I have justice on my side, and I boldly stand forward as the champion of innocence and virtue. I will speak my mind, in spite of all the consequences that may ensue to myself. Yes, I understand you, Captain Braghall, and have always done so, and it shall be no fault of mine if I do not thwart your diabolical schemes, and hold you up, as you deserve to be, to public odium and contempt! I am poor, it is true—but too proud and too honest to receive the wages of guilt. But your character is known, and therefore you may seek in vain to shelter yourself from the disgrace which your vices have entitled you to. I have now told you exactly what I think, and I therefore leave you to your own reflections, which no doubt will be of the most agreeable nature."

"Stay, Stephen Gadsby," exclaimed the confounded libertine ; " you will not surely leave me thus ; let me further explain myself, and I dare say we shall be able to come to a proper understanding."

"I have heard quite enough," replied Stephen, "and since I have fully disclosed to you my sentiments, there is not the least occasion to prolong this interview."

"Are you mad ?" demanded Braghall.

C L I N T O N.

"I think not," answered Gadsby; "but I should indeed be a villain, did I yield to your wishes. Good day, and reflect well upon what I have said, and abandon your guilty projects ere it be too late."

"One word more with you, Gadsby."

"You have already said more than enough."

"Shall I see you again ?"

"Oh, doubtless you will ; but think not to alter my determination the least in the world."

"Will no offers of reward prevail upon you ?"

"None whatever, though you had all the wealth of the universe to offer me ; and mark me, it will be well for you if you do not attempt to insult me by such a proposition."

"Threatened too," ejaculated Captain Braghall, biting his lips.

"I have no wish to do so," replied Stephen Gadsby; "but, as I have said before, nothing whatever shall prevent me from speaking my mind. But I have said all I wish to do at present, and will no longer be detained."

With these words, Stephen Gadsby abruptly quitted the room, and retired from the house, well satisfied with the manner in which he had treated the villanous proposals of Captain Braghall. For some minutes after Stephen Gadsby's departure, Braghall traversed the room in the most disordered state of mind, and muttering curses to himself. He now regretted that he had so fully divulged his thoughts and designs to Stephen Gadsby, and thus placed himself entirely in his power; for he had not the least doubt he would fully expose him, and thus the disgrace that would follow would be inevitable.

"Thwarted, despised, and dared on every side, he muttered to himself, "surely this is past all human endurance. But in spite of all the consequences that may follow they shall not escape me, notwithstanding she may flatter herself that she is safe under the protection of her friends. I have a desperate game to play, but I will not shrink from it, even though I lose my life in seeking to accomplish my wishes. I must, however, rest quiet for awhile, and they imagining that I have abandoned my designs, will be thrown off their guard, and the better be caught in my snares. Let me see, might not I gain some assistance from the rascals Hemlock and the Stunner ? They are desperate villains, and will do anything for money, especially when they know the situation they are placed in. It is unfortunate, however, that Gadsby is acquainted with their secret. I must see them upon the subject, and endeavour to ascertain what is best to be done. Let me endeavour to calm myself and reflect deliberately upon the best method to forward my designs. I must not, I will not suffer myself to be defeated easily."

He re-seated himself at the table, and quaffing off the best part of the contents of a glass of brandy and water, worked his mind up to a pitch of desperate determination. At length, however, he arose from his seat, and quitting the tavern, once more retraced his steps towards home. On arriving there he found a letter addressed to him, lying on the table, and hurriedly breaking the seal, he discovered it was from Clinton. He informed him that he had arrived safe in a remote part of the country, and succeeded in securing a retreat where he was not likely to be discovered or suspected, and that he awaited his future orders.

"Clinton would have been a useful fellow to me in this business," said Braghall, "had he not had that crime hanging over his head ; however, I may yet turn him to some account. And now I think of it, I imagine it would be no bad policy on my part to retire from London for the present, until the excitement shall have somewhat abated, and the suspicions of the friends of Laura are quieted. I can then better arrange my future plans. It shall be so; it might not be safe or prudent for me to remain here just now, and where can I better go than where Clinton is located ? I might gain much from his advice, and in all probability should be able to hit upon some plan to forward my wishes more promptly than I now anticipate. It shall be so. To-morrow, at the latest, I will take my departure, and I will immediately write off to Clinton to prepare him for my reception."

Pleased with this idea, he instantly sat down and addressed a letter to Clinton, apprising him of his intentions, and then set about making hasty preparations for his departure. These were soon completed, and the next morning, by daylight, saw him on his journey, wholly unattended.

CHAPTER XVI.

EDWARD LANGSTONE REVEALS EVERYTHING TO HIS WIFE.—LANGSTONE IS RESTORED TO THE FAVOUR OF HIS FORMER EMPLOYER.—HAPPIER DAYS SEEM TO BE IN STORE FOR ALL.—A SEPARATION.

WHEN Edward Langstone had quitted the villain, Captain Braghall, after the interview which we have described in a previous chapter, he made the best of his way towards home well satisfied with the manner in which he had acted, and his conscience relieved from an insupportable weight of care and anxiety.

"The scoundrel !" he ejaculated, "to harbour such atrocious thoughts against the peace and happiness of one so pure and innocent, but he will find himself defeated and held up to that public reprobation which he so richly deserves to be. Alas ! how could I ever have been so base as to receive accursed gold on any such monstrous and unnatural conditions? I must have been mad, and the heartless miscreant took advantage of it. But, thank heaven, I did not appropriate a single coin of the wages of guilt to my own use, and I have now returned them to their unprincipled owner, and left him to the bitter reproaches of his own conscience. And in spite of his bravado and pretended indifference, he must feel them too acutely. He will yet be punished severely for the wrongs he has inflicted upon so many of his fellow-creatures, although he may at present escape and be permitted to proceed in his guilty career with impunity. But I must disclose everything to Mary ; why should I any longer keep her in suspense? Why should I any longer hesitate, after what has already taken place, and when she must be convinced that I am truly penitent, and that no one can more deeply lament, or feel a greater horror of the guilty past than myself? She will—she must forgive me, and we shall again be happy. Something seems to assure me that our troubles are now at an end, and that I shall be again restored to that respectable position in society, from which I have so long unfortunately been estranged. Oh, God! I implore Thee most humbly but fervently to give me but the opportunity to redeem my lost character, and how gladly, how earnestly will I avail myself of it.''

Inspired with these hopeful thoughts, he increased his speed, and calming his feelings as he proceeded, he soon arrived at home. Mary received him with even more than her accustomed affection, and he returned her fond embrace with the utmost fervour.

"You have been a long time away, dear Edward,'' she said, "at least so it appears to me, and I have been most anxious for your return. But tell me, whither have you been?''

"Ah, Mary,'' replied her husband, "I have been and done that which has relieved my conscience from an insupportable burthen.''

"What mean you, Edward?'' asked his wife, eagerly.

"I have restored the hated gold which has caused you so much uneasiness and suspense, to the heartless villain from whom I received it, as the price of a crime which I cannot now reflect upon without feelings of the utmost horror and disgust.'' ʻ

"Oh, for Heaven's sake explain yourself,'' said Mrs. Langstone.

"I almost tremble to do so, Mary, for surely you must look upon me with destestation when you hear the revolting truth.''

"Oh, no, no—do not judge of me so harshly and unjustly,'' said Mary. "To what do you allude ?—Whom have you been to ?''

"To the villain, Captain Braghall,'' replied Langstone.

"Ah!'' ejaculated his wife : "and was it from him, then, you received the money ?'

"It was,'' returned Langstone.

"And for what purpose did he give it you ?''

"Alas! how shall I explain the dreadful truth ?''

"Compose yourself, Edward, and rest assured I will listen to you with patience and forbearance.''

"I will endeavour to do so, Mary,'' said her husband, "but you must prepare yourself to hear that which will shock your feelings. Listen, and you shall know all.''

Mrs. Langstone listened with breathless attention and curiosity, and then Edward, with as much composure as he could assume, related all those painful particulars with which the reader is already acquainted. Mary turned pale and trembled as he proceeded.

"Oh, Edward,'' she ejaculated, when he had concluded, "what a revolting tale indeed is that you have just related ; how grateful ought we to be to Providence that you were saved from the perpetration of a crime which must ever afterwards have pressed so heavily on your conscience.''

"We ought indeed, Mary, and I blush with shame when I reflect upon the narrow escape I have had. But can you pardon me ?''

"Oh, yes,'' replied Mary, fervently, "for I feel confident that your mind must have been disordered at the time you entered into the guilty compact, and that you knew not what you did ; and you have made all the atonement you could.''

"Heaven knows how sincerely I repent of the past,'' returned Langstone, "and the bitter agony and remorse of mind I have endured ever since.''

"Well enough am I aware of that, my husband,'' said Mary, "and never will I reproach you for your former errors, since I am satisfied that your future conduct will be such as to make the most ample amends.''

"Most earnestly will I endeavour to make it so,'' said Langstone ; "I should indeed deserve all the punishment that can befall me, could I ever again plunge into that career of vice which has been productive of so much misery.''

"But what a villain must Braghall be to entertain such monstrous designs,'' observed Mrs. Langstone.

"He is a wretch of the vilest description ; but all his intentions are now revealed ; he is rendered powerless, and we have nothing more to fear from him.   He will shrink from encountering me again after the meeting which we have had to-day, for fear that I should expose him to the world in the manner that his vices deserve.   But poor Laura, I cannot bear the thought that she should be made acquainted with that which I have just stated to you.   She could never forgive me, and must ever afterwards look upon me as a heartless and unprincipled scoundrel.''

"Oh, no, you do my affectionate sister an injustice, Edward, by such a supposition," said Mrs. Langstone; "she would never reproach you, I am convinced, greatly shocked though she must be to hear the disgusting particulars.   However, I do not see that there is any necessity to make her acquainted with them.   But I had almost forgotten, here is a letter for you which was brought by the postman soon after you left home."

"A letter !" said her husband, with some degree of surprise; "from whom can that be?"

He took the letter, and started, as he recognised the hand-writing, with mingled feelings of hope and mistrust.   Mary watched him with looks of the greatest anxiety, but he soon relieved her mind of the suspense in which it was held, when he observed—

"Why, my dear Mary, who do you suppose this is from ?"

"Heaven only knows," replied Mrs. Langstone, "but I devoutly trust that it is from a friend."

"And so do I," said her husband, "and if my ideas are correct, from the superscription, it comes from my late excellent and benevolent employer, Mr. Wyndham."

"Mr. Wyndham!" reiterated our heroine, and her eyes sparkling with expectation, "oh, what can be the purport of its contents ?"

"Nothing but good, you may rest assured, my dear girl," replied Edward, "for nothing but what is amiable and charitable can emanate from Mr. Wyndham ; but I will read the contents to you, and God grant that they may be the precursor of future happiness to us.— I have seriously, but never dishonestly offended him, and I know his character too well to imagine for a moment that he would do otherwise than deal leniently and charitably towards me."

"No, I am sure he would not, dear Edward; but the letter," said Mary Langstone eagerly.

Edward Langstone opened the letter, and read the contents aloud.   It was, as he imagined, from his late employer, and couched in the most friendly terms, congratulating him upon his restoration to liberty, trusting that he had seen the folly of his recent course, and offering him the same situation he had formerly held in his firm, as soon as he thought proper to resume it. The feelings of Mrs. Langstone and her husband were completely overpowered by this act of generosity, and tears, the tears of noble and grateful feelings, gushed to their eyes ; they sank upon their knees, and silently but devoutly returned their thanks to the Almighty for the goodness He had bestowed upon them.

"Oh, Mary, my beloved, my devoted wife," at length ejaculated Edward Langstone, "what a relief is this to my mind.   When I thought that I had by my past misconduct rendered myself an outcast upon the world, and knew not how to redeem my lost character, or to provide for you and my little ones, whom I have, unfortunately, too long neglected, to find this good, this excellent friend arise to assist me out of my difficulties and my disgrace, is indeed most overpowering.   I could cry, for very joy and gratitude, like a child.   My good, my disinterested benefactor, for such I must always consider you, never, never again will I abuse your confidence.   Oh, Mary, dear Mary, I now feel satisfied that there are happy days in store for us.   And I will be grateful for them !   Yes ; I will hourly return my thanks to that Supreme Being who has aroused me from my dream of iniquity, and mercifully taught the profligate— the reckless, maddened profligate—his lesson ! The time shall come, too, I feel confident, when we shall see the sunny fields of our native home once more ; when we shall journey on in the same innocence and purity of heart and soul that we formerly did, and look back upon the frightful past without a pang of remorse, no more than springs from the contrast of the determination of our future conduct."

"True, love," replied Mary, throwing her arms affectionately around her husband's neck ; "the happy picture you have drawn is one which my soul duly appreciates.   And it will be fulfilled, Edward, if we only persevere in the course we have resolved upon.   Oh, what joy is there in store for us—I luxuriate in the very idea!   Eternal thanks to Mr. Wyndham for his benevolence, and may every blessing attend him.   You are now reinstated in your former position of life, Edward, and I place too much reliance upon your natural probity and good sense to imagine you will for a moment abuse it."

"If I do," returned Langstone, solemnly, "may the bitterest curses that can attend human being descend upon my head.   But no, my dear Mary, I know that you cannot for an instant imagine me to be that guilty and abandoned wretch, which I should unquestionably be if I again retrograded into the paths of iniquity, and abused the confidence which Mr. Wyndham has once more so generously placed in me. Never did I expect this, and it encourages me to proceed in the proper course. Oh, would to Heaven that there were many more men in the world like Mr. Wyndham!—how many a poor wretch, who has for a time strayed from the paths of virtue and honour, might be reclaimed, and become good and useful members of society."

Heartily did Mary respond to this sentiment, and for a few minutes they remained silent, and allowed themselves to give free indulgence to the feelings which animated their breast.

"Fortune is once more placed before me," at last said Edward Langstone, "and this time, by Heaven, I will avail myself of it. Oh, Mary, what a happy man I now feel; it seems to me as though I had awakened to a new life, and may that life prove a far more happy and virtuous one than that I have hitherto pursued."

"It will, Edward," said his wife, with tears of joy glistening in her fine expressive eyes; "I am convinced it will, and that we shall all again be so happy. But, of course, you will call upon Mr. Wyndham without delay?"

"This very afternoon, my love," replied Langstone, "I should be very unmindful of my duty or the respect I owe to my honoured and generous master, were I not to do so. Employment is now offered me, after all my follies and errors, and if I do not avail myself of the happy chance, as I before said, may all the evil consequences descend upon my own head, and escape you and my innocent children, who have already suffered so much through my mad and improvident proceedings."

"Refer not to them, dear Edward," said his devoted wife, "for it only pains me. It is enough for me to know that you are now sincerely penitent, and I place a firm reliance on the goodness of Providence to prevent a recurrence of the past. But come, rid yourself of the excitement which these events have naturally created, and partake of the refreshment which I have provided for you."

Edward Langstone kissed his still beauteous wife with all the warmth of his most youthful affection, and took his seat by her side at the table, but they had scarcely commenced their humble repast, when the landlady knocked at the door, and on being admitted, informed them that Stephen Gadsby wished to speak with them.

"Oh, let him come up by all means," said Mr. Langstone, "honest Stephen Gadsby, to whom we are so deeply indebted, must ever be a welcome guest."

Mary, by her looks, sufficiently expressed the same feeling, and the landlady having retired from the room, Gadsby immediately afterwards made his appearance, and was welcomed by Langstone and his wife most cordially.

"Good day, my friend," he observed, "it rejoices me to see you so comfortable."

"Thank you, sincerely, Mr. Gadsby," said Langstone; "your words, I know, spring from your heart, and to you we owe a debt of gratitude which I fear it will never be in our power to repay."

"I must beg of you, as I have often done before," returned the honest and kind-hearted man, "to say no more upon that subject, for it makes me feel quite uncomfortable, it does, I assure you. What wretched, unworthy beings we should be, to be sure did we always forget that we are all the children of one parent, and neglected some time or the other to perform our duty towards one another. I did so at one time, I acknowledge, to my shame and sorrow, but since I have been enabled to do one or two good actions, I have felt myself one of the happiest fellows in existence, and consequently have reaped my full reward. But we will say no more upon that subject, I have something more important to converse with you about."

"We are most anxious to listen to you, Mr. Gadsby," said Langstone, "is it good or bad intelligence you have to furnish us with?"

"Why," answered Stephen, "I don't know exactly whether it partakes much of either; however, I have come to a proper understanding with a villain, and your greatest enemy, and it strikes me that he will not soon recover himself from the few home thrusts he has received from me."

"Indeed!" said Mr. and Mrs. Langstone, in a breath, "to whom do you allude, pray?"

"To that greatest of all scoundrels, Captain Braghall," replied Gadsby.

"Ah!" said Langstone, "you have justly designated him; he is indeed a scoundrel, and a most heartless one."

"I have seen him to-day," said Stephen.

"And so have I," replied Langstone.

"Indeed, at what time?"

"About three o'clock."

"I accidentally met him afterwards," said Gadsby, "and that accounts for the excitement under which he laboured. The villain, he thought to win me to his vile purposes, to make me the tool in his hands to work his diabolical designs against Miss Maysdale ; but he found himself most wofully mistaken, as all such abandoned rascals ought to do. Oh, that there were no law to prevent such an act, but I should have liked to have punished him on the spot as he deserved. However, I spoke my mind, and that is one consolation."

Edward Langstone grasped his hand, but for the moment he could make no reply.

"I suppose," said Stephen Gadsby, at length, "that you have some idea of the guilty thoughts which this Captain Braghall dared to entertain towards the amiable Miss Laura?"

"Alas! alas! too well do I know them," replied Edward Langstone with a sigh, and shuddering with shame and remorse, when he thought of the guilty part he had promised to play in that infamous plot.

"Well," said Stephen, "will you believe it, the rascal had the impudence to imagine that I would assist him in his designs, and actually offered me money to do so. D—n him, (pardon me for swearing, Mrs. Langstone,) but I could have struck him to the earth and have trampled upon him at the moment for the insult. Yes, he disclosed all his thoughts to me, and fully revealed that which I had not only long fully suspected, but felt perfectly satisfied of. But he knew not the real character of Stephen Gadsby, or it strikes me that he would not have ventured so much."

"The miscreant!" exclaimed Langstone, clenching his fists.

"Ay, you may well say that, Mr. Langstone," said Gadsby, "he is a villain, and that of the blackest character; but what think you were the replies I returned to his base overtures?"

"Oh, I can guess them shrewdly enough," replied Edward Langstone, "and you have my most unbounded thanks."

"I require them not," said Gadsby, "for I must indeed have been a scoundrel, if possible, still baser than himself, could I have yielded to the temptations he held out to me. But listen, and I will tell you all."

Edward Langstone and his wife did so accordingly, and Stephen Gadsby detailed all which had taken place at the accidental meeting between himself and Captain Braghall, for which they were fully prepared, but at the same time greatly shocked their ears to listen to it.

"The cowardly ruffian," cried the exasperated Langstone; "but he shall yet have cause to repent of his villany, if there be such a thing as justice to be obtained in the world."

"He shall—no fear of that," returned Gadsby, "but now that he has so thoroughly exposed himself, and his atrocious intentions, I question much if he will have the effrontery to annoy you again, or to pursue his infamous designs. He must feel convinced that the game is up with him, and if he is not a greater or more obstinate idiot than I take him to be, he will henceforth bury himself in obscurity. One thing, I think, is quite certain, namely, that Miss Maysdale is perfectly safe from his artifices."

"I trust to Heaven that she is," said Mrs. Langstone; "oh, what was there ever in her conduct to embolden the villain to entertain such diabolical thoughts? But to you, Mr. Gadsby, for your manly behaviour in this affair, all praise is due, and notwithstanding your modesty, myself and my husband most cordially and sincerely award it to you."

"Now pray do cease, Mrs. Lanstone," said Stephen Gadsby, "for you completely overwhelm me with your thanks. But may I ask you, Mr. Langstone, what transpired at the interview between yourself and Captain Braghall?"

"It is a confidence," replied Langstone, "that your merits and the numerous services you have rendered us, entitles you to; but still, in complying with your request, I fear that I shall inspire you with a greater disgust for my character, than that which you have probably hitherto entertained towards it."

"Do not entertain any such ideas, I beg of you," said Gadsby, "for I am only too happy to see the change which has come over you. But perhaps I am too impertinent—however, I think I need not tell you that you may confide in me; but if the explanation be at all painful to you, or such as I should not hear, I decline to listen to it."

"Again I must thank you for your consideration, Mr. Gadsby," said Langstone, "and since you do not urge me, I will claim your indulgence for the present, though at some future period, I have no doubt, I shall find courage sufficient to explain everything to you. It will, however, no doubt, gratify you to know that I have this day removed from my conscience a heavy burthen, much to the discomfiture of the unprincipled and heartless scoundrel Braghall."

"That does indeed rejoice me," said Stephen.

"One thing more I may inform you of," continued Langstone, "namely, that we came to high words, and that a struggle ensued between us, in which I hurled him to the earth like a dog."

"Bravo!" shouted Gadsby, in high glee, "that was glorious, and he dare not resent it, if even he had the power, though his will is good enough to do so, I know."

"True," said Langstone, "but notwithstanding his rank, his wealth, and station, I set him at complete defiance."

"Ay, my friend," returned Gadsby, "you may safely do so; I know the rascal is entirely defeated, and will have to sound a retreat, or I am much mistaken. I do not much fancy the idea of having received the money I have from him, and have a good mind to return it, for I do not expect that it will ever do me any good."

"Indeed I should not do anything of the kind, Mr. Gadsby," said Langstone, "it was his own voluntary gift, and is no more than a just reward for the services you have rendered in the cause of suffering humanity."

"Well, that is true, to be sure," coincided Stephen, "and as my acceptance of it has been attended with such good results, I don't know, but I might as well retain it, as to return it to him to spend in improvidence and guilt."

"A wise conclusion, Mr. Gadsby," remarked Mrs. Langstone, "and I hope that the money so honourably earned may be the means of doing you good."

"Thank you, ma'am," said Gadsby, "I will endeavour to put it to the best use, but I scarcely know how to lay it out at present—I never was so rich in all my life before. I wish you and your husband would borrow it of me for the present; I shall demand no interest for it, and it will do you much more good than me."

"What noble generosity is this!" said Edward Langtone, again grasping his hand; "how can I express my gratitude for your disinterested friendship?—but I should be mean and sordid, indeed, did I avail myself of your kindness. Keep it, my friend, and may it prosper with you—it may be the means of removing you from the difficulties in which you are now involved, and place you in that situation of life you so richly deserve to occupy."

"Well, I know it is of no use to endeavour to persuade you," said Stephen Gadsby, "though I wish I could. I do not despair, Mr. Langstone; poor devil though I now am, something strikes me that I shall one day or the other be better off, as, if all be true that I have heard, I ought to be now; and if that day should ever arrive, depend upon it, Stephen Gadsby will not forget his old friends."

"Of that I am certain," said Mr. Langstone; "and most sincerely do I trust that your hopes may not be disappointed."

"But may I ask," said Stephen, "what course you now mean to pursue?"

"Thanks to Providence," replied Edward, "the happiest prospects once more dawn upon me."

"Indeed, I am most glad to hear that," said Stephen Gadsby, fervently.

"I have received a letter from my late employer," said Langstone, "in which he expresses his forgiveness for my past conduct, and offers me once more the means of getting an honest living."

"And may God bless him for his humanity," said poor Stephen Gadsby, vehemently. "This is the best news I have heard for some time. But it is no more than I expected; I knew all would terminate happily. You will pardon me, Mr. Langstone, but I do not for a moment, after the painful experience you have had, suppose that you will abuse the kindness of Mr. Wyndham."

"Never!" replied Edward, energetically, "I must indeed be a worthless scoundrel if I could do so. No, Mr. Gadsby, I have indeed been taught a severe lesson, and I trust that my future conduct will be such as fully to redeem the past."

"I am detaining you," said Gadsby, "for I suppose you wish to see Mr. Wyndham as soon as possible?"

"This very day," answered Langstone; "it would be exceedingly wrong in me to delay it longer."

"Then I wish you good day," said Stephen, "and no one, depend upon it, can wish you better success than Stephen Gadsby."

"Of that I am thoroughly convinced, my worthy friend," replied Langstone, "and I can but again assure you of my gratitude for your good wishes."

"I will take the liberty of calling upon you again in a day or two."

"At any time, Mr. Gadsby, myself and my wife will be always most happy to see you; but, of course, I need not request that you will keep all the particulars connected with me confined to your own breast?"

"You may depend upon me," answered Stephen, "and in the meantime I will watch the actions of the worthy Captain Braghall narrowly, and make you immediately acquainted with anything that may come to my knowledge, though I rather think, after what has taken place, he will be wise enough to abandon all those guilty designs he has so long had in contemplation, in despair.''

Mr. and Mrs. Langstone again returned their acknowledgments, and after some further conversation of no importance, Stephen Gadsby took his leave, and Edward Langstone took his departure to the house of Mr. Wyndham, leaving his wife in a happier state of mind than she had been for many a day. Their troubles now seemed to be at an end, and she looked forward to the future with the most sanguine anticipations. How fervently did she return her thanks to the Supreme for His goodness, and earnestly she implored Him to guard her husband from thos fatal errors into which he had formerly fallen, and which had been productive of so much shame and misery to them.

"But I place every confidence in him," she ejaculated ; "he is truly penitent, and never, never will I reproach him for the past, but on the contrary, will do all I can to banish it from his memory. Heaven knows he has suffered enough already, and after the fearful warning he has received, and the narrow escape he has had, he will never again plunge into such a wild, such a reckless and guilty career. Oh, no, no, no—our future days will be those of happiness and sweet content—the content which is ever attendant upon acts of probity and honest industry."

Her bosom throbbed with rapture as those thoughts occurred to her mind, and so sudden was the change that had come over her and her husband's prospects, that she could scarcely keep her joy within the bounds of reason, and she felt indeed as if she were another being. In the meantime, Edward Langstone pursued his way to the house of Mr. Wyndham, his mind filled with mingled hopes and fears. Notwithstanding the kindness which his master had expressed in his letter he could not but feel a kind of dread at meeting him after the manner in which he had behaved himself; but by degrees he regained courage and confidence, and arriving at the house, was immediately ushered into the presence of Mr. Wyndham, who received him with the greatest respect and kindness. What took place at that interview it is unnecessary to state ; Mr Wyndham, perfectly satisfied of his reformation and remorse for the past, immediately re-engaged him, and promised him to promote his future welfare as much as he could, if he only continued in the same course which he had now so happily adopted. Need we say how greatful was Edward Langstone for this generosity, and how fervently he returned his thanks to Mr. Wyndham for his kindness. On quitting the house, and on his way home, he felt himself a happier man than he had been for many a day, and mentally vowed that, let the consequences be whatever they might, nothing should ever again lure him from the paths of rectitude. On reaching home, and Mary being made acquainted with all that had taken place between him and Mr. Wyndham, her heart overflowed with feelings of the most unbounded joy and hope, and she joined her husband in returning thanks to the Almighty for the mercy which he had shown to them. Soon after they were visited by Laura, and when she was made acquainted with all that had taken place, she also expressed her most unfeigned pleasure at the happy change which had taken place in their prospects, and predicted that their many troubles would now be all at an end. The next day Edward Langstone resumed his employment with a light and cheerful heart, and was welcomed by his fellow-workmen, with every demonstration of good will, while at the same time they all most sedulously forbore to make any allusion to the past, but, on the contrary, shewed every wish to encourage him in his present pursuits. What a happy man did he now feel, and how many were the solemn vows he made to continue, for the future, in the paths of rectitude and honour, and to endeavour by his future conduct to make some atonement for the former errors into which he had so unfortunately fallen. On his return home, he found his wife anxiously awaiting to welcome him, and again they mutually felt all that happiness and sweet content it had once been their lot to experience. They arranged all their plans for the future, and indulged in the brightest anticipations. In the course of the evening, they were again visited by Stephen Gadsby, who congratulated them warmly upon the fortunate change which had taken place in their circumstances.

"But I have news for you," continued the honest fellow, "which I have no doubt will afford you much satisfaction."

"Indeed," said Langstone, "and pray what may that be, my good friend ?"

"Why," answered Stephen, "your old enemy, Captain Braghall, has abruptly quitted London, no doubt afraid of the exposure of his villany, which was likely to take place, and therefore it is not likely that you will be annoyed by him again."

"That is indeed good news," said Langstone, "but is it known where he has gone ?"

"It is not," replied Gadsby, "but that matters little, so long as you have got rid of him."

"True," observed Langstone, "but still I fear that he has not made up his mind to abandon his nefarious designs altogether, and that he has merely retired from London for the present for the purpose of drowning suspicion, and in order to enable him the better to mature his plot.

MARY LANGSTONE AND LAURA MAYSDALE.

Braghall is not the sort of man, I am satisfied, who will suffer himself to be readilyd efeated in anything upon which he has fixed his mind."

"Well, that may be," returned Stephen, "and I shall not attempt to dispute it, but still I must adhere to the opinion I have before expressed, that, however evil his wishes and intentions may be, he is now rendered powerless, and will not venture to proceed in his base designs since he must be fully aware of the ignominy and the punishment he would be sure to incur were he to make any such attempt. Miss Maysdale is safe under the protection of the excellent people with whom she is living, and as for yourselves, I am confident that you may set all his guilty machinations at complete defiance. But how glad I am to think you have been once more received into the employment of Mr. Wyndham, and that you are again placed in that position of society from which the temptations of wretches, and not your own natural inclination, caused you to swerve, I am sure."

No. 17.

"How heartily do I thank you, Gadsby," replied Edward Langstone, "for that generous opinion, which I feel assured comes from your heart."

"Indeed it does," said the former, "and nothing will afford me greater pleasure than to witness your future prosperity in the world. Indeed I am indebted to you for the content of mind which I at present enjoy."

"How so?" demanded Langstone with some surprise.

"Why, you see, Mr. Langstone," replied Stephen, "before I knew you, I was nothing more than a reckless vagabond; no one respected me, every one despised me; but the sufferings which your unfortunate errors were productive of, aroused me to reason—I was shocked at that in you which at one time I could not see in myself, and I determined to try to become a better man! I trust I have succeeded, and I sincerely hope that I may continue to be so. I have already found my reward and every encouragement in the satisfaction of my own conscience, and what is more, Fortune has begun to smile upon me; I have obtained a situation as porter in the establishment of a merchant in the city, at a salary of a guinea per week, a complete fortune to a poor fellow who has hitherto been kicked and buffeted about in the world penniless. I go to it on Monday next, and I hope I shall be enabled to perform my duties as I ought to do, and to the satisfaction of my employer."

Mr. and Mrs. Langstone most cordially congratulated Stephen on this change in his circumstances, so well deserving as he was of it, and wished him every success.

"With part of the money I had by me," continued Stephen, "I have purchased a few necessary articles of decent furniture, and am about to remove into a comfortable room near the place of my employment; the remainder I have put in a savings-bank, and I hope, if all goes on well and prosperously, that I may at different times be able to add to it until it shall increase to such a sum, as may put myself and my wife in some little way of business to enable us to get a living in our old age, and when we are past labour."

"Those are excellent resolutions," said Mrs. Langstone, "and Heaven will surely enable you to carry them out."

"I trust that it will, ma'am," said Gadsby, "but I fear I am intruding on you too long."

"Not at all," replied Langstone, "your company must always be welcome to us, Mr. Gadsby. But there is one question I wish to put to you."

"What is that?" asked Stephen.

"Have you any idea where the villain Clinton has taken up his abode?"

Gadsby answered in the negative.

"But," he added, "I have no doubt that I shall be able to ascertain that before long. However, there is nothing more to be apprehended from him. He dare not reveal himself, since the vengeance of the law is hanging over his head."

"Very true," coincided Langstone; "he is, however, a desperate villain, and deserves to be brought to punishment for the crimes he has committed."

"No doubt he will not escape it," remarked Stephen Gadsby; and after a few more observations, he took his leave.

Days and weeks passed away, and nothing occurred to disturb the happiness and serenity of all parties. Edward Langstone daily grew in the favour and respect of his master, for his conduct was now most exemplary, and no man was more constant or regular at his business than he was. Mr. Wyndham shortly raised his wages considerably, so that him and his family had the means of every comfort. He placed in him every confidence, and the conduct of the past was never for a moment alluded to. And oh, how happy and grateful was Mary Langstone to Providence now, which had wrought such a blissful change. What a peaceful and cheerful home was theirs, and how great was the respect in which they were looked upon by their neighbours Laura Maysdale visited them at every opportunity, and most fully did she participate in the happiness they enjoyed, and which she fervently prayed to Heaven might continue, though she saw no reason to apprehend that it would be interrupted. Now that Captain Braghall had disappeared from London she felt a considerable weight of care and anxiety removed from her mind; but no one could form the least idea as to whither he had gone, he having taken the precaution not to make any person acquainted at the house where he had resided. Stephen Gadsby also prospered well in his new situation, and gave the utmost satisfaction; any one who had seen him now, could scarcely have believed him to be the same man, and there was no one who possessed a more cheerful or contented mind. His home, to use his own simple but expressive language, was "a perfect little palace," and his wife was a complete pattern of cleanliness and industry. No cares or anxieties troubled their minds, and had they possessed all the riches in the universe, their days could not have been passed in greater tranquillity. They frequently visited Langstone and his wife, and, as the reader may imagine, were at all times most welcome guests. Thus everything seemed going on well and prosperous with all parties, and there did not appear to be any likelihood of its being again interrupted; but an event at length occurred which cast a shadow over the sunshine of their happiness. The mistress of Laura had been for some time suffering from bad health, and the physicians at length considered it absolutely necessary, for her restoration to convalescence, that she should be removed to the sea-side, and, of course, Laura was compelled to accompany them. It was the first time that the sisters had been separated for many years, and they felt it severely, but they sought to console themselves with the reflection that it would not be for long, and that they could frequently correspond. However, when the morning arrived, they could not control their grief, and the most melancholy forebodings took possession of their minds, which they in vain endeavoured to shake off. At last they having become somewhat more reconciled, the parting took place, and Laura having rejoined her master and mistress, they proceeded on their journey.

CHAPTER XVII.

CAPTAIN BRAGHALL AND CLINTON.—THE PLOT OF VILLANY.—THE ABDUCTION.

IT so happened that the place where the villain Clinton had taken up his abode, and where Braghall had joined him on his leaving London, was in the immediate vicinity of the house where the master and mistress of Laura Maysdale had retired, and they had scarcely been there a week when that circumstance reached their knowledge, and the gratification that it afforded to Braghall may be readily imagined. Captain Braghall had taken up his residence under an assumed name, in a retired house, where he could be in constant communication with his infamous associate, and they had been for some time endeavouring to hit upon a plan by which Braghall might obtain possession of Laura, and gratify his revenge against Edward Langstone and his wife, but they had hitherto not been able to come to any satisfactory conclusion. On hearing of the arrival of his relations, and that Laura accompanied them, he immediately hastened to acquaint Clinton with the circumstance, who heard it with no little surprise.

"Is it not fortunate?" said the captain; "they can have no suspicion of the place of my concealment, and if we only set our wits to work and act with prudence, some scheme may be devised by which the girl Laura may yet fall in my power."

"True," said Clinton; "could we only catch her walking out alone some evening, this being so lonely and retired a neighbourhood, I think we should find it no very difficult matter to seize her, and convey her to your house without much fear of detection."

"That would be a bold attempt," replied Captain Braghall, "but I do not think it would be exactly safe to make it: we must endeavour to devise some other scheme; besides, we should require some assistance. Do you not know of any fellows to whom we might trust?"

"Why," answered Clinton, "you know I am a complete stranger here, and that I do not know any one or wish to be known. Now if the Stunner and Hemlock were here, they would be just the fellows for the business, and, of course, you might safely depend on them, for they are in your power, and must do your bidding for fear of offending you and thus placing themselves in the hands of the law."

"True, true," coincided Braghall, "that is a very excellent suggestion of yours, Clinton, and I will avail myself of it; I will write to them without delay, desiring their immediate attendance. They are desperate scoundrels, and will be ready enough to do anything for money."

"Oh, yes, there is no fear of that," observed Clinton.

"Could we by any means obtain a secret entrance to the house, the business might be easily accomplished," said Braghall.

"It might," said Clinton; "and I dare say, with the aid of the Stunner and Hemlock, who you are aware have had some experience in that way, we may be able to manage it. It would not be the first crib they have cracked in their time, you know."

"Exactly," returned the captain, "and therefore it is not likely that they would find much difficulty in doing this."

"Oh, no; I can answer for them."

"Then we will lose no time about it," said Captain Braghall, "for I am all impatience until my designs are put into execution. Little does Laura Maysdale suspect that I am so near her, and therefore she will be thrown off her guard, and the more readily fall in my power. Oh, I feel confident now of success, and as sure as if my plans were already accomplished."

"They will be, I think, captain, if you only act with prudence," remarked Clinton.

"And there is not much fear of my doing that."

Having come to this determination, Captain Braghall immediately dispatched a letter to the two villains whom he meant to employ, desiring them to join himself and Clinton without a moment's delay. Braghall had so disguised himself, that it would have been almost impossible for any one, even those who were most intimately acquainted with him, to recognize him, and after leaving Clinton, he walked near the house in which his relations and Laura now resided, brooding over his nefarious designs, and to see whether he could discover anything that was at all calculated to gratify his hopes. The house was surrounded by a low wall which might be easily scaled, and he thought it would be no difficult matter for the fellows he employed to conceal themselves in some part of the garden until an opportunity should present itself to obtain an entrance to the house either by stratagem or force. While he was still thus occupied, he beheld a window opened, and his feelings may be easily imagined, when the very object of his thoughts appeared at it. It was but for an instant only, and she seemed to take no notice of him, and again disappeared.

"Little do you imagine proud beauty that the man whom you have so much cause to dread, and whom you so thoroughly despise, is so near you;" he said, "and that his mind is now busy at work to get you in his power. And he will triumph too, in spite of all your efforts to the contrary. By Heaven, I would not now resign my hopes, were I by so doing to purchase a crown. In a few days, and if fortune does not frown upon me, my hopes will be realized."

Thus flattering himself, the libertine walked slowly from the spot, and retraced his steps towards home, still brooding upon his designs, and exulting in the prospect of their speedy accomplishment. Two days after this, Hemlock and the Stunner arrived, and a conference was immediately held as to what course it would be best and most expedient to pursue. They willingly agreed to do anything that Braghall required of them, but they could suggest no other means than to make a forcible entry into the house when all the family should have retired to rest, and to seize Laura, whose cries they thought might easily be quieted at all hazards; having a carriage in waiting near the spot, she might then be conveyed with all possible despatch to the house where Braghall resided, and once there, it would be no easy task they thought for any of her friends to discover her.

"Well said," observed Braghall; "I see you are determined, and I place every confidence in you."

"Why you see, captain," returned the Stunner, "that we always had a wish to serve you."

"Oh, no doubt of it," said the captain; "however, no matter how true or not that may be, only perform this business well, and you will have no cause to repent it."

"We will do our best," replied Hemlock, "and I have not the least doubt that we shall be successful. But when shall we make the attempt?"

"The sooner the better," answered Captain Braghall; "I am impatient of any delay, and as we are all prepared, I do not see that there is any occasion for it."

"Certainly not," said Clinton; "suppose we say to-morrow night then?"

"Agreed," said Braghall.

"Will you accompany us?" asked Clinton.

"Yes, I wish to be an observer of all that takes place, and you do not suppose that I am afraid to take part in the plot?"

"Certainly not," returned Clinton, "I never for a moment imagined such a thing."

"To-morrow night, then, you will all be in readiness?"

The villains replied in the affirmative.

"And something seems to convince me that we shall be successful," said the captain; "and if we are, I will not fail to reward you liberally for your services, and give you the means to retire from the country, if you think that will be the safest and most prudent plan."

"We do not doubt that, captain," said Hemlock, "but that will be a matter for after consideration."

"Of course you will have to please yourselves," said Braghall, "but remember my instructions; we must have no flinching when the time comes."

"You need not doubt us," observed the Stunner; "we never yet shrank from that which we undertook to perform."

"Enough," said the captain, "that answer satisfies me, and, of course, if you study your own interest, you will not fail to keep your word."

Having thus finally arranged their nefarious plot, Captain Braghall took his leave, and made his way towards his own residence, deeply reflecting upon the events that were likely to take place on the following night, and sanguine in his expectations of the result.

"These fellows are just the men for the business," he said, "and if they fail I shall indeed be greatly disappointed. But no, I will not entertain any such idea. To-morrow night I feel confident that Laura Maysdale will be securely in my power, and the burning desires I have so long entertained towards her will at last be gratified. Oh, how my heart exults at the thought."

Thus did the libertine continue for some time to soliloquize, and he awaited impatiently for the time to arrive when the daring attempt was to be made. The following morning he again met the three scoundrels whom he had employed to assist him in the guilty plot, and they completed all their arrangements for the expedition of the night. It came at last, and about ten o'clock they started from the house in a vehicle which Braghall had procured for the purpose, Clinton being mounted on the box in the disguise of a coachman in order to prevent any suspicion; but there was no fear of that, for the way they proceeded was lonely and little frequented, and at that hour of the night there were but few persons abroad. They were not long in reaching the place of their destination, and when they had arrived at a convenient spot, they alighted from the vehicle, which they left at a short distance, and walked up to the house. There was not a soul to be seen, and everything seemed to favour their purpose. They looked up at the house, and could only perceive a light glimmering in one of the windows.

"They seem nearly all to have retired to rest," said Captain Braghall; "I wonder if that is the chamber of Laura where the light is burning. How shall we proceed?"

"I will scale the wall," said Hemlock, "and give admittance to you by the gate. It will be all right, I feel certain."

He bounded over the wall in an instant, and cautiously unbolting the gate, gave admittance to his companions. They examined the doors, and then crept stealthily round to the back of the house.

"Ah!" said Hemlock, in a whisper, "Fortune favours us, here is a door that has been left open, probably by accident."

"By Jupiter!" returned Braghall, "this is indeed fortunate. Now courage and caution."

They entered the passage into which this door opened, and then groped their way to a flight of stairs, which they ascended with silent steps, trusting that they should be able to find their way to the room in which they had perceived the light. Laura had not retired to rest, and it was from her chamber window that the light proceeded. Not having had time during the day, she was engaged in writing a letter to her sister, and her mind was too busily occupied with the subject to permit her to take notice of any sounds that might be stirring in the house. Braghall and the others, after having groped their way about the house, at length arrived at the door of this apartment, and the captain having motioned them to silence, paused to listen; but hearing no sounds from within, he concluded that the person, whoever it was that occupied the room, had retired to bed. He laid his hand cautiously upon the handle of the door, and found that it was not fastened. Silently he ventured partially to open it and to look in, and his feelings of delight and exultation may be imagined, when he beheld the innocent girl whom he had marked for his victim. He drew himself back, and in a low voice he said to his companions—

"It is all right; she is there; now how to secure her without her creating an alarm."

"It may be easily done as she is now engaged," said Hemlock: "follow me."

They entered the room on tiptoe, but at that moment Laura happened to raise her head, and to her horror beheld the ruffians in the room. For the moment she was completely deprived of the use of her faculties, so sudden and unexpected was the circumstance, and Braghall and his infamous associates, taking advantage of the same, immediately secured her, and quite overcome with horror, she fainted.

"All is in our favour," said Braghall, in accents of delight and exultation; "quick, quick, and our prize is secure!"

Clinton and his companions raised the insensible form of Laura, and the captain leading the way, they retraced their way as well as they could, in the dark, down the stairs, and emerged from the house, but they had scarcely done so, when Laura recovered her senses, and on discovering her perilous situation, she screamed aloud for help.

"D—n!" cried Braghall, alarmed;—"stop her cries by some means or other, or we may yet be foiled in our designs. Laura Maysdale, you call in vain! At length you are in my power, and by Heaven, I will not fail to take advantage of the opportunity which kind fortune has afforded me."

"Release me, villain!—oh, help! help!" frantically shrieked Laura; but the next moment a cloak was thrown over her head, and pressed around her mouth in such a manner as to stifle all her cries, and again overpowed by her terrors, she fainted. She was conveyed with the greatest rapidity to the vehicle, and Braghall seating himself by her side, Clinton mounted the box as before, and drove off to the place of their destination with the greatest speed, the Stunner and Hemlock pursuing their way to the residence of Clinton on foot. With what feelings of triumph and delight did the libertine, Braghall, gaze upon the pale but beautiful countenance of his insensible victim, and many were the kisses that he pressed upon her lips, as the carriage proceeeded on its way to the house where he had taken up his abode.

"What a moment of happiness and exultation is this to me," he said; "oh, lovely but scornful maiden, you are now mine, mine when I least expected you to be so, and nothing whatever can save you. How kind was it of fortune to send you to the very nighbo urhood in which I was located, and thus at once to thrust you in my pywer. What have I now to care for the opposition of Langstone, or any of your friends? They can have no suspicions of where you are and it will indeed be strange to me if they can by any means discover yo u. To obtain so beauteous a prize is worth all the trouble and the risk I have run, and I am fully prepared to take all the consequences. But I do not fear that when she finds she is in my power, and that all chance of escape is at an end, she will make a virtue of necessity, and yield to my wishes. She must do so, resistance would be worse than childish."

Thus did Braghall continue to soliloquize, during the short journey, and again he pressed warm kisses upon the lips of the unfortunate girl whom he had destined to destruction. But she continued in the same state of insensibility, much to the libertine's satisfaction, as it saved him an immense deal of trouble which he might otherwise have experienced. They arrived at the house where Braghall had taken up his abode, and Laura having been lifted out of the vehicle by the captain and Clinton, was committed to the care of a female, whom the former had engaged to superintend his domestic affairs, and censigned to a comfortable apartment, where Alice (which was the name of the young woman in question) was instructed to use every means towards her restoration. Braghall retired with his ruffianly confederate to a lower room, and having produced wine and spirits upon the table, they sat themselves down to exult over the success of their infamous plot, and to discuss what was best to be done in future.

"Nothing could have been more fortunate or better managed than this night's adventure," said Captain Braghall.

"I think not, captain," replied Clinton.

"I owe you much, Clinton," remarked the Captain, "for the services you have rendered me in this busieess, and the very judicious manner in which you have acted."

"I feel proud," returned the crafty villain, "to think I have offered you satisfaction. It is always my aim to do so to those that employ me."

"You are a good fellow," said Braghall, in the height of his hilarity, "and depend upon it I will not fail to reward you well for your services."

"I do not doubt you, captain," said Clinton.

"She is a beautiful girl, is she not?"

"Very lovely."

"Worth running some risk and expense to obtain possession of—eh?"

"I should say so."

"All that I have to apprehend is, that Alice may be jealous of her."

"Why so?"

"Do you not know?"

"I certainly do not, captain," replied Clinton.

"Well, I thought I had told you that Alice is an old flame of mine; she is the daughter of an old village parson, whom my personal and intrinsic accomplishments overcame a few years ago—ha! ha! ha!—and whom I met again by accident when I came down here."

"Oh, indeed?"

"Yes, that's the fact; rather awkward though, wasn't it?"

"Very."

"Her father died some time back," continued Braghall; "they say the old fool broke his heart in consequence of the seduction of his daughter; but if he was mad enough to do so, I cannot help it, can I?"

"To be sure not," answered Clinton.

"Well," resumed the captain, "as I said before, I accidentally met her only the day after I came down here. She was wandering about destitute, absolutely begging, and in that character it was that I encountered her."

"Wonderful!" said Clinton.

"D—d unfortunate," returned Braghall.

"Rather inconvenient, I must admit," said his worthy companion.

"Well, I thought it was prudent to make the best I could of a bad job."

"Certainly."

"So I did the amiable and the penitent; took her again under my *protection*—ha! ha! ha! —and that's exactly how the business stands."

"The best way certainly, I think, that you could have acted under the circumstances, captain," observed Clinton; "but at the same time it is rather awkward as matters have turned out."

"Truly so," replied Braghall.

"But I suppose you know how to appease the jealousy of Alice?"

"Why, I will endeavour to do so, on that you may depend."

"You say she is entirely destitute?"

"Quite so."

"That she is completely dependent on your charity and protection?"

"Yes."

"Then I see no difficulty in the matter. She, of course, may not at first like the idea of your having another mistress, but, if her character is such as you have represented to me, she will not be silly enough to throw herself out of a good home."

"True," said Braghall, "there is some reason in that; and, of course, I am at no loss for argument in such affairs."

"I believe you, captain," replied Clinton.

"It is enough for me at present to know that I have Laura Maysdale securely in my power," said Captain Braghall, "and I will take good care that Alice forms no obstruction to the accomplishment of my desires. However, we will talk further of this at a future period. How lucky it was that the door should so incautiously have been left open."

"It was indeed," coincided Clinton. "In fact, fortune favoured us in every respect."

"Yes," returned Braghall, "and if the jade does not now desert me, my success will be complete. But we had better separate; I will see you and the fellows Hemlock and the Stunner to-morrow."

"Very good," replied Clinton, "and in the meantime I wish you every success with your fair prisoner."

"Thank you; we will drink towards her health in a bumper."

"With all my heart, captain."

Braghall filled their glasses, and they drank the toast which he gave in high glee.

"As an earnest of my future intentions," said the captain, "you will divide the contents of this purse between yourself and your colleagues."

"I will do myself that honour, captain," said Clinton, with an obsequious bow, and he then took his departure, and left his worthy employer to his own meditations, the nature of which the reader may very well form an idea of, without our taking the trouble to describe.

CHAPTER XVIII.

THE CONSTERNATION OF EDWARD LANGSTONE AND HIS WIFE ON LEARNING THE DISAPPEARANCE OF LAURA.—THE MEANS ADOPTED TO DISCOVER HER, AND THE RESULT.

THE house which Captain Braghall at present occupied, and to which he had conveyed Laura Maysdale, was a fine old building of the Elizabethan period, which had been for some time untenanted previous to his hiring it, and was in every respect, from its retired situation, well adapted for his purposes. The apartments it contained were numerous and capacious, and their furniture, although cumbrous, was costly, and indeed, in former days, no doubt would have been onsidered magnificent. Alice Grayson, the unfortunate female to whom the libertine, Captain Braghall, had so loosely and unfeelingly alluded in the previous chapter, although worn down with care, shame, and remorse, was still handsome, and only two or three years the senior of Laura. It was an unfortunate day for her when she first beheld Captain Braghall, for at that time she was living in innocence and peace with her only parent, an aged father, who lavished upon her every affection, and to whom she was a comfort and a blessing. Accident introduced Braghall to her, and his insinuating manners, and the graces of his person at once won her heart, and when he made an avowal of an ardent passion for her, she placed every confidence in him, and confessed with candour the impression which he had made upon her heart. The Rev. Mr. Grayson, believing in the honour and integrity of his intentions, encouraged his visits, and approved of his addresses to his daughter. Unfortunately for her, poor girl, in a moment of weakness, and by the most specious promises—which, of course, he never meant to fulfil—he triumphed over her innocence, and she eloped with him from the dwelling of her affectionate parent. Ashamed to return and ask forgiveness of that fond father who would so readily have awarded it her, she continued with her seducer, under a promise of marriage, which she too soon found to be false, for having achieved his villanous object, and gratified his lustful purposes, he cruelly abandoned her, and left her to misery and shame. For some time she wandered about the country, subsisting entirely upon the charity of strangers; but at length she formed the resolution to return home, and seek the forgiveness of her aged parent for the disgrace she had brought upon his venerable head. What a sorrowful meeting was that? She found him dying, and the day following her arrival the poor old man breathed his last, after having forgiven her for the deplorable error into which she had been seduced, and invoked the blessings of Heaven upon her head, and poor Alice was now indeed left alone in the world. Her father had died in a state of the greatest poverty, and she therefore was left entirely un-provided for. In vain she endeavoured to procure some means of employment, however humble, and those who knew her were too poor to render her the least assistance, though their will was good enough to do so, and ultimately a mercenary landlord ejected her from that dwelling in which she had been born, and where she had passed so many years of happiness, and she was cast a poor unhappy wanderer upon the earth. No one seemed to pity her; no one held out a friendly hand to help her under her overwhelming troubles. Can it then be wondered that she, in the despair of her heart, adopted the wretched course of life she did? But it was with a breaking heart she did so, and dreadful was the shame, remorse, and disgust of her feelings at the odious life she was compelled to pursue; in fact, she was at times driven to such a state of frenzy, that it was wonderful she did not lay violent hands upon herself. When driven to the last stage of destitution and misery, it was that she accidentally encountered her seducer. To avoid him as something loathsome, to heap the most bitter reproaches upon his head, were her first impulses, but, in spite of all the injuries he had done her, she could not forget the old passion with which he had, so fatally for herself, inspired her; and when he pleaded so many excuses, professed to be so truly penitent, and offered to take her again under his protection, shuddering at the recollection of the horrors she had already experienced, she yielded to his persuasions, and it was thus that she became placed in the position in which we have introduced her to the reader. The feelings of this unfortunate female on the arrival of Laura Maysdale, may be readily imagined. She deeply sympathised with Laura, while at the same time her bosom swelled with disgust and indignation at the atrocious conduct of Captain Braghall, and she determined to frustrate the villanous designs she had no doubt he contemplated against her, if possible. But she knew that, in order to accomplish that praiseworthy object, it would be necessary to conceal her real thoughts and feelings from Braghall, so that his suspicions might be quieted.

"The villain!" she ejaculated, as she gazed upon the insensible form of Laura; "and so he would add you, poor girl, to the dark list of his victims, and make you the same wretched and degraded creature that he has made me. But if kind Heaven will only aid me in my good intentions, he shall find himself deceived. Unfortunate girl, your countenance convinces me that you are now good and innocent, and surely it will be some atonement for the fatal errors I have committed if I can but rescue you from the snares and power of the base and heartless seducer. I will do so, to your shame and confusion, Braghall, or perish in the attempt."

Thus determined, Alice became calm and collected, and exerted her best efforts to restore Laura to animation, in which it was not long before she succeeded; but the astonishment, alarm, and bewilderment of Laura, on recovering her senses, needs no description at our hands. But the whole truth immediately rushed upon her brain, and starting frantically to her feet, and gazing wildly at Alice, she exclaimed—

'For the love of God, tell me where I am, and why I am detained here?"

"Calm your feelings, miss," replied Alice, "and rest assured that you have a friend in me. You are in the power of Captain Braghall, whose unhappy victim I am; but he shall not triumph over your innocence, if Providence will only aid me in my good intentions."

"Heaven bless you for that assurance," said Laura, fervently, "but is the villain Braghall in this house?"

"He is," answered Alice, "but in order to aid you, it will be necessary for me to dissem-ble to him, and to appear to enter willingly into his projects. Fear not, I will be the means of rescuing you at all hazards."

Laura grasped the hand of Alice vehemently, as she thus spoke, in accents which proved at once the sincerity of her protestations.

"Oh, thanks, thanks," she said, "for that assurance; but tell me, who are you who thus expresses so much sympathy in my misfortunes?"

"Alas!" replied Alice, "as I have before informed you, I am a poor fallen creature, and owe my shame and misery to that unprincipled man who has committed this brutal outrage against you, and who, no doubt, flatters himself with the idea that his triumph is certain. But what is your name, and from whence do you come?"

Laura briefly informed her, and then Alice, in as few words as possible, told her own

BRAGHALL PRESENTS GADSBY WITH A CHEQUE FOR £80.

melancholy story, and repeated her determination to be the means of saving Laura at all hazards.

"But," she continued, "as I have before said, it will be necessary for me to dissemble in order to put him off his guard; and when I have succeeded in rescuing you, and restoring you to your friends, I will abandon this accursed place, again cast myself upon the world, and if I cannot honestly obtain the means of existence, calmly resign myself to my fate, trusting that the Almighty in His mercy will at least put a speedy termination to my sufferings by death."

Laura was deeply affected by the observations of Alice, and sought to calm her feelings.

"Nay, my unfortunate friend," she said, "for such indeed I must consider you, after the promises you have just now held out to me, you must not give way to these dismal thoughts, indeed you must not. Heaven will not permit you to perish in the miserable manner you have pourtrayed, and something will yet occur to restore you to happiness. Encourage hope, and depend upon it that you will not be disappointed."

"Happiness!" sighed Alice, "ah, no—that can never again be mine; but I will not trouble you with my sorrows; rest assured that what I have promised I will perform, and therefore do not give way to any unnecessary care or anxiety."

"Your words inspire me indeed with confidence," said Laura, "and I place every reliance on you."

"You may safely do so, miss," replied Alice, "for I should indeed be a disgrace to my sex were I for a moment to attempt to deceive you. At the earliest opportunity I will contrive to make your friends acquainted with your situation, and of course they will lose no time in effecting your liberation. In tee meantime you will muster all your fortitude to meet Braghall, who no doubt will seek an early interview with you."

"Thank you kindly for this advice," said Laura; "I will endeavour strictly to follow it, and I feel confident that by your humane assistance, the infamous designs of Captain Braghall will be defeated."

"They shall," returned Alice, confidently; "and his crimes shall be fully exposed to the world. Oh, miss, what a wretched degraded creature has he made of me; death would indeed be a mercy to me, for must not all my fellow creatures in future look upon me with disgust and contempt?"

"Oh, no," answered Laura; "the charitable will look upon you with pity and respect: it is Braghall alone that must be held up to the opprobrium and detestation of the world; it is he alone who must ultimately suffer for the many wrongs he has inflicted on his fellow creatures. But what is now the time? Surely it must now be getting late?"

"It is past midnight," answered Alice.

"But shall I be left alone, here?" eagerly inquired Laura.

"No," replied Alice, "I will remain with you, and you need not apprehend anything. It is not likely that Braghall will obtrude his presence upon you just yet, and I will take good care to represent the condition in which you are in such a way as to induce him to act with forbearance."

Again Laura returned her heartfelt acknowldgements for the kind promises of Alice, and, re-assured by her observations, she became much more calm than could have been expected under the circumstances.

"But," said Alice, at length, after a pause, "it is necessary that I should see Braghall before he retires to rest, in order that I may endeavour to satisfy him that I have carried out his instructions, and that I entertain no feelings of jealousy or malice in consequence of his present villanous transaction. Be not alarmed, but wait patiently till I return, which will be in as short a time as possible."

Laura again returned her thanks, and Alice retired from the room. What a weight of care had that kind but unfortunate female removed from her breast; she could entertain not the least doubt of her sincerity, and therefore she looked forward to her speedy restoration to liberty with certainty. Ardently she returned her thanks to the Supreme for His merciful interposition to save her from the revolting fate to which the libertine Braghall had destined her, and by the time Alice returned, which was in about a quarter of an hour, she had become quite calm and collected.

"Have you seen the captain?" she eagerly inquired.

"I have," replied Alice, "and though the part was a difficult one for me to play, I think I have succeeded in deceiving the villain, and making him believe that I felt no sympathy towards you. Oh, Miss Maysdale, you may judge of my feelings while thus conversing with him to whom I owe all my shame and misery. Had he possessed one spark of honour or humanity, he must have shrunk abashed with shame and remorse in my presence. However, he shall find, at any rate, that I am not exactly the poor degraded tool in his hands that he takes me to be. Rest assured that I will keep my promise to you, and that if fortune favour my efforts, you shall shortly be restored to liberty and your friends."

"How can I ever sufficiently thank you for this kindness towards one who is a complete stranger to you?" said Laura.

"Do not thank me, miss," said Alice, "for performing what is no more than a common ac of humanity towards one of my own sex. I must indeed be an abandoned wretch, unworthy of the name of woman, could I lend myself to the villanous designs of my seducer against you. May heaven receive it as some atonement for the fatal errors I have committed."

"Do not reproach yourself too severely, my good Alice," observed Laura; "for surely it is Braghall who is alone to blame; he is the author of all your misfortunes, and upon his head sooner or later will descend the just retribution of outraged Heaven."

Tears started to the eyes of Alice. It was some time since she had before heard the words of kindness and sympathy addressed to her, and it overpowered her. She pressed the hand of Laura warmly and gratefully, and it was some time ere she could give utterance to another word.

"Alas!" she sighed at last, and her eyes still overflowing with tears, "when I think of that poor broken-hearted father, from whom I ever experienced such unbounded affection and indulgence, how can I help most bitterly reproaching myself? Surely I deserve to suffer all the agony of conscience I now experience."

"Banish such melancholy thoughts from your mind," said Laura, in her kindest accents; "the compunction you feel for the unfortunate errors into which you were seduced will surely be recieved by Heaven as ample atonement, and you will again be restored to happiness and a proper position in society."

"It is in vain that I may endeavour to hope so," returned Alice; "but alas! what prospect is there of my ever being so?—When I abandon Braghall, which I am determined to do at all hazards, for I can no longer endure to lead this life of degradation wh,at will become of me, without friends, without a place to which I can direct my wandering footsteps or seek a refuge? Who will pity or relieve me? No, Miss Maysdale, peace and happiness, as I have before said, must henceforth be unknown to me, and I shall have nothing left but to lay me down and die."

"Would that I could persuade you to divest your mind of such sad ideas," said Laura, "oh, what a villain must Braghall be to have been the cause of all this misery."

"He has," returned Alice, "and he would doom you to the same fate; but he shall be frustrated, and that when he least expects it. Let that assurance console you and inspire you with confidence. But come, it is very late, and you must need some repose, especially after the unusual fatigue and excitement you have undergone. Let us retire to rest, and look forward to to-morrow or the next day with every hope."

"Your kind assurances have indeed removed much of my anxiety and apprehensions," observed Laura, "and I cannot but place every reliance in you."

"Oh, yes, you may, indeed," returned Alice; "Heaven forbid that I should seek to flatter and deceive you by holding out to you false hopes and promises."

Laura once more returned her acknowledgments to her unfortunate companion, and all being silent in the house, after having invoked the protection of the supreme, her and Alice sought their pillow, having first secured themselves against intrusion by locking and bolting the chamber door. Notwithstanding the behaviour which his unfortunate victim, Alice Grayson had assumed before him, Captain Braghall felt convinced in his own mind that she must feel disgust and abhorrence at his conduct; that a feeling of revenge must naturally be excited in her breast, and therefore, that while he affected not to suspect her real thoughts, it would be necessary to keep a strict watch upon her, and to guard himself against any designs she might have in contemplation to frustrate all his nefarious intentions.

"It will not do to trust her, I am certain," he replied, "and it would be the height of madness in me by any neglect of due precaution to suffer Laura Maysdale to have an opportunity of escaping from me after I have been at so much trouble, and ran so many risks to obtain possession of her. It will not be safe to trust them alone in the house together, or there is no knowing what might be the consequences. Laura will be sure to exert all her eloquence and powers of persuasion to enlist her sympathies, and induce her to connive at and assist her to escape, and it is but too probable, under all the circumstances, that Alice would be only too ready to yield to her supplications, for I know that she must now view me with feelings of the greatest detestation. I must take prompt measures to prevent this, or all the business that has so far been so well executed will be undone, and I shall be exposed to shame and degradation. However, I shall be sure to see Clinton and the other fellows in the morning, and then I can consult with them what is best to be done, and arrange all my future plans. Oh, yes, I have nothing to apprehend if I only use common prudence. Laura cannot escape me, and without anyone here to stand up in her defence, resistance to my will on her part would be completely useless. That thought emboldens me, and since I have dared so far, it is not likely that I am going to retrace my steps. I should only be laughed at and despised were I to do so. In a few days at latest Laura Maysdale shall be wholly mine, and I will not hesitate to brave all the consequences that may follow."

Having given vent to his guilty feelings, Captain Braghall being tired from the adventure of the the night, sought his couch. In the morning almost as soon as he had arisen, he summoned Alice into his presence, and she met him with the same calmness of demeanour that she had done the night before. There was nothing whatever in the expression of her countenance or her behaviour to excite the least suspicion; but the captain was not to be so easily deceived, though he pretended to place every confidence in her. He eagerly inquired after the health of Laura, and was glad to hear that she was much more composed and resigned than he could at all have expected her to be; and after a few more observations, he dismissed Alice with a determination to visit his fair prisoner, if nothing occurred to prevent him, in the course of the day. He had scarcely finished his breakfast, and was weighing all these matters over in his mind, when Clinton (whom we aught to have before stated, had assumed the name of Mark Redford since he had taken up his residence in that part of the country) was announced, and was immediately ushered into the presence of his gutlay employer. Captain Braghall motioned to him to be seated, and Clinton having done as he was desired, the former having satisfied himself that Alice was not listening, observed—

"Jack Clinton, you are the very man I wish to see."

"Indeed, captain," said Clinton, "has anything unpleasant occurred."

"No—no, but I wished to consult you."

"Of course you are aware that I am at your service, captain. How fares Miss Maysdale?"

"Why, from all that has been represented to me, much better than I could, under the circumstance, have expected."

"That is all right," remarked Clinton, "but I suppose you have not had an interview with her yet?"

"No," replied Braghall, "but it is not at all improbable that I may do so in the course of the day. Where did you leave Hemlock and the Stunner?"

"At my 'snuggery!' Dou you require their services?"

"Why, it is not at all unlikely that I may do so. As I before told you, I think, Alice Grayson is an old flame of mine, and although she affects to do so, it is not at all likely that she can view the arrival of Laura here, and my future intentions as regards her, with any amiable feelings towards me."

"I should think not, captain.

"It would not be safe for me to be absent from the house, and to leave them without a guard upon their actions

"By no means.

"Consequently, I think, that it will be more prudent for yourself and your associates to take up your residence here for the present, to prevent all accidents which might otherwise arise."

"Very good," coincided Clinton, "and depend upon it whatever the wishes of Alice may be, she will have not the least opportunity of revealing them while we are present."

"I believe you," said captain Braghall; "so now we both perfectly well understand each other."

"We do, I believe," answered Clinton.

"Have you heard anything relating to the excitement which has been naturally caused at the house where my relations, Mr. and Mrs. Maynard, have taken up their present abode, by the disappearance of Laura Maysdale?"

"I have not; but no doubt it will soon be considerable all over the neighbourhood."

"Oh, I dare say; but it strikes me they will remain involved in s state of mystery; at any rate till after I have accomplished my object; they can have no means of discovering her."

"They cannot," said Clinton; "we managed the business with such skill that no one can have the least suspicon as to what has become of her, and ignorant as they are of your being in this neighbourhood, that she has fallen into your power."

"Very true," said Braghall, "and therefore do I flatter myself that my triumph will be the more complete."

"Certainly; I see nothing whatever to prevent it."

"Then, on your return home, you will make the necessary arrangements with your associates and return here as speedily possible?"

"I will."

"And in the meantime endeavour to ascertain what kind of a sensation the abduction of Laura Maysdale has caused in the neighbourhood; so that by that means we may be the better enabled to arrange our plans for the future."

"Your wishes shall be attended to, captain," answered Clinton. "Have you any further commands for me?"

"None, at present."

"Then I wish you a very good morning."

"Stay; you must not depart until we have drunk success to our future undertakings."

"Very good, captain," agreed; the villain and Braghall having filled their glasses from a decanter of brandy on the sideboard, they drank the toast accordingly, and Clinton then took his departure, leaving Braghall to his own reflections, the guilty nature of which there is no occasion for us to particularise. Although the captain had flattered himself with the notion that the conversation which had taken place between himself and Clinton at this interview had not been overheard, Alice Grayson had listened to the greater portion of it, secreted in an adjoining room, which was only divided by a slight partition, and had, therefore, become acquainted with the principal of their future designs, and was resolved to frustrate them, if there were a possibility of so doing; but still she felt annoyed and vexed at the trouble and delay which were likely to occur before she could put her praiseworthy designs into execution. The presence of Clinton and his infamous colleagues in the house would present an almtos insurmountable obstacle, so watchful and wary as they would be of her and Laura, but notwithstanding all she determined to persevere, and she trusted that Providence would not fail to assist her in her endeavours to rescue an innocent female from the revolting fate to which the heartless and unprincipled libertine, Braghall had destined her. On her return to the apartment in which Laura was confined, the latter anxiously inquired of her what had been the result of her inquiries.

"Why," replied Alice, "unfortunately I have unwelcome news for you, but keep up your spirits, and depend upon it, all will yet be well; at all hazards, I will perform the promse I have made to you."

"Oh, what is it you have to tell me?" inquired Laura.

"Why," replied Alice, "that the visitor who was here just now, was the villain, Clinton, that Braghall suspects me, and intends to place that ruffian, and the two other miscreants who assisted in your abduction in the place to prevent, if possible, your escape.'"

"Oh, God!" sighed Laura, "then, indeed, I am lost!"

"Nay, say not so," returned Alice, "do not give way to despair, unfavourable as your prospects may at the present appear. At most, I flatter myself that it will only cause a delay of the execution of my plot for a day or two, but something will, I feel convinced, occur to enable me to either make your friends acquainted with you situation, or to deliver you at once to liberty."

"And in the meantime," remarked Laura, with a shudder of horror and disgust as the terrible idea flashed upon her brain, "to what fearful and disgusting insults may I not be exposed by the cruel and unprincipled man who holds me in his power? Alas! I see clearly that all hope is at an end."

"Indeed! it is not," replied Alice, "for great a villain as Captain Braghall is, and impetuous as are his passions, he will, if you acquire courage and confidence, surely be awed into forbearance, and meanwhile something may occur to frustrate his intentions and to release you from his power."

Laura shook her head, and in spite of all the efforts of her kind-hearted companion, she in vain tried to think as she suggested. When she thought of the anxiety which her amiable master and mistress must be enduring at her disappearance, and the grief which her sister and her husband were in when made acquainted with the occurrence, her own anguish of mind was increased tenfold, and she gave herself up, notwithstanding the sincere and humane exertions of Alice to compose her almost entirely to despair. The day passed over, however, and fortunately for her as her mind was distracted at that time, Captain Braghall did not offer to obtrude upon her, and she and Alice were left to their own reflections and conversation; and gradually by the good advice of her companion, Laura became more calm, and awaited the issue of the fate which now seemed to be impending over her with all the fortitude she could muster to her aid. Clinton and the other villains arrived at the house, and every arrangement was made for their taking up their residence there for the present; and Captain Braghall now feeling himself secure of his victim, exulted at the success of his infamous plot, and resolved that nothing whatever should prevent him from the consummation o it at the very earliest opportunity.

"I should be a fool, indeed," he remarked to Clinton, "if I let the chance, the glorious chance for which I have so long panted, and which kind fortune has at last placed in my hands, now slip through my fingers.'"

"Ay, Captain," coincided Clinton, "but there is no fear of that, I should imagine, and I only wish I had the same opportunity as you have with the wife of Ned Langstone. It would be a glorious gratification to my revenge; but the time will yet come for me, I trust.'"

"Yes, yes," said Braghall, "and, as you faithfully perform your promises towards me, so will I assist you all that is in my power in the furtherance of your designs."

"Thank you, captain; you shall have no cause to complain of me, assure you."

"Well, I do not doubt you," returned the captain, "and as for Hemlock and the Stunner, I think I have them secure enough in my service."

"Oh, yes, they are perfectly secure. They dare not act contrary to your wishes; and why should they wish to do so when you reward them so well for their services?"

"Why, that is true," said Braghall; "they must be fools indeed if they did so."

"To be sure they must," agreed Clinton; "but there is no fear of that."

"Then all goes on as well as could be wished?"

"Why, I should think so, captain; "the girl is your's beyond a doubt, and you have not the least cause to apprehend detection."

"I think not, for the present."

"Think? I am positive of it," said Clinton. "The friends of Laura Maysdale may suspect that you have her in your power, as doubtless they will; but what will that avail them, since they have not the slightest opportunity of discovering where you have her concealed?"

"Ah! that is fortunate; I had no idea that the game would have been played so well into my hands. Who would have thought for a moment that they would come to the very neighbourhood in which I had taken up my temporary abode?"

"No one. Fortune has favoured you throughout, captain, and you ought to thank the fickle dame for it."

"And so I most heartily do," replied Braghall; "indeed, I had almost began to despair of the ultimate success of my designs."

"I do not doubt it," remarked Clinton; "but you have no cause for any such feelings now; the bird is fairly caught, and it will be your own fault entirely if you allow her to escape you."

"Oh, I will take good care of that; I would lose my life sooner than that she should be now taken from my power; and, with the assistance of you and your associates, I have not the least doubt that I shall be able to retain her in my power. But this business will be sure to cause the greatest sensation in the neighbourhood."

"Certainly—you must always have expected that," said Clinton; "but what occasion have you to care about that? All that you have to do is to keep yourself as much concealed as possible for the present."

"Of course I shall do that, though I do not entertain much fear that I should be recognised in my present disguise."

"Well, that might be; however, it is as well to avoid the risk."

"Yes," returned Braghall, "I agree with you there; too much precaution cannot be used. But I long to see my beauteous prisoner, that I may breathe my sentiments in her ears, and gloat over her various beauties with delight."

"I dare say the reception she will give you, captain, will not be one of the most agreeable description."

"Why, for that matter, I do not expect that it will; no doubt she will heap upon me her reproaches; but they will not have the least effect on me—they will not cool the ardour of my passion the least in the world, or intimidate me from the execution of my purpose."

"It is well that you are so determined," observed the ruffian Clinton, "and I wish you every success, which I do not see how you can fail to meet with, if you only act with common prudence; but when do you propose to pay your respects to her?"

"Why, I should like to do so without delay," answered Captain Braghall, "this very day, for I am all impatience." "Excuse me, captain," said Clinton, "but I can't help saying that I consider that would be rather premature; however, you know best, but for my own part, however impatient I might be for the consummation of my wishes, I think I should give her some short time to collect herself, and in the meantime I should watch the behaviour of Alice narrowly, and if you have any good reason to suspect that she is playing you a false game, which I have not the least doubt she will, if she have the opportunity, of course, you will know how to deal with her, and to prevent her from doing you any mischief."

"Why," returned Braghall, after a pause, "perhaps that would be as well, and, the delay of a short time will not be of much consequence. Your advice respecting Alice is prudent, and you may be sure that I will not fail to attend to it. She must never be suffered to leave the house, or I have no doubt that she would not for a moment hesitate to betray us."

"That, I think, is certain," said Clinton, "and must be carefully avoided. It would indeed be awkward to be now discovered, after we have so far succeeded."

"It would," replied Braghall; "but have you anything more to suggest?"

Clinton replied in the negative, and Captain Braghall having expressed a wish to be alone, he quitted the room and rejoined Hemlock and the Stunner, with instructions from Braghall that they were to enjoy themselves in the best manner they could, and to make themselves quite at home; orders, which the reader may be sure the ruffians did not fail to obey. But we will leave Braghall and them for the present, and return to the residence of Mr. and Mrs. Maynard.

The cries of Laura, has been shewn, did not arouse her master and mistress on the night of her seizure, and they slept to their usual hour on the following morning; but Mrs. Maynard finding that Laura did not make her appearance to assist her to dress, she summoned Susan, a young girl whom they had hired during their residence, in the country and desired her to go to her chamber, thinking that she had probably overslept herself. In a few moments Susan returned, and her looks shewed that she had something particular to communicate. Mrs. Maynard eagerly questioned her, and she replied, " that Laura was not in her chamber; that the room was in the greatest disorder, and that the bed had evidently not been slept in during the night." Mrs. Maynard was greatly alarmed.

" But have you searched any other part of the house, Susan ?" she demanded.

"Yes, ma'am," answered Susan, " I have examined every room in the house; but I could see nothing of her."

" This is most strange and alarming," said Mrs. Maynard ; " what can have become of her ?"

" May she not have gone to ake an early morning walk, Ma'am ?" suggested Susan.

" Oh, no," said her mistress, " it is never her practice to do so till after she has attended upon me. I fear that something has happened to her. Did you hear any noises in the night, Susan ?"

Susan replied in the negative, but added that she found one of the back doors open.

" Ah!" ejaculated Mrs. Maynard, " that looks suspicious."

Mr. Maynard now entered the room, and on being made acquainted with the circumstance, he became as much alarmed as his wife. They immediately commenced a strict examination of the premises, and the confusion into which the furniture of her chamber was thrown, increased their apprehensions and suspicions.

" It seems," remarked Mr. Maynard, " as if a desperate struggle had taken place here. What can be the meaning of this ?"

" I am completely lost in amazement," said Mrs. Maynard ; " is it possible that the house can have been entered in the silence of the night, by villains, who have borne Laura away ?"

" Oh, what wretches would have been daring enough for that ?" said Mr. Maynard ; " and yet there is enough to excite such suspicions ; one circumstance which is of considerable importance, is, the back door being found open ; but still is it not likely that her cries for help would have alarmed us ?"

Mrs. Maynard made no reply, but her fears became strengthened every minute, and her worst surmises confirmed, when on examining the stairs more closely they discovered several footmarks upon them, and a ring which they knew belonged to Laura, and which had probably been torn from her finger in her struggles to release herself from the hold of the ruffians who had seized her.

" Unfortunate girl," said Mrs. Maynard, who was deeply affected, " she has too surely fallen into the power of villains ; but who can they be, and by what means have they been able to accomplish their diabolical designs ?"

" I am astounded," said her husband ; " but no time must be lost ; every inquiry must be instituted that may lead to their detection, and her restoration to liberty."

Search was instantly made all over the neighbourhood, but no one could give them any information that was calculated to throw the least light upon the subject ; and it seemed but too probable that they would be unable to penetrate the painful mystery. We need not state the agitation into which the master and mistress of Laura Maysdale were thrown by this unexpected event, and they fell completely at a loss what course it would be most prudent to adopt under the circumstances ; neither could they form the least conjecture as to who was the perpetrator of such an atrocious outrage. Their suspicions never for a moment lighted upon Captain Braghall, for although they knew his character well, they could not believe him to be so thoroughly base and abandoned as to commit such an offence as this. But the longer they endeavoured to fathom the mystery, the more bewildered did they become ; but when the day wore away, and still they could hear nothing of the poor girl, their anxiety may be well imagined. They did not retire to bed till a late hour that night, with the hope of receiving some tidings of her; but none came, and they gave themselves up to despair. They had now no other alternative than to write immediately to Mr. Langstone and his wife to inform them of the melancholy and alarming event that had taken place ; and they felt keenly the anguish which they would be sure to experience, when they became acquainted with it; but, of course, they could not attach the least blame to them. Having despatched this letter, they awaited with the utmost anxiety an answer; but they continued to adopt every means in their power to discover the unfortunate girl, notwithstanding the almost utter hopelessness of the task. The letter reached Langstone and his wife in due time, and it would be utterly impossible to find language sufficiently powerful to describe their astonishment and consternation on perusing the contents.

"Good God!" exclaimed Mary, clasping her hands, and looking up towards Heaven with an expression of countenance that was truly painful to behold, "when will our troubles be at an end? My poor sister; what can have become of you, and who are the villains who have committed this monstrous outrage?—Oh, Edward, what is to be done?—How can we act?"

"I am completely at a loss, dear Mary," replied her husband; "but whatever we do must be done promptly. Little did I ever expect to hear of such a calamity as this."

"Alas, no!" said Mrs. Langstone; "and unless we quickly obtain some clue to the discovery of my poor sister, I fear the shock will be more than I can well sustain.

"Courage, courage, Mary," said Langstone, "and success may attend our exertions sooner than we expect. It does not appear probable that whoever the villains are who have been guilty of this daring outrage they will long be able to keep her concealed from us."

"But oh, what may not have happened to her in the meantime?" said Mary; "I shudder to think."

"Providence will, I trust, protect her," returned Mr. Langstone; "but who can the villain be who has committed this atrocious offence but Captain Braghall? and his sudden and secret departure from London, all but confirm my suspicions."

"Can it be possible that he has thus dared?" said Mrs. Langstone; "and if Laura is indeed in his power, have we not every reason to dread the worst that can befall her?—"

"I will depart immediately to the place where Mr. and Mrs. Maynard are residing, said Langstone; "and in the meantime keep up your spirits, Mary, for something seems to assure me that I shall be successful, and that Laura will be restored to us uninjured."

"God grant that your hopes may be realized, Edward," replied his wife; "but oh, how little was I prepared for intelligence such as this. Dear Laura, most affectionate of sisters, how terrible must be your feelings wherever you are."

Langstone tried all he could to soothe her,—but although he pretended differently, he could not but entertain apprehensions as powerful as her own. While they were still conversing upon the painful subject, Stephen Gadsby made his appearance, it being his custom to call every evening on his way home, to pass away an hour or two in conversation with Langstone and his wife. Noticing their melancholy looks, he eagerly inquired the cause, and when he was informed of it, his astonishment and indignation were as great as theirs.

"Poor girl! poor girl!" ejaculated the kind-hearted man, "most heartily do I pity her and execrate the wretches who have been guilty of this abominable crime. But mark me Langstone; depend upon it that Captain Braghall is the author of it all."

"Yes," coincided Mr. Langstone; "that is decidedly my opinion. On whom else can my suspicions fall?"

"Certainly not," replied Gadsby; "and I have no doubt that he has been assisted in the execution of the infamous plot by that arrant rascal Jack Clinton."

"That is very probable," observed Langstone, "especially goaded on as the villain Clinton would be by his feelings of revenge against me."

"True," said Stephen, "and if I had only been made acquainted by Braghall with the place where he had taken up his abode, there might not be much difficulty in discovering them. But there is no time to be lost, for there is no knowing the danger that may threaten Laura Maysdale. What course do you propose to pursue?"

"Why, to take my departure as quickly as possible to the residence of Mr. and Mrs. Maynard," answered Langstone; "and then I can consult with them how it will be best pro- ceed."

"I should like to accompany you," said Gadsby; "and to aid you in your search."

"Nothing would give me greater satisfaction," remarked Mr. Langstone; "but I am afraid your business will prevent you."

"Oh, no," replied Stephen; "I feel certain that my employer, with whom I am already a favourite, will excuse me for a few days. I will return immediately to him, and seek his permission."

"And I will accompany you, as it is all in my way to my employers" observed Mr. Langstone; "and I must apprise him of what has taken place, and inform him of my intentions. As I said before, there must be no delay in this business, for every moment may be fraught with danger to Laura. I will depart on my journey at an early hour in the morning."

"You will find me ready to attend you," said Gadsby; and Langstone, having embraced his wife, and bade her be of good cheer, they took their departure. When they were gone Mrs. Langstone gave free indulgence to the feelings which the melancholy intelligence had naturally created in her breast; and fervently she supplicated the protection of Heaven for her unfortunate sister, though she could not but entertain the most painful apprehensions, when she took all the circumstances into consideration. If she was indeed in the power of Braghall, she felt convinced, that unless Providence should interpose to save her, he would never rest

EDWARD LANGSTONE RE-ENGAGED BY MR. WYNDHAM.

until he had accomplished his diabolical designs; and the delay that might occur before they could discover Laura, might render it too late to save her from the fate with which she was threatened. These thoughts greatly distressed Mrs. Langstone, and it was some time before she could in the least compose her feelings. She would have liked to accompanied her husband; but her domestic duties at home would not permit her to do so; and she endeavoured to console herself with the assurance that Edward would constantly communicate with her; and she tried to hope that many days would not elapse before she received some favourable intelligence from him. Langstone and Stephen Gadsby were not absent long, and they having both got permission from their employers to absent themselves for a time, and the few arrangements that were necessary being speedily made, almost as soon as it was daylight the following morning, Gadsby and Langstone both took their seats upon the coach, and were soon proceeding on their important journey,

CHAPTER XIX.

THE UNEXPECTED METEING.—VILLANY DEFEATED.—THE RESCUE.—THE RESTORATION.—STEPHEN GADSBY'S GOOD FORTUNE.—PROSPEROUS TIMES WITH ALL; AND CONCLUSION.

As Langstone and Stephen Gadsby proceeded on their way, they consulted together what it would be best for them to do on their arrival at the place of their destination, and they formed many schemes which they as quickly rejected as impracticable. But at length they arrived at the residence of Mr. and Mrs. Maynard; where they were received with the greatest hospitality, and they expressed their deep regret at what had occurred in such ardent terms, that it was impossible to doubt their sincerity. Various plans were arranged which seemed likely to prove successful, and no time was lost in putting them into execution; and in their operations they had the assistance of the magistrates. But all their endeavours were unavailing, and Langstone and his companion began to despair. But a circumstance occurred, when they had only arrived there two days, which brought about the consummation of their wishes in a manner they least expected. Langstone and Gadsby had been walking all day, and very tired and dissatisfied with the result of their exertions, they were returning home in the evening, and in doing so it was necessary for them to cross one side of a wood. At length, having yet some distance farther to go, they resolved to rest themselves for a few minutes and accordingly seated themselves beneath the shady branches of a noble tree. They had not been long there when they heard the voices of men in earnest conversation, and which seemed to proceed from a clustre of trees behind which they were sitting. They started to their feet, and the voices appearing to be familiar to them, their curiosity was excited, and they listened attentively.

"Yes," said one of them; "I think as you do, that it would be imprudent to delay; for there is no knowing what accident might occur to rescue my prize out of my hands."

"By Heaven!" whispered Langstone to his companion, "that is the voice of Braghall."

Stephen Gadsby nodded assent, but at the same time motioned him to silence, and then they heard the following answer returned—

"Why, as for that matter, captain, I do not think you need entertain any fear. They may search as long as they like, but if you only act with common prudence, it will be totally impossible for them to discover you. But come, I think it is time to return home."

They now heard them moving from the spot on which they had been conversing; and no longer doubting that it was Braghall and the villain Clinton, and that it was the former who held Laura in his power, they determined to seize them immediately, and to force the whole truth from them. But Langstone's feelings of delight were so great at this unexpected meeting, that he could scarcely contain himself; but he had not much time for thought; they emerged into sight, and the instant they did so Langstone and his companion darted from the place of their concealment, and before Braghall and Clinton could recover themselves from their astonishment and confusion, Clinton was felled to the earth by a blow from a heavy stick which Stephen Gadsby had with him, and Edward Langstone, grasping the captain by the collar with irresistible force, exclaimed—

"Villain! cowardly ruffian! I have discovered you at last then? Where is the innocent girl whom you have dared to deprive of her liberty? answer me, for it is only by so doing that you may expect any mercy to be shwon to you."

"Leave go your hold, insolent, presumptuous beggar!" cried the enraged captain, at the same time producing a pistol; "you see I am armed, and by all my hopes, I will not fail to avail myself of the means I have at my command, if you seek to detain me."

Langstone grasped his wrist with the only hand he had at liberty, and endeavoured to make him resign the deadly weapon; but in the struggle, just as the muzzle, by accident, was turned towards the body of Braghall, it went off, and with a bitter oath, he exclaimed, as he sank from the hold of the astonished Langstone to the earth—

"Ah! I am shot! Curses light upon the hand which did this!"

Clinton still remained on the ground, stunned by the blow which Gadsby had given him, and Captain Braghall, from the effects of the wound he had received, fainted. Langstone and his companion stood for a few moments completely dumb-founded by the unexpected events that had taken place; but at length the former said—

"Good God! who could have anticipated this? What is to be done?—We are yet some distance from the place of our destination, and we cannot convey the captain there without assistance; besides, he would most likely die before we could reach there."

At this moment they heard the voices of men approaching, and instantly afterwards three stout rustics made their appearance, and approached the spot. The singular scene which presented itself, as may be expected, not a little astonished them; but Langstone, having briefly explained everything, begged them to direct him to the nearest house, where they might procure some assistance for the wounded man.

"Why, my cottage is close handy," said one of the men, "and you are welcome to take him there, if you please. Perhaps, Robin, you wouldn't mind running for the doctor?"

Robin agreed, and Langstone, having thanked him, bound up the wound as well as he co uld and then he and Gadsby raised the captain from the ground, and prepared to convey him from the spot.

"What shall we do with this one?" said the man to whom Langstone had first spoken, pointing to Clinton.

"Oh, convey that rascal to the nearest prison," said Stephen Gadsby in reply; "is there one handy?"

"There is the lock-up," said the man; "so we can lodge him there for the present."

"Ay, that will do," observed Langstone; "but pray let us be going, for we have not a moment to spare."

"D—n you all!" growled Clinton, in a savage voice, as the men seized him; "but I will deceive ye yet."

They were only a few minutes in reaching the cottage, and Robin having used the utmost expedition, the doctor arrived almost at the same moment, and immediately proceeded to attend to the wound of the captain. Clinton was safely lodged in the lock-up, and Stephen Gadsby, at the request of Langstone, hastened to the residence of Mr. and Mrs. Maynard to make them acquainted with what had happened. Langstone waited with the greatest impatience and anxiety the restoration of the captain to his senses, that he might endeavour to elicit from him the place where Laura was concealed, but he remained in the same state of unconsciousness till after the arrival of Mr. and Mrs. Maynard, who were very much shocked to behold that their suspicions were correct, as regarded their guilty relation, and to find him in the state he was. However, by the attentions of the medical gentleman he was at length restored to sensibility; and on beholding Mr. Maynard and his wife, he evinced much confusion and groaned.

"I have erred, greatly erred," he at last said in a faint voice; "but I not regret my misconduct, and would fain make all the reparation I can. Laura Maysdale is my prisoner."

"Where—where?" eagerly inquired Langstone; "tell me that, and I shall be satisfied and will freely forgive you.'

Braghall informed him, and he then became too faint to speak further for the present, and he was suffered to remain quiet. In a short time he again revived, and he then fully explained everything to his relations and Langstone, and supplicated their forgiveness, which was readily granted him. That very night, late as it was, Laura and the unfortunate Alice Grayson were restored to liberty; and the meeting that took place was all that the most vivid imagination could conjecture. Hemlock and the Stunner were secured and sent to prison.

*　　　　*　　　　*　　　　*

The wound of Captain Braghall was by no means dangerous, and in the course of a few weeks he was restored to convalescence and returned to London with his relations, quite an altered man. Only a few days after his return from the country, Stephen Gadsby received the welcome intelligence that he was discovered to be the only surviving heir to large estates in Norfolk, and immediately departed from London to take possession of them. Captain Braghall never again swerved from the paths of rectitude and honour; and the natural qualities of his mind being now displayed to full advantage, a sincere passion sprung up between him and Laura Maysdale, and in a few months afterwards he had the happiness of leading her to the hymeneal altar. Clinton, Hemlock, and the Stunner, were tried and convicted of the burglary before mentioned, and were sentenced to be transported for life. Alice Grayson was amply provided for by Braghall, and about two years afterwards she married a respectable tradesman, and is now living surrounded by every happiness. Edward Langstone continued every day to grow in the favour of his employer, who at length took him into the establishment as his partner, and dying in a year or two afterwards, having no relations of his own, bequeathed him the whole of his large property. One portion of this was an estate only a few miles from that of Stephen, now Squire Gadsby; and the friends often meet to enjoy themselves, to talk over the past, and to recal to their memory all the circumstances connected with "THE WIFE'S DREAM" AND "THE PROFLIGATE'S LESSON."